I0636443

SPECTERS
FROM A
DREAM

SPECTERS FROM A DREAM

The Enchanter's Web, Book I

M Turville Heitz

This book is a work of fiction. Names, characters, places, and incidents are the product of the author's imagination or are used fictitiously. Any resemblance to actual events, locales, or persons living or dead is coincidental.

Copyright © 2025 by M. Turville Heitz
979-8-9918853-3-1

First Edition

All rights reserved. No part of this book may be used or reproduced in any

manner without written permission except in the case of brief quotations embodied in critical articles and reviews.

For information address Oakland Hills at P.O. Box 531, Cambridge, WI 53523
Oaklandhillsfarm.com

Cover art and design by Ingrid Kallick https://ikallick.com

For David who wanted to see this in print and didn't, and for Morgan who will.

Acknowledgements

Thanks to all those who provided feedback and insight as this work took its long journey from a college writing thesis to novel. Special thanks for in-depth review by Jay Clayton, Kandis Eliott, Hal Gillam, Kathleen Massie-Ferch, Steven Rogers, Fred Schepartz and Morgan Turville-Heitz.

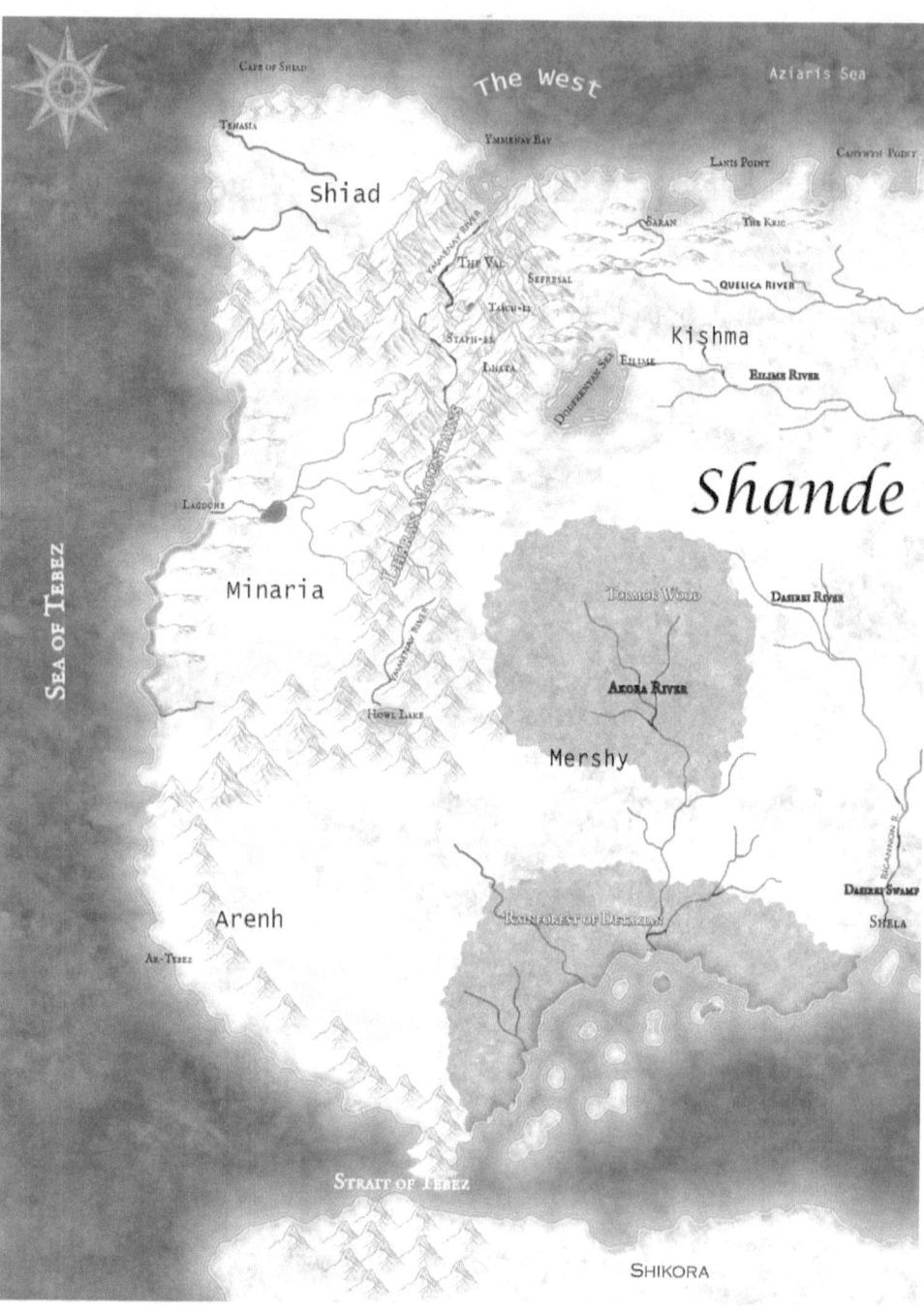

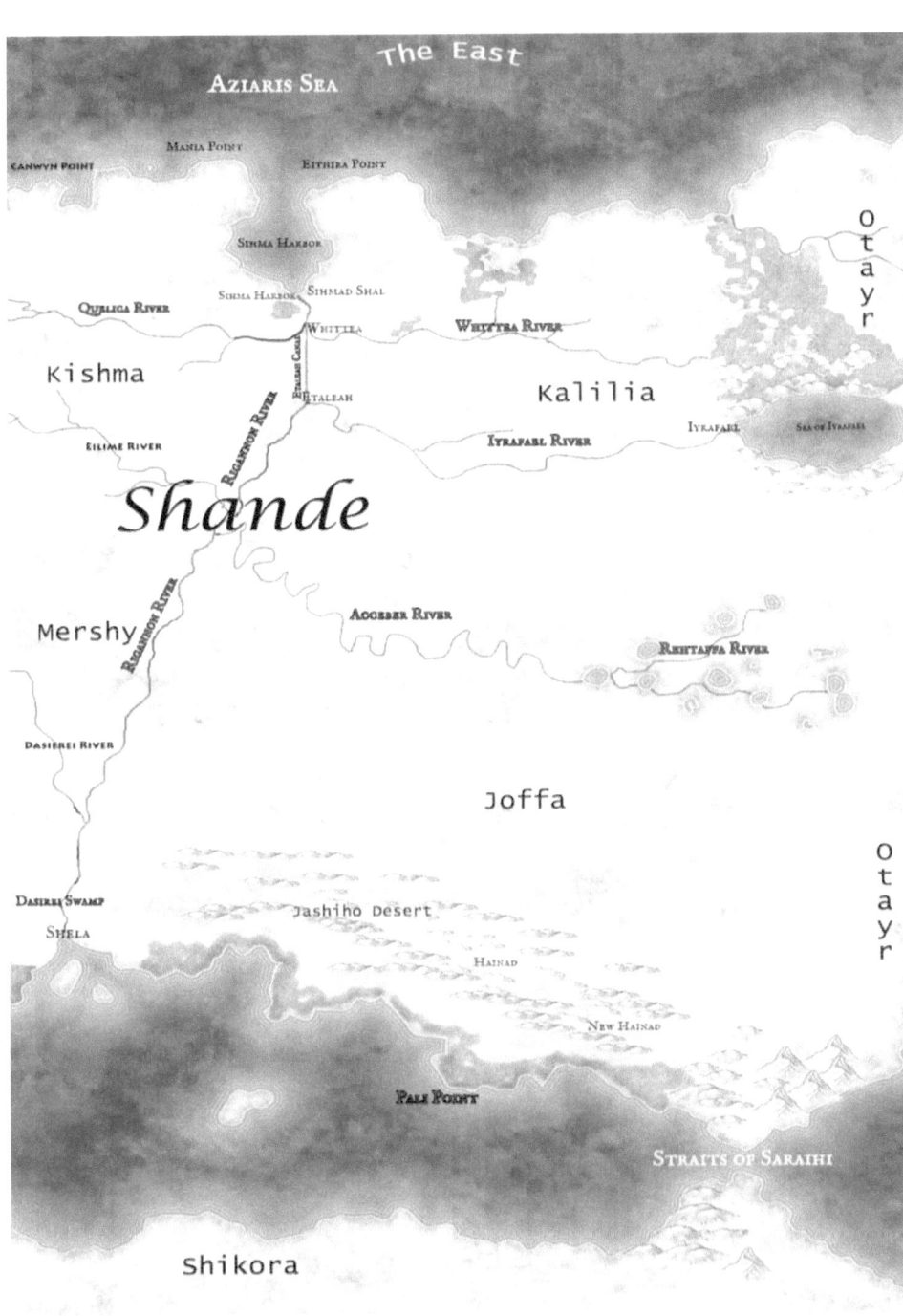

PART 1: COMMENCEMENT – THE WEST

1: A Cry on the Wind

"Why do I have to do this?" Khoti asked the slate in front of him as he used the heel of his palm to smear out an answer he didn't like.

"So you can be my Second!" Von said as he slid down the ladder from the loft where they worked their figures. "I'll have important things to do. Taxes'll be your job!"

Khoti let out long sigh. His effort to erase had smudged an earlier answer. What had he put? The numbers blurred in the flickering candlelight of the loft as the wick sank into a pool of wax.

He startled at the soft bump of a branch against the cottage roof then felt the brief prickle of goosebumps at what sounded like a distant wail coiling along the valley floor, like some injured beast or maybe a tempest wind rushing through a canyon. He cocked his head to listen but heard only the constant whoosh of water over the cascades in the valley bottom and the snap of an ember in the fireplace.

He should be on the road with Fa, hunting maybe, or tracking game that sprinted across rocky mountainsides, hooves clacking against stone, but never too swift to escape his perfectly aimed arrow. Or maybe the icy spray of a rapids would mist him as he cast his net to snag a fish leaping forward in search of its birthplace; he'd scoop it from the icy waters with his bare hands and wrestle it to shore, a wriggling beast larger than anyone had

1

seen before. Fa would hold it up for the whole village to see and praise Khoti –

Again he thought he heard something in the wind that made the hairs on the back of his neck crawl. Did he imagine it?

He let out another deep sigh. Number of villagers by bales of fleece times tenths to province, subtract cleaning and transport fees and ...

"Maybe someone else can be your Second," he muttered toward his brother's empty mattress crowding the other half of the loft. "I'll be filling the barrels with game and too busy for taxes."

He stole a glance over the loft edge to see if Von still worked his problems. Drawn curtains hid a niche where Mam slept alone with Fa away, as well as the other one where Grandmam snored so softly her night voice sighed like the pines swaying in the Tasch-el Valley. The table in the middle of the room stood empty but for Von's now washed slate and his stack of answers awaiting their father's return.

Of course Von finished first; then his older brother would climb into the loft and blow out the candle whether or not Khoti had finished. Soon the lambing would begin with too much work to trouble with learning to Second his brother, especially when it could be years before Von took their father's place. Distant rulers, who only remembered Tasch-el to collect the tax or demand more metals from the mines, had named Tsevon of Tasch-el, like his fathers before him, headman of the mountain region. It's just a title Fa told them; the man in the job had to earn the people's respect. Khoti didn't want to be a Second. What did he care about sheep or mines or taxes? Fa's sour-faced cousin and Second, Tegi, likely got that way from figuring the village tax.

Outside, a horse whickered. Again, something hollow sounded just beneath the wind, low and urgent, not quite right, not quite wrong. Maybe he hadn't heard it at all.

He dug his bare toes beneath the straw covering the floor. He squinted at the slate as the silence in the cottage built. His eyes drifted shut as he imagined his father in a distant hunting camp with his fellows enjoying a laugh as they roasted fresh –

"Khoti," Von whispered from the top of the ladder. Khoti yanked his head up. "C'mon sluggard, move your bony butt," Von jabbed Khoti's backside with a stick from the wood box. "Something's stirring up the horses and it looks like one's loose in the paddock."

"Are you afraid of the night without me to protect you?" The candle fizzled out.

Von tapped the tattoo at the base of his neck. The three parallel black slashes marked him a man of Tasch-el. Khoti would have no voice among men for several more months.

"Come child," Von gave him another playful jab with the stick then slid down the ladder with a barely audible thump.

Khoti had no excuse to complain. The village stables were their responsibility. A tawnkat or some other wild beast among the horses could cause devastating harm in minutes.

A piece of bark flew up into the loft in a perfect arc that landed on Khoti's head. Khoti peered over the edge to find Von's broad grin beneath a mop of unruly hair. Von stabbed the stick upward like a pitchfork aimed for a mound of hay.

In bare feet and night shirt, Khoti slid down the ladder. If they hurried, his bed would remain warm. He quickly pulled on lambskin boots and followed Von, bare-legged, into the cold of a mid-spring night. He cursed the wail of wind that raised a cold shiver as it fell from the snowy peaks above. Von disappeared through the dark hole of the stable's side door, Khoti stumbling into him.

With his eyes still adjusting to the dark, Khoti at first could only hear the chorus of stomps, snorts and whickers of restive horses and mark the scents of oiled leather and manure reaching him like a warm breath in his face. Then he noticed the paddock door askew. The plank used to bar it had snapped in two. The door banged a little further open with each gust of wind. Beyond, a pony trotted around the paddock, trailing a broken lead.

Von stood out in silhouette for a moment as he lit a lantern and began checking the line of stalls.

"I see nothing to fear, Von. Still need me to hold your hand?" He peeked over a couple of stall doors to ensure no wild animals had crept in. "I hear my warm bed calling and I still need to finish my figures."

Von turned to grin at him. "What a wee cub you are! Can't handle a bit of cold. Here –" he pushed the lantern into Khoti's hands. "All better now, boy?"

"Who needed his little brother to protect him? Just wait until I've my marks and we'll see who's a cub!"

Von laughed at that as he pulled a second lantern down from a hook to light it from the first. "Men earn their marks. They don't just give 'em to you. And you'll always be Second to me."

"You're the one that has to show up for all the rites and keep the peace. I'll be taking my ease hunting and fishing."

Von laughed, gesturing toward the paddock and the loose pony as he headed for the ladder into the hay mow.

As Khoti hung his lantern from a peg he heard it: a rumble at first, like a rockslide on the mountainside breaking free in the thaw. Hooves pounded frozen ground, growing louder. He turned toward the closed stable doors that opened out onto the village green and main road beside it, wondering if the Duke of Lharan's Guard raced to some tragedy at one of the mines.

An undulating shriek, like wind furies in the peaks ripped at the night raising the hair on Khoti's neck and renewing the stomps and snorts of the horses in their stalls.

"Khoti!" Von shouted from above. "The bell! Raise the alarm!"

Khoti ran for the stable doors onto the green and yanked one open so he could dash to the well where the bell hung. He heard shouts coming from the northeast road toward Sefresal, and saw the bob of lamps as villagers emerged from the cottages fronting the narrow green that ran along the swift creek in the valley floor. A hound bayed and someone screamed. His eyes still blinded by the lantern, he thought he made out the shape of horsemen, cloaks flying out behind them as they raced down the road against the wind, their faces hidden in the shadow of hoods or masks.

Suddenly a torch fell in the stable doorway, quickly igniting a pile of straw near the door. For an instant, Khoti froze, too stunned to move as shadowy figures pounded through the village. He stepped back to look up the ladder into the mow.

"Von! Fire!" Khoti shouted, not sure if his brother could even hear him over the growing din in the village. Turning back, he found the fire already growing out of control. He tried to kick at the edges and grabbed a nearby bucket but the few inches of half frozen water had no effect. "Von!"

Horses neighed as smoke gathered in the low stable rafters. Think! He needed to reach the green and ring the bell. The flames grew so quickly they already blocked the path to the doorway.

He backed away, his limbs trembling. "Von!" He heard no reply but a crash of wood splintering somewhere, like a cottage door burst open, followed by a shriek.

He dashed back through the barn, pulling up the bars from as many stall doors as he could as he headed for the paddock. Several horses, freed, slammed him against the planks as they fled by. He reached the paddock, slipping in the thin layer of frozen mud over the thawing ground and fell to his knees. The village alarm bell tolled out twice then fell silent with a metallic clang.

Smoke poured out of the lower barn windows now and fire snapped at the planks. He fought down the desire to cough, which might reveal him, as his panting breath drew in cold and smoke. His heart pounded in his ears as he struggled to his feet. Horses that hadn't fled the stable squealed in terror. The handful that had escaped had quickly leaped over the paddock rails, leaving behind the smaller pony that frantically trotted along the far side of the paddock trailing her broken lead.

He should have freed all the horses. He should have gone for the bell instead of hesitating. Von knew they needed to raise the alarm – Von!

He heard a clatter of pots somewhere falling from a hearth pole and the din of wood smashing and people shouting. He could just make out that the door to his own cottage hung askew. If he could just get to his knife and bow–

Suddenly a dark figure filled the doorway of his cottage, hood thrown back to reveal a helmeted head and a face concealed by a mask shaped like the skull of some fanged beast. The man yanked hard and pulled his mother from the cottage barefoot and in her nightdress. She grasped at the door frame a moment as another shadowy figure lobbed a torch within.

He couldn't breathe. Mam screamed his name, Von's and for Grandmam. Her captor pulled her toward the road by her dark braids as she kicked and clawed him. Khoti wanted to run to her, his entire body tensed to move but stayed. What could he do? He could only watch as the marauders gathered the village's women and children on the green around the stone wall encircling the well. The bell swayed there, silent. The village burned, roofs crashing inward, flames roaring, horses screaming, hooves beating against plank walls, the shouts of neighbors and cries of children –

A cloaked figure swung a club at the tanner, splitting his head open. The man crumpled to the ground in front of his cottage.

Khoti backed into the shadows where the forest leaned over the paddock. Finding his wits, he looked around franticly for a club, a stone, something he could wield. He couldn't take his eyes off his mother, where she now comforted a neighbor, lit by the glow of fire. Another marauder dragged a young man, a friend of Von's, from the side of his life mate who clutched their newborn and thrust a sword into the man's chest. Khoti stuffed his muddy fist into his mouth and bit down, concentrating on his need to remain silent and keep his wits. The marauders continued to race through the village, running down those trying to escape into the wild and towing women and children to the green where they were bound together in a line to march into the dark night, mothers grasping small children to their chests to hide them from the horror, other youngsters clinging to their mothers' nightdresses. He watched his mother, back straight and hands bound before her, as marauders led her out of sight.

"Think," he whispered to himself. He couldn't just foolishly race into a sword. He couldn't do anything alone.

At the sound of splintering boards Khoti looked up to see the silhouette of his brother framed in an opening pried in the wall of the hay mow as he tried to kick his way free. About to shout, to race to Von's aid, Khoti stumbled to a stop and dropped to the ground as two marauders, swords glinting orange in the firelight, rounded the side of the barn.

"Khoti! Help –" Von's voice cracked as arrows drove him back into the flames.

Von! Khoti choked on his breath, lying still in the muddy paddock, feeling nothing, feeling frozen. Help. He needed help. What could he do?

Rising to all fours as the marauders moved on, he scooted backward into the shadows. Gaze locked on the burning mow, he stumbled into the shaggy gray-black sides of the pony. He swiftly took up her lead and towed the skittish mare deeper into the dark. Von didn't reappear. The village grew eerily quiet except for the suck of flames. No scream of horses or crying children. He needed to think. He needed help to go after what remained of his world. He needed to reach Sefresal and the Lharan Guard. They were hours away on a fast horse.

He couldn't think about it. He gripped the lead on the pony as he carefully dropped two paddock rails. His breath ripped the air. He could barely move his trembling limbs, certain his heartbeat would give him away. He led the pony over the rails then leaped onto her bare back. The cold wind stung tears from his eyes and pulled his breath in sobs as he urged her quietly along the forest edge until well beyond the smoldering village, then raced east as fast as she could carry him.

2: In the Ashes of Tasch-el

A day's ride southwest of home Tsevon of Tasch-el tended a small fire beside the Staph-el road. He hummed a bit to himself, an old ditty his mother used to sing to him as a child when summer storms sent cracks of thunder echoing down the valley. Now, the tune fought against the odd silence of a crisp spring evening. The Lharan Mountains, which ran like a wall down the western boundary of Shande, usually hummed with the pips of night birds and the early frogs emerging from the ponds of snowmelt alongside the road. Silence felt unusual and heavy, gathering despite the sigh of wind among the rocks and stirring the tree tops in the valley. A dark and moonless night huddled around the edges of the hollow where he'd lit his fire.

He took a steaming bite from the loin of the mountbuck he'd shot, then skewered another chunk of venison and set it just above the flames. He crowded the fire a little, his sheepskin blanket and fur-lined boots and heavy winter gear felt too thin against the cold wind falling from the snowpack above. After a winter in the mines, working ten away for every four home, he should savor the wild air he drew with each breath. Soon the blossom moon would herald the return of all the miners for the lambing and the labors of summer, and he'd have all the little disputes that wore a headman's patience, plus initiations to oversee, birth names to give, rites of passing to utter, joinings to perform and taxes to gather. A night like this, with just his horse Kivik and the spirits for company, should have him at his ease.

But he wasn't. And it made no sense. He moved on to hum a greening song as he scanned the pine fringed valley below where the road plunged deep into darkness at the mountains' feet. Outside of his hollow, a few twisted trees fought for a foothold, but much of the road from Tasch-el south to the Staph-el Falls on the wild Ymmenay River ran through the barren passes and

7

narrow stream gorges just above the tree line.

He plucked the hot chunk of roasted venison and juggled it between his hands for a few moments before it was cool enough to stuff into his mouth. Then he turned back to his work of quartering, boning and salting the mountbuck and packing it and the hide into the saddle bags hanging from Kivik's back. The mare stomped, shifted and snorted a little before nudging him with a little nervous murmur. He studied her a moment. She seemed as out of sorts this night as him.

The wind swirled a moment, then slapped back at him from the north. It carried a hint of smoke. He glanced at his fire, which cast its sparks south along the stony ground, away from him. He swung around and stared into the dark northern reaches. He thought he detected a faint glow reaching skyward toward Tasch-el.

He quickly rummaged in the medicine pouch hanging at his side for his tapping stones. Finding the palm-sized rocks – worn and smooth with years of use – he swiftly rapped the stones together, sending a message that snapped like rocks cooling with the night, rhythmic and sharp, so loud that it could bound off mountain sides and carry into valleys. The stones could always find the ear of some mountain folk. He listened intently for a reply. None came.

He tapped again and still nothing, not even from Staph-el or Lhata to the south. In a quiet night with only a weak wind the sound should carry. He glanced at the Spirit's Guardian striding above him in the night sky. Did all sleep?

Northward the light continued to grow against the sky. Amhese, Von, Khoti. Did his little family watch helplessly as the village storehouses rose in smoke?

Did he hear a tap? He listened again, straining his ears against the silence for a distant rap of stone. Only the wind in the pines and the snap of the cook fire returned, mere whispers. Did a forest fire rage, surrounding his village and leaving them nowhere to go? Likely some fool would try to form a bucket brigade from the stream and well, elders haggling over who should lead in this moment, instead of guiding the people to safety first.

Amhese would end the bickering, he assured himself, as he loaded the last of the venison into his packs. As strong as her lifemate and almost as stubborn, Amhese would force the people to hear reason. They'd flee with only their needs, and lead the livestock to the open ground above the tree line. Someone would ride to Sefresal and call upon the Duke of Lharan's Guard for help. That's how it would be. Amhese would know what to do. Even the dream reader saw wisdom in Amhese's night visions. The old woman had nodded sagely and proclaimed Tsevon's Staphian bride a wise woman. She had shown her wisdom, knowing just what to do when the wolvers threatened the livestock that hard winter when Von first walked, and again in the year when Tsevon couldn't heal the death in his father and a blizzard closed the valley.

He swiftly gathered up his gear and repacked it on the mare. Some stubborn fool likely would panic and not listen. Tsevon didn't have enough medicine in his blood to treat more than one or two injured if foolishness led them astray. He kicked out his fire and emptied his bladder on the last embers. Then he slung his bow at his back and stuffed the last bit of venison in his mouth. He chewed furiously as he swung into the saddle and goaded Kivik to gallop north on the Staph-el road toward the ever-growing glow.

The road – really only a marked path cleared of debris and just wide enough for wagons from the mines – at last dipped below the tree line and ran beneath the arches of massive pines with wind-tossed tops. Rushing streams in rocky courses bearing snowmelt toward the plains, the clatter of Kivik's hooves on stone, the wind – none of it could compete with the roar of blood in his ears.

He reined in among the deep shadows beneath the boughs, breath rapid as Kivik snorted and blew, steam rising from her shaggy black sides. He walked her through the darkness, occasionally tapping his stones, with no reply.

"Easy, Kivik," he told the horse in an impatient whisper, willing her to regain her wind. "Needs be, we'll be going yet into dawn." He buried one hand in the wavy mat of her winter hair to the gritty heat of her sweat. When the mare had cooled, he mounted and goaded her on. Each time he'd rest her beneath some dark forest arbor, let her take only a little water from the roadside stream, and each time they continued on they'd emerge above the tree line to find the glow brighter, nearer. Tasch-el burned. He knew it now.

When at last Tsevon rode down into the Tasch-el Valley, the glow abated as morning neared. Trees closed about him, a smoky, acrid fog clinging about their trunks. The odor grasped at him, of char, and worse.

The tightness in his throat made it hard to breathe and the

9

smoke brought a thirst he couldn't quench with the water in his skins. He came upon a few outlying cottages. They smoldered, roofs fallen in and doors gaping. Here and there in the road lay bits and pieces of villagers' belongings: a shoe, a cloak, a ribbon.

Amhese, Von, Khoti.

Gone. Everything. More than sixty cottages had surrounded the green and the cascade that flowed through it, and more straggled out along the Staph-el Road to the southwest, or the Tasch-el road to the northeast. Nothing remained. The fires died away in the dim dawn, an eerie silence falling as Tsevon emerged from the shadows clutching the forest's edge. He left Kivik on the outskirts of the village, the mare already tossing her head and stomping at the mordant odors.

He tried to find rational answers. Amhese must have led the people to safety above the tree line, where they waited for the fires to abate before rescuing what they could from the ash that now slithered into pools of snowmelt. Or maybe she had simply marched them straight away toward Sefresal in search of the duke's aid, knowing elders and infant would need shelter and food. Amhese, wiser than he, would accept the charity of a lowland duke that a stubborn man like Tsevon would refuse. She would tell her people to hold their heads high despite the disparaging remarks of lowlanders staring at them with awe and pity and assuming them ignorant fools for living so deep in the wild.

But the forest around the village remained green. Inviting. Unburned. Only the homes –

He shivered in a snowpack wind that for a moment brought the comforting scent of pine, before the stench of burned flesh overwhelmed his senses again. He hurried past the collapsed walls of the stable, then stopped and stared, his heart thrumming harder in his chest. Those tannin-stained hands had to belong to the old leather-worker. He lay face down in the mud, no sign of burns on him. Tsevon scanned the green. Here and there bodies lay at grotesque angles, some clutching the ground with frozen fingers. Others sprawled as if they fell while running.

An arrow made of some dark pitch-stained wood protruded from the back of one man, fletched with two black feathers to one fiery orange. Who would do this? Why?

He clenched his fists at his sides, trying to control the rage that made his limbs tremble and his breaths pull from him in gasps. His cottage had burned to a shell. Where were his sons, Amhese, her mam?

He forced himself to stop and listen to the pop and hiss of the dying fires and the wind in the trees. He heard no voices of the living. The fires had burned for at least eight hours now. Even if he hadn't rested Kivik, he couldn't have arrived in time.

He followed the Tasch-el Road to the edge of the village. One horse had reached the road beyond the last of the houses and made for Sefresal at a run. All other sign led into Tasch-el, that of more than two dozen horses. Though shod, like the mounts of the Lharan Guard, these horseshoes were heavier and wider than anything the Guard's blacksmiths forged. The Guard couldn't have come so soon. His people hadn't taken the road to Sefresal. And they hadn't taken the road to Staph-el.

He needed to find the survivors. But the dead needed their rites to free them to join the spirits. He couldn't fail in this last of his duties to them. He swiftly searched the village, finding small clues here and there in a wound, an arrow, in belongings cast aside. They had even toppled the spirit pole in the gods' garden in the common and hacked it to pieces.

He dragged the bodies of seventeen men and three older women behind the burned-out shell of the stables where the forest came closest to the village edge. He stared at each face, remembering a laugh or a smile, the skill of their craft as baker or harness maker, or some strange quirk of habit. The tanner used to yell at Tsevon's boys for playing outside his window, though quick to offer a fine knife sheath to Von when Tsevon marked Von's neck to name him a man. The women had gathered each morning by the well, their gossip like bird chatter, pausing now and then to scold a child or tease a young man for his interest in some woman pretending to ignore him. The elder of the three always held Tsevon's hand when he visited, chattering away about events of the far past as pat, pat, pat, she punctuated her tales on his hand.

He wanted to keen, to mourn them as he should, to provide for each a wooden platform in a quiet glade, padded with hides to comfort their journey, sealed with soil, raised high above the snuffling of mice and wriggling of worms and planted with flower seed gathered by their kin. He could only assemble a single crude platform of charred planks – some still steaming hot so that they blistered his hands – and branches he cut from the trees and pine boughs. He couldn't spare the time to remove the dead from a place where people lived. The platform he erected behind the stable stated he would never return. No one would. One didn't live among the platforms of the dead.

Amhese, Von, Khoti, her mam? Where were they?

He stared at the smoldering ruins of his cottage as he bound the platform together with green bark, ripping each strip with a knife as sharp as his rage. He hefted each body up to the low platform as the morning crept by. His gaze kept returning to his cottage. Every person he had ever loved had crossed that threshold. He had brought Amhese and her mam here to share his hearth from their people in Staph-el. His fa had helped him lay the cottage's supports. His own mam had provided the first hearthstone. His sons were born here. Every villager had come here, for rites or medicine or to talk the small chatter of their lives.

At last, he ducked beneath the fallen timbers, only to trip over something soft, yet solid. He gagged then stumbled out into the muddy street staring down at his blackened hands as the world spun around him and threatened to bring his stomach into his throat. Did Amhese wander somewhere, grieving, knowing her mam's fate? Who burned old women in their beds? He forced himself to return and bear the body to join the others atop the platform.

Hours had passed. He needed to find his people. He couldn't search each cottage, nor rummage through the ruins of the stable and storehouses. More might remain, not freed to join the spirits, forever chained to the moment of death. He wanted to bellow into the trees, to the peaks of the mountains to free the knot of grief in his throat. But already a day had passed. He needed to find the survivors and ensure their safety. Facing the platform, he spread his arms wide, freeing his village, calling the spirits with one clear note from his throat. Then he tossed a handful of soil on the platform.

He drew his knife again, jabbed it into the platform's support and made his mark: claw-shaped gouges like the tawnkat he revered as a kindred spirit. He traced the mark with his fingers, drawing on the ferocity and cunning of that predator to harden his resolve.

Again, he slowly circled the village, knowing he couldn't miss the path of horsed marauders and dozens of villagers. Soon he saw the clear trail, heading northwest straight up the mountain's side. He ran back to Kivik, swiftly mounted and galloped back through the village. At the trailhead, he paused to mark a tree, before he sped up the trail without looking back.

3: The Lharan Guard

A cold spring night had crept into the Duke of Lharan's hall, which, though sheltered within the city walls of Sefresal in the foothills of the Lharan Mountains, felt as cold as if open to the winds on some snow-covered peak. A servant scrambled to stoke the fire higher as Duke Eithurdon glanced at scribbled notes his younger brother Steadon had left him.

A server refreshed the mug of Eithurdon's guest, a Minarian envoy and long-time friend and occasional hunting companion. But the man worked on his third beer, and doing business over his morning meal put the duke in a sour mood. His bread had gone cool and the butter wouldn't spread properly and Steadon usually handled discussions of labor and production. But he'd sent Steadon to a provincial meeting, which he now regretted.

"Look, Ozer," Eithurdon said with a sigh, setting aside Steadon's notes as his guest quaffed his beer. "We negotiated a five-year production and compensation plan less than two years ago. And you want changes already? We certainly cannot meet compensation, or even consider an increase, if your laborers fail to produce the raw materials. Deliveries are down forty percent over last year."

"It is really out of my hands," Ozer said around a piece of apple cake. "Labor is an issue everywhere. We had this conversation with Shiad and Arenh recently." At Eithurdon's raised eyebrows Ozer took a deep drink then shrugged. "An element among the Hogde demand change and this kind of change elevated Mol Azezial. He needs to show himself worthy of the support."

"The Hogde? They already oppose your king? It has been, what, a year, two, since his coronation? I thought only the Pladde worked the mines."

"King Mol Azezial remains popular," Ozer returned with a

13

dismissive wave. "He assures the people that they are chosen for a higher calling and we Hogde are favored by a living god, not the dead ones that fathered the shawnsi." Ozer paused and laughed at Eithurdon's frown. "It has been centuries, Eithur, the powers of the shawnsi are much muted from the nursery tales of ancient times. We do not see you magically bringing rain to break the Minarian drought, or recall the fish that abandoned the Tebez reefs." He laughed again, as if reassuring Eithurdon that he intended his comments, though biting, in jest. "Our king tells the people that with the guidance of a living god he will lead the Hogde to a new prosperous future as the shawnsi fade into the dirt as their dead gods have done."

Eithurdon's pshaw at that claim hung for a moment, Ozer smiling a little as he glanced at him sidelong.

"I merely relate the politic. Some of his advisors accuse Shande of flooding markets with fish and wine, making it even harder for our producers when they are still smarting over your king's claim that we produce inferior fish oil. The rains have yet to come, so who knows how long before they see through all these promises."

"You are not wooed by them?"

"He has big ideas. If he succeeds, I will pledge my life to him. But, well, we shall see."

"It does not explain the decline in production."

"It does. Hogde serve as overseers in the mines and have resurrected that old argument about the drawing of borders. You have to admit Shande took the best mineral resources. They want better pay and favors and refuse to push their charges until they have them. And the Pladde are quick to lean on their picks and pine for their lifemates while taking advantage of the moment. As summer comes on, I am certain we will see change." He gave Eithurdon another sidelong glance and a quick smile tugged at his lips as he toyed with the crumbs on the platter between them. His knife scraped them into a pile, where a small dab of butter adhered them. "But, yes, I shall send word that the Duke of Lharan frets at how few wagons of ore arrived at the smithies when the roads opened."

"It affects your share, Ozer. I would think Minaria would see that it serves us both to see more production –"

"Does it?" Ozer let the knife drop on the platter, a little too loudly. "Of course, of course." He drank the last of the beer and gestured toward the servant for more. "Our ... ten percent, is it? And the meager wages and rations our laborers send home. How could we ever survive without the largesse of Shande and her magnanimous shawnsi leaders?"

"Ozer. Your tone –"

"It is not as if the Shandean laborers stay through the summer."

"That, too, was a negotiation and no easy contract. The Independent Lharan Tribes insisted on a labor schedule that allows them home for lambing and –"

"So, you will of course have lamb on your board while Minaria is paid in ... Shandean grain, wine? It is quite a benevolent trade system, for you. Perhaps we should have been as intransigent as the Independent Lharan Tribes."

"Look, I did not create these treaties. I am obligated only to uphold them. We negotiated with Otayr, Arenh, Shiad, even Shikora, fairly, just as –"

"The last fully executed agreement with us was before King Ebon took the throne. What, thirty years ago? Things change, Eithur. You and I are friends and I respect Steadon. We have worked well together. But things change and it is time Shande does not look at Minaria like a poor laborer to whom you offer alms."

"Is this a threat? Are they planning to walk off?"

Ozer suddenly laughed, one hand waving away the comment as Eithurdon joined him a little more cautiously.

"Your brewer makes a strong beer," Ozer said at last. "I'll convey your concerns."

The doors of the hall suddenly banged open, striking against fieldstone walls to send an echo through the chamber. A door warden leaped forward with a bared sword to block a figure that rushed through the opening, trailed by a squire who cursed and limped as he rubbed a bruised shin. Eithurdon and Ozer rose from the table as the cold morning wind swept in and ripped at the candles in the hall. The newcomer lost his footing and stumbled as he entered, the door warden catching him by an arm.

"It's just a boy," the warden called out.

"Tasch-el!" The youth gasped as the warden steadied him.

Through the open door, Eithurdon could see beyond to the courtyard where a shaggy pony stood, head down, bare sides lathered and only a lead rope trailing in the dusty yard. Its shed coat clung to the insides of the youth's bare, scratched legs. The youth wore only a nightshirt and boots against the cold.

"Mine collapse?" Eithurdon asked as he signaled for a servant to fetch a heavy cloak. The warden wrapped it around the Taschian's shoulders, gripping the youth with his arms to help him put down a violent shiver as the youth shook his head, teeth chattering, his skin and cheeks bright red.

"They ... they burned it. Everyone, they killed them ... and took them away."

Eithurdon lay a hand on a scratched arm and felt the deep cold of mountain night. He nodded at the limping squire. "Send for Kefta." He glanced at Ozer, who sat back down at the table with his beer, his face puckered up in thought.

"Who burned it? What happened?"

"I don't know. We were in the stables. They rode in on the wind. Von ... They burned ... They killed people. Drug my mam out. Von tried to get out but they shot him and –" The youth paused. He'd been staring at his feet, shaking his head, the words tumbling out with each breath. But suddenly he looked up at Eithurdon with a disquieting stare. "I grabbed a pony and rode for help." His tone had gone flat. "They gathered them all on the green. Killed the men. They burned everything and took everyone else away."

"Outlaws? Did you mark their affiliation? How many were there?"

"They wore masks and hoods. More than I could count."

"Lhatan, maybe?" Ozer asked, from the table. "Thieves? Were they not part of the troubles when you negotiated that generous work agreement with the Lharan tribes?"

Eithurdon raised an eyebrow at Ozer's tone.

"They weren't Lhatan." The youth's tone had gone icy. "These weren't mountain folk. Lharan tribes are brothers, not enemies."

Ozer shrugged his doubt. "Outlaws then. Did Shikora ever hunt down all of its bonded who escaped during their war with Arenh?"

Eithurdon stared at the boy, wishing he could see through his eyes what had truly happened. Clearly, whatever had happened had terrified him. It was rare that a Lharan tribe member would ask for anything from Sefresal, especially a Taschian.

His captain of the Lharan Guard hurried up the steps. "Kefta, I need twenty Guardsmen ready to ride with me to Tasch-el," Eithurdon said, then turned and ordered his servants to ready his horse and fetch his gear. "Send for my daughter. With Steadon away, she will need to manage the household alone. Get this boy some food and clothes. He can wait here for my return."

The youth was shaking his head and pulled free of the

warden. He squared his shoulders, somehow appearing more composed despite standing before the duke in a nightshirt.

"I'm coming with you," he said. "My fa will have gotten there by now. I need to find him, and my mam. I can show you the way —"

"I know where Tasch-el is." Eithurdon said, dismissing the boy with a wave as he donned the gear offered by his chamberlain, including a finely woven buff and pewter cloak, heavy sword and a dagger sheath strapped to his boot. Ozer sat back with – was that his fourth beer? – seeming to enjoy too much the excitement of the morning, despite the gravity of an apparent tragedy.

The boy hadn't taken the dismissal. "I'm Tsevon's second ... son," he said. "He'll have gone after them. You don't know the mountains as I do. I can guide you and read Fa's marks."

"And why did you come to us if you thought we could not find our way? Where do you think they went?" He didn't expect a useful answer and was tiring of bantering with some backward shepherd's get. "You wanted a Guard response. Do you now recant your tale? You nearly kill a beast with your race to get here and now you only delay us?"

"Let me join you. You'll need my guidance," Tsevon's son insisted.

As outside the Guard gathered in the yard Eithurdon could feel the youth's rigid, impatient gaze on him as the boy quickly put away a warm cider and hunk of bread from Eithurdon's table.

"I am no stranger to these mountains," Eithurdon said as evenly as he could, despite his rising irritation.

"Oh, Eithur, let the boy play Guardsman. It could be amusing," Ozer offered.

"You don't even know who you're to look for and once you're above the tree line you'll need a tracker. I know my Fa. He'll be hard on the trail and he'll leave sign only a Lharan can follow."

"I am the Duke of Lharan," Eithurdon returned more coldly than he intended, eliciting a chuckle from Ozer.

The Guardsmen assembling at the monument to Terremar in the yard appeared fierce and any fool would parlay on seeing them. But every one of them hailed from the lowlands. During all their disputes with the Lharan tribes it had never come to killing; it had only taken the show of force to break the impasse. Now and then they had to deal with escaped foreign bondsmen, even Minarian Pladde trying to break their contracts who turned outlaw to survive. If outlaws had taken to marauding, then the might of the Lharan Guard would make things right. He would serve justice, free captives, gain restitution and end this foolishness. And in doing so, maybe he'd earn enough gratitude from Tsevon of Tasch-el to at least gain some of the cooperation and respect owed a lord of the region when the tax came due.

Easily Tsevon's son mirrored his father, with tawny hair and the hint of fire burning behind green eyes, like those of a cat gathering the small light of darkness. Perhaps such a brash young man might one day be an asset if encouraged. He might even earn a place as an attendant to a Guardsman. He might just be the tool Eithur needed to build a bond with the tribes and soften Tsevon.

"Get him a mount," Eithurdon ordered as an aide returned with breeches, a woolen tunic and cloak for the youth. The aide ran off again as Ozer openly guffawed with what Eithurdon thought surely was a little too much pleasure at his discomfiture. "I expect obedience. Absolute. You will not get in the way."

He threw a glance at Ozer, then brushed the youth aside and strode for the door. He caught the glint in the Taschian's gaze and felt an odd sense of apprehension race up his spine as the boy turned to follow, as if stalked by a predator.

Despite their haste, it was well into the afternoon before they reached Tasch-el. Khoti Tsevon's son demonstrated none of the weariness evident in the dark smudges beneath his eyes. He sat stiffly in the high-backed buff and pewter cloth saddle. The heavy gray cloak he wore blew back to reveal a Guard dagger tucked in his belt, one he evidently knew how to use.

Eithurdon's eyebrows hooked up when he saw the platform at forest's edge. Khoti reined in at the sight of it, going no closer than the shaggy and trampled green around the well. The village's silence muted even the wind in the pines.

"My fa's work," Khoti said.

"It could have been anyone," Eithurdon said.

"If you know Tsevon, as you say, you'd recognize his mark. No one else would use it."

Kefta nudged Geleg, and soon all the Guardsmen stared at the youth, who remained oblivious to the impropriety of his behavior. Eithurdon smiled and shook his head at Kefta, who then laughed aloud, his face almost as red as his beard. The remaining Guardsmen chuckled in the boy's direction. The youth echoed Tsevon from his looks to the way he displayed absolutely no respect for the duke, lord of the region and nephew of the King of Shande. Not even the deference owed an elder.

"Typical of the Independent Tribes," the duke told Kefta in a voice he didn't think would carry.

"And like his fa," Kefta agreed. "That man's as stubborn and hard to move as a mountain."

Khoti glared at the chuckling Guardsmen, who shifted under his gaze and fell silent in a little knot behind the duke. Some studied the platform, but most watched Khoti as if they examined some new device they hadn't quite figured out.

"I do recognize his mark," Eithurdon admitted. Called to his attention, he clearly saw the crude Vs carved at the base of the platform.

"They went northwest," Khoti said. He gestured toward a tree at the village edge where a fresh scar in the bark looked like a W on its side. The Vs pointed north. "He's got no plans of coming back here. We don't live among our dead like you lowlanders."

"Your father must have educated you," Eithurdon said, nodding.

"Of course. Your children are taught we're no better than our livestock."

"I am sure our children are taught no such thing," Eithurdon returned, feeling a rush of heat at the insolence. "That he educated you speaks well of your father. However, he appears to have neglected teaching you social graces." He scanned the charred village, his gaze finally resting on the youth who showed no sign of the fear, grief and loss he must feel, but had easily picked out a mark on the west edge of the green that had eluded Eithurdon.

He gave a sharp hand signal to Kefta. "Khoti, you will ride ahead with the scouts to watch for your father's marks."

The youth joined two of Eithurdon's best, barrel-chested Toban and slender Ytri at the head of the company. Khoti stared at them a long moment, as if he'd long ago proven his right to ride with the Guard. Eithurdon found something endearing in that cocky certainty. The duke grinned at Kefta, who merely laughed on cue, his red beard quivering.

The trail they followed led straight up the mountain side. Soon, they left the protection of the forest with its pockets of snow. The horses scrambled over barren rock edged by early wildflowers. The trail of almost one hundred captives and their mounted captors soon crossed trackless stretches of bare rock or loose slopes that sent them off the trail to find firmer footing.

Khoti paused often to study the small signs left behind. At last, as darkness fell, Khoti lingered long enough on a ridge for the rest of the party to catch up.

"They will have to –" Kefta began, but Khoti put up his hand with the Guard signal for silence.

The Taschian peered into the darkening mountains, his eyes narrowing to cat-like slits, his head tilted, as if he listened to the wind. Suddenly he dismounted to dig amongst the loose rock at his feet to find two palm-sized stones. He struck one to the other, sending a large piece of the rock slivering up at his face. He cursed, trying again, rapping out several quick beats before one of the stones broke in half. He threw them to the ground, his fists clenched as he stared into the growing darkness.

"What is it?" Kefta asked at last.

"Worthless rock," Khoti said. "I lost my stones. Fa's trying to let the captives know he's following. They don't respond and the wind's all wrong. This is the worst part of the mountains for tapping –"

"Tapping?"

"You pass news with stones." Eithurdon said, stunned. It explained so many odd exchanges with the tribes when they seemed to already know what others had just learned.

"How else would you send word?"

"So did you tell him we follow?"

"I tried. This stuff just crumbles." He kicked at the stones he had rejected. "He thinks he hears a reply but isn't sure." Khoti hadn't taken his eyes off the horizon ahead of them.

"Lord, should we find a place to camp for the night?" Toban asked.

Khoti was shaking his head. "They're travelling into the night. We'll lose them."

"Can't follow a trail in the dark, boy," Ytri said.

"And if they've near a hundred folk, as you say, they won't get far ahead," Kefta said.

"They marched 'em out in darkness, why would they stop now?" Khoti gestured ahead. "And if you miss signs on this broad of a trail you might as well retire to the hearth. Besides, they show no mountain sense. They should be keeping to the valleys and passes. They aren't even smart enough to slow down. They're going to end up in a rock slide or going over a cliff."

Eithurdon peered into the gloaming. "While we're above the tree line, I doubt you would miss a sign. We can rest when we find a stream and make camp when the trail next takes us into the forest."

Khoti nudged his mount ahead. The Guardsmen followed without a word from their duke.

They had ridden several hours into the night before Toban and Ytri halted, Khoti quickly dismounting. Eithurdon listened, expecting to hear tapping in the wind. Instead, a soft sigh told him they neared the eaves of the forest again. He caught then a smell that first resembled a pungent wildflower of the plains then became unmistakably bitter.

"Several days old," Toban agreed with the youth as Eithurdon reached them. Khoti scooped up a stone and threw it into the trees, unsettling carrion birds, which squawked, then again fell silent in the darkness. Some scavenger scurried away in the dark, bounding across stones with a growl.

The stench made Eithurdon's eyes water. "Animal?" he asked.

"No, Lord," Toban said.

"We'll need to camp nearby, upwind," Ytri said. "The trail goes into the forest where it's too dark to follow."

Khoti remained as the Guardsmen set up a camp several hundred paces away, with a small fire sheltered by the trees. Kefta and Eithurdon returned with a torch. The duke stifled a gasp when they illuminated the body lying trailside. Though scavengers had worked it, they could still see the face, darkened with a crust of blood where a triangle inside of a circle had been branded on the cheek. A miner's spike protruded from the man's forehead.

Khoti pulled aside long dark plaits to reveal a tiny triangle tattooed on the man's neck. "Lhatan."

"Any other signs?" Eithurdon's thoughts raced as Kefta shook his head. Lhata. Had other villages suffered Tasch-el's fate?

They struck camp before dawn. For almost two days they pushed on from dawn until well after dusk, stopping at night now for fear they'd miss markers as they closed on the marauders. On the second day they came across the first Taschians. An older woman clearly had died from the injuries sustained in the raid on the village; the other, with a shriveled leg, Khoti identified as his aunt. The marauders had carved a bloody mark in her forehead and slit her throat. The marauders had clearly made a short-lived camp there. Tsevon, following, had pulled the dead closer together and made a small mound that served as a fruitless gesture to lift them above the reach of scavengers.

In the following days, they found more Taschians, as if the

marauders herded the villagers deep into the mountains merely to kill them. In each case, Tsevon had paused to perform the rites of a headman and free their spirits. Eithurdon wondered if Tsevon would perform rites for his entire village before he caught up to the marauders.

Having hunted on the slopes above Sefresal since childhood, Eithurdon had thought himself capable in the mountains. He was mistaken. Many times, only Khoti knew north from south as they circled into some deep valley or could mark from a long distance where they would find a pass to avoid a dangerous part of the trail, or a stream to replenish their skins and rest their mounts.

"Fa used his medicine here." Khoti said on the afternoon of the fourth day. The youth studied the blackened cinders of a campfire as Eithurdon caught up to the scouts.

"He hasn't lit a fire yet. Why now?" Toban asked.

"He's with someone." Khoti rummaged in the brush, gesturing at beaten soil, trampled weeds and scuffed lichen.

"The marauders camped here before him." Toban pointed out signs that illustrated that story.

"Fa found someone hiding here and made medicine. He'd need a fire for that. He's just about on top of them now." Khoti looked up at the duke, for the first time appearing concerned. "What can he do alone?"

Eithurdon didn't have an answer and they had little time to ponder it. They needed to keep moving. The scarred face of a mountain loomed just to the south as they rode on, a rough wagon-rutted path zigzagging like dirty holiday ribbon across its sides leading up to the Tasch-el mine. The marauders' trail circled north, then west to avoid it. Likely miners still labored there, unaware of what had happened to Tasch-el. At times, Khoti stopped, putting his hand up for silence as he listened for a tap or voice on the wind.

As dusk closed and the wind died, a voice carried back to Eithurdon. "Ah, Khoti, if only there was a glimmer of a camp fire. We could sweep right in," Geleg said in a companionable tone. "And what if other raiding parties are out here attacking other villages and we're just heading farther away from places where we could be defending them?"

What if, Eithurdon wondered, again, as he lost Khoti's reply to Geleg in the breeze. What had become of his ordered and ordinary world when a mountain boy could teach a lord, that someone dared raise a weapon against Shandeans under his watch and that he, the Duke of Lharan, could feel such a disquieting sense of foreboding in all of it?

As the last rays of sunlight tinged the mountain top, Khoti reined in and dropped to the ground to study the marks at his mount's feet, the horse immediately reaching out to tug at the sparse greenery emerging with the first days of the blossom moon.

"What does it mean?" Kefta asked, as he and the duke arrived to stare at the marks.

"The single mark west, the trail continues. Double mark either says number in his party, or emphasizes direction, or both. I think he found someone alive and to follow him we head for the mine."

Kefta scratched at his beard, his brow furrowed. "But he was almost on top of them when he left the trail."

"He knows he needs help." Khoti seemed to choke on the word 'help' and turned away from them to stare at the mountain. "There's probably fifty Taschian miners finishing up the winter work in the mine. He probably thought to reach them before they headed ... home. He's marking the trail because he hopes someone is following. All those rites he's done. He might have used up his medicine. There's a couple other Taschians in the mines with medicine, though not as good as Fa's."

"Medicine? You mean herbs and extracts?"

Khoti didn't answer and pursed his lips. Eithurdon gave him a long measuring look before he decided that maybe, finally, it all caught up to the youth.

"I will take Khoti and my unit on the route Tsevon took," Eithurdon said. "They may need help. We can look for sign he came back this way. The rest of you push on after them, faster. You may come upon them before full darkness. Engage only if necessary! We should be at full force in the event they are well armed."

As they diverged, Eithurdon urged them on faster, Khoti scanning the trail for signs, his head turning from side to side as if following a fly's flight through a pantry, each sighting of a sign swiftly signaled with a Guard hand signal, and the youth already expertly guiding his mount over treacherous terrain that the Guardsmen struggled to follow.

Khoti had already demonstrated to the duke that he belonged in the Lharan Guard. He was just what Eithurdon needed to gain control over the Lharan tribes: Tsevon's own son sworn to him.

4: Night of the Cat

Amhese studied the east rim of the valley where pines painted the sky, made into silhouettes by a waxing moon that lurked out of sight and deepened the valley's shadows. A crawling sensation of being watched tickled her scalp as she methodically worked the rope binding her arms, now rubbing the binding against a sharp rock then plucking at it with her teeth. The skin on her wrists had rubbed away from days of walking, bound, on unstable ground. Only mothers carrying small children went hands free, though bound together at the waist and closely watched.

The marauders' campfire revealed a stony stream course. Dark water boiled through the center and the forest hung back, with logs from past floods piled up far beyond the reach of the fire's light. Wind sighed in the pines, as if Tsevon whispered from the ridge above her to be patient and await him.

Her braids had come loose and now her long hair spilled into her lap where it hid the frayed rope at her wrists. Head bowed, she sneaked a peek at the fire where their captors gathered. Only a few dozen in all, they bore swords and bows, axes and knives, and wore armor beneath their black cloaks and tunics, appearing like shadows that had broken free of the forest. She had seen their brutality and did not doubt they would kill again, as they had killed Tsevon's sister when she moved too slowly and complained too loudly. They spoke to one another in a thick dialect, muffled by the grotesque masks they wore, both familiar and not. She couldn't place them: no mountain-born would stumble so foolishly into locked valleys like this one. Yet, they strutted, intimidating and relishing it. They didn't care that they herded children into the cold without cloak or blanket. They tossed food at their captives as if they fed livestock and left them bound through the night, child and adult alike, ignoring

Amhese's appeals for mercy for the sick and young, and answered questions with fists.

The captives knew Tsevon followed. His taps, barely heard on the night wind, went unanswered but for an occasional covert acknowledgement. They dragged their feet, slowing to keen over the dead, hoping Tsevon would have time to gather help and follow.

Beside Amhese, Latra stared silently at the ground. Fearing the worst intent of their captors, she had left her daughter Jiata hidden in a cleft along the trail, hoping Tsevon would find her. When their captors discovered the child missing – dead, Latra claimed – they struck the woman until her eyes swelled shut. Clearly, they wanted the children alive, but it didn't matter in what condition. That worried Amhese most.

A covert glance told Amhese no marauder looked her direction. She pulled at the rope with her teeth, breaking a few more strands, aided by the sharp edges of a tooth chipped by a captor's fist. Again, she plucked at the rope, thinking herself like the mice that had nibbled holes in the grain casks in her larder, each day gnawing away a few more shavings. More than halfway through the rope now, she wanted to be ready for what she expected: Tsevon.

"It's a night of the cat, Latra, I know it," Amhese whispered as she rubbed the frayed rope against a rock.

Latra scanned the bright rim to the east where the moon hesitated to crest. She squinted as if she could see Tsevon's lithe frame silhouetted against the sky. "You've so much faith? Can he do anything alone? Has he found Jiata? Ahrwesz will hate me for leaving our daughter –" When one of their captors turned, Latra lowered her head again and fell silent.

"He will come. And he'll show no mercy." Amhese stared at the backs of her captors and again plucked the cords with her teeth.

A shriek erupted from the tree shadows edging the campsite. Amhese's head snapped up. The call trailed away into the low whining growl of a tawnkat. With a wrench, she yanked her arms apart, snapping the final cords securing her wrists. Gaining her knees, she freed Latra, even as a quick rapping of stones ordered the Taschians to cover. Amhese and Latra, joined by others, freed the remaining prisoners to dash into the shadows.

The captors leaped up to stop the fleeing captives. At that moment, the canyon erupted with a shrill yell that brought heat into Amhese's face and lifted the hairs on her arms. Captives threw themselves behind rocks in the stream course or rolled

25

behind logs as arrows whistled by to find targets in the light thrown by the fire.

Some of the captors fell to the ground, not to rise again. Amhese shrieked a warning when she glimpsed a marauder aiming a throwing knife at Tegi, Tsevon's Second, as the man rushed the clearing. The warning came too late. Tegi fell with the knife in his chest. As quickly, Tsevon grappled the marauder to the ground and slit his throat. For an instant Amhese couldn't move, transfixed by the blood on Tsevon's hands, on the fallen warrior's throat, Tegi's still form. Her lifemate had always been capable of this. He had slit a man's throat like he would a lamb's for the midsummer feast.

She quickly recovered. He'd done what he must, as she must. She called her people to rally to her. On her signal, women and children collected a store of rocks, some for throwing, and some fragments as sharp as knives. They would not be captives again.

Some twenty raiders remained. Their armor turned miners' arrows as they confronted the sixty men Tsevon had found at the Tasch-el mine. Even if they could penetrate that armor, their bows were now mostly useless in the close quarters. Now they faced their better-armed opponents almost bare-handed but for a few picks and knives.

Amhese ordered children to hide, instructed to race to her if she called for them. A word held most silent, the elder youths keeping the younger quiet, the mothers gripping stones in their white-knuckled hands. She crouched behind a large boulder near the stream, her heart pounding. Jaw clenched, she stared out at the camp now brightly lit by moonlight bounding from the grey-white stones of the stream course. Tsevon had come. Where were her sons? Had Tsevon sent Von and Khoti to gather the livestock and shepherds scattered in the valleys near Tasch-el? Von had a voice and one day must lead the Taschians. Why didn't he fight beside his fa? Even Khoti would certainly have insisted he fight for his village.

Unless they'd been killed like the tanner, or been asleep in the loft and trapped in the burning cottage with Mam. No. Her sons waited among the trees for the turn of the fight. Taschians outnumbered the warriors three to one. Why send youth into a battle for which their elders were no better prepared? It was enough Tsevon had come. It would end soon. Hadn't Tsevon just slit a man's throat like a lamb's?

She crept toward the bow Tegi had dropped, then darted out to grab it and scoop up the scattered arrows, before dashing back behind the boulder. If her lifemate, a healer and spirit talker, could take a life in defense of his people, then a mother could take a life in defense of children. Trusting her mountain-born skills, Amhese picked a mark from the shadows darting in and out of the trees and tumbled boulders, or briefly silhouetted against the fire. The light fell on a conical helm. She sucked in a breath then loosed an arrow. It bounded off the marauder's chest and clattered to the stony ground. He turned toward her, knife raised. Her heart rose in her throat as a miner's pick slammed into the man's face.

She must pick her targets more carefully. She wouldn't make that mistake again.

The skills that had earned Tsevon the respect of the northern tribes were no match against warriors. He couldn't use his hunting bow in a melee; his dagger turned like straw against armor. His foe lolled his tongue out of his fanged mask with the laughter and confidence of a man to a child as they circled one another. It felt futile and yet Tsevon had no choice.

"Who are you?" Tsevon demanded as they circled. "What've we done to deserve such malice?"

His foe let out a humorless laugh, revealing a gap-toothed grin behind the mask, and lunged, missing, as Tsevon darted closer to the campfire. Young. The laugh sounded like that of a youth. Tsevon set his back to the fire to light his foe's movements. Gap-Tooth lunged again, his blade slicing Tsevon's upper arm as the older man leapt away. Tsevon tried to call up the instincts and predator skill of his patron tawnkat as he darted just out of Gap-Tooth's reach, but he was exhausted from his pursuit, and now clearly overmatched. Around him, others struggled, some two-to-a man, while yet others hurried to aid their lifemates and children.

His people stumbled to escape the reach of swords and struck with the clumsy blows of men accustomed to attacking rock and tree, or pursuing game, not fighting to the death. Their breaths ripped from them in gasps, like Tsevon's own.

Tsevon lunged. His dagger turned on the warrior's metal shell, which had no weak point. Gap-Tooth spun, slicing upward. Tsevon ducked, a hair's breadth between the blade and the flesh of his neck. Taschians fell about him. Gap-Tooth didn't fear him, even toyed with him. The eyes behind the mask were cold even as that mouth grinned behind its fanged façade.

As Gap-Tooth lunged again, Tsevon tripped in the clutter of cooking gear, bedrolls and packs around the campfire. He struggled to regain his footing as the man rushed him. He stabbed upward for the man's neck, only to have his dagger again turn on metal and bound back as Gap-Tooth came on again. Tsevon rolled away, escaping with a minor cut from his own dagger, a cut that burned as hot as his temper.

Suddenly a horn call echoed up the valley, chasing around tree trunks and bounding from the boulders. A clatter of hooves against stone rose to a din. Tsevon wanted his back to the fire again, too pressed to dare hope it wasn't more marauders. Gap-Tooth pushed him backward, trying to force him down into the fire. Tsevon swept up a burning branch and thrust it toward that sneer. The throb of hoofbeats built like thunder in the narrow canyon, followed by a shout rising from the shadows of boulders and logs and the boles of trees.

The Lharan Guard galloped toward them in a wash of moonlight, the white light glinting from drawn swords. A red bearded Guardsman rode straight at Gap-Tooth and drove the warrior to the ground, splitting his black shield with a single blow. Tsevon leaped to make the man his prisoner. But just then Gap-Tooth dragged his own knife across his throat.

Tsevon fell back in shock. "They slay themselves!" he shouted. His call came too late. When he scanned the battleground, only miners and Guardsmen stood in the moonlit stream course as the captives stole from hiding. Only one marauder remained alive, too injured to harm himself.

For a long moment Tsevon could do nothing more than try to find his breath, to slow his heart before he stumbled the few feet to where his cousin, friend and Second lay but one more still lump among the boulders. Tegi's hand still clutched the dagger in his chest. If only he had been bolder against a foe so weak he would slay himself. If he had arrived sooner, perhaps his medicine could have saved Tegi. He wanted to keen, to roar. Tasch-el had lost so many. For what?

"I have someone here for you," said a voice behind him.

Tsevon turned to find the Duke of Lharan, jaw set in a tight smile. The duke nodded over his shoulder, where Tsevon could see Khoti astride one of the duke's fine beasts. His son appeared dwarfed by an animal that stood easily a forearm's length above Tsevon's own weary Kivik, its sleek coat shining in the moonlight, not dull with the heavy garb of winter. Tsevon scanned the milling Guardsmen for Von, then the gathering of captives hugging and crying as they reunited with sons, fathers and lifemates in the moon's glow. In the chaos of men and horses, he didn't see his elder son. His gaze fell on Amhese, who regarded him with her arms crossed on her chest from across the dark distance of the stream course. She stood safe, and strong. What remained of his home stood there, proud and undaunted, hair loose to the wind as it had been long ago when they first danced together around a Long Day fire.

He forced his attention back to the duke and Khoti, feeling the weariness of sleepless pursuit and obligation as Khoti slipped from his mount. The youth merely looked into Tsevon's face with an expression lost in shadow and the flickering gold of campfire. Something was missing. Gone was the light-hearted youth Tsevon had despaired of taming to serve as his brother's Second. Tsevon pulled Khoti to him roughly then pushed him away to regard him.

"I thought I heard a rap of stones behind me, but lost the song in the wind," Tsevon stated. "Your brother?"

Khoti looked away. "The stables," he said in a near whisper. "He was in the mow. The fire – they drove him back in."

Tsevon took a breath that hissed like a wind full of snow. His fists clenched at his sides. He hadn't freed him. Von remained chained to that moment of suffering, unable to rejoin his people among the spirits. He had failed his own son. He turned his back on the duke and Khoti, overwhelmed by the rush of his grief, the wail of denial inside him that wanted to rip the night sky. Von's face loomed before him, broad grin and twinkling eyes staring from the door of the stables, flecks of hay clinging to his hair as he leaned on the hay fork. The stables. The stench of burnt horseflesh had made Tsevon retch. The musky scent of his son working beside him. His laugh echoed into the rafters of the cottage. Von. The stables, smoking and sputtering, sending their acrid stench in search of him no matter where he had worked in Tasch-el.

All of his people had lost someone. He had gathered them, freed them to the spirits, done his final duty. But not for his own son. He could not keen now for just one of many. Not yet. Not until they all gathered safe again, their wounded healed, their children warmed.

Khoti stared at his back. He felt him there, changed somehow, a blast of heat and cold and anger at his back.

"Find your mam and see that she's well," Tsevon said through clenched teeth, the words barely passing the knot in his throat.

29

As Khoti ran to his father's bidding, Eithurdon dismounted and put a hand on Tsevon's shoulder. "You are no easy man to follow, Tsevon of Tasch-el. If not for Khoti, we would have missed the marks and lost the trail. He has the best of his father in him."

The knot in Tsevon's throat remained, though he tried to swallow it away, tried to fill his lungs and regain the lost sense of balance that threatened to bring him to his knees.

"We need his kind in the Guard," the duke continued. "With his woodcraft and tracking skills he will be an asset to my house."

Tsevon stiffened. He scanned the clearing, finding Khoti wandering among the milling villagers. He had stopped beside Tsevon's nephew Ahrwesz, who hugged Latra to him, the woman gone limp with relief to learn their daughter lived. Konner, the man who would now be Tsevon's Second, tended their wounded, his medicine no match for Tsevon's. Quiet Segan had already set about building litters to bear those most grievously injured, if given a place to take them. They had no home. Tasch-el was no more. They were people bound only by the memory of who they had once been. Now Eithurdon offered an honor about which most parents dreamed, one that would further tatter Tsevon's world.

Tsevon shook his head. "He has a lot of learning to do among his own folk. There's a village to settle, livestock to gather. We don't even know who it was attacked us and we'll need to secure our people. And now I've only one son to train for headman."

"I think he belongs with me. Once your people are safe, we can discuss this further."

"I've given you the final word. He's my son, now my only son, and hasn't even earned his marks yet. He stays with me!"

The red-bearded Guardsman interrupted them to whisper in the duke's ear. "Bring him," Eithurdon snapped, scowling as two Guardsmen brought forward the surviving prisoner and set him at the duke's feet. The man's helm and mask had been removed to reveal youthful features, but not that of a local tribe. Thick dark hair hung in braids so tight they pulled his skin taut.

"He dies," Tsevon said softly, seeing it as certainly as he could see the death in a parched plant or the eyes of the mountbuck he'd shot. It was in Tsevon's blood to know this, in the gift of the spirits. "He drowns in his own blood."

The wounded raider sneered as the red-bearded Guardsman yanked the man's head up to force him to look at Eithurdon as blood seeped from an arrow wound at the base of the man's neck.

"I will have none of that, Kefta," Eithurdon said.

The man struggled to wrench his head free of Kefta's grasp as if he didn't feel the pain that Tsevon could see in him, or sense the death that stalked him.

"It is too late for you. You cannot stop us," the prisoner said, each word shooting a fine spray of blood.

"Why? Who are you?!" the duke demanded.

"Victory is ours," he said with his dying breath. Kefta let the man fall face forward to the ground with a thump.

"What is happening in this world?" the duke scanned the circle of Taschians forming around them. "Kefta, take five men and ride to Lhata and Staph-el. Watch yourself. If there are other raiding parties hitting other villages, the attackers could still be in the area." He turned to face Tsevon, his shawnsi features somehow haunting in the spare light of moon and fire, as if he were a man on his death walk, though the duke certainly stood strong and hale and little older than Tsevon himself. "And what are we to do with you?" he asked of Tsevon.

"Do with us?" Tsevon echoed. "I'm honored a man such as the Duke of Lharan troubles himself with assaults on mountain folk he knows only to collect the tax."

The silence around them fell sudden and deep.

"I came on your son's request. I feared for the lives of Shandeans. Mountain folk or not, you are still Shandean. Your trail awed me, Tsevon of Tasch-el. I saw your skill and dedication, and how wisely you taught your son. I am amazed you let your prejudices steer you at such a time, when even Khoti thought first of his village."

Tsevon straightened. This duke wore no armor to turn a dagger.

"Why would we not care?" the duke went on. "People died in attacks unprecedented by strangers who claim they are victorious even in their death throes, who would slay themselves to hide their identities, who have waged battle against children and elders."

Tsevon studied the duke, certain the man knew, or thought, something he didn't say. If nothing else, that gave Tsevon a crawling feeling in his gut. Tsevon inclined his head.

"Well, what do you suggest?" Eithurdon demanded. "We cannot be everywhere at once, nor await direction from the king. That will take months. We must find out who these people are, their affiliation, what their goals are in attacking your village. Are they some overlooked mountain tribe?"

"They aren't mountain born, that's certain," Tsevon said. He remained silent a long time as the moon rose higher above them. The people of his village had sorted themselves into families, their features stark in the faint light. Herbalists, wise women and lesser healers such as Konner tended the wounded until Tsevon could spare his medicine for the worst of the injuries. He could only do so much before it would wear him to nothing. His people had no home. They needed the strength of health to survive, and they wouldn't have that health long without shelter, livestock and the stores that burned away in Tasch-el. He eased himself down onto a massive boulder as his people gathered around, and stared into the last of the marauder's campfire. The smell of blood filled his nostrils, seeming to cling there as had the odor of burned horseflesh.

In the stables, Khoti had said.

He sensed Eithurdon staring at him impatiently, and the uncertainty of his people, and felt his muscles tensing beneath his hide shirt. Inside he felt the tawnkat's urge to spring.

He gestured his head toward his constable, Konner, whose good-natured face had a sharp edge usually softened by a slashing grin. Now he stood bloody and weary of healing, something brutal in his features.

"How many men did we lose?" Tsevon asked, determined to keep his tone even and not betray the emotions that threatened to overwhelm him.

"Eight, with ten wounded. Eleven if you count you." Konner gestured at Tsevon's bloody arm.

"Amhese," Tsevon called across the fire to where she stood, her arms again crossed, her dark hair blowing like a veil. "How many lost?"

"Twenty-two in Tasch-el, fourteen on the march, if Latra's child is truly safe with her grandfa."

"Almost a quarter of Tasch-el dead!" That familiar knot built in his throat again. Unbidden the feel of his foot against Amhese's mother – "And half of those left are injured. Our homes gone. Who knows what livestock remains." Amhese had move to his side. She took his hand, anchoring him. "And other villages could be facing the same? I won't stop here and admit losses. Nor can I rebuild Tasch-el beside the platforms of the dead. If there's more of these raiders, I'll find them. I'll kill every last one of 'em."

"Not alone you won't," Konner said.

Tsevon stroked the bloody wounds on Amhese's wrist. "They've taken everything from us. We won't accept defeat. But first we need to make what remains of us safe."

"Do you know where they were taking you?" the duke asked. All looked at Amhese, who shook her head. "Clearly you need shelter, not too distant for your injured to travel."

"We're not people of the city or lowlands –" Tsevon began.

"I know that. Sefresal would be an unacceptable direction. It would cause only more grief for your people. We need both a safe place, but also a base from which we can search for more raiders and protect the region. They can be one in the same."

Tsevon stiffened at the duke's tone, recognizing a task assigned to a subject.

"There is a sheltered valley, the one deep up on the Shiadin border west of the Sefresal Pass that empties directly into the Ymmenay River. It must be only a few days' travel from here and is close enough Sefresal can send support and there are grazing areas for livestock. Until we are sure we have secured the mountains it is not safe for you to settle again on traveled roads and passes that are easy to attack. I recall caves that should be large enough to shelter all your people, and there is a ready supply of fresh water," the duke stated in a tone that suggested he had already made the decision. "You will need supplies: what you can gather from the mine and Tasch-el and what we can bring to you. We will keep your location ... secret. There we can decide what is to be done."

As Tsevon prepared to retort that he needed no duke ordering his people around, Kefta arrived to announce his departure with the men to Lhata and Staph-el. With a shiver of revulsion, Kefta held up several chains with medallions hanging from them. Glittering in the dying firelight, rubies, like eyes, were set in a raised imprint of a disk with many rays pointing downward. The star-like imprint stood out in a dull black alloy of adanan, the hardest of metals, pressed into a gold triangle etched with the imprint of flames, surrounded by other symbols.

"Found these on the dead," Kefta said.

Tsevon leaned forward, studying the shape. "This mark was on the bodies along the trail." The glitter of the rubies made his heart skip with revulsion and he swept them from Kefta's arm and tossed them into the fire. The embers seemed to make the gems glow more intensely. "They thought themselves martyrs for some idol! They aren't going to stop at any small show of force."

33

"Well, Tsevon," Konner said, straightening. "We know you're a bit of a lone hunter, but I gather we might have better luck in a pack. This foe aims to make trouble in our mountains? We'll harass them back to wherever they came from, or into their graves."

Tsevon studied his hand. He could still feel the so-brief sensation of the medallions in his palm. They hadn't been cold like metal, but warm to the touch as if from the passion driving their bearers.

"Yes," Tsevon admitted, "we might have the better luck in a pack." He glanced at Eithurdon who blanched at the Taschian's expression. "We'll go to the duke's valley, get our people mended then prepare our hunt."

"If these are foreigners, I must await the official word of the king before I can take any overt action beyond detaining any we capture," Eithurdon said.

"Then you may wait," Tsevon said. "We will not."

THE EAST

5: A Warning

Sihma Harbor baked in the first hot afternoon of spring. The rolling hills and cliffs on the north east coast of Shande seemed to hold the sea's breeze at bay at the edge of the salt-whitened and barnacled pilings of the docks, allowing barely a leaf to stir here on the trampled green of the common. A hubbub rose as townsfolk gathered to gossip and wager on the pending wrestling match between Harbor champion, Prince Arshaldon Dyndevas, and a stranger who all agreed should know better.

"Make it a good contest, Arshal," his friend Javan called, his Shikoran captain's cap tilted to shield his face from the sun. "I owe that robber Jan a ship's purse for a single ale."

A round of laughter followed as Jan the Innkeeper sputtered his denial, declaring loudly and repeatedly that Javan ordered a single ale for every member of the Shikoran's crew.

"And I owe that rascal Javan for our wager on how slow Aron Keeper would be to meet my vessel," his fellow captain Azuth agreed, as the lighthouse keeper both laughed and whined that Minarian ships had too deep of a draft for most of the harbor.

The banter buzzed in Arshal's ears as he nursed a headache he'd had since waking from yet another restless night of bad dreams. Somehow wave sparkle glittered too much like the nightmare's image of fire on swords. A sour gut from too many ales with Azuth and Javan at Jan's inn the night before only added to his bad humor.

As he scanned the onlookers, his gaze fell on one sailor who stood stone-faced, arms akimbo. Something unsettled him in the way the man stared at the prince, something that reminded Arshal of one of his nightmares –

He shook his head and arms and tried to loosen up. He needed to focus on the match. He had a record to uphold. Dreams were just dreams, his tutor Cree kept telling him.

Despite the racket of onlookers and the seabirds lining the clutter of benches, net-drying racks and small boats pulled up for repair, the common felt like a peaceful oasis, unlike the king's echoing halls where petitioners, clerks, and courtiers lurked around every corner in the midst of the teeming royal seat of Sihmad Shal. The common bordered a seaside village that by turns felt sleepy or clamorous, and today chaotic, as market vendors lured sailors from the five ships new to port this morning. Carts and teams crawled westward into Sihma Harbor along the crushed shell road from Sihmad Shal to line up along the waterfront boardwalk as the boats of fisher and trader jockeyed for position at docks where cargo stood, sailors yarned, and fishwives hawked the catch of the day, their racket blending with the ever-present and impelling cries of gulls hovering above the fishing boats. Strains of music and laughter filtered from inns lining the boardwalk, which followed the harbor's natural curve from the west to end at the common. The clamor gave Arshal promise of an ale, a tale, and a hearty song to laud his exploits this afternoon.

The growing crowd formed a circle around Arshal, held at bay by the small flags Reve Pedr lay upon the grass to mark the boundaries of the match. Arshal took note of the fluttering ribbons from a gaggle of young women arriving, their cheeks flushed from hurrying to the green, as they giggled and preened and posed, each vying for his eye.

Jan nudged him and jerked his head toward the women with a conspiratorial grin. Arshal merely nodded.

"Where's that famous princely grin?" Jan asked. "You can't be afraid of this newcomer. He's got no reputation."

"I'm not really in the mood for wrestling today, Jan. Perhaps we should call it."

"Mood? Mood! It'll come to you in moments. It's the competition you live for and you know it. I can't imagine you walking away from a match or a race or even a bet on the fastest beetle –"

"You know Azuth dunked that beetle in ale first. It was too

drunk to move."

Jan waved away his protest. "You just need to shake off the memory of last night's drink and set your mind to the battle in front of you." He thunked Arshal on the back. "And look at all those ladies, all dreaming they'll catch the eye of Shande's most eligible undefeated matchman. You can't let all those faces turn sad for you."

Arshal snorted at that.

"There now, no more frowning and spoiling folks' fun. In a few minutes it'll be over and you can nurse your headache with an ale. We can't be letting you lose to anyone but those mercy matches to your brothers. You've a reputation to uphold."

Arshal laughed then, just as his opponent arrived in the ring. The prince made a ceremony of bowing to his foe. The burly stranger from the countryside had begun to sweat in the afternoon heat, leaving dark stains on his brown tunic.

"Farm laborer from down near Whittea," Jan whispered as he brushed by Arshal in a hurry to join Javan and Azuth among the onlookers so he could get in on their side bet over how long the match would last.

So, his opponent would be accustomed to controlling a plow team or tossing sacks of feed. He'd be the kind who pinned with a crushing strength, rather than the quick agility in which Arshal specialized. Arshal would have to knock the man off his balance first, leaving him slow to rise and orient himself each time Arshal moved. If the stranger even placed a hand on him, the prince might lose.

Arshal shook his head as he took the man in. Maura's breath! The farmer was huge, tall, like a shawnsi, though no drop of shawnsi showed in his broad features. The shawnsi birthmark on Arshal's temple itched as the heat brought a thin sheen of sweat to his face.

"We've never wrestled," Arshal called to the man by greeting, who gave him a stiff nod.

"Once is usually enough!" Pedr called from his place at the ring's center. A few whoops of laughter erupted in the crowd and Arshal's opponent gave a nervous smile as Pedr doffed his constable's cap to acknowledge the laughter.

Arshal puffed up. "Are you fearing my superior skill?"

The man laughed, a friendly sound. "No, Lord, only what'll happen when I win."

"Confidence doesn't become you," Arshal returned. "I'll have to do something about that."

He pulled off his heavy blue surcoat to reveal the blousy white tunic beneath, which hung halfway to his knees. Pedr recited the rules of contest, assuring Arshal's opponent that in the match the prince had no privilege above others. Not that Arshal wanted or took advantage of his rank. Privilege belonged to the Shande of old, taught by historians, a world unlike today's rule of titled clerks in their sumptuous halls. Privilege, certainly, spawned too many of the pointless traditions he had to observe.

He had already kicked off his boots. Mapping the small bumps and pits in the ground of the wrestling ring, he paced the soft grass in just his stocking feet. He cast a glance at the young women watching him. Though not dressed in the finery of his father's halls he found their bold smiles more engaging and their humor less feigned. Grinning at the attention, he strapped his belt at his waist with a purposeful slowness, stretching and twisting his back to mark his wrestler's build. In reward, a titter of giggles erupted, swiftly silenced by the scolds of elders.

The ring had tightened now, leaving Arshal and his opponent in the sun while the crowd kept to the shade of a few trees. The buzz of laughter, boasts and wagers finally had Arshal grinning so broadly his cheeks hurt. He felt at home here among dockworkers and fishers more than among nobles and their servants, who fretted over a little dirt or sweat.

Pedr raised an arm and the crowd fell silent. Pedr scratched his dark beard a moment, grinning at Arshal and his opponent. Arshal tensed, his calves knotting as he braced to launch at his foe, his gaze locking on Pedr's arm reaching toward the sky. He rocked on the balls of his feet. He needed to be fast, pin the man and take his points before the Whittean could lay a finger on him. His opponent appeared unmoved but for the sweat trickling down his neck.

Pedr's arm dropped and Arshal lunged, head down, his arms locked across his chest. The Whittean tried to turn aside, but Arshal's momentum caught him in the chest and stomach. As the Whittean stumbled backward, Arshal brought his locked arms up to strike his foe on the chin. The Whittean tried to catch himself from falling, his face slack in the stunned expression that preceded most of Arshal's triumphs. The Whittean caught a heel in a small depression and before he could recover, Arshal had grasped him around the torso, pulling him down in the same fluid movement. He used the momentum of the fall to roll so the Whittean lay face up on the ground. Arshal scrambled to his knees in the middle of the man's chest. His foe writhed a moment as if finally realizing he'd fallen and just now thought to defend himself.

Pedr intoned the count.

"Hah!" Arshal hopped up as the count reached four. He held out his hand to the man, who accepted it sourly, almost pulling Arshal down when he stood and offering his mumbled concession.

Arshal could hear among the chatter his friends settling their bets and crowing that with this five-point match, under three minutes and no demerits, the prince would draw comers from far provinces and they would have some real matches to bet on. As the crowd dispersed, Javan made a show of handing over his debt to Jan one coin at a time.

"You must have worked up a powerful thirst in so lengthy a match as that," Azuth crowed. As he spoke the sailor Arshal had noted before brushed hard against Azuth's shoulder, turning to stare back at the Minarian sea captain as he continued on toward the docks. The sailor put his hand to his chest in an odd gesture then disappeared in the dispersing crowds.

"What was that all about?" Arshal asked.

"Looks like your crew thinks they need a coin or two from those winnings," Javan offered.

Azuth wasn't smiling.

"Come, let's go over every detail at my place. My treat," Jan offered. Arshal's stomach growled at the thought of a dented metal bowl full of Cookie's rich chowder. "I'm not proud you're my best business asset, but there you have it. Pedr, join us," Jan said to the reve, who held Arshal's coat for him. "I owe you for breaking up that brawl last night. Thought they might bust right through my window, cost me a year's earnings last time, and true I was fearin' one of them might actually hurt himself, drunk as they were."

"Didn't know a man could drink so much and still stand," Pedr said as Arshal settled his clothing. "It's a wonder he could swing to hit anything, though he really didn't try to. And when his lady seen him hanging' from the arm of the constable, he was wishin' I'd spare him from his lady!"

Pedr retrieved Arshal's boots and the decorative sword of rank that Arshal buckled at his side, an accessory for which he'd never determined a purpose. Though handy when prying a knot or lopping an apple from a high branch, it could just as easily turn on a slender bough. The histories told of wars thousands of years ago when the shawnsi had magical gifts and had worn heavy swords made of adanan that took two hands to wield as they sought to bring order to Shande in the wake of a war among the gods. He doubted half of what he'd been taught, and thought the tradition entirely ridiculous. In the far west, his cousin Eithurdon might need to have an armed guard against the occasional outlaw, but in Sihmad Shal? Sihma Harbor? Maybe if discarded these silly accessories wouldn't trouble his dreams the way they did.

"We'll make a celebration of it," Jan told Pedr and Javan as he led them across the common. "This is the twelfth comer in a row he's tossed without so much as breakin' a sweat. He must be above fifty points by now."

"Forty-seven, in five months," Pedr corrected.

"And twelve times in a row folk gathered at The Old Scow to hear the story! Next, we need to get him settled with a good Harbor woman to keep him honest."

"I swear, Jan, someday you're going to remember who I am. Your future king! How likely would my father see me joined to a Harbor girl when there are so many boring noblewomen in line?"

Jan executed a stiff bow and fell behind him in passable imitation of a trailing retainer like those who had followed the Otayran king on his official visit. The feigned humility on Jan's broad and bearded face left the reve snorting through his nose as he struggled to maintain the serious guise of a respected Harbor citizen. As Jan bowed and groveled, with many a "your magnificence" and "your grace," a man nearing his fortieth year cavorting behind the prince like a child, a sailor dressed in the florid trousers of an Otayran dropped to one knee and bowed as Arshal passed. Pedr's guffaws rang out above the Harbor din as Arshal tried, unsuccessfully to glare at them.

"Ah, will you be in trouble for muckin' about with the poor likes of us? Keepin' company with us lesser folk?" Jan teased. "Seriously, you've come an age most Harbor men have a cottage, lifemate, and a crib full of minnows."

As they reached the dockside boardwalk, Arshal felt a tug at his sleeve. Azuth pulled him aside, his expression serious, gaze locked on the pier where several sailors waited beside a tender serving Azuth's ship. They stared back, unsmiling.

"I need to say good bye," Azuth said.

"What? You aren't sailing tonight, are you? Didn't you just port yesterday?"

"Things are ... difficult." He glanced along the waterfront. "Look, you are a good man and a good friend. You need to listen closely. I am being watched, even by my own crew. They think they will be heroes and kings. Things are happening in the world that you and Shande are not ready for. I had hoped it was all talk, but things have been set in motion that –"

"What are you saying? Come, let's have a drink on your winnings that I've earned for you!"

"You are young and impetuous –"

"You sound like Cree –"

"Perhaps you might ask Cree for some insight into the history of Minaria. It might make more sense. There is a movement in my country –" he paused as one of his men stiffly brushed by him on the way to the tender. "I should say nothing, but whatever comes, know our friendship has been genuine. Know that I have told you to be wary."

"Wary of what? You're speaking in riddles."

"I cannot say more. This," he gestured at Arshal's decorative sword. "Will not serve you. We sail in the morning. I wish you well. We will likely never meet again."

Azuth spun on his heel and headed for the tender, leaving Arshal standing in confusion for a moment, shaking his head as he tried to understand what he had just been told. He couldn't imagine that asking Cree, king's advisor and Arshal's tutor, about the history of Minaria would make any of this conversation make sense. What would he make of any talk following a match? "Someday you will wish to lead them, and they will not respect you enough to follow," Cree had told him after one late night of revelry in the Harbor inns. For some reason those words always echoed some dream image he had of his father bent with sorrow.

The dreams. Again.

He scanned the brightly lit waterfront. Azuth, back stiff, sat in the bow of the tender as sailors rowed toward their moored ship. Too easily he pictured ships flitting in and out of firelight as waves tinged with crimson foam rose up to cross the reef. He gasped in thick, fog-wet air tasting of smoke.

"Eh, there you are, daydreaming again," Jan motioned for the prince to lead the way to The Old Scow. Arshal jostled his way through the crowded market at the heart of town where it opened onto docks that stabbed toward the lighthouse, reefs and breakwater, as if daring the sea to batter them.

As they left behind the last market stalls, Arshal caught a glimpse of the far west end of the boardwalk where it became a dusty track heading out toward Mania Point. A sprawling shack stood there where a Minarian merchant operated "The Beach

Head," a place as foul as the waste that washed up against the pilings supporting it. The harbor current carried all of the city's waste toward The Beach Head before flowing out to sea, leaving a green and mucky mess at low tide, and a lingering stench on anyone who dared go so far west along the shore. Arshal had entered The Beach Head once, on a dare, and fortunately his friends had whisked him out of the place before an encounter he would have regretted. He remembered it had stunk of flowers. Though very drunk, he recalled the sad eyes of an unsmiling Pladde woman who had beckoned him toward a curtained alcove. He'd once asked Azuth about the place, but the sea captain had frowned and told him Minarian sailors expected Pladde to provide the entertainment in such establishments and that the prince wouldn't understand, or be welcome. He considered the dare one of the stupider things he had done. Imagine the scandal: future king frequents The Beach Head! Oddly, the place now gave him the crawling sensation of being watched, as if behind each of the shack's shutters some evil intent lurked. The floral scent, pungent, sickeningly sweet – almost the odor of decay – had filtered into his nightmares and even in waking wriggled under his skin like a chigger.

As they reached The Old Scow, Arshal noticed a small boy of six or seven playing with a cat on the edge of the boardwalk. The boy swung his short legs over the water and giggled as he teased the cat with a bit of rope. Something felt hauntingly familiar about him from his thick dark hair, in needed a good brushing, to his features, fleshy with youth that hinted of someone Arshal should know: the oval shape, the angle from cheek to chin, the deep set of his eyes. Arshal's mouth went dry. An image reared up, then slipped away.

"Who is that?" Arshal asked of Pedr, who waited for him to enter the inn.

"Nali's son, Bertal. Good lad, probably waitin' on his fa."

"Nali?" The name lurched out at him. "Do I know him?" Instantly he pictured a man his own age, dark hair, dark trimmed beard, deep-set hawkish green eyes and a spare smile. Certainly, he knew him. How could he picture a man he didn't know? The boy looked like his father. Surely, he'd met this Nali in the inn over an ale.

Pedr shrugged. "Doubt it. Fisher, so he's out early and doesn't come around the inns much. If he has a spare moment he's studyin'. For the dernailye, you know."

"A fisher!" The certificates dernailye went to scholars who

worked for years to become advisors, readers of signs, master teachers, seers. But a fisher?

"Ah, Nali," Jan gestured for Arshal to enter the inn. "He's a bright lad. How Drul ever got so bright a son, I don't know. Must'a been his mam as got him some smarts. His babes, they're near as sharp as Nali. Maybe he's just tried harder to prove he isn't star-crossed like the midwife said."

"Star-crossed?" Something jolted ahead in Arshal's thoughts. He lost it as Jan pulled him inside, where Aron Keeper strummed a tune and the aroma of chowder wafted from the kitchen fire out back. Arshal stared over his shoulder at young Bertal. Nali. Certainly, he'd remember if he'd met a fisher scholar. Where had he heard that name before?

6: Visitors in the Night

He stood upon a rampart. Behind him somewhere a stronghold loomed. A scrap of flag he knew to be his fluttered upon its tower. The odor of fear hung thick on dewy air as gray clouds rolled away. Orange dawn stabbed through smoke coiling up from hundreds of fires on the plain below.

Arshal gasped. A dream! he shouted at himself, struggling to break free of it. Something gripped his belly as silhouettes crept from the ink of the field to lift sun-gilt swords. The angry eyes of a medallion's gemstones glowed red on mailed chests. Taunts filtered up from shadows that shifted and swirled with the mists. Behind him mountains fought skyward, clouds boiling about their peaks. An angry yell rolled toward him like the sea against a cliff. Grappling hooks and ladders clattered about him. Catapults cast flaming shot over the rampart.

"No way to hold! Prepare to retreat!" A shout rose from the rock and earth around him.

The blast of a horn herded him up twisting paths into the wind and sleet. Heart pounding, he lumbered through snow, climbing the steep sides of narrow valleys to escape dark figures of pursuit. His enemy hewed his comrades. Blood dripped from rocky precipices. Snow swirled about them. He climbed the sharp face of a scarp, slipping in the beaten snow of those before him. Pushing upward with one hand, he sent a kicking, unsupported foot above him over the ledge then felt himself pulled over the lip. A dark flag replaced his on the stronghold.

The pink stain of bloody footprints marked the path ahead, but he dropped down beside a figure buried deep in bloody snow. He must dig to find and turn the body, recognize the face. He pulled a gnarled hand from where it clutched a protruding arrow. The ring on the dead hand gleamed faintly.

"Gods!" Arshal whispered and opened his eyes.

He still smelled sword metal on his hands, the tang of pine on mountain air and the stench of smoke in his clothes. Must these nightmares always play out to completion? He felt as if he were awake through them, eyes closed but awake. He couldn't stop them. His sweat-damp bedclothes went cold as the fire in his room had burned low.

About to reach for a robe, a red flash stunned him, forcing him to shield his eyes. A shadow behind the light directed it at him, willing him to untangle himself from the bed covers, to approach, to listen, to respond, impelling him to obey, to hear.

He shook his head. Riveted. Was this part of the dream? The light blazed and a shadowy creature emerged from it with outstretched claws. Fire gathered in the creature's eyes. Words came from a pit where the face should be. Something metallic flashed crimson, reflecting like blood sheathing a blade. An almost morbid curiosity drew him, made him want to listen and obey. His heart pounded in his chest. His breaths ripped from him in ragged gasps.

No! He wouldn't listen! It was wrong! The image in his head, a face, made him squirm on his bed. He must do as he was told. But it was wrong!

The heavy silence of the room crackled, hesitated a moment, then burst into fragments that raced to pierce him like shards of shattered stone. Arshal wrenched upright with a shout. In that instant, the light winked out and the shadow dissolved. Stone scraped. Then footsteps departed with a soft, furtive sound. He sank back, his arm shielding his face.

A dream? Again? It had to be. Like all of them, if he got up and looked out his small square of window he'd see a normal world, no armies arrayed on a snowy plain.

But he'd been awake this time, hadn't he? And the red glitter of medallion light had remained.

The door opened and a rustle of satiny robes identified his visitor. The prince sighed and stared wordlessly at the piercing eyes in the Visionary Cree's haggard face. White wisps of hair clung to a creased dark forehead, half-hidden in the shade of the hood of his blue-black robes. Arshal turned away awkwardly, his bedclothes tangled around him. He shivered as he resisted the old man's gaze, tucking his icy bare feet under a corner of blanket.

"Another dream?" Cree demanded, his voice resonant with the power of his station.

Arshal shrugged, his teeth chattered. The Visionary thrust his face into view, a face too like that which had urged him to do ... something. Arshal's heart still pounded, his gut twisted and he felt vulnerable, as if he'd bared himself, soiled himself. It had gloated, hadn't it? His head throbbed. Nausea rose in his mouth. Star-crossed they called him. He was going insane.

The Visionary still stared at him. The old title that some said meant nothing in these years so distant from the Making implied one who could see all. Did Cree see into him, see the humiliation he felt?

For what? What had he done?

Cree studied him as if contemplating a mad man. Arshal had long ago given up trying to explain the dreams. Cree always dismissed them with a wave of his hand. Then he'd again change Arshal's training, weigh him with even more lessons as if to punish him for having so little to do he could waste a Visionary's time on dreams.

Cree added kindling to the fire, sending up a flurry of sparks.

The flash of light had shone from something familiar that terrified him and dominated his dreams. The medallion.

Feet slapped flagstones in the corridor outside his rooms like those he'd heard after he shouted himself awake. No, he'd already been awake. He'd seen the signet ring and awakened to the red glow in his chambers. Had he heard his own feet running? That idea rankled, as did the murmur of speculating servants outside his door.

"Cree –"

Cree raised a hand for silence. He lit a taper from the fire and edged the door open to cast faint light on a cluster of faces pressed to peer around the tutor.

"Return to your beds and duties. It is nothing. A bad dream."

As they shuffled away a low oath and the muttered speculation of star-crossed filtered in from the hallway.

The old man turned, his piercing eyes now fired by growing flames in the grate. He had an uncanny resemblance to the one that reached out to him from a red haze: dark eyes set in the dark center of something – He shivered again.

Cree untangled his covers and wrapped a blanket around his shoulders.

"I can take care of myself. I'm not some Otayran lordling needing servants to dress and wash me. And I certainly don't need a tutor bundling me up like a child going out to play."

Arshal shoved his feet into slippers, pulled the blanket about him like a cloak and paced to the divan Cree pushed closer to the fire. Cree uncorked a flask and poured amber spirits and offered it with a perfunctory gesture that assumed acceptance. Arshal had to grasp it with both trembling hands and took its contents at once. The sweet liquor hit his knotted stomach like a hot coal.

Cree's gaze on him felt like judgment.

"It isn't what you think."

"That you poisoned yourself on ale or spirits in that wallow of a tavern? To hear that the crown prince needed a bucket of water to rouse him home, that the reve had to saddle the prince's horse –"

"Where's my horse?"

Cree glared at him.

"Oh, leave me be old man. You know these nightmares have nothing to do with drink. I drink to escape them."

"Your behavior is unbecoming your position. You bring shame on the house of Dyndevas! Your line comes so close to ancient nobility you and your siblings could be mistaken for the first shawnsi, the near gods they were. And you waste yourself on Harbor inns and matches. Besting poor farmers and dockworkers of their hard-earned coin. I know what you do!"

"I have to! Don't you see? No, you don't. I keep telling you, but you don't hear me. It's all part of the dreams. Everything is." Arshal wiped at the cold sweat on his face, and felt how his damp hair had tousled into the fair ringlets he hated.

"Arshaldon –"

"Maybe I am star-crossed and losing my mind. These dreams. I'm certainly not normal."

"Of course you are not normal. No one expects a future king to be normal." Cree's tone had gathered more than its usual arrogance. "I have dreams. I am not losing my mind. Neither am I normal." A gray eyebrow had hooked up over his stern countenance, a face that in this moment seemed as dark and weathered as the trunk of an old swamp oak. He saw warning in this expression. The folk tales and even the histories claimed the first Visionaries were gods who remained in the devastation after the Great War, most of the gods' war waged with mortals' blood. Most knew this was absurd. Visionaries were merely derna of great skill and experience. But if any could give off a greater air of power than Cree, Arshal would know that indeed Terremar or even One had come into the world. Cree was an old man. A most insufferable old man.

Cree splashed more spirits in Arshal's cup. "Leave the dream behind," he offered in a softer voice than his expression. "It will not seem so terrible in the morning."

Arshal downed the contents, Cree, retrieving the empty cup. Arshal scrunched lower in the divan. "It'll trouble me no less tomorrow. It'll continue to haunt me like a premonition."

"And I have told you I see nothing but history in their content. Dreams are largely symbolic. You may not understand the signs."

"They're more frequent. And urgent. Your assurances are meaningless." He jumped up and paced to the other side of the hearth to relieve himself in a chamber pot of at least half a dozen tankards of ale. "You talk of symbols," he said to the wall, his back to his tutor. "Yet explain none of them. Unless you're simply afraid to tell me I really am mad." Resettling his clothes, he turned, half expecting the Visionary to finally admit the prince's frailty.

"Perhaps you are not ready –"

"Maura's breath! You just said they don't matter. Now you say I'm not ready to understand them. Which is it, old man –"

"Arshaldon!"

"Why would I dream of battle? It's been thousands of years since the Great War! I dream it like I know it. I can smell it. Feel it. I see mountains, not the rolling hills of Kalilia. And the Dyndevas ring on a dead hand lying in the snow. That vision must mean something! Yet you tell me nothing."

"There are many possible meanings. It could even reference lost lines to the throne or natural succession. Leaping to conclusions is fruitless."

Arshal grasped the mantelpiece and let his head drop onto his arms. "You despair of my nights at the inns. Don't you understand? I'm trying to silence the voices warring in my head."

"Voices?"

Arshal lifted his head to glare at him. "I told you about the warnings. To be alert to something. Just now I awoke to someone watching me, compelling me to do … something."

Cree's brows hooked up into the crinkle of his forehead. He was silent an uncomfortably long minute. "Your shawnsi line is among the purest," he said, repeating empty words Arshal had heard since childhood about how gods had taken lifemates among the mortal shal tribes, their children known as shawnsi who supposedly inherited special gifts from the deities who had long since abandoned them. All folktales and nonsense it felt so meaningless thousands of years later and far removed from Shande's origin story. He'd often asked about the people who existed before Shande, but Cree claimed it didn't matter. What mattered was Shande. How did he know?

"There is a distinction to being first born," Cree said. "Bloodline and order combine in your fate."

"More likely being star-crossed is the bigger thing," Arshal said.

"Perhaps," Cree said with a shrug. "I can guide you only based on long study and service to kings, and study of the Lierye. I am not the mind of the gods." His humble tone rang insincere. "Most likely your dreams are revealing wisdom great leaders of the past drew from the osfothye."

"Food seasoning and elixirs to calm the nerves? I've never heard of osfothye leading to nightmares about war. More likely they make you sleepy. "

"You do not know all things, Arshaldon. Neither do I. There is much about you that has not made sense to me and I may not be meant to know. Now, you must sleep."

Cree guided Arshal to his bed and blew out the sputtering candle with unusual patience. But as the old tutor settled into the divan, Arshal thought he caught a speculative gleam in the Visionary's fire-lit eyes. He felt a shiver of apprehension. What wasn't Cree telling him? And why did it feel like something had changed tonight and the furtive sounds he had heard slipping away had been no part of a dream?

He woke alone and like so many mornings, climbing upon a chair and leaning on the sill of his chamber window assured him that his dreams hadn't come to pass. A warm breeze wafted over the cold damp of stone barely heated by the now cold fire and tapestries strung from his chamber walls. Royal blue pennants on the towers snapped in the vigorous ocean wind that carried just a hint of salt damp and the fading scent of the kitchens. Below, ponds glittered darkly in morning shadows, reflecting heavy blossoms in the pools and gardens crafted to honor the gods.

A commotion rose beyond the wall; he ignored it. Likely, court idlers and petitioners had gleaned some tidbit of gossip as crowds gathered for today's ceremony. Today the king would issue certificates of dernailye to a new crop of scholars.

From his tower window he could see the succession of eight city walls marching away below him until the far-flung outermost wall of black granite secured tens of thousands. When he climbed up to the Window of the Sun – that uppermost central tower of the palace – he often felt a giddy sense that he stood at the center of a tightening coil.

A sudden yell brought Arshal's attention to the nearest wall. A man in the royal blue livery of an officer of the exchequer pointed up at a figure darting among the flower gardens that grew atop the battlements. Other officers and passersby rushed up ramps and stairs in pursuit. The commotion on the ground grew as court idlers called to their fellows and pointed.

The pursued figure reached the narrow space arching over the gate. Just as an officer grasped for the man's arm, the figure tumbled from the wall onto the mosaic path below. Pushed! Arshal thought in horror. The officer's startled gestures told him otherwise.

With a sense of foreboding, Arshal rushed from his rooms for the gateway. A circle of onlookers stared at the broken figure in silence. The officer who had reached for him related to his superior how the man had thrown himself from the wall when his capture seemed certain. The group parted, clearing a path as Arshal approached. Clearly dead, the man's head twisted to one side, his arms and legs flung out in a sprawl. Blood pooled beneath his head and spread across the mosaic path. Arshal couldn't look away from the first dead body he'd seen, in his waking hours.

"My lord," a clerk held a pouch taken from the body.

A man's life had poured out at Arshal's very feet and seeped into the dry earth between the stones. It stained the bag the officer held.

"What is it? What happened here?" the prince asked, not taking the proffered pouch.

"He ran from the offices of the exchequer upon discovery, Lord," the clerk said as he dug through the pouch.

"What was he doing?"

"Stealing." He held up the bulky black exchequer's seal and a fistful of blood-smeared papers. "I don't understand, Lord. Where did he think he could use these? Perhaps he's deranged? Pay rosters. Merchant itineraries and harbor fees. What would anyone want with these?"

Arshal shook his head. The dead man's expression seemed relaxed, careless. In dreams, the dead appeared rigid, grasping, resisting to the last. How could he entertain such foolishness? If a treasury clerk could search the dead, certainly he could look upon the remains without yielding to such mad fancy.

"Send the people about their business," Arshal directed an officer as the chatter continued to grow. The officer spread his arms and shooed the onlookers toward the gate. There, they continued to crane their necks to see what the prince would do.

"Where is he from? Does he have a purse, papers?"

"Just smiled and leaped, Lord. Nothing else on him."

"No personal items? Jewelry? Anything?" Arshal pushed a toe against the dead man's chest but felt nothing solid or large enough to be the medallion in his dreams. What craziness to think such a thing!

"Lord!" an officer shouted as he ran down the ramp from the wall. "A man's dead! His throat was cut!"

A burning knot restricted Arshal's breath. Murder? In the upper boroughs? Unheard of. "Remove him," he said, turning away from the body. "I want an explanation. See that the treasury and exchequer are secured and account for all who work there."

He turned on his heel to return to the palace, unable to wipe the scowl from his face. Too many things about this tickled his memory as if something lived or dreams dreamt. If so – Maura's breath! How could he even contemplate such foolishness? If only he hadn't been born beneath Kedtair, that one proscribed time the sooths claimed served only Fyraer. The mere thought turned the fresh breeze acrid in his throat.

The fisher scholar: they claimed him star-crossed as well.

7: Specter from a Dream

Sihma Harbor stretched below Nali Drulson like a pearl nestled against black, moonlit waters. Soon, dawn would stripe the waters aqua and dark purple from the massive reefs in the depths, as a host of colorful fishing boats raced to the best spots to set their nets. From Nali's vantage, the moon lit the statue of Maura looming over the boardwalk. Her arm outstretched in warning to calm the sea, her figure wrapped in a wave-like robe depicting sealife, had led generations of seafarers to touch her well-worn hand before leaving port in hopes of her blessing. Something about the statue kept drawing his gaze, something he should see.

Behind him, Olna giggled in her sleep and rolled over, snoring softly. He rubbed tired eyes, wishing his dreams made him giggle and chuckle. Instead, he stood at his window most of the night trying to unravel yet another nightmare.

The gloaming dimmed the moonlight and the village began to stir. The lone light of Aron Keeper's pilot boat lurched from his home in the lighthouse, each powerful pull on the oars bringing him nearer the first merchant ship he would guide through the narrow strait between the sea wall and reefs. Neighbors stirred in their white-washed soddies that clung to the limestone bluffs. Narrow alleys paved with crushed shell glowed, the ribbon of road zigzagging up the steep face like a drunken sailor. His neighbor's footsteps crunched on the shell as the man made for his boat, where Nali should be. He heard the man hail another. Nali couldn't force himself to move.

He couldn't stop replaying the images of the latest twist on his dreams. Dream warriors fought in unbearable heat beside fetid marshes that spewed biting flies. Of the enemy he discerned only the medallion, its rubies like eyes that watched him, judged him, made him want to run. He needed more than his will to force himself to stay. Then the familiar dream took a twist: His brother commanded the Shandean army. Nali had no brothers. A horn blast rang out. In the melee that followed the metal cap fell from his brother's head to reveal Prince Arshaldon Dyndevas. The prince's features stood out, stark and highlighted: an important clue. The prince had grinned at him like a life-long comrade. In the strange white light falling on the battlefield, the prince's hair shone white, his gray eyes deep and penetrating in a battle-scarred face.

The dream's meaning grew more elusive the more Nali tried to make sense of it.

While the prince spent more time in the Harbor than any other royal in memory, Nali had never met the man. He remembered seeing him in a horse race, where the prince's mount left the others far behind, to the roaring approval of his friends. Friends, he called innkeepers, seafarers and merchants who spoke of little more important than weather or shipping or the gossip of who fancied whom. Arshal, they called him, not lord or prince. While the Dyndevas family had never stood on formality, in the prince emerged an odd connection to the people that hadn't existed since the darkest days of Shande's beginnings when the shawnsi leaders rose out of the chaos of destruction.

Now, in a land where war's artifacts could be found only in the dusty corners of ceremonial halls, Nali fought dream-battles beside a prince he called "Arshal." They campaigned through country Nali had never seen before on the backs of war horses, when he'd only ever ridden his father's donkey or Cousin Tel's plow horse. How could he believe such visions? Yet, as vivid on waking as when he slept, how could he deny them?

He rationalized that long hours of study led him to dream himself into the Great War. But in some dreams they fought in Sihmad Shal, a city built in the aftermath of the Great War. The past clearly mattered: he could see it in the hints of godly rivalries, a sense a fisher had that Maura grew restless. Nali scanned the high cliffs to the east where he could see only the topmost tower of the city of Sihmad Shal, a tiny silhouette in the distance against the reddish glow of sunrise. Brothers.

Olna sat up suddenly, startling him. "You're back! Why didn't you wake me?" She said as she rubbed the sleep from her eyes. "I don't even have biscuits mixed. Now I'll make us late and I won't have a space at the market. Has the catch improved?" As she spoke, she slipped into the long, faded green tunic she'd worn to morning market ever since he'd known her. The drabber brown and beige of everyday hung like sacks from a peg, no more faded than her best.

"You didn't oversleep. I haven't gone out yet," Nali said, thinking they'd need a seamstress soon. Already her stomach nudged threadbare fabric with the hint of their fourth child.

She stared at him, pausing with her brush tangled in long dark hair.

"I overslept," he lied, feeling guilty as he did so.

"Nali, we need something for market. You've been studying so much there's been barely enough to live on." He hated the hint of fear in her expression. "I made promises of payment for the first of the blossom moon, and here we're in the second week already. I wouldn't want folk thinking we can't make good on our debts."

"Well, I'm done with the studying," Nali said with a sigh. "If I don't pass today I never will. We can't make do a few more days?" Olna shook her head as he shed his nightshirt and donned clothes smelling slightly of brine and fish. "I'm never going to have time to set and pull nets and get up to the city."

Why did it have to be the night before the biggest test of his life? People claimed the seldom-held oral exams so difficult only one in ten could pass and he could only try once. In only a few hours he'd stand before a Visionary to argue his knowledges. Sure, he'd do well in the histories. He lived them in his sleep. But what about the herb lore, the cultures, the hierarchies of gods and symbols, the humors, the transmutables, the elements, the natures, the numbers, the prophylaxes and curatives? What if they asked something as simple as which fish oil prevented conception and he couldn't utter its name?

Derna seemed an odd second profession for a fisher. But he felt oddly called to it. The Harbor needed more derna to read birth signs, cast auguries and prevent conception prior to Kedtair, and offer curatives beyond the knowledge of wise women. But what kind of derna couldn't even read his own dreams? And where did warrior fit into this future? He shook the thought away as he rushed for the quay.

Puffing and sweaty, Nali slammed into the scholars' hall later that morning with all of the decorum of his toddler. The examining Visionary, whose accent and features placed him from one of the southeastern tribes, sat before him like an unscaleable wall in the face of Nali's nervous apologies and stammered greetings.

The Visionary raised a judgmental brow when Nali grinned at

the first questions: Explain the causes and effects of the Great War, including the major players from all lands, the gods involved and the portents they set for the future. The next question also seemed simple, involving fish-based oils. He felt less confident on symbols and numbers had always given him trouble, but the majority of the focus covered a history that Nali knew best. It felt too easy.

He walked out of the hall into a blaze of mid-day to find Olna, his children and his fa waiting for him. It had been her confidence that propelled him to sign up for the exam, one of the youngest applicants. She'd never believed the talk of star-crossed, swearing she'd know Fyraer's mark in him. She held his hand, confident, smiling, as they waited that longest hour for the herald to post the list and merely said, 'as I expected,' when they found his name on it.

In one short morning he went from fisher to wise man. He began his training as a teen, when he still courted Olna, and after a third of his life spent preparing for this day it rushed by in a blur. It felt surreal to step into the king's long reception hall and pace the polished flagstone to the long narrow bench an usher led him to. Whispers from his fellow scholars and the gallery of onlookers – where he knew Olna clutched her knees in nervous pride – echoed up into the dark rafters and scurried among the shifting feet. Near the front of the hall, two tall windows threw natural light on white marble steps that led to a stellan chair, glittering against a blue velvet drape. Blue cushions padded the roomy seat and high back, and gems edged the cushions, which were embroidered in white with the Dyndevas coat of arms.

Nali shifted nervously, bumping against the arm of a southerner beside him, who startled and pulled away. Nali stiffened. Certainly, some merchant's son disdained an honest fisher. Or maybe his tribe disliked northerners like Nali – but that should be no excuse for someone versed in the cultures. The man wore fine clothes, his hair and skin scented with an extract that reminded Nali of toasted nuts. The heat rose in Nali's cheeks. He'd washed up as quickly as he could and dressed in his best. Yet his hands still stunk of fish, his best faded and stained. Somehow, he thought such things wouldn't matter among scholars. Nali scanned the row of seated scholars opposite him, but realized several appeared to be regarding him with amusement. He clenched his fists and glared back. They squirmed and looked away.

At the king's arrival, Nali jumped up as the rest of the hall rose, his stomach churning as King Ebon Dyndevas stepped from behind the blue curtain and stood before his seat five steps above, but only a few paces distant. The king's features struck Nali as seeming much older than his years. Certainly, his bloodline suggested another hale forty years before him, yet his hair had grayed and thinned beneath the gold and stellan-braided circlet with its large central sapphire. His deeply creased face made him look used up. It gave Nali the queasy feeling in his stomach he often felt after a dream. The gleam of the signet ring on King Ebon's leathery finger struck a familiar chord Nali couldn't quite place.

The hall fell silent as the king waited, impatiently, for the herald to intone the crown prince's name and titles. Nali steeled himself for what he knew would come next. This would be his greatest moment, the equal of his joining day with Olna and the births of his children.

But the sight of Prince Arshaldon changed everything.

With an air of disinterest, the prince took up his station at a blue velvet pillow two steps down from the throne as the king finally sat, so close to Nali that he could hear the rustle of his blue satin mantle. With a somber nod from the king, the petitioners took their seats.

But Nali couldn't take his gaze off the man who had fought battles in his head. Long legs sprawling across the lower step so close Nali could have reached out to touch them, the prince leaned back on his pillow and yawned behind his hand.

Nali had dreamed of hearing the king tell the traditional tale of the mortal scholars who learned from the first god-born Visionaries. But it felt too long in this moment, not when Nali needed to sort out the prince's place in his dreams. He caught snippets of the narrative, mention of the osfothye plant, the rise and set of the star Kedtair and the immortal blood, diluted by millennia, in the veins of the shawnsi. All these were key parts of the lore to which derna belonged, kept alive to remind them of One and Terremar, and the critical role derna had in preventing childbirth during the time of Kedtair, when Fyraer, Terremar's jealous alter ego, could corrupt a child. Nali's head swam with the images of history and dream merging into a chaotic mush of symbol and portent. The king then commended the scholars on their admission to an elite corps, reading the names of derna who would receive their certificates, starting with the fifth and lowest level among the assembled scholars.

Nali heard the words, an ear cocked for his name, but he couldn't take his gaze from the prince. He noticed the moment the prince's nostrils flared and he sniffed, his forehead crinkling as if he smelled something familiar and unnerving. The prince scanned the hall, his gaze at last falling on Nali. The man's jaw dropped open and his eyes widened. Nali felt as if he'd had a torch jabbed into his face under that gaze.

The prince recognized him.

Images raced through his thoughts: a helm tumbling from the prince's head, a bright sword shining in battle, a companionable arm across his shoulders.

Nali sucked in a breath. It felt like the first he'd taken in minutes. The prince knew him. And Nali knew what thoughts rushed the prince, whose hand jerked as if to ward himself. The shawnsi's gray gaze ran him through like the sword he bore.

"Nali Drulson, Sihma Harbor. First Degree Dernailye."

Nali almost missed his name. He jumped to his feet at the prod of the southlander beside him. He'd earned the highest order of rank. Yet he struggled to hear the king's congratulations through the rush of blood in his ears, barely felt the scroll in his hand, the king grasp his arm, the blue robe placed about his shoulders. Nali felt as if he observed himself from the gallery.

The prince's expression muted the impact of it all. Years of dreams meshed into a pattern. If he could just think on it. He knew he could find an answer. It would all come clear. Their eyes meeting and recognition had unlocked something. His heart pounded. He had a crawling feeling beneath his skin of something ominous, yet at the same time it felt like elements that belonged together had suddenly reunited, as if he had waited his entire life for this one thing that would make him whole. He knew the prince stared after him as he led the processional from the hall.

Nali walked with three others granted the First Degree. They stepped into bright afternoon that fell on the wide, open-air passage outside the reception hall where the procession dissolved and scholars turned to congratulate one another, voices high with excitement as families streamed out to gather in the courtyards below. Shandeans gathered from every tribe, from every province, young and old. And Nali, the youngest to pass, made the First Degree. Each answer he'd felt as if he knew exactly what the examiners sought.

It was meant to be. That thought stopped him for an instant. The prince recognized him.

Nali stood in a cluster of newly ordained derna, including those who had sniffed at him before. His deep blue satin robe contrasted with the pale blue coarser linens and wools of the lesser degrees. Several slapped him on the back, curried his favor, asked if they could consult with him on difficult auguries. Suddenly he commanded respect. His young age meant he might even one day be called Sage or Visionary, one whose work bordered on prophecy. Though Nali thought "Visonary" a term best left to the legends of the Great War, he wouldn't sneer at "Sage." His new colleagues no longer noted the fishy smell lingering on his hands and shoes, nor the faded trousers peaking from beneath his blue robe.

The prince had stared at him wide-eyed and open-mouthed. He knew.

Nali smiled at a young woman, a third degree, who congratulated him, asking with red cheeks if she could touch the sleeve of his robe to feel the richness of the weave. He let himself bask in the moment. From the corner of his eye, he saw his family waiting on the edge of the gardens. They would want to hear every detail, but he knew he couldn't tell them the most important. How the prince recognizing him changed everything. He didn't understand it yet himself. But it was right. By the gods, that was the scary part. It felt right.

He saw the prince emerge from a side door. When the prince met his gaze, he knew. The man sought him. But at that moment, the prince looked over his shoulder and disappeared back into the hall. For an instant, Nali considered following. Maybe the prince didn't know why Nali seemed familiar to him. Nali could just imagine how odd the meeting would be in that case. He had no reputation yet among scholars. What if he dismissed his dreams as the star-crossed eccentricities of a fool?

He turned from the excited talk of scholars. More than ever, he had that queasy sensation the dreams gave him, something that made him want to purge everything from his body and cleanse himself in the sea. He shook his head at the turn of his thoughts. Not now. His family awaited him, Olna breathless with anticipation, his fa, feeling awkward, having pulled his cap low over his forehead. The children strained against Olna's grip on their shoulders. He had work to do yet to support his little family. He took the stairs down to the mosaic path and in an uncharacteristic move, pulled Olna into his arms.

"It's done. Thank you for believing in me," he whispered. Grasping her hand, he hurried them through the gate to an alley and side streets and finally the long flights of steps that wound down through laborers' neighborhoods, bypassing the longer Sijway that ran by busy shops and markets. He needed to find the time to piece together all this strangeness and steel himself for what it meant. For now, he let himself grin under Olna's praise and breathe. It felt right. That it felt right sent a brief shiver up his spine. He wished he understood what that meant.

8: Storm Warning

Arshal stared after a man he knew but had never met. The prince had his fists clenched and had to force himself to loosen them. The derna had stared back as if seeing the shade of a dead man. Arshal knew how the man's eyes would widen, how his cheeks would stretch beneath his dark beard when he smiled, how those green eyes would speculate on this encounter. The prince couldn't stop his feet from following. When he picked the derna out of the crowd, Arshal's heart had stopped, a pause followed by a thunderous beat. Mad he must be, surely, to even think such things. The man stared back with that same haunting gaze. Arshal had to understand!

A servant called to him from the hall. "Lord, the king calls!"

Arshal turned away, impatient and suddenly afraid. It would make it all real, wouldn't it, if not alone in his madness? Each step felt heavier. He wanted to run back and press the derna against a wall and demand he explain himself, force him to reveal what trickery had placed him in the prince's head. Even as he thought it, Arshal knew this Nali Drulson felt no less confused.

The king waited in an alcove behind the curtain of the dais as Arshal emerged from the side corridor. His gray brows arched. "You can't be rushing off on childish whims," he said in a voice hushed so it wouldn't carry to the hall beyond. "I know it's spring and the days are pleasant –"

"I'm not a child, father. I needed to speak with one of the new derna."

"We have petitioners to hear yet. You must earn the respect of the people by taking an interest in their concerns, or they'll never trust your judgment. First, before us is a legal matter of fault. *Maura's Heart* ran aground with the loss of twenty bushels of osfothye. The merchant wants guarantees for his losses, but both

60

captain and ship owner claim it an accident. The village ruled the owner erred, but the province ruled that the captain erred, as the charts marked the depth and thus he shouldn't be paid for his journey and –"

"Make Arelson pay the merchant," Arshal interrupted with a dismissive wave. "You know Captain Bruder was steeped in brew and Arelson should never have hired him. He idles his days in The Old Scow. It's the only that still takes his credit."

"See here! This is exactly the kind of thing you must learn," the king snapped. "You can't just deal out judgments like that. No one claims Bruder was drinking. There was a storm. Maybe he would have run aground sober or not. Decisions must be made on the evidence. We judge responsibility in the matter. Whether an accident is the fault of the ship owner –"

"Father, there are more important things than whether the gods or Bruder ran the ship aground. A thief died falling from the wall today. Had you heard that? An officer of the exchequer was killed, his throat slit, likely by the man who fell."

The king took a breath as if about to reprimand Arshal again. Instead, the king's shoulders sagged. "I heard. I'm told we'll have a report soon."

"Something feels wrong about it. About all of it. I had the oddest conversation with a friend yesterday. He told me to be wary, that there are things happening. And then this. It's like something from a dream. Something bad. Something that demands a response."

"I thought Cree had settled the matter of your dreams."

"By ignoring them? They might be something, might not. Now there's an answer I can work with! Dreams are supposed to help us solve our daily riddles. By dreaming of battlefields? And these are more than dreams. I'm awake, or I awake and remember –"

"So, you remember dreaming a man fell from the wall?" The king's voice rose slightly, a servant looking up sharply to peek around a curtain into the hall to see if anyone had heard.

"No, more like I remembered it in a dream."

"Arshal, we have duties to attend to now. We can discuss this later."

"You may be in danger, Father! Have you considered that? Someone killed a man for those papers. What next? Assassins? We should order additional protection for you."

"Oh, Arshaldon, now you're chasing shadows again. Months ago you claimed an assault was imminent because you dreamed masked raiders attacked a village and burned it. Where are your dream raiders? You were wrong then, as now. I'm tired of this." The king thrust aside the curtain. The crowd beyond hushed.

Arshal knew he should just go listen to the petition to please his father. He couldn't. He had felt certain about the masked raiders and the burning village. It felt too real! He needed to find that derna. He needed to understand. He hurried down the hall to the portico but couldn't find Drulson among the milling scholars and their families.

He hesitated too long. His sister Resala called to him from the arm of her suitor, Zopher don Saran, a man a few years older than Arshal and once the prince's friend and idol, a scruffy companion. Now, with Resala on his arm, Zopher appeared the picture of noble arrogance, perfumed and draped in the fine satins and ribbons that made Arshal's Harbor friends laugh.

"How do you mend or wash it?" Cookie had laughed, making her aside to Jan that afternoon Resala appeared at The Old Scow to warn Arshal an angry Cree sought his wayward pupil. Resala had stood in The Old Scow in this very gown, a stark green with lace, brocade and small satin flowers sewn onto the ends of ribbons that streamed from every seam, giving her the appearance of a field of waving wildflowers.

"Arshal," she called, pulling Zopher along.

He glanced out over the gardens toward the gate, noting the spot where the thief had fallen that morning near the pillar to Terremar in the gods' garden. A cart had taken the body away hours ago.

Just smiled and jumped. He had to find that derna!

"No time for you dear," Arshal told her, smiling sweetly and tweaking her cheek in a manner he knew would infuriate her. "There's ale to be drunk and bragging to be done."

"Oh, you embarrass us at every turn," she said as she raised her hand to ward off his tweak. "You promised you'd speak with us today, about approaching Father. Remember?

"I don't have time today." He brushed by her.

"There's no call to be rude. You promised to help. Father can shorten it. He has that right. We shouldn't have to wait a year when I'll accept no other suitors. It's a stupid tradition."

"I really am in a hurry. Maybe Father has good reason for following the traditions." He took in the way Zopher's unruly brown hair and been powdered and pasted into place with herb water and bound up in a green ribbon that matched Resala's dress, right down to the silly flower on its end. His blouse remained unrumpled by the heat as he stood idly examining a spot on his sleeve. "Maybe he expects to learn something unsavory about Zopher. That he's a changeling or something star-crossed."

Zopher stiffened and narrowed his gaze on the prince. "And who's to talk of star-crossed?"

"He certainly isn't the man I once knew. Perhaps I don't feel my help is appropriate."

He knew they stared after him as he turned on his heel and took the steps to the gardens two at a time. He felt petty and wished he hadn't said it. He knew her cheeks had flushed, that her hair blew into her face unattended, her expression shocked. He knew it because he knew his little sister, the same way he'd known how Nali Drulson would react, this Nali he'd never met, but knew would chastise him for so callous a remark to his sister. But Zopher! How he stunk now of flower extract – a man who had taught Arshal to race and wrestle, drink and wager – he deserved derision. Resala seemed to find something likeable in Zopher this way, both as palatable as stale bread.

At the archway from the gardens into the next borough, he waited impatiently for a groom to fetch his horse, the heat of the city seeming to press the air from his lungs. The palace's mosaic path opened here onto the Sijway, a cobblestone road that became crushed shell outside the city's last borough of Shanai. The more people who passed him on their way to court – all greeting him with a bob of head or a small bow – the more irritated he grew at the delay.

At last, the groom brought Booty, his best horse, a chestnut gelding he'd won from Zopher's father in the autumn races. Crowds thronged the Sijway, which curved through each gate to traverse the boroughs the long way, forcing him to walk Booty to avoid bowling over some merchant or shopper. The sun glared from the multi-hued walls covered in flower boxes and gardens that lined towers and battlements and the multi-storied homes and businesses along the way. Every breath of the heavy floral air seemed to weigh him down, like his dreams. It all needled him as if he missed something, but his sour humor had him too impatient to ponder it. When at last he reached the archway of the vine-clad outer wall of the city and finally the borough Shanai outside the walls, he mounted and took the road at a gallop, maneuvering around carts and other travelers on the wider streets and ignoring the startled looks of those darting out of his path.

A man had been murdered. A thief jumped from the wall. He

knew that derna!

None of the travelers on the road wore a dark blue robe. What if Nali had taken off the robe for his travels home and he'd already missed him in the press on the Sijway? What if the man stopped to enjoy his success at one of the city's inns? He dismissed the thought. Nali would be with family. He knew.

He had to slow Booty to a walk long before he'd passed by all the farmsteads, walls and ditches carving up the countryside and reached the loops of road descending from the plateau down to the bridge over the river and at last to Sihma Harbor. The derna must have ridden to the city. Or had he remained in Sihmad Shal after all, joining his fellow scholars for an ale before begging off? Or maybe he stopped at the market. Once in the Harbor where then? The docks? If a derna, would he still fish? Maybe a Harbor inn, just to celebrate. Arshal scowled at himself. He let the stableman lead Booty away before he even decided what he should do. What he should do was return to the palace and talk his sister out of seeing Zopher. At least he should sit in his father's court and make Bruder admit his fault, or check the exchequer to see if they had secured the offices as he'd ordered.

Then he saw him, still in his robe. He bent to speak with the boy, Bertal. The boy grinned and dashed up a narrow alleyway toward the cottages on the bluff. The derna turned and walked across the common toward small triangular shelters where fishers stowed their gear. He heard a woman pulling her fishing vessel ashore call out congratulations. Elders sitting on shaded benches teased. Nali smiled at them the way Arshal knew he would – a spare smile, one side up, in a dark beard, his head thrown back just a little to one side when he laughed aloud.

Arshal strode across the grass, barely acknowledging the greetings of those he knew, ignoring everything but the back of that familiar head. Nali stopped at a little shelter with 'Drulson' painted on it, removed the blue robe and stowed it. Suddenly he straightened, turning to look right at Arshal.

"Nali Drulson, is it? Congratulations on attaining First Degree!" Arshal said when the silence grew awkward.

That spare smile again. "I'm honored the prince comes so far to wish me well," Nali said with a slight bow. Sweat sprouted on the derna's brow.

"Yes, indeed. A worthy achievement."

As the silence again grew awkward with a shrug and a cock of his head, Nali kicked off his shoes into the little shelter and pulled out a wooden pail stained black with pitch.

"Forgive me, Lord. I'm overdue on some repairs to my boat. You're welcome to watch." His tone sounded strained. At least he, too, felt nervous.

"I thought you'd be celebrating."

Nali grinned. "Olna shooed me away so she can ready a surprise."

"You seem very familiar to me."

The derna's glance went swiftly to the elders on the bench and the woman lingering around her fishing boat, barely hiding her attempt to eavesdrop.

"I don't believe we've ever met, Lord," he said quietly, handing Arshal oars before grabbing a trowel and heading for his boat.

Arshal scowled. Certainly, he made a fool of himself. Nali stopped on the common in the open space between the last of the trees and benches and the stony shore. He appeared to readjust the items he carried as Arshal caught him up.

"In person, Lord," the derna said softly. "I don't think we ever met in person. You're going to think I've spent too much time at sea –"

"Maybe not."

A smile barely lifted the corner of his mouth. "Maybe not."

"Perhaps we should talk."

"Indeed. But I don't want my neighbors thinking I'm an oar short. Or telling my young ones their fa's star-crossed. Lord, we do need to talk and I think you know why."

Arshal stared at him.

"Or, maybe not." Nali made for his boat again, leaving Arshal to catch up.

"Wait," Arshal called. The elders and the fisherwoman all watched with unabashed curiosity now. Nali set down his bucket, hawkish gaze measuring him. "Is that boat seaworthy?"

"I'd be hard put to make a living in a boat that isn't. It's a small leak."

"Would you take me for a sail?"

Nali tilted his head slightly in ascent and carried his trowel and pail back to his little shelter. Arshal fell in step beside him. "We should go fishing," he blurted. "I'd like to throw one to this dandy suitor of my sister's. Zopher's fine hosiery dripping fish scales might shake that fake pomposity out of him." Arshal laughed, but quickly sobered at Nali's serious expression. "Not that I have anything against fish."

The common had grown quiet. A few more people gathered to stare at them openly now. Several fishers, having left their catch at the docks, arrived to pull their boats up above the waves on the quay beside Nali's or tie them to the pier where they bobbed and chunked against one another.

As Nali stowed the pitch in the shelter, a speculative glance at Arshal sent both of Nali's eyebrows arching. "Are you going in a boat dressed like that, Lord?" Arshal looked down at himself, then at Nali. "This isn't a ship. If you went overboard, you'd sink like a rock."

"I'd sink anyway. I don't swim." Swiftly, he pulled off his boots, unbuckled his dress sword and stowed them in the shelter before hurrying after the derna in his stocking feet, trying mostly successfully to dodge the leavings of seabirds.

Despite the leak, Nali's craft seemed in better repair than many others. He pushed it off and guided it to the pier where he studied the sky. Arshal shaded his eyes against the sun to follow Nali's gaze.

"Storm coming, Lord. It'll be here by nightfall."

"There isn't a cloud in the sky!"

"I'd be a pretty poor fisher if I couldn't recognize a change in the weather and the behavior of the birds and sea life in advance of it."

Nali helped him into the rickety craft, which threatened to tip as the prince stepped in. Arshal thumped hard on the bare seat toward the bow to avoid falling.

"Careful of me boat, Lord! You're liable to punch a hole right on through!" Nali's indignant tone had a keen teasing edge that accentuated a bit of a seafarer's lilt he hadn't heard before. The derna stepped aboard more lightly and unfolded a tiller. He turned it hard to the side and secured it, gesturing for Arshal to stow the oars as he untied the sail from the boom, clipped it to the halyard and drew it part way up the mast, the loose boom bobbing as the shortened sail luffed. He signaled for Arshal to loosen the bow line and with a shove of his foot against the pier, he pointed them away from its bobbing neighbors. In moments, he had freed the tiller, and adjusted the sail to capture the shore wind that would push them into deeper water away from the piers. In the distance, growing waves built against the breakwater, throwing spray high in the air, though the harbor remained almost calm.

"Maura's restless," Nali said, almost to himself. He motioned with his toe to a small storage compartment beneath Arshal's seat where the prince found a full wineskin. He took a swig of warm, burning wine and passed it across to Nali.

66

"So, you believe Maura's here, beneath us? A god just sort of lounging about in the sea?"

"The sea is Maura's world. There's a reason sailors honor her." He gestured toward the large statue of Maura that overlooked the harbor. "They say she refused One's call home out of sheer cussedness. If not for her, we'd have no warning before the storm." Nali paused, his brow creasing as if he'd just had a profound thought. He shook his head then, as if it had eluded him. "But yes, I believe it, Lord, as a scholar and as a fisher. Maura's here, more than Terremar. He remained with One. But Maura's love of the Merien kept her here."

"Don't the children's stories say she stayed for a lover?"

Nali shook his head. "Aziaris threw himself into her sea when Maura refused to return to One. At least that's how the scholars tell it. Maura's a far more complex god than that. Her passion began a war! When Fyraer began destroying everything Terremar commissioned, Maura dared to confront One."

"I've never heard a claim that Maura started the Great War," Arshal scoffed.

"It's a scholar's tale, Lord, recorded, as they say, in the Lierye. We folk just learn the short version. Scholars find meaning in all the little details that they argue about for centuries. For example, One's intent. We know One is every element, every thought and deed and the Maker of what Is. But when One brought One's hands together, the brothers Terremar and Fyraer burst from One's hands in ways that have plagued us since the Making. Some scholars insist an error divided the elements between them that way. Others say it had to be part of One's intent, if we're to believe that One is the Maker of all history and future. So, maybe even the Great War was part of the plan."

"I can't believe that. They say it almost destroyed Ea!"

Nali shrugged and smiled a little. "It's a scholar's argument. Terremar favored quiet making and beauty, thus we honor him with gardens. But Fyraer thrived on ambition, chaos, and jealousy. They were bound to conflict. Fyraer destroyed everything of other gods' making for spite and sport. Think of it! We were some of those creations. If Fyraer passed as we awaited the Making the peoples of Ea wouldn't exist! Terremar, they say, gave Ea and the shal tribes especially, the endurance to thrive and survive despite Fryaer. It made our early days quarrelsome and scattered us across creation, because we misinterpreted the gods' wishes and always look at each other with distrust or jealousy. At least, so says the lore."

67

Nali's brow was again furled, as if something in the story reminded him of something.

"Where does Maura come into it?" Arshal asked, interested despite himself. This version of Shande's origin story held something different, more foreboding, than he had heard before.

"The Lierye says Maura's was a mother's love. She went to One, bearing the broken body of the last Merien, the people of her sea, that Fyraer had boiled, burned, and mutilated for his amusement. She demanded One stop his destruction. Maura is terrifying, like the sea itself. They say her heart, and the power of her tears falling on the body of the last Merien reached One's intent." Nali shrugged a little. "So, that began the Great War, they say." He gazed on distant sea as he spoke. "It's said during the war Fyraer singled out Maura's seas for his worst assaults. After the war ended, Maura remained behind to tend what little survived."

The snap of the wind in the lines and chunk of the waves against the boat seemed to add something more real and alive than the stories he'd grown up on. A giant wave struck the breakwater, sending a plume so high the mist carried to them, punctuating the end of Nali's tale. It gave Arshal the strange feeling that Maura listened. No wonder seafarers revered her.

"There's something about Maura's story," Nali said, with a shake of his head. "It, well, even telling it now, I feel like it's relevant to our ... dilemma."

"Dilemma," Arshal echoed. What exactly had he experienced in the reception hall today? The silence grew awkward. At last, Nali took a deep draw from the wineskin passed it to him and set his shoulders as if he'd resolved a debate with himself about what to say.

"I don't know where to begin, Lord."

"With Arshal."

"Arshal ... Well, out with it then. I have these dreams. You're in them with me. And, well, they're odd dreams."

"It is the dreams, then."

Nali slowly inclined his head. "I dream that, well, we're friends and – Maura's breath! – battle comrades. This sounds so strange to say aloud. In all my study of the histories, I can find nothing that matches these dreams. There's things in them I just don't understand, or maybe I do, and I'm afraid of what I see."

"I recognized you," Arshal admitted softly. "Even your son."

"They feel more urgent lately. As if I'm running out of time to figure it out."

"I guess I hoped you had the answers."

"Well, maybe a few." Nali's hands shook a little as he took the wine again and took a long pull. "I think it's Kedtair."

Arshal straightened and frowned. "I assume you know Kedtair's my birthstar. Star-crossed, somehow I knew that would come up."

Nali nodded. "In the dream, you're my brother – blood and spiritual twin – like the binding holding my twins Bertal and Kia together, but not as much with lone Rena. It's a deeper bond. What makes twins? First, naturally, is they're born together. You and I were born within minutes of each other at the rising of Kedtair twenty-four years ago. Different parents, but perhaps the same intent. Star-crossed."

"The same day! But how?"

"The histories say you were late. I was early, healthy and over a month before my time, though left a bit short for my liking. In both cases, reportedly, our mothers conceived despite all the preventatives." He took another swig of wine. "I don't buy into all the proscriptions, even though it's the calling of the derna to make a good living at it. But Kedtair and all it stands for is a powerful metaphor, a symbol, a message. I haven't deciphered it yet, but it's there. I'm sure it's what connects us."

The silence felt on the verge of becoming awkward again. Folklore claimed the gods decreed that no child be born during the month when Kedtair rose overhead. Many, including Arshal, thought it mostly superstitious. Midwives and seers grew wealthy casting auguries and prescribing a fish oil that prevented conception, the oil so scarce around Kedtair it became expensive, and the year after Kedtair always saw a spike in births. Kedtair pulled the world awry when it rose, like a smaller sun in the sky it lit the night and added its heat to the sun's, driving horrible storms and droughts. It was a curse.

"My tutor, Cree, mentioned omens at my birth," Arshal said at last. "I don't know if I like the implication behind this coincidence. It feels like a sign of doom, of –" he looked up sharply. "Have you dreamt of my death?"

Nali shook his head.

"My father's?" Nali's intake of breath propelled Arshal forward, his face thrust almost into Nali's.

"What did you see?"

"I didn't see anything, Lord, but that you wore the signet ring and the king's circlet crown."

Arshal sat back and lowered his gaze. "I dream of finding a

body. I never saw his face, but he wore the ring."

"It could be far in the future. It's dangerous to plan life on dreams, Lord ... Arshal. It always impressed me that you wore the ring because it drew my attention, specifically, as a sign. Like ... Like the red eyes."

"I've seen them!"

"Part of a medallion," Nali said. "Rubies, I think. They shine with their own light, as if the medallion is the evil, not those wearing it."

"It always leaves me feeling sick. Kedtair explains so much. Cree told me it's a message to the people that the gods remember us. Maybe the gods send the dreams. And here I let him convince me the dreams mean nothing, not that I ever believed that." He sat back and looked up at the sky, which began to darken a little with a growing haze to the west. Suddenly he slammed his fist against his knee, the motion causing the little boat to pitch. "You're a derna and you can't make sense of all this? And a Visionary let me wander far from the mark."

"A Visionary's got no special route to the gods' intents. I can't imagine why he would dismiss your dreams, unless he's so baffled by them he doesn't want to admit it, or maybe even so frightened by them, that he fears the truth. Dream symbols are powerful. If we're to believe they come from the gods, they must know our failure to read them."

"But wouldn't gods intervening go against One's intent? What could even prompt such a challenge?"

"Last time it was the destruction of a people: the Merien."

Arshal stared at the surf spraying over the breakwater. "I don't know what to do. Are there Visionaries with greater dream-reading skills? Could we even dare ask?"

"I can't imagine that Cree would have his position if better derna existed." Nali motioned that he was about to change tack, moving the little boat farther into the harbor. As the waves built against the breakwater they passed the wineskin.

"Ever fish before?" Nali asked, breaking another awkward silence.

"Not on the ocean. I imagine it's easier than with line, nets and all."

"Compare Maura's sea to fishing a lake or river with line? Really, Lord ... Arshal. With all the sea to play in, all its depth to hide in, fish can't really be counted on to be anywhere. We often set our nets off the reef beyond the breakwater, but it's outside the safety of the harbor where the seas are more unpredictable and the fish respond to all that and the weather, too. It's Maura's way of protecting 'em."

Nali hove to just inside of the breakwater, the boat stopped, bobbing in the waves as the sails luffed, the vessel slowly drifting back toward shore with the swells. A wave struck the breakwater, sending heavy spray over the men. Startled and laughing, they wiped the water from their faces and hurried to rescue the wineskin from the water around their feet.

"I'm kind of disappointed," Arshal said. "I hoped to catch a fish. If nothing else so I could smell truly offensive when I see my sister and Zopher."

"Oh, I think I can help you with this," Nali said with a laugh. "I'm bettin' I can find a day-old layin' about, or snag a floater around the docks. In this heat, you'll be pretty ripe by the time you get home."

As the wind picked up, Nali tied down the sail and boom and dropped oars into place and began to row toward shore, most of the effort left to wind and wave.

"So, do you know how to use that fancy sword you wear?" Nali asked as they neared shore. "You seem to handle it pretty well in my dreams."

Arshal stared at him and Nali appeared to flush, perhaps with wine or embarrassment. Neither spoke again until the boat bumped against the pier.

"I'll send a messenger for you as soon as I can set up a meeting with my father and Cree," Arshal said as he stumbled up onto the pier. Nali drew the little boat over to the quay and pulled it up above the waves and more. People had begun to gather on the common to secure their boats against the coming weather, packing up nets and rinsing out fish crates. Arshal led the way back to the triangular shelter.

"We need to find you a fish," Nali said, moving off toward market as soon as they'd collected their shoes and his derna robe. Arshal fell in step beside him feeling it both familiar and not yet quite right. Brothers, he'd said. He had the crawling sense of something pending – maybe the storm about to break – but Arshal sensed a different kind of storm.

Arshal reached the city as evening fell. As he waited for the groom the air grew oppressive with the storm Nali had promised. The gleaming white palace towers took on an eerie glow in the fading light as clouds overtook the setting sun. A last ray of sunlight shone on the Window of the Sun in its high tower, the prismed glass glowing red-gold. The westward towers stood out stark against the approaching storm clouds. Thunderheads spread upward, taking on a pink cast as they obscured the sun.

A distant fork of lightning seemed to pierce a pennant on a tower. A low roll of thunder drifted across the sea and struck the cliffs, sending echoes reverberating back out to the storm. A gust of cold air made him shiver before the trapped heat returned.

Perfect. Resala and Zopher scurried toward him, trying to make the palace before the storm struck. He unhooked a stringer from his saddle and held up a large fish that had grown offensive in the heat.

"Resala you must try this!" he called. "It's a new scent, all the style!" He tried to force the stringer into her hand. Resala backed away in disgust then hurried by him, throwing him a murderous look as she did so. He laughed, but it felt forced. He had hoped for a more gratifying reaction and now it felt a bit beneath even him.

"Why do you work so hard to embarrass this family?" she demanded. "At least act like someone who could be king. Here Cree's been looking for you all afternoon and you broke your promise to meet with us, just to play a disgusting prank."

Arshal let the fish fall to his side. He vaguely remembered Cree saying something about a change in his training, again. The intrigue of meeting Nali had driven all that from his mind.

Resala's hair danced in a gust of wind as heat alternated with a cold blast. She took Zopher by the arm and aimed for the palace, calling over her shoulder, "Maybe next time I'll let Cree find you at The Old Scow instead of fetching you myself!"

"You have grown sniping and petty, haven't you, Arshal," Zopher called back, his dark hair unmoved by the wind.

"Better than being a Jashiho lizard. Go ahead, change your color to whatever hue the princess demands today!"

"Talk of changed," Zopher began, but Resala dragged him out of earshot.

Finally, a groom arrived to take Booty. Arshal scowled. He didn't feel like dealing with Cree just yet. A tavern, maybe a game of dice-and-spinners might be just the thing to make him forget all the day's strange things, allow him to ignore the ominous press of storm about to break that felt like more than a mere storm. He started to turn back toward town when a flash overhead and earth-shaking crack jolted him. A rolling boom followed, echoing over and over again. Rain splatted the stone in isolated, fat drops as Arshal instead dashed toward the safety of the palace with long-legged strides.

He'd only taken a few paces along the slick path when he slipped, falling near where the thief had died that morning. When he recognized blood in the cracks between the tiles, nausea rose in his stomach. Reaching out a hand to steady himself as he scrambled to his feet, he spotted an odd shape that lurched out at him from his dreams. A medallion glittered in a crevice between the path and a low stone curb. The rubies glowed in the dim light, burning, hot. He expected to feel the humiliating wash of red light fall upon him. Reaching for it, his hand brushed hot metal. His hair lifted and a prickle ran up his spine, followed by the sizzle of lightning and crack of thunder above him. He dropped the medallion and dashed for shelter, rubbing his hand as he went. It stung as if burned. He dashed through a door into the palace, looking back at where he'd dropped it. He'd send someone to fetch it after the storm, if he dared look on it again.

He again studied the odd burn on his hand as he turned, only to find Cree glaring at him from the shadows. Arshal gasped as the old man yanked the stringer from Arshal's other hand and threw it out into the rain.

"I thought you had grown out of such childishness. You disappoint me." Cree turned away. "We will discuss this later."

Arshal grabbed him by the arm, something he instantly regretted. "It was important. We must talk. I need your advice."

"What you need. It is always what you need. We are stuck with a spoiled prince." The Visionary's glare made Arshal feel like he was twelve again, not a man well beyond the age of being scolded by his tutor.

"Please, it's important."

"Important? Do you need advice on baiting your hook? I am here to train you to become king, not how to entertain yourself. You already know how to do that." The Visionary removed his arm from Arshal's grip and turned to leave.

"It's about the dreams!"

"How does fishing have anything to do with your dreams?"

"The fisher does."

"Explain!"

"We weren't fishing," Arshal told Cree's turned back. "It was a place to talk. He has dreams like mine. I suggested he meet with us, that you might know someone who could help read dream messages from the gods."

"And what am I? A Visionary. And I have told you what can be told of your dreams. So, you shame yourself to some Harbor scoundrel to make a mockery of –"

"No. He's a derna, First Degree. And I trust him. He spoke first. There's more. Just now I saw a medallion near where the man fell this morning, one I've seen in my dreams. It burned my hand." He held out his hand to show the faint red burn, but Cree didn't turn, his back a wall.

After a long moment the Visionary nodded. "I planned to teach you things today, to perhaps find some of those latent shawnsi skills I am certain you possess. I think we will begin differently, after your evening meal. We will send a servant to fetch your fisher later."

Cree sped away on ageless legs as if Arshal represented a trifling delay and more important things required attention. Arshal sensed he had surprised his tutor more than the Visionary wanted him to know.

Late that night Cree arrived at Arshal's chambers, ceremoniously producing a small vial of blue liquid from a locked box. He set the vial on the table for the prince's inspection.

"What is it?" Arshal's heart pounded in his chest with some instinctive reaction, his nostrils flaring at the scent.

"Osfothye." Cree took a small drop from the vial and let it fall into a clear glass of wine. The wine instantly turned blue.

"I've never seen osfothye like this!"

"It is the secret of kings, what the Dyndevas line was built upon," Cree said. "It is the royal blue of the Saran strain. It is not made from the leaves like the powders, elixirs, and seasonings. This extract comes from the flower, and the plant requires six years to grow to flowering maturity. Remove the flower and you destroy the plant, which makes this extract a costly tool. This potion will bring dreams to guide those with the power to see them. If you have some Visionary powers, as I suspect, you will learn for certain. If not, Shande's kings have always found gems of wisdom in osfothye dreams. You must become familiar with this extract and the people who can make it for you when you become king. Few know the process. If not made properly the extract can kill, or do nothing at all."

Arshal stared at Cree, having to force himself to not let his jaw gape open in shock. He understood for the first time from where the royal blue colors of the family had been derived. He vaguely remembered childhood tales where kings relied on drug-induced dreams to solve dilemmas.

"It takes only one drop. But it takes a bushel of plants to produce the flowers for just that one drop." Cree said as Arshal studied the wine, somehow expecting it to animate or continue shifting colors.

"A bushel! That could buy the finest horse in our stables!"

Cree gave him a grave nod. "It is special. Drink the wine. Your father survived it and his before him, all the way back to the great leaders of the early times. Dynfearn the Lost relied on it. One drop should be enough to determine your strengths. Later, as you gain skill and know yourself better, you can take more. The more you take, the longer the vision, and the greater the risk that you will never wake again. This drop should allow you to wake in a few days –"

"Days!"

"In a few days with, perhaps, new insight into your dreams. You sought answers. You asked for help. I offer help. You may learn you have powers of prescience or skill. Or maybe you will discover nothing, which has been true of many before you. In the meantime," Cree gestured to Arshal's bed, "Make yourself comfortable and drink this entire glass."

Cree pulled up the divan closer to Arshal's bed. He waited as Arshal sniffed the wine.

"You said it can kill."

"If not made well or if you take too much. This is made correctly and is not too much."

"You said it could change things. Will it change me?"

Arshal waited, glass poised near his lips. The pungent aroma of the extract cleared his lungs. It had a minty scent, not as strong as the leaves, with a slight floral note that completely overwhelmed any scent of wine. His father had tasted this, and his grandfather. Was it just one more strange tradition, or would he truly see the future as the lore claimed of Dynfearn? Could it show him the answers he and Nali sought?

"I cannot say it will not change you. I do not know what it will do. Now drink. It cannot be worse than the swill you put down in the Harbor inns."

He eyed the liquid a moment more. "Nali," he said. "Nali Drulson, derna, Sihma Harbor. I promised I'd set up a meeting between us and the king."

Cree inclined his head. Arshal shrugged, then, with a last wary glance at Cree, he gulped. No taste of wine touched his tongue, only the minty flavor of osfothye. He lay back, feeling it

hit his stomach then course through his body. He closed his eyes
to the sound of distant thunder and rain, seeing soft snow falling
in the mountains.

9: Visionary

When a king's messenger knocked on Nali's humble plank door, at first he thought it a response to the news he'd sent to the prince that the body of a sailor had been found floating in the harbor the day after their meeting. Pedr and Aron, as Harbor officials had come to Nali for his first official paid task as a derna: to review their findings and conclusion. The two Harbor officials, had accounted for all the sailors on the manifest of each ported ship and all the local mariners. Only one ship had departed recently, a Minarian vessel, the morning of the dernailye awards. The man wore captain's epaulets and the black breeches preferred by Minarian sailors. Pedr noted he thought he looked like Azuth, known captain of the departed ship, but the man's face had been mutilated, compounded by the time he'd been in the water at the mercy of hungry fish. Nali had been struck by the marks on the dead man's face and added to the report that it appeared to be a brand, a triangle inside of a circle, but otherwise remained indistinct.

Now, several days later, a messenger found the derna in his cottage, mending Rena's toy fishing boat. He donned his blue robe to follow. The messenger merely grunted or shrugged to each of Nali's questions as they rode to the city at a full gallop, Nali clinging to the horse's mane as the ground sped by beneath him, quite certain any moment he'd fall.

The trembling from the breakneck ride didn't stop when they reached the palace. Nali's stomach fluttered and soon even his fingers and toes tingled as a page led him through the palace. Three days had passed since he and Arshal had met and the prince hadn't appeared in the Harbor or responded to Nali's note. What if Arshal had reconsidered their conversation? Did they call him to a tribunal to rescind his certificate? His racing thoughts and the many corridors, turns and flights of stairs in the palace soon had him hopelessly turned around.

Finally, they reached a non-descript door. "King's study," the page told him and motioned for him to enter, the door closing behind him.

The modest space stunned the derna. A small fire in a grate sent a spiral of smoke into the eaves before it found its way out a high window that served as a chimney. The fire barely touched the damp chill of several days' rain. Nali didn't dare sit at the table where a flagon of wine and four cups sat or on the bench lining the wall beside the door. Standing drew him to touch the dusty, hand-copied books cramming shelves, or peer at crudely drawn maps of the world. A stack of recently consulted tomes crowded the writing desk beneath the window. Small and cluttered, the room didn't feel regal enough for a king. Just as Nali had thumbed open a thick map collection askew on the desk, the door opened to admit the Visionary, Cree. Nali froze. Cree's mere presence insinuated command, the old man's mouth souring with judgment before he motioned Nali to a chair, which Nali quickly took.

"Nali Drulson?"

He heard a hint of unfamiliar dialect.

"Lord?" Nali ventured.

Cree stiffened. "I am no more a Lord than you." Before Nali could stammer an apology, the king arrived. Nali jumped back up so quickly he almost overturned his chair. The king measured him with a glance before sitting at the table with the Visionary beside him. With a sharp gesture, Cree signaled Nali back to his seat. Nali let out an uneasy breath. Any moment he expected the king or Cree to demand an explanation of why this lowly fisher had troubled the prince.

At last, when the awkward silence seemed like it would become unbearable, Arshal arrived and sagged into the empty chair at the king's right, across from Cree. Face drawn and pale, eyes ringed by shadows, the prince glared at Cree a moment before greeting Nali with a spare smile, looking nothing like the youthful prankster Nali had sent home with a rotten fish just a few days prior.

"Sorry to leave you waiting with these stern old men, Nali," Arshal said. "A seer's potion scrambled my mind for days."

"Arshaldon," Cree cautioned.

"I'd have refused it if I'd known. I suppose it's better that I didn't." Arshal waved away Cree's angry gesture toward Nali. "Who is he going to tell? Do you really think a First Degree derna would gain something by embarrassing me? I trust him. We share the dilemma and he deserves to know anything we learn. Besides, Nali's future and mine, our survival, depend upon each other."

"Not that I doubt your character, or that you are a learned man, Drulson," the king said with a nod. "It's no small feat to attain First Degree. But, Arshaldon, you make incredible statements. By your own account the two of you just met. You make sweeping judgments based on dreams Cree has dismissed. Your prophecies have not come to pass. You trust a young, inexperienced derna at the expense of a Visionary. Certainly, you hear how outrageous your claims sound."

"No, I do not. You don't understand the dreams."

"So, you both have dreams you cannot fathom. Nothing unusual. When you first spoke of them, Cree said they are from your study of history."

"Father, we don't dream history. We dream future."

Nali tried to take a deep breath but found his throat closed. This was too much. They would never listen if Arshal made unsupported statements.

"Murder and thievery have come within our own halls. I've just learned that my friend Azuth, the man who warned me of some coming trouble, turned up dead in the Harbor with a brand on his face similar to an image both Nali and I have seen in our dreams and that were on a medallion I found in the gardens near where the man fell. Our future bodes so ill it paralyzes me to contemplate it." Arshal paused dramatically. "The osfothye made this clearer."

"So, what did you see?" King Ebon demanded. "What prophecy that Cree has not found in months and months of reading your dreams?"

"I don't know if they show what will, or what could pass if we don't heed the signs. Clearly, they warn we aren't prepared for what is about to –"

"Again, what can we say that we haven't before?" The king's voice had risen. Nali's heart pounded. "Cree sees nothing in these dreams –"

"He doesn't? He'd have us believe that, this Visionary left behind in the gods' rush to escape Ea."

Nali wanted to just creep out of the room. Really, Arshal went too far. The king appeared stunned as anger gathered in Cree's dark eyes.

"Admit it Cree! Or is that Idenai?" Cree blanched at the name.

"Wasn't that your name? Perhaps you're our enemy, Idenai!"

"Arshaldon! What are you talking about?" In the same breath the king turned to the Visionary. "Cree?"

"It's all about that," Arshal said. "They exiled their enemy. They didn't vanquish him. Our future's wrapped up in the errors made by our ancestors, Cree's brethren. Maybe we should hear this from one who lived it?" He turned to Cree, expectant.

"Do not be ridiculous. It is a distant past and I hardly see what it has to do with anything."

Arshal leaned toward Nali, fair eyebrows raised, though his words directed to Cree. "He doesn't deny he's a witness."

Nali peered at the Visionary. Did a deathless being sit beside him? Wouldn't people notice over time? Wouldn't a true Visionary emanate something more god-like? A god.

Cree sighed and poured himself a cup of wine. "Once I was named Idenai. Now only Cree."

The king opened his mouth but said nothing. Nali couldn't find his breath.

"So much forgotten. This is what you learned? That I am nothing now? Odd that this is what the osfothye should show you."

"Clearly because it's the only way to get you to tell us what you know." The squall line that had crossed Cree's face abated as Arshal's shoulders sagged and he let his head fall onto his folded arms on the table. He looked up at Cree, his voice almost plaintive with fatigue. "Please, you recorded omens at my birth, a day I share with Nali. What does it all mean?"

"To ask is to question One's intent," Cree said dismissively. For a moment Nali thought the Visionary intended to leave. Instead, he braced himself. At last, with a prod from the king, Cree slowly nodded. "The root is One. We all know this." Cree said, his voice low and quiet, reminding Nali of the distant sound of surf on the headland. "Before the Making, before there was Ea, was simply One. From One's first Making sprung the father to all, Terremar, and his brother Fyraer, to embody the unseeable One." Cree paused for a long moment, drinking deeply then shook his head.

"They are halves out of balance that cannot exist without each other, skewed toward chaos. If one brother ceases to exist, One will unmake creation to return order to all that Is. This is key. Fyraer cannot be destroyed without destroying everything the gods created."

Cree glanced at Nali out of the corner of his eye as if to gauge how much Nali knew of this part of the story. If one read deeply enough, they would find it in the Lierye. He gave Cree the barest nod of acknowledgement.

"Fyraer will always seek to defeat Terremar and Terremar will remain undefeatable. Even in the Great War we knew we could only hope to contain Fyraer, not destroy him." Cree again fell silent for a long moment, his gaze on some distant point in the past. "What a world Ea might have become had things divided otherwise. Of all the gods Maura's realm is richest, water critical to everything on Ea. Fyraer took his chaos there to break the thing that supported all that survived in Ea. For all that she threw at him to defend it, he still left her creations decaying on the sea floor or washed upon the beaches. Maura demanded of One some punishment for the wanton destruction.

"All Ea shook when at last Terremar faced Fyraer with One's banishment, Maura's price for the destruction of the Merien. Fyraer's own creatures and corruptions he sent against Shande – slaughtering, raping, pillaging, burning – to destroy all that Terremar and his children had made. The gods' hearts went out to the shals, their shawnsi offspring, to the lands they so lovingly crafted. With One's intent behind him, at last Terremar drove Fyraer and his corruptions to the edge of creation where they remain, nursing their hatred, plotting their revenge."

Cree looked from Arshal to the king, the latter appearing stunned. "This is the key to your dilemma, perhaps: the fear that they would return with vengeance. One called the gods to him to remove the temptation for Fyraer to return. A few, those first called Visionaries, defied One and remained. What foolishness, that. The lore claims Maura refused to relinquish her world, and stayed to heal and guard what remained and the waters Ea needs. They say even Aziaris gave up One's gardens to join her rather than pine for her for eternity. Even I do not know if the tales are true. You must see: I know only what I knew then. Once a Visionary defied One they no longer shared the privilege of seeing One's intent. Those who stayed hoped to help the shawnsi rebuild the torn lands, settle the tribal wars and guide Shande back to some kind of peace. One demanded a promise from the gods not to interfere with Ea, but only to watch it, leaving behind only the blood of gods in shawnsi veins, a few Visionaries, and the osfothye plant, a gift from One's gardens."

Arshal's brow had furled, his eyebrows touching as he peered at a stain on the table. "So, the osfothye's strength lies there."

Cree inclined his head. "But the power of Visionaries and

shawnsi weakened over time. We lost or forgot much: the magic of the shawnsi, the role of the city of Sihmad Shal – Hope of the People – and the unity of Shande's tribes."

"And what has this to do with the dreams?" the king prompted.

"Kedtair," Cree said. "Terremar had his son Kedtair create a star to rise every ninth year as a message that the gods remembered us and that Terremar watches. Nine years, like the nine years of battle against Fyraer. Terremar decreed no child be born during the month the star rose overhead – a reminder that no child survived Fyraer's war, each corrupted in the womb. Only Kedtair could prevent such a child from being marked evil. Only auguries would name which were blessed, which cursed. During its time overhead, Kedtair would wreak havoc over the world to remind us of the way the gods had so tortured Ea in their battles. Kedtair of all of them has proven too powerful a symbol to forget.

"And thus, at the rising of Kedtair twenty-four years ago, I cast an augury for the first child born to King Ebon and Queen Sala, a child who defied all contraceptives and refused all urgings to enter the world before that fated day. The auguries told us Kedtair blessed this child. The signs pointed to greatness ... and to change."

Cree shifted in his chair, silent a moment as evening settled outside. "I was Idenai, a lesser god of small wisdoms," Cree again admitted, his voice suddenly booming in the room. It startled Arshal from the images playing through his mind. "Powers wane. I fear for the place I chose to remain. I grieve for the lost Merien and all the other creatures like them. I grieve for my dead children. I may know the events of the past, but I never knew all. I once knew the future, One's intent, but the future changes with every act of the present and many acts have occurred since I last knew it."

A log split and fell in the grate, sending a shower of sparks rushing upward. The Visionary emptied his wine, poured another cup then stared across the table at Arshal.

The osfothye vision had left Arshal unlike himself, as if a candle within had blown out, no longer illuminating some element, some strength, and leaving behind the germ of fear. Azuth had warned him. And Azuth was now dead. His scalp tingled, a strange lifting of the hairs he couldn't seem to shed.

Had the elixir changed him as he feared? He remembered the cloud of blue sinking into the wine ...

"Terremar spoke to me," Arshal said at last, sitting up to recall that brief sense of wholeness.

Cree peered at him. The king stared at his tented fingers. Nali watched him closely, eyes wide and bright, unreadable. How much had Nali known and what had he learned from Cree's tale? What else did a derna know?

"Many things make more sense now. The osfothye showed me that the visions are the future and perhaps even the now, but clearly built upon the past." Arshal ignored his father's loud exhalation.

"Terremar showed me mountains where people starved and hunters sought them; a woman in white whose face hid in a hood, grieving; rivers and floods; blood raining from the sky. I saw a young Idenai watching a ship depart, an aged Cree watching a ship arrive. All the while Terremar told me to look to the people of Ea for help, especially Nali. Because shal and shawnsi fates are interwoven, so are our destinies. He revealed us in dreams so we would seek and recognize one another. Born in the same hour at the rising of Kedtair, the gods' influence would be strong. Then," Arshal's hands jerked on the table as he relived the vision. "Then I saw someone holding an inferno in his hand, ashes blowing away as if a whirlwind encircled him. This being held the flames out to another whose words – I can't recall them now – soothed. They drew me, thick and sweet, like honey, entrancing. They sounded almost familiar. Then the one with the fire pointed at me and ordered me destroyed, passing the flame to the honey-tongued companion. Then I saw only the medallion. It filled my vision, so bright it burned my eyes. I woke sick, as if fevered. Then Terremar touched me. The shadow lifted, but I felt so empty."

Nali had shivered visibly at mention of the medallion. The king turned to him, a question mark in his graying brows.

"Lord, that medallion terrifies me more than any other symbol," Nali said. "I even felt it, muted, when I saw what I'm sure is that same image imprinted on that sea captain's face. Not for its look, but, well, it just feels evil, as if it's opened you up and climbed inside, pawing through your private thoughts." Nali wrung his hands in the loose robe gathered in his lap, palms leaving a sweaty stain and wrinkles in the fine fabric.

Cree studied Nali, frowning. The derna straightened and stared back with a stony gaze better suited to a hawk eyeing prey.

Cree rose to stir the fire. "Perhaps Arshaldon saw an image meant to warn that Fyraer has broken his banishment," he said as sparks rose from the grate. "I do not know. Apparently, I erred in my judgments of Arshaldon's dreams. I now wonder at my own conclusions. That," he jabbed the poker hard into the white ash of a log, "Is one reason I was less than candid with you. Another? I have forgotten. Almost three thousand years is a long time distant from One's intent. Besides, prudence tells me a young prince does not need to know everything the wise know."

As Cree again settled at the table, his gaze seemed to pierce Arshal as he asked, "The honey-tongued one, how did he appear?"

The image leapt out at Arshal, leaving him again feeling soiled and uncertain, as he had when the red glow filled his chambers and – What had the creature in his dreams said to him, done to him? Not a dream, real. Arshal ran a sweaty and trembling hand through his hair. "He seemed almost fair at first. A sense only since I couldn't see him clearly. If he looked like anyone, he looked like you. Different, yet very much the same. When he turned to me, I saw only the medallion."

Cree arched a brow, scrutinized Arshal a moment then looked away, his expression a mask. Again, that crawling sensation worked through Arshal's gut. What speculation did Cree entertain that he wouldn't voice?

"Certainly, your dreams are a warning, and god-sent: no one else could give my name," Cree said at last. "I have lost so much of what I once knew! Terremar's message sounds symbolic. It would be like him. But what could lead Terremar to disobey One's intent? Do I even correctly assume Fyraer attracts new followers?"

"The medallion," Nali blurted. "If it's a talisman his followers would carry it with them." He reddened as all eyes turned to him. "And sailors are quick to pick up anything new they think will bring them luck. The Minarian sea captain had this mark branded on him. We might look for other sailors who seem to show unusual hostility or openly wear the medallion."

Arshal nodded. "Azuth even suggested I ask for a history of Minaria to understand troubles he apparently had with his crew. Did they mutiny? Was it the entire crew, or just one sailor adding his own mark to their work."

"All this assumes your conclusions are correct and not merely based on coincidence," King Ebon said, rousing himself from his deep contemplation of his tented fingers.

"Lord, I agree that conclusions are premature and we have few options until we know more or understand the dreams," Cree said. He gestured at Nali. "Clearly, no coincidence led these two to share a borning day, nor that a fisher became a seer of a caliber to advise a prince, to whom he has symbolic connection. Nor could coincidence also make him appear in the dreams and visions of a man he has not yet met."

"So, a warning then?" The king shrugged, a less than regal bewilderment lining his brow. "Perhaps the visions represent the far future. Maybe they'll only happen if we don't take some action. I can imagine no course. I think Nali's recommendation to gather information is sound. We shall see."

"I don't think this is the distant future, father," Arshal said. "Remember the man who fell from the wall? I found a medallion near where he died. When I went back to look for it, I couldn't find it. Someone must have returned to fetch it. The man appears to have some friends."

"You did not tell me you looked for it," Cree said.

"I had no chance. You plied me with osfothye. The papers he stole included officers' payroll. I can't help but think he meant to identify targets for some evil intent." Arshal said.

"If these are related issues at all," the king cautioned.

Arshal rose and stretched, feeling too weary for someone who had been asleep for several days. He could see his father's doubt in the set of the king's jaw.

"I'm quite certain they are," Arshal returned.

"I have no suggestions," the king admitted. "It was wise to bring this to me," he said with the same officious tone he used with petitioners. "We'll assign observers in the consulates and I assume Nali will report if he notes anything unusual in the Harbor. It's premature for any of this to otherwise leave this room."

Arshal nodded, turning at the dismissal. Nali jumped up to follow, bowing to the king in nervous afterthought.

When they reached the corridor outside the king's study, Arshal pulled Nali aside. "I trust you Nali," he said. "Terremar made it clear that I'll need to. I'll tell Cree that I expect you to be part of any more discussions involving our dreams or any other findings related to this." He gripped Nali's arm, the parting of long-time friends, comrades, as he nodded to a waiting page who led Nali away.

Arshal should feel happy that they were finally taking action.

Instead, he felt the crawl of dread in his gut. They moved too slowly.

10: Unmasked

As two days passed, Nali watched the Harbor for some sign of change, clueless about what he sought. He knew from a note from Arshal that among the consuls, too, nothing appeared unusual.

As he left the market on the third day, he heard a clamor from around the corner near The Old Scow: rude taunts and angry bellowing; wood splintering and a woman's screech of dismay; Reve Pedr demanding order and a drunken sailor egging someone on as an illusionist cursed and chased after several birds freed from his cape in the fray. Brawls weren't uncommon when tribal tensions flared or a ship arrived after months at sea. But they usually ended as soon as Pedr arrived.

Nali leaned against a boardwalk railing, expecting to see Pedr emerge from the crowd at any moment leading two sheepish drunks. Instead, Pedr's voice rose, angry. More sailors shoved and shouted. A table of pottery overturned. A tinker bellowed a warning.

"Congratulations, Wise One," Nali startled to find Jan at his elbow, sporting a grin. "Deep thinkin' and daydreamin' never got an honest day's work." He plucked at Nali's robe. "I hear you're already suppin' with royalty. Is the prince any better at fishin' than huntin'?"

Nali forced a smile he didn't feel. "Guess not. Didn't you say he carried an empty bag when you guided his hunt?"

Jan bobbed his head. But before he could respond Pedr's horn blasted from the midst of the brawl, calling up his volunteer deputies. Clearly no friendly scuffle, half a dozen Minarian merchantmen had drawn daggers. Several more grabbed broken bottles from an overturned table and others grabbed balusters for clubs. They faced a dozen Shiadin sailors, their heads wrapped in florid scarves, as they, too, quickly armed themselves. While Shiad and Minaria had never been friendly, it appeared the Minarians directed their anger at a pair of Shandean mariners who shrugged off their vests and rolled up their sleeves to the elbows, backed up by the Shiadins.

Pedr stood alone now in the center of a hostile ring, threatening to deport all of them if they didn't stand down immediately as deputies pressed through the crowd of onlookers to join him. Two sailors helped a third who bled from a gash on his head. Pedr's warning could barely be heard over the bellowing threat of one Minarian sailor who bled from a gash on his cheek.

"You have no right to order us from port!" the man bellowed, shaking a broken bottle at Pedr. "You will pay for this injustice! You will –"

The man stopped as a fellow sailor nudged him hard and said something that couldn't be heard. Sputtering a brief protest, the sailor then paused and smiled instead. He scanned the watching crowd, his gaze falling on Nali. "This will not be forgotten!" he shouted and whirled to sweep his companions before him toward the pier where their tenders awaited. Laughter and jeers snapped at their heels, but the sailors didn't turn and soon the crowd drifted away.

"Well, that was odd," Jan said. "The last time Pedr had to call up deputies was for that fire last year." When Nali didn't respond Jan nudged him. "Now that oaf's boasts don't scare a wise man like you, do they?"

"Not at all," Nali said without conviction. Did this brawl fit any of his dream fragments? Nali let out an uneasy breath. "That dead man found in the Harbor, Minarian, wasn't he?"

"Aye, and a friend," Jan said. "Do you think a Shiadin killed him and the Minarians want revenge?"

Nali shrugged, forcing a smile as Aron Keeper gestured from across the milling crowd, holding his fist in the air and tipping it as if he held an ale.

"Let me treat you," Jan said, trying to guide Nali toward The Old Scow. "Won't hurt business to have a derna visit. I'll tell you the tale of the wrestling match between Arshal and his brothers, two on one. They almost won, had Arshal on three demerits –"

"Jan, I just remembered an appointment in the city. Can I borrow your pony?" Jan bobbed his head and gestured to a small stable behind his inn. Brawls might not be unusual, but drawing a weapon on the reve and forcing him to call on deputies could be something, or nothing. A feud between Minarians and

Shiadins might explain Azuth's death, but not the medallion mark on his face. Shiadins backing up Shandean sailors didn't suggest medallion carrying thieves breaking into the exchequer. Nali had that under-the-skin feeling that the Minarian had almost said something very important.

As Nali led Jan's fat paint out to the street, he saw the innkeeper standing in front of his tavern, stroking his beard as he stared after him. Aron joined him with a snubbed scowl on his face. He'd have to make it up another time. As he passed by, he barely took note of a sailor in the alley beside the inn whose gaze on him felt less than friendly, as if noting his derna's attire with disdain. As Nali rounded a corner, he threw a glance back down the street, wondering why he felt as if he'd missed something as the sailor emerged from the alley and followed Jan and Aron into The Old Scow.

Nali wasn't sure what to expect when a king's messenger fetched him the next day from where he worked on his boat, given only enough time to grab his derna robe before they raced to the city. As he entered the king's study, he noted the room's neatness had given way to tomes open and spilling from the desk to the floor, and signs of a meal mingled with a litter of papers shoved to one corner of the table. The room felt crowded as all three of the king's sons joined Cree and King Ebon.

Esthenshaldon, the king's second son, leaned against the wall by the cold grate, thick arms crossed on his chest. He favored his mother's darker southern features, unlike his towheaded siblings. Appearing on the verge of saying something wry or clever, the bottom right corner of Esthen's mouth drooped as he spoke to Arshal, his lop-sided grin hinting of a deeper bemusement just shy of scorn.

Peshaldon, King Ebon's youngest son, sat on the wall bench, his quiet demeanor like a gray shade between two charismatic brothers. Nali settled beside Peshal as a servant ushered in a Shiadin emissary.

The emissary appeared uncomfortable in the king's more intimate study, not his public hall. A few dark wisps of hair escaped a bright green head scarf, and the purple, red and gold brocade of his outfit made a colorful anomaly in the more austere company of the Shandeans. Naming himself Yechan, he greeted them with a sweeping bow. With a nod from King Ebon, he gently set on the table the stellan disk with the image of Shiad's king imprinted on it, marking him the bearer of King Keyen's words.

"I asked for an audience, Lord, as the bearer of sad news," Yechan said. "Two shawnsi leaders of the Shandean trade merchant guild were found murdered in the city of Tenasia. A third is missing and feared dead."

"Murder," King Ebon said, studying his hands folded on the table. "Shandeans have always felt safe in Shiad. There has been an investigation?"

'Yes, Lord. We learned of attempts on the lives of Shandean consuls in Arenh as well. We suspect we know who is responsible." Yechan waited for King Ebon's nod for him to continue. "We have come by information that Minaria is producing arms that are being sent to ships in Ymmenay Bay. We have yet to apprehend a spy alive." Arshal sat up straighter, the king briefly looking up from his hands. "Then King Mol Azezial warned us we must suspend trade with Shande or be thought of as having chosen to ally ourselves against Minaria in its dispute with you. Thus," Yechan took a deep breath. "King Keyen has ordered Shandeans to leave Shiad and suspends open trade with Shande. We have no desire to become embroiled in another country's dispute. King Keyen suggests trade might still be accomplished through an intermediary."

Nali felt each heartbeat in his temples. It was not the future, but the now. The stricken faces of King Ebon and his sons gave him no comfort. Who would nobles raised to clerk call upon to counsel them about war? War. Shande had no army, no military, only gossipy officers who let thieves into the exchequer.

"King Keyen believes no ill of the House of Dyndevas, so long generous to its neighbors," Yechan continued. "We beg for an explanation of the charges Minaria levels against you."

"What charge do they make against us? For we've heard no word of it," King Ebon said.

"They claim Shande has stolen the labor of Minaria and wrongfully taken possession of Minaria's land and property." Yechan said. "King Keyen remains skeptical," he added in haste as Esthen began to sputter a denial.

"Silence!" Cree directed his ire at Esthen. "It is not your position to respond to any allegation."

"Our dealings with Minaria are no different than those with Shiad or any other nation," King Ebon said. "We apprentice Minarians in our forges and mines. We tried to help them cultivate osfothye, one of our principal exports to Minaria. The plant did not take to their soil. I don't understand these allegations. We hosted Mol Azezial's predecessor for a state visit and I was that king's guest in Minaria. We've had only good trade relations."

Yechan nodded. "Things have changed in Minaria since the Hogde coup that led to Mol Azezial's rise. He quotes often from the philosophy they name Ghyldism, which claims they are the true chosen people of Ea and have a special covenant with the divine."

"Tell us more of this Ghyldism," Cree said softly.

"I know little about it. I have heard that Ghyldism rejects One and One's children as false gods. We know some Hogde warriors believe they must go to battle or make blood sacrifices to demonstrate their commitment to this philosophy and their king appears to reward this behavior. Soldiers now skirmish openly along our borders even though we have sound treaties that have not been contested. Hogde factions have brutalized the lowland Pladde who have refused to denounce One. If their lot was hard before, that caste is now punished for being nonbelievers." Yechan's voice had grown soft.

Nali couldn't find his breath. How could no word of any of this have reached the king's ears before now? If Shiad and Arenh saw this, certainly the western provinces of Shande had to have some inkling. Or, like King Ebon, could they not imagine anyone would raise a hand against Shande?

"Do they wear any talisman?" Nali ventured.

"I have seen none." Yechan gave him a deferent nod. "They have changed their seal, to a triangle within a circle, ringed with flame and wind symbols."

Nali looked to Arshal, but the prince scowled at the ceiling.

"Return to King Keyen with our assurance we've done no harm to the Minarians," King Ebon said. "If anything, we're the victims of misdirected jealousy, blamed for their misfortunes because the gods once dwelt here and their blood runs in shawnsi veins. It seems they worship a vengeful Fyraer."

"Lord, if I may, they do not worship Fyraer, at least to their knowledge," Cree corrected with the delicacy of one who must correct a king before others. "They cannot perceive Fyraer. More likely he has corrupted an emissary who stole the identity of a lesser god, known as Ghyldus, who earned the love of the Minarian people during the Great War and remains a hero in their lore. And those symbols on the seal, they are ancient markers as well."

Nali narrowed his gaze on the Visionary, who ignored Nali's

interest. Did Cree intend to hide from them that all the gods had their own identifying marks? Even Nali knew that from his studies of the Making. And he knew, too, flame and wind symbols didn't belong to the god Ghyldus. For a moment he considered speaking up. But Cree had been a god. Certainly, he had a reason for his silence.

"Warn your king, Yechan," King Ebon said, dismissing the emissary. "He may yet become involved. If this is Fyraer's work, through an emissary or not, his efforts won't stop with suspending trade with Shande."

The unspoken remained. Did another Great War loom? Would the unfinished business of the gods be fought again, but now among people who had forgotten the gods and lost their ancient powers?

As Yechan departed, Arshal leaned over the table to face his father.

Only the pennants flapping outside the king's chamber window broke the silence, the faint cinnamon aroma from a popular Shiadin hair scent all that remained behind to mark the change their world had undergone.

Nali studied the prince, sensing a hesitation that seemed to run counter to the Arshal of Harbor matches and bravado, of the warrior brother he knew from his dreams.

"We must plan," Arshal said at last. "Before war catches us unawares."

King Ebon let out a slow breath. With a motion of his head, he sent Esthen to fetch a decanter of wine and goblets, the prince's hand trembling as he poured, spilling drops of red wine on the table. A few drops struck Nali's leg, soaking the fabric like droplets of blood as Esthen shifted his gaze from his elder brother to his father and back.

"Certainly, this news adds only more fuel to your speculation," the king said. "But we still need verification. We can't chase phantom enemies, alarming the people over nothing."

"Nothing? We need to prepare a defense, and offense."

"We have diplomatic means for dealing with issues of trade and treaty. The Minarians have presented no claim, and we've no proof they've harmed our people."

"Dead aren't proof? We had murders here! And possible spies. And deaths in two countries. We can't lose the advantage of advance warning. They likely have a plan in place and we need one as well."

"We have procedures, protocol, treaties. You don't take a war footing because of a disturbing dream, a defensive hunch and hearsay. That's all we have. We must treat with Mol Azezial's consul and peacefully resolve the dispute. This is how civilized people behave and have done so for hundreds of years. We discuss difference and reach compromise –"

"Compromise? What, shall we give them the land they claim is theirs because some god named Ghyldus told them so? You'd have us stand by defenseless until an act of war comes, and it'll be too late then. If they felt like negotiating, I'm sure we would have heard from them before they murdered our people and harassed King Keyen."

"You accuse without proof! To even begin to arm for defense can be construed as hostile."

Arshal waved his hand in dismissal. "I'm not saying start a war. But be prepared. The dreams warn us. Shiad warns us. Terremar warns us. What more do you need to feel threatened? Warships in the Harbor?"

"Don't take that tone with me!" The king rose abruptly, his chair slamming to the floor.

"What do we do then?" Arshal's hands were clenched at his sides. "Preparations can't hurt, Father. I'm not saying march on Minaria. If they come here, we should at least be ready to defend ourselves. All that we've seen and heard makes that prudent. We once maintained armies with garrisons all over the country and it didn't provoke war with our neighbors. It's why past kings disbanded them."

The king didn't respond, staring at Arshal until he could no longer hold the gaze and instead looked down as the westering sun marked a path across the table.

"With this warning we can be prepared, and stronger!" Esthen said. "No one will challenge us if we appear unassailable. We have nothing to fear. Cousin Eithur keeps a standing guard. No country views it as a threat. And all those countries have at least a militia."

"Past kings disbanded those garrisons because they were costly, very costly, and a need never arose for them," King Ebon said as he regained his seat. "I don't know that there's one now that can justify the expense if we must raise the tax. We can consider options under the conditions we state no intent of starting anything. Discreet. It serves no purpose to alarm people. But they'll eventually demand to know why we spend the treasures of the realm and demand more from them, on defenses we haven't seen the need for in generations."

"At some point, Father, we may have to call the people to arms," Arshal said.

"Perhaps. What can we do that won't provoke hostility?"

"I'm not sure," Arshal admitted. "What do I know of battle tactics, defense, weaponry?"

"We'll just pin them," Esthen said with a grin. "Think of the tales! The glory!"

"I can't imagine it," Peshal said. "That's history."

"I hardly think glory –" Arshal began.

"You've heard the histories, Arshal!" Esthen returned. "Dynfearn the Lost rode to war surrounded by one thousand spears, pennants of every hue flapping in the winds of battle. Ten thousand horsemen charged at his call. The warring tribes fled before him!"

"Dynfearn had the new blood of gods in him," Cree said.

Esthen waved the caution away. "In the city alone we must have thirty thousand who could fight, three times what Dynfearn took to the field against gods, not Minarians."

"Men die in war," Nali said softly.

"A few, yes, for the greater good of Shande. Look how Otayr has built on its military, to its benefit with only a few men lost. We'll be stronger. We have a far larger population to draw from and many more resources. The people will be angry that anyone would dare challenge the peace. Minaria thinks we're weak because we haven't wasted our resources on armies. We'll sweep the field."

"Inexperienced and untrained Shandeans sweep a nation of warriors?" Nali returned, surprising himself at his own tone.

"If we practice –"

"The Minarians have practiced for generations. Their professional army will face innkeepers, fishers and clerks. Defending ourselves is one thing. I don't think Dynfearn saw much glory in the Great War, only tremendous suffering."

"No –" Esthen began.

"We must defend ourselves, yes," Arshal said. "That's a given. If Esthen gains glory from it he'll have a bonus. I don't desire glory."

"Oh, so nobly said," Esthen returned. "Then what do you seek in those Harbor matches and races and –"

"The win, Esthen. Something quite different."

"Do we even have a place to begin?" Peshal asked. "If, as I understand it, the gods warn us with Arshal's dreams, wouldn't they tell us what we need to do?"

"The gods likely expect us to rely on our own devices and won't render any aid but warning," Nali said.

"They cannot lead us, only guide us," Cree agreed.

"Why not tell us what the gods want us to do, Cree?" Esthen demanded. "You're immortal, I hear."

"Such insolence!" Cree glared at Esthen. "A Visionary is not privy to the mind of One, nor the counsel of gods. Here I am nothing, not a god, not mortal, nothing. I outlive those I love with no hope for peace in passing, burying lifemates, children. I guide some king and his insolent sons a few decades, then retreat in exchange with another, returning with a new name, a new history, to continue atop the bones of those before. Each time, a little more of what I knew is gone. Arshaldon makes only the fiftieth royal I've tutored. I remember what came before. To covet my former position would be to welcome the seed sown by Fyraer's ambition. I no longer see the future. I remember many of the signs. Likely the future's path changed since I last saw it. It is not a thing carved in stone, but as variable as those who make a mark on the world. My wisdom is nothing here."

Esthen mumbled an apology, but Cree waved it away. "I remember the Great War. It was not glorious, but tragic, bloody and the fuel for nightmares. I know Ghyldus. I knew him once as Athlen, a fellow and friend, a keeper of the peace who took to the Minarians as a shepherd. This Ghyldism must be some slanderous name. Athlen rejected Fyraer. His own blood runs in the veins of Shawnsi. He tended the battered shal tribes. He was stronger than I, more powerful, and felt he could help heal the battered Minarian lands that were one of the last battlefields, blasted. His words soothed their wounds and he convinced them to set aside their anger at the destruction of their world. But I am sure he departed when One called the gods to return."

"And yet," Nali said carefully, "Arshal's medallion dream described a creature that sounds much like Ghyldus. Could he have turned, been convinced to serve in Fyraer's place?"

"I do not believe it."

"Yet, it would be a fit, wouldn't it, for a frustrated shepherd who sees his people still struggling to make that blasted land support them?"

Cree's glare made Nali's heart skip a beat, but after a moment the Visionary inclined his head slightly. "It is possible. I do not believe it. If true, it would be a god that we face, one whose words are spells and whose power is more than any Visionary or shawnsi can match. If he turned to Fyraer, he would bear that god's grievances. He would stoke a hatred of shawnsi. It would not be difficult. All he would need to do is stir up ancient tribal rivalries and jealousies. They would hate Shande for how the gods favored it and they would seek out Visionaries to destroy. For Fyraer, it would be revenge to stoke greed in the peoples of Ea for what Shande has and to turn her people against their gods. But I do not believe Fyraer would have convinced Ghyldus to destroy his own descendants."

"Whose blood, much diluted, he may not recognize," Nali said softly.

"How," Peshal ventured, "Can we hope to defeat an enemy with stronger forces than we are likely to gather?"

"Determination," Nali said. "They'll have theirs, but ours must be stronger. We're defending our homes. They're driven by an idea and a sense of injustice – powerful motivations – but we've something deeper, the tangible of home and family."

"And," Cree added, "Even if Fyraer or even Ghyldus drives this movement, they will not have legions of gods behind them with their powers to unmake what has been made, only shals with their crude weapons."

"We hope," Nali added, feeling a sense of dread creeping over him.

"So," Esthen said, crossing his arms over his chest. "What do we do? If an enemy arms against us, should we, as Arshal said, set up defenses? Do we know when this dream war will find us?"

Arshal gave his brother a sidelong glance. "We don't know what they intend or when they'll attack."

The king's brows hooked up.

"If," Arshal added.

"What about a messenger to Sefresal? Nali asked. "Certainly, the Lharan miners would notice things unusual on the border and among the Minarian laborers. The Duke of Lharan might have some captain he could spare to advise us on defense." Nali pulled a chair up to the table and set up parchment, pen and ink under the approving eye of Cree. He scribbled notes in a sprawling hand.

"As well," King Ebon mused, "We should send a delegation to the Minarian Consul to ask about the rumors, and dispatch a message to our consul in Minaria and ask him what news there is."

"Lord," Nali asked carefully. "Should we show our dice?"

"No, of course," the king conceded.

"Does the armory have weapons we can use?" Peshal asked.

"Or should the mines increase production? Our swords are certainly not of Dynfearn's quality."

Arshal tapped the parchment in front of Nali, nodding.

"Ah, worthless," Esthen said, slapping his hand on the back of Nali's chair. "It'll take a courier over a month to reach Sefresal, near three to get there and back. He could return to say Sefresal is in ashes."

"By express stations, a rider might make it in twenty days," said Peshal.

"Twenty out, twenty back, that's the record," the king said. "Three horses lost, but I imagine the urgency requires it. Time is the unknown. We'll dispatch a messenger tonight."

"What about the city? What do we know of defenses but that I'm sure flower gardens on the walls have no defensive value?" Dismay had begun to creep into Arshal's tone.

"We have eight walls!" said Esthen. "What army could breach them? A siege might be of more concern."

"The Otayran Consul might have some ideas," Nali said. "They've skirmished in their eastern wildlands for years." Arshal nodded as Nali added the item to his list.

"Is there anyone we can summon to this – I guess this is a defense council – who knows anything?" Peshal gave Arshal a wry smile.

"Council?" Arshal returned. "I suppose that's what we are. I hesitate to trust many people, especially until we know what we face. And to tell you the truth, I don't know who we could call on other than Eithur. Even the constables and their deputies are more about keeping the peace among their neighbors and responding to flood and fire, not taking up arms –"

"Zopher?" Peshal asked. "Didn't he train in the Lharan Guard?"

Arshal's lip curled.

"It's best to keep our circle small for now," King Ebon stated. "I expect queries to be made with the utmost discretion. The risk of a rumor could lead to a public panic."

"Not to mention tell a foe we're prepared," Esthen added. "We'll do fine, Arshal. We're not idiots here. We'll be ready when the time comes and they'll flee before us."

Cree shook his head but said nothing. Nali wondered how inept they must sound to someone who had witnessed the Great War. If he knew, why didn't he speak up?

"Shall we tell Mother? Resala?" Peshal asked. "Do we dare trust servants to carry our messages? Do we keep this quiet even in the household?"

"For now, unless we've authorized it, it shouldn't leave this room," the king said.

"Resala will have a fit," Peshal muttered under his breath.

"Provisions. And horses. And cattle," Esthen said, pacing now, his face set in an eager expression, seeming oblivious to them all. "Didn't Dynfearn lose one hundred men to starvation in the siege of Shela?"

"Why would your victorious army worry about a siege?" Arshal said. "Though, an inventory of supplies and an idea of what the city consumes in a week would be wise. Not to mention having a sense of where the provinces stand and what they would need."

Nali added the item to his growing list.

Afternoon, evening and night passed as ideas became a sketchy plan. Early morning had come before Nali set down his pen and rubbed tired eyes. Dawn neared. Arshal stood by the window, gulping deep breaths of the cool air. It began. Daybreak hadn't come and already messengers scurried throughout the city and countryside.

Paper crackled in the still room as Cree studied Nali's notes and copied them, adding a comment here and there and placing them on a stack beside empty mugs and platters from meals taken as they worked. Nali massaged his hand and tried to wipe the ink stains from his fingers. Peshal shifted in a doze on the wall bench and deep breathing signaled Esthen had nodded off at the secretary. Cree pushed his chair away from the table with a loud scrape, startling King Ebon from where he'd buried his head in folded arms. Peshal stirred and yawned, blinking his eyes open as Esthen began to snore.

"Well, in a few hours, with all the messengers racing about, any spy will notice we are up to something," Cree said.

"Nothing can be done about it," the king said around a yawn.

"Perhaps I can learn something." Cree's ominous tone made Arshal turn from the window.

"Osfothye," Arshal said.

"I once stood among gods. Perhaps I will find answers if I see the signs."

"I'll sit with you, Cree."

"We have more important things needing your attention, and perhaps you may yet glean other news from your dreams."

King Ebon stood and stretched, his joints snapping in the still room as Cree left in a swirl of robes. "We might as well sleep for an hour or so," he said, yawning again and dismissing them with a wave. He gathered the notes and set them atop the secretary, waking Esthen to send him away bleary-eyed as he prepared to pore over the night's work.

As Arshal closed the door, Nali glimpsed the king turning the first page of notes, shoulders bowed and sagging with the defeat of a man who witnessed his world falling apart.

An hour later, weary feet took Nali up the lane from where he'd left a king's servant with an extra horse and a whispered goodbye. It felt like ages since he'd been home and here dawn already chased the night away. He should be going the other way.

The cliffs above kept the neighborhood dark with inky shadows. A few voices rose, waking, and on other lanes, feet crunched stone. His cottage yard remained silent.

As he entered the low gate into the bare, hard-packed yard, he caught a small glimmer of red in the shadows, moving beneath his bedroom window. Startled, he called out, thinking it some drunken sailor or errant youth. He rushed forward, aiming to nab the culprit, only his family in his thoughts.

The shape leapt over a rack and raced at him. Two red glimmers, like eyes rushed him from the dark. Before he could react, Nali had fallen in the dirt of his yard, crumpled up like a drunk on Midsummer.

PART 2. AWAKENING – THE WEST

11: Alliance

Encumbered by sick and injured, it took a week to reach the sheltered valley Eithurdon had promised. A few men slipped back to the Tasch-el mine for supplies, returning with teams of horses hauling sledges that ground over the rocky trail, laden with all the Taschians could salvage, and trailed by others who worked to conceal their passage. Still others searched the valleys near Tasch-el for scattered livestock and the shepherds who had already taken the village's sheep to the spring range and might have escaped the marauders.

When the refugees crested the last ridge and looked upon the enclosed valley encircling a still lake, they caught their breaths. Nestled to the northwest of Tasch-el in a remote part of the mountains, the little valley glimmered like a jewel. The deep hollow muted the harsh winds. Wildflowers carpeted the hillsides and shoreline in the sunshine of the first weeks of the blossom moon.

From the jut of shelf outside the entrance of a deep stream-carved cavern, Tsevon looked out over the place they had come to call the Val. Behind him chased the echoes of Taschians making of musty caves a home. Trees fell for furnishings and fuel. Boughs and reeds became mats for floors and walls. Woven aspen branches fenced off crevices and pits and gave an illusion of privacy to families assigned cramped quarters. The valley vibrated with an alien racket.

Northwest, the morning sun gilt Shiad's mountain peaks, while nearer, the four mountains whose feet made the valley threw blue shadows at Lharan Guardsmen assembling in the lush meadow lakeside.

Spring melt rushed from the snow pack down cascades and dozens of waterfalls before reaching the rocky lakeshore, creating an undercurrent of rushing thunder, like the low snore of some massive beast that sheltered the Val between its tremendous paws. A marshy area at the west end held back the lake, allowing a small stream to feed a boulder strewn gorge that ended in a drop of more than a hundred paces to the Ymmenay River, the western border of Shande.

Children shrieked as they tested the frigid waters, fishing in the shadow of aspens leafing out. The sound of axes on trees and miners' picks leveling a cooking area bounced from the peaks, the resonant echo like a lifebeat.

It was not home.

The giggles of women picking stones for a communal hearth fell hollow in Tsevon's ears, forced and shrill. He noticed when his people paused in their work to stare east with a distant gaze, or startled at a sudden noise, or turned from some unbidden memory with reddened eyes. In others, Tsevon found barely suppressed rage that emerged in scowls, in tools thrown in anger and icy stares, or in the particular vehemence with which one might attack the rock with pick or a tree with axe.

This latter group – haunted, like Tsevon, by what they had seen or lost – he marked for the tasks he had in mind. Unbidden, he had an image of Von dropping from the loft with a sleepy smile on his face – and the stench of burned horseflesh. He kept those thoughts to himself like a burning ember he sheltered for when he needed fire to fuel his vengeance.

As the Lharan Guard released spare horses into the Val's lush meadow, Tsevon marked where Eithurdon sat his horse, a tall figure as he readied his men for their return to Sefresal through some of the mountain range's roughest terrain.

He felt his heart lurch at the sound of hoofbeats and calls echoing among the rocks. He made out a cluster of figures trotting toward them from the west along the lakeshore riding two to a horse. Eithurdon rode up the path with the new arrivals to where Tsevon waited with his eyes shielded against the sparkle of the sun on the lake.

"Tsevon your ranks swell," red-bearded Kefta said, his tone

sour, as he rode out of the glare. "We bring the entire population of the villages of Lhata and Staph-el to crowd you."

A half dozen ragged miners slid from their perches behind the Guardsmen accompanying Kefta and nodded to the mountain leader. Their darker hair and eyes marked their more southerly tribes. Tsevon recognized one or two men he'd met at festfires, harvest councils, or official visits to other mines. They regarded him with stony expressions. What loved ones did they think on as they begged a neighbor for aid? They stood before Tsevon with only the clothing they wore and the bitterness in which they'd wrapped themselves.

"We came too late," Kefta said. "The raiders escaped with about a hundred captives from Staph-el and we lost their trail at the river. They hit the mines this time." Kefta's indignation had crept into his voice as he swung an expansive arm across the sole six survivors. "All that remains of two tribes. Five from Staph-el." He jabbed a finger toward a particularly dour and wild-eyed figure whose face wore a crosshatch of scabbing cuts. "They trapped Halieri here in the Lhata mine when they pulled the braces on a side shaft. He's Lhata's only known survivor."

Tsevon went cold. Kefta's words hung in the space between them.

Eithurdon regarded Tsevon for a long minute before turning his mount's head.

"I will send notice to the king. Before his response, I cannot sanction anything that might be construed as aggressive if it involves foreigners. You might want to double your sentries in case trouble happens upon this valley. I left some of our spare horses to help speed messages to Sefresal. I wish I could do more. I will send supplies as soon as we reach the city. I still think we need to keep this place secret. We need not offer them new targets, or allow them to recognize a threat."

After punctuating this last with a raised eyebrow, Eithurdon goaded his horse down the slope at a gallop, trailed by his Guard.

Tsevon stared after the duke as Amhese ordered comforts and quarters for the newcomers. The way the duke had looked at him: Eithurdon expected him to protect the region. The duke knew well Tsevon would not be content until he'd avenged his village.

Tsevon turned his back on the sparkling waterfalls. "Konner!" he shouted. His new Second stuck his head over the ledge above the cave mouth where he sat watch, his mousy hair grown unruly and hanging in his eyes. "Let's call a council. Invite the newcomers."

"It's time," Konner agreed.

Tsevon nodded to himself. "It's time." He strode into the candle-lit darkness of the caves, trailed by dour Halieri, the man's presence at his back a goad.

Unlike the duke, Tsevon had no protocols to follow. It took only a few hours for his council to mobilize a plan.

Thus, when three days later Tsevon tapped a summons, he drew a handful of Shandeans from their scouting assignments to a point several days south of the Val, at the foot of the last large waterfall on the Ymmenay, a river only navigable from the Staph-el Falls north to the river mouth.

As they scouted for raiding parties or their captives, Tsevon hadn't expected to find torches on both sides of the river flickering off metals hauled by the wagon load from Shandean mines to cross a rickety bridge devised from the halves of tree trunks. Teams of draft horses hauled wagons over a pass and out of sight to the west, and canvas-bottomed barges filled with just forged weaponry and metal fittings floated down river over dozens of rapids to Ymmenay Bay.

"So, that's what they wanted," Konner said with a low whistle as he peered down on the torch lit scene below. "Minarians. After all we've given them! All those apprentices I trained. Makes my blood boil!"

A slither of stones shifted from beneath Konner's feet. The scouting party crouched lower, but the river thundering over the Staph-el Falls absorbed the sound. Besides, the Minarian sentries clearly feared no discovery as they lounged against trees or drank around their watch fires.

"Looks like they're plannin' a war," Tsevon said through clenched teeth.

Tsevon turned, hand going to his knife, at the sound of something scuttling over the stone. Khoti crawled out of the shadows to his father's elbow.

"Wondered what kept you," Tsevon whispered. "Well? What did the mines look like?"

"Forge going full fire at Staph-el. Mostly weapons and armor. There's ship fittings, wheel rims, barrel rings." Khoti looked down at the torch-lit scene below, his eyes widening. "Well, that explains where all the wagons were going. One headed up the Staph-el road toward Sefresal."

Tsevon's Tawnkats as they fashioned themselves, stared at

him. He couldn't let them down with indecision. But they faced an army! What did they want with the women and children of Tasch-el and Staph-el? Did Amhese's Staphian cousins now toil in some Minarian camp?

"Well, if it's a war they want," he said at last. "Khoti, take my mount and Konner's and ride to Sefresal as fast as you can. Tell the duke what we found. And don't be keepin' yourself for promises of glory in the Lharan Guard! I need you here!" He squeezed Khoti's arm, then with a light shove sent him into the night.

Konner's smile was a slash of white. "Are we taking on all of Minaria? Shiad and Arenh paid pretty dear for getting in their way before!"

"And we've paid too dear to let 'em pass. They'll rue the day they crossed the Ymmenay."

As a Minarian guard finally shifted and looked up at the dark mountain sides, as if he felt himself being watched, the Tawnkats padded softly into the night.

Tsevon led Konner on foot along the trail back to the Val as the rest of his Tawnkats slipped away to various scouting positions, the occasional rap of stone carrying through the valleys and up the passes as they reported in. What they dared, a bunch of miners and shepherds taking on professional warriors, Tsevon refused to think about. He wouldn't rest as long as Von still remained unreleased to the spirits.

A day north of the Staph-el Falls, Tsevon sensed someone on the trail behind them. He'd heard no tapping for hours. A rock skittered down the mountain side only a short distance behind. A swift signal sent Konner scampering into the rocks overhead. Tsevon pulled himself back into the shadows thrown by a precipice over the narrow trail they followed. A silhouetted figure neared. In the moonless night, Tsevon just discerned a man's shape crouching at Tsevon's slight shift on the stony ground. As the figure turned, Tsevon pounced, throwing the man to the ground in one fluid movement.

The man squinted up at him, likely seeing only a shadow against the sky. He held out empty hands, placating. Tsevon pressed a knife against the stranger's throat.

"I have done you no wrong!"

Tsevon peered at the man. "You don't sound Minarian. What, is all the west our enemy? Why are you following us?" Tsevon demanded. He leaned back to let the man take a breath.

The man kept his hands out, but sat up, peering in the dark

at Tsevon. "Aibak, Shiadin. I have no battle with you." He lowered his hands slowly, keeping a wary eye on Tsevon's knife.

Tsevon didn't hear deceit in Aibak's tone. "Then what brings you from your coasts to dog our heels?"

"Border patrol. I look for Minarians who have crossed into Shiad in raids several times now. We thought our old foe hoped to again claim Shiad for its own. They have always envied our fishing grounds. I think with their skirmishes they intend to keep us from noticing other things. They seek bigger fish it seems."

Tsevon hesitated. It could be a trap. He knew enough Minarians to know an alliance between Minaria and Shiad would stand like fleece before the shears. He sheathed his dagger and put out a hand to help Aibak to his feet. He meant his grip to make an impression. Aibak merely bobbed his head in greeting.

"So why do you follow us?" Tsevon's hand rested on his dagger.

"We merely monitor the situation so we know what we face. It is fortunate your people are alert to stop them."

"Alert? Maybe. I don't know about stopping 'em."

"Our king suspended dealings with Shande when Minaria threatened to attack anyone that still trades with you. They killed several shawnsi in Tenasia."

"They killed more than a few folk here, and took captives."

"Labor, to serve their warriors," Aibak said with a nod. "There are not enough Pladde to serve an army. They took hundreds of captives in our last war with them. But you prepare to fight and defend yourself? This is good. Long ago, they attacked us without warning. Eventually we drove them off. They had attacked Arenh as well and were unable to maintain two fronts. We still lost most of a generation. Their advantage lies in surprise and overrunning –"

"We've nothing to fight with," Tsevon protested. "Likely our king is clueless, if he remembers such lowly tax payers so far from his fine halls. It takes a fast rider to reach Sihmad Shal in under a month." Tsevon stabbed a hand at the air. "We lost everything! They control the mines. We've nothing but a few pick-axes against swords and armor. We're almost out of arrows and bowstring. And we still need to feed and guard our people."

"If you do not stop them, they will simply annihilate you. Then they will come for us. It is selfish, but true." Aibak stared at his feet a moment. "Dealing with Shandeans is forbidden now. But perhaps, between mountain neighbors, something can be arranged. You need weapons? Supplies? Perhaps we can spare your time from provisioning, to fight."

"Your price? We've nothing to exchange."

"Oh, but you do. We ask anonymity, and will give the same. We must tread carefully because we are unprepared to join a war and they outnumber us. You need us to supply you. We need you to fight them, or at least distract them long enough to give both our lands time to arm." Aibak paced in the darkness. "You must defeat them. We never recovered from their last war and now whatever drives them makes them even more perilous in their reckless –"

A hist from above cut Aibak off. Tsevon and Aibak crept beneath the shadow of the ledge. Above, Konner threw himself flat. Tsevon drew his dagger. To his surprise, Aibak had freed a sword from beneath his cloak.

Booted feet crunched the stony trail and squished in snowmelt puddles. Two shapes rose out of the night, their heads oddly misshapen by their helms. Aibak tensed, bending forward as Tsevon crouched, ready to pounce.

Air shifted as Konner leapt to land on the rear figure and as quickly slit his throat, the body falling with a soft gasp. As the other turned, Aibak leapt out and thrust his sword into the man's neck before Tsevon could react.

Tsevon stared at the medallion glinting from the dead man's chest. He had an instant's memory of the heat in his fingers as he'd tossed medallions in the fire.

"We're not the type to seek others' help, but this," with his foot he nudged the medallion, "This is beyond me. Maybe we can use some help."

Aibak laid a hand on Tsevon's shoulder in a sign of pact. As Konner rolled the bodies down the slope, Aibak detailed where he lived, and where he'd make his mark when he had supplies for them. Tsevon merely nodded, finding an irony in traveling so far south to meet a man who made his camp across the Ymmenay from the Val. Did the valley remain unknown to the Shiadins? Could the racket of their community be heard above the roar of the river? He needed to post sentries on the river side now, another thing he should have thought of before this.

As Aibak gave a cheery wave and strode into the night, Tsevon noticed other movement in the rocks around them. In a fluid move, before he even took his breath, his bow came up to train on a figure. Aibak stopped and grinned at him, motioning toward the rocks. In an instant, two more Shiadins joined Aibak. As they slipped into the night, Tsevon, realized they'd been stalked and the meeting no accident.

A week later, a newly posted Val sentry summoned Tsevon, who laughed to watch Aibak work. The Shiadin and a companion crossed the river into Shande to hew at the base of a giant pine, finally pulling the wedge to let if fall across the river channel.

At first, Tsevon thought the plan had failed as the tree didn't quite reach the far shore. But Aibak fastened a rope to a protruding branch, tossing the end to a third Shiadin on the opposite shore. When pulled taut, the rope ran neck high across the river. When night fell, Aibak's men paddled into the river, tied their boat in the lee of the pine and hid behind its branches.

Tsevon almost cheered when the first Minarian raft rounded a slight bend in the river and came upon the felled tree. The current swept the craft toward the Shiad side as the Minarians maneuvered to pass by the tip. Just as they shot through the narrow gap, Aibak yanked the rope. The three men on the raft spilled into the water, one dead with his neck snapped, the other two dispatched by archers hidden among the boulders on the shore. As the raft spun past, the Shiadins threw a hook onto it and towed it into the calmer waters of the Shande shoreline where they unloaded it, concealed the cargo, then busted the raft to pieces. When they finished, they returned to wait for the next raft.

By late night, the Shiadins had piled the cargo of three Minarian rafts upon the Shande shore. Before departing at dawn, Aibak tied a strip of cloth to a branch on the Shande shore by the cache. Such a simple plan, Tsevon wished he'd thought of it himself. He grinned as he held up a newly forged sword, his men hauling chests of arrowheads, metal balls and sling shots, daggers, pike heads, oil-cloth wrapped swords and bags of Shiadin barley up the long slope to the Val. He had a target, a base and a supply line. Now he would have a war.

12: Tsevon's Medicine

In the dark of an overcast night, Khoti, Konner and a dozen Tawnkats crept to the bridge at the foot of the Staph-el Falls. Crouched among the boulders, they waited as a raft drifted down river and a wagon crossed the crude, torch-lit bridge to the camp on the other side before they moved again.

Khoti, newly returned from Sefresal, tried to fight the weariness of his break-neck race through the mountains, barely pausing to switch from Kivik to Konner's sturdy bay and back. Each moment he had feared discovery; each time he rested the horses felt too long lest he arrive too late. Now, his limbs felt slow and his head thick as the torch light quivered, creating phantom figures in the dark. He struggled to remain alert. He had to earn the role he so desperately wanted: to fight beside his fa as a trusted man of Tasch-el, to make up for not being the son Tsevon had wanted to succeed him, to make up for his failure to save Von and Grandmam and fight for his village.

Konner padded up behind the sentry at the east end of the bridge. When the man's head turned, Konner reached out and slit the sentry's throat. Konner's hand and the roar of the falls muffled the man's cry as Konner dragged him into the shadows. The one-time Constable of Tasch-el gave an approving nod to Khoti's close scrutiny. Khoti must first learn from Tsevon's Second, who demonstrated a brutal side Khoti wasn't sure he could emulate.

Konner gave the signal and the Tawnkats waded into glacier-fed waters, pulling themselves along the rough bark of the bridge as they held to the deep shadows thrown by the torches. Slipping on stones, gasping as the cold sucked the breath from them, they clung to the logs at the deepest point, their feet swinging up behind them as they moved hand-over-hand along the bridge.

Suddenly, Khoti lost his grip. He flailed his freed hand against the rush of water, struggling to gain a stub of branch before his other hand gave way. His arms felt like logs at his sides. Clenching his teeth, he expected at any moment to be dashed against the rocks or pulled under the boil of turbulent rapids. Konner gripped him by the belt. Khoti opened his mouth to gasp for breath. A wheeze of water rushed in. He buried his face in Konner's shoulder, trying to clear the water from his lungs as silently as possible. At last, his hand brushed the log and he grasped the bridge, finding a hold.

The Tawnkats watched with stony expressions as the falls muffled his hacking coughs. After what seemed minutes, though only painful seconds, he nodded and the Tawnkats continued their slow passage across the river.

Once they found their footing again and the current waned, they broke for the dark line of bank and threw themselves among the boulders, movements stilted as they tried to gain their breath and push blood back into their limbs.

"You all know your assignments?" Konner whispered around chattering teeth. "You come around from the south," Konner motioned to the last four men to cross." And you, he signaled another four men, "circle 'round to the north. Gotta hit hard, fast, and slip back before they know what hit 'em. Remember, stealth, you're a Tawnkat!"

Konner turned to Khoti, his forced smile like a grimace. "Ready, boy?"

Khoti scanned the sputtering torches of the camp where Minarian sentries lounged in wait for another load of metals from the mines. Konner for the third time measured the length of rope and attached grappling hook hanging from his side as he waited for Segan's signal.

Peering into the dark, his eyes still seeing the ghosts of torches, Khoti searched for the silhouette of Segan sawing the bridge supports and the thick ropes binding the logs together and to the pilings. For just an instant he thought he heard the squeak of wood in the saw's teeth, but the water swept the sound away. It felt like forever as they dripped and shivered in the shadows.

"Set?" Konner whispered at last.

With barely perceptible nods, the men beside Khoti nocked their arrows. Khoti crept to the top of the bank and crawled to the edge of the torch-lit ring of the camp.

When he heard arrows swish over his head to sink into soft targets, Khoti dashed to the nearest fire, wrapping a hide around his hand as he went. He grabbed a burning branch and tossed it onto the canvas roof of the largest tent. Other Tawnkats scattered the sentries' horses, slashed harnesses and dropped sputtering torches into wagon beds. Arrows whistled by as Tawnkats picked off startled Minarians stumbling from their bedrolls, running for weapons or staggering from burning tents. Khoti continued to lob burning brands at the tents, dashing from fire to shadow.

Segan made a final pull on the saw and lofted it to the Shandean side. As he did so, Konner let out a tawnkat shriek, a wail so loud and full of menace the Minarians briefly faltered in their race for their weapons. As the echoing wail trailed away, Konner tossed his hook to Segan, who lobbed it onto the rocky Shandean shore and tugged the rope until set.

The Tawnkats rushed back to the shore and the only hope of escape.

"Anchor!" Konner called as the camp organized pursuit.

"Wagon coming!" Ahrwesz shouted as he tossed his bow to Halieri then wound the end of the rope around his waist.

"Two archers, cover us, go!" Konner shoved young Davin toward the water, breaking the Taschian's concentration on the Minarian soldiers running at them. Two dozen, maybe three, closed. Seconds separated them. Davin, little older than Khoti himself, let his last arrow fly into the throat of the lead man with a calm Khoti needed to learn. As the Minarian's hands rose to his throat, Davin plunged into the roiling river, his fair head disappearing beneath the current before he could pull himself above the surface and drag himself along the rope.

Segan pulled himself up on the far bank and readied a bow as Davin reached the middle of the river. Minarian arrows began to fall among the Tawnkats, some splashing into the river.

At last, Khoti plunged into the water, feeling the breath catch up in his throat. Ahrwesz braced against the weight as the current pulled the Tawnkats downstream. More arrows whizzed overhead as two more Tawnkat archers joined Segan. Konner plunged into the water behind Khoti as Ahrwesz waded in behind them, at last letting the Tawnkats on the Shandean side pull them across. Without Ahrwesz anchoring them, the current swept them down river and into the cover of darkness as Minarian arrows splashed around them, the river boiling into their faces as Tawnkats towed them against the current.

Panting, lungs aching, Khoti at last found his feet among the slippery boulders. Stumbling for shore, he unslung his bow, abandoning the rope, ready to fire an arrow at the first open target. Wagon wheels rumbled over the road from the Staph-el mine and began to cross the bridge, blocking pursuit.

He looked back to check Konner's progress, Ahrwesz behind him. Ahrwesz floundered in the shallows, alternately pulling at the rope and clutching at an arrow in his shoulder.

"Ahrwesz!" Khoti shouted, as he raced to Ahrwesz to haul his cousin from the water.

"Go, go!" Konner ordered as Khoti and Ahrwesz reached the firmer ground of the shore where Segan and Halieri took Ahrwesz's weight between them as the man's legs gave way. Khoti unwound the rope from Ahrwesz's waist as the other Tawnkats slipped away.

They trotted along the broken ground only a short distance before they heard over the sound of the falls a loud creak, then snap. A man shouted. Horses screamed. The log bridge lay collapsed in the middle of the river, the wagon lifting in the water and the horses flailing in their traces. When the current caught the edges of the bridge logs, they, too, drifted downstream, slamming into the teamster as his wagon broke against a boulder.

Konner snorted at the helpless stares of the Minarians on the western shore. The Second sobered the moment his gaze fell on the slumped figure of Ahrwesz. Hadn't Latra warned that she saw tragedy befalling Ahrwesz if he left the safety of the Val?

They didn't travel far. Barely a day north they had to stop as Ahrwesz continued to lose blood and a fever threatened to take another of their dwindling people. Konner tapped out an urgent message to Tsevon, reaching him on the Staph-el Road where he scouted with another Tawnkat unit.

Tsevon's medicine and ability to recover from using it far exceeded Konner's. Their headman sped to reach them, unrested, with the intent of expending strength it might take weeks for him to completely regain. Khoti felt certain his father hadn't recovered yet from all the medicine he'd spent mending his people after the attack on Tasch-el.

As Konner readied Ahrwesz, baring and bathing his wound and building up the fire, Khoti begged his father to a hear a plan he'd been thinking about since seeing the Staph-el mine. He was sure it would work and would strike a tremendous blow.

"And we've a plan crafted by men who've seen twice your years and possess twice the life's wisdom," Tsevon said. "A boy with no voice thinks he's got a better strategy then men who've earned their marks? I've no time for it Khoti."

"Fa, it's a sound plan. I know! I feel it!"

"I rode hard to get here, son. We've had no rest in a month. You're trying my temper. It's enough I've let you take on these dangerous missions. Ahrwesz could have been killed! We're just too few to lose now. I trust Konner to keep you in line –"

"But –"

"I'll have no more! I'll send you back to the Val and you can stand watch at the caverns!"

Tsevon glared at him, all the other Tawnkats watching, as Khoti kept a healer from an injured man who tossed in fever and pain, whose sickness Khoti could *see*.

Tsevon lightly pushed his son aside as he tried to reach the cleft where they tended Ahrwesz. Khoti stumbled, tripping and falling to his knees. He heard the chuckles of the older men. His face burned with humiliation.

"A boy in years, but with his fa's instinct for the fight," he heard Konner say.

Khoti knew he had proven himself a Tawnkat worthy of the altered tattoo his fa's best now sported. The three slashes on Konner's neck, and the necks of many other Taschian Tawnkats, had been linked into the shape of a Tawnkat's fangs, Tsevon's mark. Tsevon had even transformed Halieri's triangular Lhatan tattoo. Khoti's neck remained bare. The rapport Khoti had earned in his skirmishes with Konner's squad evaporated with his fa's arrival. Instead of a mountain man who could run into an enemy camp dodging arrows to lob torches, or scout out a mine crawling with Minarians, or race the long hours to Sefresal via dangerous paths patrolled by armed soldiers, they saw a youth. They laughed at his ideas because his fa made light of them, his voice disregarded as if a child, a second son and second choice.

Khoti became an impatient scowl as the tera sticks moved in his father's hands. The medicine sticks hummed and whistled as the three narrow, forearm-long strips of wood twirled faster and faster on their leather thongs. They ripped the air to call the wind, slapped together with the crack of stone, urging the spirits to aid a mountain life threatened. Shadows hung about his father's face, his skin shimmering and pale.

The sticks disappeared in a blur, as now he swung them over the fire, now over Ahrwesz. Instead of the crack of wood against wood, Khoti heard in them the wind in the peaks and the snap of sun-heated stone. Certainly, the spirits took over the tera sticks to have them sing so in Tsevon's grasp, sing with the mountain's voice.

Tsevon loosed one stick to fall in the coals of the fire while the other two continued to rap a pulse. Konner plucked the stick from the flames with a flourish, guarding the bright ember at its tip then swished it through the air so it flared and spit out a spark before Konner at last quenched the flame between his fingers.

The rhythm slowed as Tsevon tapped and brushed the remaining two tera sticks together. Finally, the sticks fell silent and Tsevon took the burned stick from Konner. Ahrewsz's wound festered. Khoti could *see* it. Tsevon marked a line along his nephew's wound with the burned end, leaving a dark smudge of ash beside the arrow wound. Then he sliced his palm to draw blood and lay his hand on Ahrwesz's injury.

Ahrwesz gasped. Khoti could *see* his father weakening as the poisons passed through him on their way to the spirits. Ahrwesz tensed to receive a hot knife pulled from the fire. Segan placed a rag in Ahrwesz's mouth to muffle any cry and held his head. Konner kneeled on the man's legs. Tsevon, his mouth twisted and sweat running from his brow, bent to cauterize the wound.

As the knife pressed flesh, Khoti pressed his hands against his ears, hearing instead of Ahrwesz's cry of pain, Von's screams from the burning stable, his grandmam's wail as fire engulfed their cottage, tongues of flame boiling from the windows. Khoti grabbed his dagger and bow and stalked into the night, his ears echoing the cries of the dead and his lungs constricting at the hint of burned flesh.

Looking back, Khoti saw his fa note his retreat. Scowling, Tsevon stood, Konner gripping his arm to hold him steady.

"I can't be chasing after a boy's fits of temper when we've an enemy to fight and warriors to heal." Tsevon's voice carried, medicine-weary and angry. "Does he think such pouts make him look strong?"

"No, Tsevon," Konner said. "Don't let your anger draw words you'll both regret. It's the age. He's just months from his rites. Remember when you weren't quite a boy and not yet a man? He's got all that and a fury he hasn't let out. I'll keep an eye on him."

Tsevon pulled his arm free. He sat, staring into the dark, an older image of Von, a little of Von in his movements and wiry build. Almost, Khoti thought his father could see right into him. If so, he should understand. But the headman shook his head after a moment and turned back to Ahrwesz to study his wound, which Khoti could see no longer festered. Within, the muscle would mend swiftly, the spirits working with Tsevon's blood. And, as swiftly, his father had dismissed him.

Far from the sheltered light of the campfire, hidden by the steep walls of the defile, Khoti heard the banter of Tawnkats teasing Khoti's fickle adolescence. Khoti watched a while, feeling in his heart his father's magic as the healer tapped a song of tribute to the spirits for healing Ahrwesz. Khoti wondered if he would ever make such music. His father had given him sticks last Long Day, but they burned away in Tasch-el and he still awaited completion of his replacement set. Would he have the healer's gift to bring spirits to his aid? He doubted it when the sight of the dead and dying Minarians raised the bile in his throat. If he possessed the skill, he wouldn't know until he had a voice and earned a spot in the guild of medicine wielders. His fa had told him once that his ability to recognize illness showed the potential of a healer. He wondered if they would ever again have a settled time when Tsevon could teach him the sticks' secrets.

Tsevon's tapping ended, and with it Khoti's compulsion to watch. Konner led Tsevon to a bedroll, the concerns of a mere boy too much to trouble him.

Khoti reached into his haversack and weighed the few handfuls of nuts, dried meats and roots, and two hard biscuits Segan had baked over the fire. He hadn't felt hungry since the moment the blood welled up around the arrow embedded just below Ahrwesz's collar bone. He needed to force himself to eat. He needed his wits about him to carry out his plan. Without the help of the Tawnkats could he even do it?

"I'm no cub, Fa," he whispered. "They'll call me Tawnkat. I'll earn it and I'll have that mark on my neck, no other."

He dipped his water skin in the icy spring a few yards away and with a backward glance at his father settling into his bedroll, slipped into the night.

13: The Staph-el Mine

Khoti peered from the cover of weathered pine clinging to moonlit, wind-battered slopes outside of the Staph-el mine. He waited for a laden wagon to clear the mine's entrance and the Minarian laborers to disappear back into the shaft, carrying their torches with them. Draft horses huddled in their traces, heads bowed into the worst gusts of a cold wind, awaiting the next load to fill their empty wagons.

Orange light flickered skyward from a dell a short way down the mountainside where the clang of a forge rang up into the heights. To Khoti, they appeared unconcerned about detection. Shouldn't they be wary after the Tawnkat raid two nights ago?

He tried to calm the pound of blood in his ears with a deep breath. He shouldn't be doing this alone. Why hadn't they listened? He wiped sweaty palms on his hide shirt before tucking his dagger in his belt. Fearing his bow and quiver might rattle, he left them beneath the pines. No light or sound of sentries came from the mine. He darted across the wagon-rutted road to duck behind the nearest empty wagon waiting just beyond the mouth of the shaft.

He had to move quickly before the next load of ore or teamsters arrived. He gathered four sets of reins and unhitched the horses from the wagon, then swiftly worked the heavy beasts into position at the mouth of the mine. His breath came in short puffs, the horses shifting nervously and tangling the reins as they sensed the fear in his trembling hands. Could four horses even do the job?

When at last he steadied the beasts, he hooked heavy wagon chains to iron rings on the whiffletree with the quickness and certainty of a miner's son. The horses snorted. Chains rattled and harnesses creaked. His ears strained for the sounds he feared most. Did he hear wagon wheels? The crush of booted feet? He just needed a few more minutes.

The outline of the first roof brace loomed before him. A narrow crevice between wood and the rough-cut stone revealed weathered and time-built cracks up into the ceiling. He quickly tucked the chain around the beam. After an instant's hesitation, he dashed back to attach the second chain to a brace deeper in the shaft. Any moment a new dray of metals would arrive, his timing crucial. The second chain barely reached. He could only slip it around the beam high off the floor. He struggled on tiptoes to reach the ceiling support above him, push the taut chain through and clasp it. He shouldn't be working alone.

Listening a moment, he heard only silence. He pulled up the slack on the first chain and looped it around several times near the bottom of the beam. At last, he maneuvered the team out of the shaft until the tree hung suspended above the stone floor. He had to fight the urge to rush. He couldn't risk a mistake.

A noise echoed up the shaft and he caught the faint flicker of torches approaching from the mountain's heart. He snapped the whip across the horses' flanks then rushed to beat them out of the mine's entrance as they strained in their harnesses to escape.

A loud wooden creak echoed down the shaft as the chains dug into the beams, the noise spooking the horses. With growing agitation, the team pulled first one way, then another, as Khoti scrambled across the moonlit open roadway to the safety of the pines and snatched up his bow. The horses' heads stood out of the shadow of the mine, the wavering light glowing on the whites of their eyes. Torches closed from behind, filling the animals with fear.

"C'mon, c'mon," Khoti urged under his breath as he heard the unmistakable rumble of a wagon negotiating the steep road. The torches in the shaft stopped for a heartbeat before bobbing with the gait of running miners.

At what seemed the last possible moment before failure, something gave and first one half of the team, and then those yoked beside it broke free. Khoti held his breath. Nothing. They must have broken the traces, or the tree, or the chains had snapped or the miners had cut them, or he'd misjudged the weaknesses in the stone or –

A slow rumble beneath his feet told him his intuition had served: The crevices in the ceiling, the extra brace. A cloud of dust chased the horses from the shaft and soon the first cascade of pebbles fell from the opening. Then the entire mouth of the mine disappeared in a roll of dust as the horses bolted down the road to collide with the oncoming wagon.

With a triumphant grin, Khoti slung his bow at his back and turned. He froze at the glint of an axe about to fall on him. His heart thumped hard. In that same instant the weapon fell.

Khoti stumbled sideways. The blade sliced through his haversack and tangled in his bow. The arrows clattered to the ground, worthless. He gasped, trying to correct his fall. Instead, he came down hard on his side. He rolled away as the sentry swung at him again, axe striking hard against stone. Khoti strove to pull the dagger from his belt. His hand came away bloody, from either the axe edge or the unsheathed dagger. He scrambled to his feet and crouched, waiting for the next swing of the axe. The sentry had dropped it, the head having broken from the shaft. And he saw that unlike those who guarded the bridge and attacked Tasch-el, the sentry wore no armor.

The sentry circled Khoti now. A dagger flashed as the man twitched his wrist from side to side in search of an opening. Khoti's insides turned to water when he saw the purposeful, trained, movements. Standing a head taller, even in the dark the man's silhouette marked the frame of a warrior, not a youth.

Khoti tried to remember all he'd learned from his father, to move like a tawnkat as the sentry lunged, turning the dagger in search of a mark. Again, Khoti jumped away, now standing on the higher ground where he almost reached his foe's eye level.

Without thinking, letting instinct propel him, Khoti lunged. As his head met the man's mid-section he sunk his dagger into the man's abdomen. Using the momentum of his fall, Khoti pulled upward with all his strength, ripping the man open as if he dressed a mountbuck.

The sentry's gasp howled in Khoti's ear as blood stained the ground and Khoti's momentum sent him skidding down the slope a few feet beyond the Minarian. Khoti felt a tremor in his chest when he saw the man's eyes glaring back at him. But soon they glazed and Khoti allowed himself to breathe. He gasped at the effort to pull a breath, suddenly aware of the fire in his side. The sentry's dagger protruded from Khoti's blood-stained buckskin shirt.

Khoti groaned and almost cried his dismay when he realized he was alone and likely dying, more than a day on healthy feet from his father's last-known camp and a healer's blood.

He stumbled down the slope away from the scarred mountainside where dust still hung in the air. Almost doubled over, one hand clutched the knife in his side. The other still held his own dagger, smeared with the sentry's blood. He staggered down into the valley with no sense of where his feet took him.

Stumbling for what seemed hours, he tripped over every branch and bumped into each outcrop of rock as the moon sank west and dawn broadened. Not knowing where he walked or how far he'd gone, he couldn't allow himself to stop, even as the fire in his side burned and blood soaked his shirt and crept down his leg. He couldn't die alone, desperate with thirst as carrion birds whirled overhead and the tawnkat leered at him from the dark. No one would find him to free him to the spirits. He would remain, forever, chained to this moment, his flesh the fodder of worms. He imagined them coiling through his guts, flies settling on him, his deserved end for disappointing his people, his fa.

He realized he couldn't take another step. His body confirmed this one lucid thought and he collapsed, still clinging to his dagger, within yards of a stream, the cool and liquid babble of it taunting his nightmares.

14: Scavengers

"'I'm dead.' Makes no sense, Tsevon. Who'd be tapping such a story, asking us to come free him to the spirits?" Konner whispered as the Tawnkats strained to make out what sounded like the distant call of stones. Konner watched a scowl spread across Tsevon's face.

All morning Tsevon had continued to insist that Khoti, who they hadn't seen since the night before had, in a childish pout, headed home to the Val. The entire unit spent half the day waiting for his return, risking discovery this close to Staph-el. But Konner felt equally certain Khoti, no longer the child his fa thought him, wouldn't just leave his fellows like that. Again, they heard the faintest hint on the wind of tapping.

"It's stones, too rhythmic to be random," someone said.

Tsevon motioned his Tawnkats to silence with an impatient slash of his arm.

"Khoti sign with a two-tap?" Konner asked Tsevon.

"I wondered when you'd say it. You're so certain Khoti didn't head home?"

The tapping had stopped, lost somewhere in the folds of the mountain range.

"I'm thinking you haven't been around the boy much since the attack on Tasch-el. Seems changed from the lad I knew." Tsevon shot a glare at his Second but Konner plunged in. "The boy's growing up the hard way, fast. It's sour mash to be both child and man and, honestly, he's more man than you think. You're going to get a bad brew if you don't handle it proper. I know he didn't take to our teasing. He's got his mind set on a plan to get his own revenge for the horrors he's seen."

"You think Khoti's so frail he'd lose all the sense he's got? We've all seen horrors."

"I'm telling you he's got something to prove, especially being the younger."

Tsevon let out a long breath. "Maybe you're right. I haven't had it in me to talk to him about it. But –"

"But does the boy sign off with a two-tap?"

Tsevon nodded into his chest, eyes closed.

"Then even if he didn't take it in his head to go off alone to the Staph-el mine, he could've taken a fall, or met an enemy patrol. Your boy thinks we're looking for him. And we're not. And he's saying it's too late to do anything but release to the spirits."

"Khoti wouldn't give up."

"And I'm betting he didn't go home," Konner continued. "He's not a child, Tsevon, with more experience than most men have at his age. He's as much a man in heart as you and I, as brave as any Tawnkat, having the sense to fetch the Lharan Guard and lead them through the mountains. You know it."

Tsevon dropped his head into his hands. "Konner, how can I drop everything we've set in motion to chase after one boy and not save every other Lharan who might yet fall in battle?"

Konner knew it couldn't be justified. That was the special knowledge of healers, who spent years learning to be callous and compassionate in the same breath, deciding for whom the initial ruling of the spirits would stand, and for whom they would appeal for a reversal. He could read Tsevon's weariness like he read disease in the ill. He clearly hadn't recovered from all the medicine he'd already doled out to keep their dwindling people alive. But Konner couldn't let it go. Finally, he signaled for Segan to rap out an urgent rhythm demanding more information. They listened intently, but no response came.

Tsevon paced. They should have left for the Val yesterday eve. But they kept expecting Khoti to wander into camp hungry and apologetic. But that was the Khoti of before.

"Maybe we should look for signs leading to Staph-el," Konner urged.

"He wouldn't deliberately defy me."

Konner steeled himself. How far could he push Tsevon before he risked their friendship? Just then, a sentry pointed to the figure of Teckhan trudging up the defile. Though only a few minutes, it seemed like it took hours for the Taschian to reach them.

Teckhan looked from Konner to Tsevon, the silence hanging between them like a sentence.

"Spit it out," Tsevon demanded, his voice carrying up into the rocks and startling a raptor from its perch.

"No sign toward the Val," he said, going red under Tsevon's scrutiny. "I, uh, backtracked to Staph-el."

"Are you saying you tracked my son to the Staph-el mine?"

Teckhan shook his head. "I lost his trail. But it heads that way. So, I scouted the mine. The area's crawling. Seems there's been a cave in. I couldn't get near enough to search for sign. The rain last night didn't help."

"His plan worked!" Konner crowed, slapping Tsevon's back.

"Did it?" Tsevon returned. "Then where is he? Did he get himself killed makin' his point?"

"How far did the trail take you?" Konner asked.

"Most of the way. I lost it in the rocks up around Redside." He gestured toward a steep mountain about three hours distant. The mountain glowed red as the sun lit its rusty face where a slide had bared a vein of rock.

"The most direct route," Konner said, nodding. "You saw no trace beyond?" Konner hoisted his pack. "I guess I'll just be hiking over by Redside then."

Konner nodded for Segan and Teckhan to join him. His last glance at Tsevon revealing a man whose sagging shoulders, back turned and head in his hands, told the grief he contemplated: both his sons.

The tapping came so infrequently and faint they could barely hear it over the wind. Konner grew more certain than ever Khoti called for help from somewhere in the valleys rippling at some mountain's feet. Sound deceived; they needed the tapper to provide a position. Faint replies reported a valley of moss-covered stones by a stream, describing virtually every valley and stream in the mountains.

They had wandered half a dozen valleys running along the feet of Redside and about to cross the next slope to look further east, when Segan looked up and pointed. A circle of carrion birds winged lower and lower toward a defile due west of them. The birds swam in and out of the westering sun's glare, but appeared to descend only a short distance away. They hurried now, making for where the birds' loops brought them down into a gorge spilling from a valley at Redside's feet that seemed impossible for Khoti to have intentionally entered.

Konner peered into the afternoon shadows filling the gorge, finally seeing movement. He couldn't discern a figure, but birds gathered, screeching and flying short distances, only to slowly walk back toward a hollow in the rocks.

The descent was treacherous among boulders strewn like the toys of restless giants, many moss-covered and slippery from the spray of a waterfall. Konner tensed as they neared, fearing they came too late, or if in time, still too late.

"Ah, now why did you get yourself like that," Konner cooed when he crouched beside the still figure who so closely resembled his father.

Segan beat away scavengers that screeched at the robbery as Teckhan searched for branches to make a litter. Khoti burned with fever, his eyes glazed as he swatted at Konner as if he thought the constable another bird harrying its victim to death.

Konner studied the knife embedded in Khoti's side. While one hand still held the stone he had used to rap against a boulder, the other clutched a bloody dagger. He saw no dead birds nor wounded animals. Konner knew no scavenger's blood darkened the blade. Then he saw the waterskin and haversack, slashed and empty. He quickly fetched water and tried to force Khoti to drink. Most of the water dribbled from his mouth.

"I'm not carrying this news to your fa, so you'd best just hang on. I can't do it for you," Konner said.

Khoti's eyes seemed to focus on him a moment and he dropped the dagger to clutch his arm.

"Free me. It'll kill him."

"Don't be stupid. Just stay with me, boy. You're a Tawnkat!"

Konner quickly cut away clothing from Khoti's wound and poured spirits over it to cleanse it. Khoti let out a small gasp and closed his eyes, barely shaking his head, not reacting as Konner drew the dagger from his side. He applied a healing salve and packed the wound as best he could from what he had in his pack. Konner didn't have the medicine in him to treat this wound more effectively. He could see the infection and damage and knew Khoti walked the edge of a vast spaciousness from which he doubted even Tsevon could fetch the boy. What wrong did they do to return a dead son to a healer who would expend all his strength to bring him back?

It took an hour for the three of them to maneuver the litter bearing Khoti out of the gorge, then hours more to carefully bear him through treacherous valleys. When at last they bore Khoti up the defile to Tsevon's camp, evening had fallen.

"What's their burden!" Tsevon demanded in a rasp that carried down the slope, his hands cupped around his eyes as he tried to peer into the long shadows.

The men around Tsevon turned away, leaving Tsevon standing alone with his hands clenched at his sides as Konner, Segan and Teckan neared with the litter.

When at last they reached the camp, they gently settled Khoti's litter beside the fire.

"He's bled so much, Tsevon, I don't know that medicine can save him. I know mine can't." Konner felt as taut as a bowstring as Segan set about building up the fire and Teckhan again tried to get Khoti to take water. Konner knew what Tsevon saw: his stubbornness had let his son suffer. They might have reached him sooner.

"He shouldn't have been alone. I should have listened –"

"We can pass out blame later," Konner said. When Tsevon didn't respond immediately, Konner yanked Tsevon around to face him, his hands balling into fists. "He dies! I'm not the healer you are! He hasn't given up. If you won't at least try for the boy, I will, but you know I'll die trying because I don't want this on my heart!"

A shiver took Tsevon as he finally turned and knelt at Khoti's side.

"Get my sticks," he ordered as he probed the wound with his fingers. Only Tsevon among them had medicine strong enough to mend such a wound. He had it in his hands and heart, mountain folk said. As never before, Tsevon would have to call on those spirits to bring his son back to life. What Tsevon, or even Khoti, might be after such a journey, only the spirits knew.

15: The Hunt

"If Khoti can take it in his head to attack the Staph-el mine alone, then maybe we can go bigger and better ourselves. We got to pay 'em back for what they done to us, all of us." Tsevon's hoarse voice boomed off walls, wheedling into a world not quite solid in Khoti's mind.

His fa's call had pulled him from the edge of the chasm more than a week ago, before the three-day journey that Khoti had endured in a haze of pain and fever. His fa couldn't take all of it, only the worst. He'd administered his medicine so sparingly Khoti's limbs remained leaden, though the strange world Khoti wandered in now felt less frightening. A mush of sounds like voices heard through a wall – things to react to if he could just make himself – replaced the terrifying silence in his head. Like Mam's voice, confiding the helpless dismay she'd felt when dragged from the cottage, her mam left to die within, how she couldn't bear in her heart the loss of another son. He wanted to comfort her, to apologize for not saving Grandmam and Von, for the recklessness that brought her grief. Each time he tried to move or speak, the spirits called in sweet wordless voices, like earth and sky, soothing his fears and urging him to set aside his burdens and just be still.

The voices intruded again. The passion Tsevon expressed at the destruction of Tasch-el couldn't compare to the cold fury Khoti heard in the tone of a father contemplating the death of his remaining son.

"These demons," Tsevon's voice trembled. "All we've done so far is insignificant, barely troubles them. What Khoti did, that hurt. Not just in lost laborers, but it stung them in the soft parts: weapons production. It proved that we got fangs and claws and we aren't going out without a fight. We got weapons now and a steady supply of food from our friends across the river. Now that it's summer, we won't need to leave as many behind to protect and provision the Val. I think we need to go bigger. Stop them if we can. Slow them we must."

Murmurs of agreement filtered from the common area of Tsevon's alcove through a rush curtain into the niche where Khoti slept. His mother's hope-filled words so close at hand tumbled over a waterfall in his head. She soothed as she bathed him. Her words mingled with the spirits' song. And battle plans.

"I gathered you to make a decision," Tsevon said. "We either continue to pick away at the enemy or try for something big enough to make our time and losses worth it."

"I say we put 'em right in the dirt. Let the spirits have at 'em," Konner said.

"You set yourself quite a task!" a booming voice, familiar, proclaimed.

Stools scraped as the Tawnkats jumped to their feet. Khoti felt his awareness lurch ahead, the mush of noise clearer.

"I hope I am not interrupting." He recognized Eithurdon's voice.

"Why, we're just discussing a little housekeepin'," Konner replied. Stools creaked as those gathered retook their seats. "You know, Duke, sweeping away all the little vermin that crept in during the winter."

Eithurdon laughed, but it held a keen edge. "I understand you have been doing quite a bit of 'housekeeping' and I hope it continues. I must take your mind away from all that –"

"Tsevon!" his mother's shriek ripped through the curtain of sound. The noise abated. He heard each footstep, each breath. A chair crashed to the floor. As if surfacing from a deep dive into the Ymmenay, the cold rush of liquid into his lungs, he couldn't take the breath he needed.

Everything in him went still but his mother's grip on his wrist. Last, he heard her desperate words to his father.

"He's cold! No lifebeat."

Tsevon knelt and listened to Khoti's chest.

"What happened to the boy?" Eithurdon asked.

As Konner explained, Tsevon shushed him, so that Konner's voice dropped to a bare whisper, just enough to make the duke's eyes widen and his features harden until they appeared sculpted from mountain granite.

"Fever's broke," Tsevon said as he stood and took Amhese's

shaking hand in his. "But his chest rattles. The breath barely passes through him. That, not the wound, may yet undo him. There's little more my medicine will do but kill us both."

"I know this is an awkward time," Eithurdon said, placing a bold hand on Tsevon's shoulder. "I know your thoughts are rather with your son than with plans for battle –"

"My thoughts are in both places," Tsevon interrupted. "If it weren't for battle the boy wouldn't need my worries. What's so pressing it brings the Duke of Lharan from his comfortable halls to my miserable cave?" Tsevon's question might have held a touch of bitterness, a hint of challenge. He didn't care. Courtesy was an inconvenience that kept men from the truth.

Eithurdon gestured for them to return to the common room. The duke righted a chair and held it for Tsevon, motioning for the rest of those gathered to take their seats. He pulled a stool up for himself.

"I made as much haste as I could," the duke said. "After Khoti's warning about the Minarian camp at the falls, I sent a messenger to the king with the utmost speed, sacrificing mounts and almost riders. My messenger returns already: the king warns we must prepare for possible war." Eithurdon accepted a mug of cavern-cooled ale proffered by Amhese.

"Then he knows," Tsevon mused.

The duke nodded. "They had word from Shiad, and went on about omens and seers' musings about what may or may not be imminent. I am instructed to prepare, not necessarily to take any action, but to plan to arm my people, protect those unable to fight, and," he waited for Tsevon to meet his gaze. "And, I am warned that the most endangered Shandeans are shawnsi and royal employees. I must find safe refuge for these people as well as defend the city. I think that refuge, for all, is here."

Tsevon narrowed his gaze on the duke. "Shawnsi? Who's been doing most of the dying but mountain folk? Abandon us, is that it? Sacrifice our people for yours? Ah, we're but mountain folk, of no worth to lowlanders and shawnsi but to bleed and serve as your alarm bell."

Konner and the other Tawnkats had straightened in their chairs. Amhese's glance darted from lifemate to duke like a rabbit spied by a fox.

"It is not as you make it sound, Tsevon. I am told their king pushes this belief in Ghyldism. It stokes hatred toward the shawnsi leadership of Shande. Do not hate me because my blood is mixed, is not Taschian, or Lhatan, or Staphian, but of plains tribes and ancient gods."

Tsevon forced down the urge to drive the duke from his alcove with his fists. No shawnsi lay on his deathbed behind the rush curtain! Tsevon rubbed his face furiously with both hands. He still felt so medicine-weary long after he should have recovered. He leaned back and took a small sip of his ale. Amhese let out her breath and the other Tawnkats leaned back. He knew Eithurdon read him. He could see it in the wariness of the duke's posture. Good. Let him know how perilous was this ask.

"I've yet to repay my debt to you, Eithur." Tsevon's familiarity went unchallenged. "So, I've got to take your folk into my care."

"I do not want this to be a grudging favor perceived as an undeserved burden," Eithurdon protested. "You must understand. Of the hundreds of Shandeans living and working in Shiad and Arenh, only shawnsi and royal officers have been targeted. An officer of the exchequer was killed in Sihmad Shal and pay rosters stolen. They believe they were dealt with unfairly in the Great War –"

"We didn't fight Minarians in the Great War!"

"Of course not. But if you were a banished god, who better to serve as your tool of vengeance than a Minarian? In the wake of the wars their homelands remained blasted and desolate. Who else would be most open to the seeds of hatred than those with the least? They went to war over fish! We have a fat and complacent country that has rested on its plenty with no thought to how it might feed that jealousy. All they need is a small push to believe we have spent all history subordinating Minaria. It is not abandonment for shawnsi to go into hiding. It is us they seek to kill. Look how they have enslaved the Pladde! Shande's people are too valuable to them as laborers to destroy them in their conquest. Do you think people will not die if they harbor shawnsi fugitives in such a war? Our people must go where they will not endanger others."

Eithurdon's hands lay palms up on the rough table that dominated Tsevon's alcove.

"And you expect us to do the dirty work of fighting and protecting you while you hide? How does this make us better than the Pladde? Maybe all we're doing is giving up one master for another."

Eithurdon leaned in and peered at Tsevon. "We will fight for our homes and families beside you. But we will suffer inevitable defeats where shawnsi noncombatants face a greater risk than shals. It will take time to build defenses, but once we do, we will outnumber them. They know that. It is why they hope to catch us by surprise. If you can imagine," Eithurdon's tone turned bitter, the tone that had followed him into the alcove. "The king and his council debate whether the Minarians really intend war. They fumble through their defense like children selecting teams for Capture the Flag with no strategy. I warned them of what passes here. They do not see charred villages, or the platforms of the dead, or the faces of mothers mourning children. So, they continue to debate. Well, I am a better student of conflict. I know what comes and what we must do, but I cannot do it without you, Tsevon. We must set aside our differences. My men are warriors raised in the shadows of the mountains. But they do not know them like your people. My Guard will fight to save Sefresal, Eilime, any village they can. They will keep your flank guarded and keep you supplied. But you, Tsevon, must protect the mountains and provide a safe refuge for the region's noncombatants. We need each other Tsevon. You need me to protect you. I need you to protect me." Eithurdon fell silent, staring into his mug.

"The king really don't think war's coming, with all the weapons we seen?" Konner asked, rubbing his mousy beard. "What else does he s'pose they want with our mines but to work 'em?"

"They are probably just receiving my message. King Ebon is a just ruler. But I do not think he can contemplate war."

"Then, gods save us, he'd better learn!" Tsevon returned. "You and I know there's a war on. We don't need to wait for messengers from Shiad. We can see it in our destroyed homes, in our," he jutted a thumb over his shoulder at the niche where Khoti slept, "Dead and injured."

"We'll find room for the duke's folk," Amhese said, laying her hands on Tsevon's shoulders. "I trust the duke's counsel. If all we've heard doesn't support his word, then you must still trust him because his trust in you deserves the honor."

While she spoke to her lifemate, Tsevon knew she directed her words to the duke, who inclined his head toward her. Tsevon harrumphed, but as he tilted his head up at her, he smiled. For the first time in days her forehead didn't furrow in fear for Khoti.

"Amhese is the better side of my nature," Tsevon said. "She knows I'm unlikely to back down from my stand even when I find I'm wrong. That's why Khoti lies there, because Tsevon of Taschel wouldn't retreat from a bad decision. She's right. I have to trust you, because you've trusted me, my son, my people. I'll force myself to understand your need. But you talk of noncombatants. The old, ill, children, how will they adjust to these high valleys, the depth of winter, the dangerous pass, these barren caves? If we're spending all our efforts keeping them safe, we'll be too busy to deal with the Minarians. I can't see how they would be better off in our care."

"They will adjust," Eithurdon said. "We will send them slowly, protected by Guardsmen, to give them time to fit into your community. Some may be more help than burden. We will send supplies so they don't place a demand on your stores."

Konner's face split into his slashing grin. "We've more here, Duke, than we know what to do with! While I admit the Minarians make lousy weapons, they do in a fix. And we're fond of that Shiadin smoked fish from the coast. And their grain, oh that makes a fine loaf of bread, and an ale that's fit for even a duke." Konner laughed at Eithurdon's confusion, as the Second gestured at the mug the duke had just emptied. "Ah, Lord, we backward tribes can forge our alliances, even here in the mountains. We'll take some of your stores. For now, Shiad has us well provisioned. Seems they don't take to the idea that when Minaria's done with us, they'll be back looking for those fine fishing holes."

Eithurdon leaned back, letting his surprise show for a moment before it turned to the first genuine smile Tsevon had seen on the man.

"If the duke's delivered his messages, perhaps now we can get back to business," Tsevon said. "You're welcome to stay, but time's passing. And time's something short."

Eithurdon watched in evident fascination as the Tawnkats hashed out their plans. What Tsevon hoped to achieve would make the collapse of the Staph-el mine seem like a minor inconvenience. If one boy could take out a mine and twenty Minarians in one stroke, certainly a force of less than a hundred could take on an army. At least, on its face, Tsevon's plan appeared crazy enough to work. In the next few days they would need victories like none they'd had before.

It began several days south of the Val, on the Staph-el Road, the main route the enemy used to enter Shande and rob her mines. Small squads of Tawnkats stationed themselves throughout the region. Like their patron cat, they slipped in and out on predator feet.

On a curve of the Staph-el Road, Segan tossed a last handful of pine needles over the scuffed spot in the road, then using a pine branch swept away all sign he had stood there. He waved up at the shelf of rock where Tsevon hid with Konner and Ahrwesz.

As Ahrwesz stood lookout, Tsevon nodded to Konner and between them they worked levers into a crevice near the edge of a shelf clinging to the sheer mountainside. Weather-loosened gravel and small boulders from the cliffs above became a loose slope below. Finally, they wiggled the ledge a little. A clatter of stones slid down into the road.

Segan scrambled away from the soft turf beside the road, backing toward the narrow stream flowing just a short distance away. After a glance west, he signed up to Ahrwesz then disappeared into a stand of pine.

Ahrwesz added his weight to Konner's on the lever and suddenly the slab of rock gave way, throwing the three men backward. Slowly at first, then gaining momentum, the weight of the slab pulled a slide down into the road. The entire road blocked, the only passage lay across Segan's trap.

The Tawnkats melted away, unable to stay to witness the fruits of their labors.

As a column of Minarian reinforcements marched toward the Staph-el mine, they detoured around the slide to Segan's trap. Branches collapsed beneath the first ranks, which fell with a rush of pine needles to be impaled on spears pressed into the muddy bottom of the pit. The following ranks, in disarray, tried to pass closer to the stream, where knives swung at them from tensed branches and stakes tipped with a slow poison pierced the soles of feet. At last, a cluster of soldiers ran back the way they had come, only to hit full force a wire, strung neck level, across the road behind them.

As Teckhan and Davin retreated up the hillside from where they had strung the wire, they stopped a moment to look back. With a brief touch of his fingers to his forehead, young Davin gave a Taschian salute to the Minarians' valiant efforts to escape: the remaining soldiers stood agape and quaking in the center of the road, too frightened to move, and likely to stay there until someone came for them.

Elsewhere along the Staph-el Road, windfall tossed into the roadway stalled teamsters long enough for Tawnkats to poison the goods stolen from Shande, its osfothye, ales or wines. Each evening a squad crept upon the Minarians; each day the Minarians grew more skittish.

Soon, the Minarians threw together a small stone redoubt overlooking the rebuilt bridge over the Ymmenay River, its only entrance from the upslope rear with its overlook commanding a view of the road and bridge.

One night, as half a dozen sentries lounged against the walls in the redoubt, calling to comrades as the second watch approached, Ahrwesz crept up onto the slopes above, careful how he held a writhing sack Konner had handed over with his customary grin. The Minarians' banter grew louder as they reinforced each other to diminish the fears that came with darkness. When the six replacements arrived, the redoubt became crowded as they continued to chat amiably before the first watch prepared to depart.

A small noise in the rocks above caused one sentry to spin and stare up. After a moment, his fellows laughed at his skittishness.

Ahrwesz looked down at the watch fire in the redoubt, breathing easier to know his misstep hadn't revealed him. He held the bag by one end, hoping the adders within weren't too sluggish from the cool evening to do their work or unable to move in the dark. Striking only a few sentries would be worth the effort that had been spent catching them and carrying them up the mountain. He shook the bag. An assortment of hisses, rattles and strikes made the bag writhe.

Clinging to a corner of the bag's mouth, Ahrwesz loosed the tie. The mouth flopped open. Several snakes surged toward the opening. He tossed the bag, hoping it wouldn't land in the fire, or fall short. Sinewy shapes broke free mid-air to slap the ground among the sentries. When the bag hit, a few more slithered out. As one man reached for what struck his neck, he screamed.

Ahrwesz almost laughed aloud as the Minarians tried to retreat from the redoubt. But now he had to pick a path through the rocks among those same snakes.

Not far away, on another night, Konner and a squad of Tawnkats crept upon a Minarian camp, struggling to keep their burden from clanking together.

Konner looked with regret at the pottery jars filled with distilled Shiadin grains topped with a wick. Konner touched a wick to a sputtering torch on the outer perimeter of the Minarian camp. The wick flared, burning toward the wax-sealed jar as Konner lobbed it at the Minarian captain speaking expansively to a circle of low-spirited sentries, assuring them no resistance existed.

The jar struck the captain in the small of the back, the jar's thin skin breaking. Almost immediately, the captain's clothing burst into flames. With his customary grin, Konner and the rest of his squad sent several more jars flying among the scattering soldiers.

Like the others before it, Konner's raid succeeded.

Tawnkat skirmishes had left the Minarians shy to the least noises, the most innocent looking windfalls or piles of boulders. They skittishly approached overhangs and eyed the cliff ledges. And in their own camp they still feared the ghostly attacks where Tawnkats melted into the night, with the Minarians never seeing a one, only hearing the trailing shriek of a tawnkat that marked most raids.

And so with this assault. Before the Minarians could determine the source of the jars, the Tawnkats melted away with the wild cat's growl, to slip down river and cross in Aibak's raft. It felt so easy. Certainly nothing could stop them now.

At last came the boldest part of Tsevon's plan, a plan born of grief. In weeks of terrorizing their foe, they had slowed the conquest of the mountains and the manufacture of weapons. But Tsevon wanted to take a bolder step. As they performed their grisly tasks, they scavenged not simply the weapons of the dead, but their uniforms as well. Now they were poised to perform what Tsevon considered not only the most deceitful of tasks, but the one he expected would win his war without need for kings and dukes. He would avenge his sons.

On a rainy morning in the beginning of the light moon, Tsevon squirmed into the ill-fitting Minarian clothing that Konner had stripped from some unwitting sentry. A sentry's boiled leather armor, reinforced with thin metal strips, restricted Tsevon's movements and he found the heavy wool cloak too hot for one accustomed to the cool mountains. He fastened the sword belt and walked around his alcove to adjust to the constraints. Already he missed his soft hide shirt and trousers, and here he hadn't left yet.

He pushed aside the curtain and clumsily knelt beside Khoti's bed. Weeks without fresh air had paled Khoti's skin to a thin film over the youth's cheekbones, like the first hesitant layers of ice on a still lake in the autumn. Resting a hand on Khoti's chest, he felt the slight lift as his son took a breath. Tsevon said his small appeal to the spirits who had brought Khoti back from death, yet still kept him from the living.

He jumped when he heard the curtain behind him yanked

aside, almost stumbling onto the bed in his clumsy Minarian garb.

Amhese stood in the opening, jaw clenched, hair wound into two braids and wearing the gear of a Minarian sentry.

"What on Ea," Tsevon sputtered, and then began to laugh in great gasps. His laugh trailed away to tense silence as Amheses's eyes flared and the color rose in her cheeks.

"I'm not staying," she said.

"I'm not taking you. It's suicide to try this in the first place. I'll not make my son an orphan."

"Oh, get off your martyr's plank, Tsevon." Her voice cut like a shard of ice.

"Amhese, he needs someone to care for him."

"My life role isn't nursemaid. If anyone should remain it should be a healer, one with responsibilities for an uprooted people. Since that's unlikely from a stubborn man like you, I told Ahrwesz he's to remain to help Konner."

"How dare you! To countermand my orders! My own lifemate!" Her coolness checked his fury. "How could you think such a thing?"

"You'll never understand, Tsevon, the things mountain women know, just as I'll never understand the mind of a healer. I only know I must join you or never see you again. Perhaps you'll find a need for me before the end."

"You dreamt this?" His heart went into his throat when she merely squared herself before him. "Did you read your dream, or Latra?" Could fate intend her to join him? All of his best couldn't abandon Konner. Certainly, she'd chosen the most suited to remain behind. Ahrwesz and Amhese were his most skilled archers. She'd trapped him.

"You warned me this plan could lead to your death. I'm going to see to it that doesn't happen, and if it does, I'll join you. Like Khoti, I'm small in your shadow, Tsevon. You can either permit me to join you, or I'll come on my own. It's up to you."

On the verge of a biting retort, Tsevon glanced at Khoti and checked himself. He saw clearly the actions that led to his son's injury. He should have encouraged the boy to think like a leader. Tsevon hadn't listened. And with Khoti's determination, a stubborn will like his parents' –

"Would you really follow on your own?" he asked.

She inclined her head.

"Then I'm stuck with you. But Khoti –"

"Konner will care for him." Her voice had softened. Khoti had cleared the way. Could Tsevon ever again act on impulse, with no thought to others' counsel?

"Then it's settled. To Lagdche then. We take our battle to Mol Azezial. Remove the head and the body dies. Khoti's near a man. If he survives, and his parents don't, it'll make him hard, strong, better to lead his people to war when his time comes." Tsevon grasped Amhese's sword arm, noting firm muscles as he guided her from their alcove, leaving behind the son he sought to avenge.

At the mouth of the caverns, Konner waited, huddled against a storm rolling down from Shiad's peaks as Tsevon's party checked their gear and adjusted their Minarian attire.

"I sent Ahrwesz to Sefresal to tell the duke about your fool plan," Konner said.

Tsevon double-checked his pack and secured the cape with a clasp at his neck, refraining from the rebuke he'd almost let escape. Konner was complicit. With Ahrwesz gone he couldn't deny Amhese. He couldn't even express the knot in his throat.

"You look good enough to kill," Konner said. "Khoti's gonna rage when he wakes. So, you better prove yourselves."

The nine Tawnkats and Amhese finished their goodbyes and settled their packs on their backs. Rain slanted at them with a vengeance.

"Go get 'im!" Konner called through chattering teeth as they turned their back on the warm caves. "Make 'im pay for what he's done to us!"

"We won't come back 'less we're bringing Mol Azezial's head with us!" Tsevon called over his shoulder.

"Oh, you're gonna have a good time," Konner said with a dry chuckle.

Tsevon knew Konner stared after them, his eyes closed in entreaty to the spirits as the inviting aroma of breakfast cakes taunted them like the rain. Was it a fool's errand? Would Amhese only join him to see him fail so utterly he died far from his people with no one to return him to the spirits?

In their first days of travel, Tsevon kept expecting, not quite hoping, Amhese would give up. He watched her struggle among the rocks on the river bank and clench her teeth when the bitter pain of icy water turned her limbs crimson as they crossed the Ymmenay. He watched her tense when Segan approached a sentry, the heavy war helm concealing his Taschian features, his blue eyes lost in shadow. Then, in the midst of casual conversation, Segan slit the man's throat, Amhese blanching as blood splattered the rocky ground. He watched her rise, stiff, from fireless camps, pacing and slapping her hands together to warm the night chill from them. He waited for the day when she would prove a burden, when trouble surrounded them. Then he would say: it's your own fault.

Yet, Amhese would not give up and seemed determined to prove wrong his every expectation.

He tried to remember she had her own score to keep. She'd related a few things from her captivity: of Latra being beaten until she fell unconscious, of the brutal murder of those like Tsevon's sister. And like so many others, with no effort, often unbidden, she would recall the power-drunk and twisted pleasure in her captor's eyes when they tortured some poor soul until left for dead on the trail. She easily relived a fist smashing into her face and recounted nightmares that made Tsevon's simmering anger boil. He remembered the feel of her bloody wrist in his hand, the strength in her posture, glimpses of her shepherding the captives to shelter. He knew her desire for revenge could be no less than his. For these same reasons he thought she should remain behind: their people needed her steady strength.

But she didn't yield. And if anything, she seemed stronger each day.

It took several days through rough terrain before the furtive band of pseudo-Minarians crested the final buttress of the Lharan Mountains. Below, Minaria opened up before them, a plain sloping down to the Sea of Tebez so far distant they saw no hint of of it even from this great height. At their feet, barren brown hills carved by snowmelt and knots of brambles gave little hope of easy travel. The heat of summer gasped up at them from a scrub desert. They saw no sign of the rumored irrigated farm fields further west, or the low hills lining the coast and acting like a wall holding the bulk of Minaria's habitation along the coast.

Only the light moon of Long Day had arrived. What would the heat moon bring? As far as they could see, no hint of tree or sign of life showed itself. The blast of heat that slapped them with each gust of wind made them wonder, not for the first time, if they would fail before they ever even reached their goal.

They finally turned south along the feet of the Lharans, seeking one of the tributaries to the great river that lazed from the mountain snows to Lagdche so far west. While they hadn't seen a Minarian patrol for days, they had no doubt their enemy lurked somewhere nearby. They only hoped the road along the river remained open.

As they at last took the Lagdche road, facing straight into the enemy they hoped to destroy, and passed the last foothills into the desolate deserts of eastern Minaria, Tsevon reached for the sword at his side, sensing someone watched him. If so, there was no sign. He looked to Amhese beside him. She seemed to thrive on some inner strength he had never before seen. The fire in her eyes startled him, and he thought if they should survive this journey, he had better step more carefully around his changed lifemate. Her hand, he saw, rested on the dagger at her side. Her glance darted up to the peaks above and stabbed into the valleys and gorges they passed. The back of his neck tingled as if someone glared at him, reminiscent of the strange feeling that had lingered after he touched the enemy's medallion. The crawling sensation came and went, as if the mountains themselves had eyes, as if someone's attention touched on them and found them unimportant. He hoped from a distance they looked only like a Minarian patrol to whomever watched as they picked their way into an alien land.

16: The Bridge

A few days after Tsevon's departure on a fool's mission to Minaria, Konner entered Khoti's alcove to discover his charge – so long unconscious and all but dead – staring back with clear and open eyes. Khoti didn't speak, though his gaze followed the Second's movements without comment.

Konner feared the reaction meant all those days of fever had stolen the youth's wits. How would he tell Tsevon? Konner paced the alcove, Khoti watching him like a cat on a fly without expression or reaction. It had taken Konner and Tsevon together to mend his physical injuries. The fever had run its course and the hollow rattle Tsevon had so feared taking into himself had gone. And now, the boy merely stared, silent.

Konner called in wise women and dream readers, even a loremaster who might understand some oddity in the Staphian blood from his mother's tribe. No one could explain Khoti's silence, nor recall a precedent in the histories of healing. In the end, Konner stood at the foot of Khoti's bed, staring back at the youth's doggedly blank gaze, waiting for a great idea to come to him. He stood so long, and so silent, that when he finally and suddenly cursed and turned, he could swear he saw Khoti blink and flinch. Konner peered at him, waved his hands in front of Khoti's face, pretended to jab his fingers towards the boy's eyes. Nothing.

In the days that followed an uncomfortable intuition became deep suspicion. Konner tried, unsuccessfully, to catch Khoti doing more than following him with that vacant stare. But Konner found tiny signs the youth moved about his niche, the outer alcove, likely even the drafty cavern corridors in the deep of late night. For some reason Khoti wanted to play him for a fool.

Long Day and another week passed while relatives and neighbors fed and washed Khoti as if helpless. Konner spent his idle hours listening for movement in the alcove and slept on a mat outside the doorway. At some point, Khoti would emerge and Konner intended to catch him.

Fast asleep one night, Konner dreamt of the old days when his monthly shift at the mine, mediating an occasional domestic squabble and wandering with Tsevon and Tegi through their old mountain haunts summed up his concerns. Something stirred him and he awoke with a comfortable smile on his lips, which turned to a scowl when the dream left him. The tug on his sleeve came again.

Khoti crouched over him, studying him with eyes penetrating in their lack of expression.

"Finally coming out in the open are ye?" Konner growled, sitting up. He rubbed the sleep from his eyes, stretched and yawned as Khoti disappeared within the alcove. With a groan, Konner gathered up his mat and followed.

Konner's mouth fell open to see Khoti with a Minarian sword, darting around the alcove, jabbing and dodging some imaginary enemy. Surely the boy had lost his wits.

Khoti laughed at Konner's expression. His laughter sounded different somehow, genuine, yet forced. Despite his unhealthy color and gaunt cheeks, the youth appeared both confident and unreadable. By the gods, Konner thought, the boy had died. A man had stolen him.

"You little sneak, you. You've been well a lot longer than you let on, haven't you? I knew you were up to something. You don't look like you just rose from your death bed." Konner tweaked the muscle of Khoti's sword arm.

Khoti shook his head. "Not that long, really, Konner," he said in a voice raspy with lack of use. "I didn't know how determined you were, 'til I saw you sleeping like a fool outside my door." Khoti cleared his throat several times as he tried to find his voice.

"What then, since your fever broke? You just wanted to lie abed and let everyone wait on you, worry on you?" Konner felt heat rising to his cheeks. How many times had he sat and talked to the sleeping youth, telling secrets on himself?

"I woke when my parents argued over me, the day they left. Then you just happened to catch me when I wasn't paying attention."

"So, you been playing this game of yours –"

"It's no game, Konner. If I'd told you I aimed to follow my fa, you'd have tied me to my bed. You can't now. I'm too strong.

Besides, you might as well help me as stop me."

"You aren't going anywhere, boy," Konner growled as he reached for Khoti's arm. Khoti brought up the sword, resting the tip in the center of Konner's chest. The Second's eyes widened. "You dare threaten me? Who's never been anything but a friend to you and your family, who's always stood up for you? Your fa's own Second? You threaten me when 'twas me that forced a search to find your miserable bones, that risked your fa's life-long hatred? When 'twas me as made him heal you, knowing it could steal his spirit away, giving you my own blood when your fa's medicine couldn't mend no more? You dare to threaten me, you whelp? I'll call every curse on you, Tsevon's son or not." Konner's voice rang shrill with his hurt. The boy was willful!

Khoti let the sword tip drop a bit. "I don't want to threaten you, or any Shandean. But I won't let you stop me. Don't force me to. I – I care for you Konner. But you're as stubborn as Fa."

"It's you that's stubborn," Konner knew he sounded surly, but he couldn't stay angry, just so relieved the boy appeared to still have his wits.

"Just let me be. Trust my judgment again, like you did before." His forehead scrunched at a memory. "It's odd. I remember hearing things folks said, but as much as I tried, I couldn't answer. So, I know you trust me, Konner. Prove it."

"You heard things?"

"Everything," Khoti's emerald eyes twinkled. He turned his back on Konner to rummage through his father's small chest of belongings while the Second tried to recall his words.

Khoti pulled out a ragged Minarian uniform from among the rejected clutter of their raids and checked it for damage.

"Ah, Khoti, don't do it. Tsevon'll never forgive me."

"He'll forgive you."

"They're weeks ahead of you. You can't go at that wilderness alone. You may have been up and about longer than we thought, but you still – you just don't look right, Khoti. You might fall into fever again."

Khoti didn't answer.

After several minutes, Khoti's back a wall, Konner left, torn by his inability to reach through to that something so different from the Khoti he'd watch blossom in Tawnkat raids. It was a suicide for Tsevon and Amhese to go, and no less for their son to strike out alone. But Konner doubted anything would stop Khoti once he set his mind to it. He was too much like his fa, this one.

The next day, Khoti shivered as he emerged from the caves into the pre-dawn chill of the Val, the warm exhalation of his village within trailing him like a plea to return to the comfort of home. He would be stronger this time. He had to be. Though right now he felt as vulnerable as he had when the sentry smiled that gruesome smile at him, as when the terrible loneliness overcame him in the gorge. He'd survived that lonely fear of dying far from his people – the fear of scavengers hurrying his death – he would again. Every time he lifted his arm he felt a tug in his side, an ache pinching his breath. Each morning, though easier, he found it difficult to rise, to shed the grogginess from his head and force his limbs to respond. He knew he still needed to mend, but he just had to follow. All that remained of his family had raced headlong to Minaria. He didn't know what he would do if he ever caught up to them. But he had to try.

It only took a few minutes to capture a gelding among the horses the Guard left behind. After packing his saddlebags and assuring himself he'd selected a sound mount, he left the valley with the first streaks of dawn behind him. He knew Konner watched from just inside the cave, and wondered only briefly what favors the Second begged of the spirits. It would be only the spirits who could help him now.

He had no clue which path his fa had followed. He knew only one route into Minaria, a busy road that ran from the oft-destroyed bridge. He would need to find a way to slip by an enemy far more likely to spook at the least shadow or noise than they had been before they came to recognize the shriek of an angry Tawnkat.

Two long days in the saddle brought him to a vantage point where he could see the Minarian camp at the foot of the Staph-el Falls. He left his horse, blowing and stamping, in a small cleft beside the trail as he crept forward on his belly to peer down upon the river valley. He froze, his breath locking up in that stitch in his side. A mass of armament stretched below him like nothing he had ever seen before.

So many warriors assembled beside the Staph-el Falls Khoti couldn't count them, couldn't absorb the meaning of the machines, couldn't contemplate facing such might. A swarm of Minarian carpenters reinforced the oft-reconstructed log bridge over the Ymmenay, while huge catapults crowded over the mountain pass and lined up to cross the river. Giant towers, several stories high, rolled on massive, metal-rimmed wheels.

From the arrow loops, the ledges and ladders, he knew engineers built these machines to assail a city. Cavalry trotted in rank with machinery as pikemen, archers and support troops streamed behind. Tents popped up along the banks of both sides of the river, and still the army poured over the pass from the Minarian plains beyond.

He had to do something. Khoti's head ached just to look upon the scene of black, red and orange banners standing out in the wind, the dark helms glinting dully, the crush of stone beneath wheels and pound of hammers on the bridge. Konner was right. Khoti couldn't face this. He stanched his first sense of panic with deep breaths. He needed to calmly assess what he saw.

They didn't need towers and catapults to put down Tawnkats. This army marched for Sefresal. He couldn't imagine any other worthy target of strategic value. Certainly, they didn't aim for Eilime, a sleepy fishing village and exchange hub for barges shipping mountain goods by river to the Rigannon. Even Sefresal with its Guard could never face such an onslaught. They would all be destroyed.

He forced himself to take a deep breath and hold it, willing his heartbeat to slow. Only a few days ago he felt strong enough to face Konner with a bared sword and a vow to follow his fa into the heart of Minaria. How could he let weakness take him now?

Clearly the Minarians knew a bunch of mountain folk couldn't stop an army. And what would a warning to Sefresal and Eilime accomplish? Shande had no army but the hundred-member Guard, no great leaders that could promise help even if they could erase the weeks of distance between them. Neither city could throw together defenses capable of slowing such a mass of warriors and machines so quickly. Eilime didn't even have walls. Khoti knew this host exceeded anything even Eithurdon expected. There could do absolutely nothing. It was over.

He vaguely recalled Eithurdon and Tsevon arguing, their voices muffled by a wash of sound and spirit song. The duke planned withdrawal to the Val. He knew Sefresal couldn't hold! Did he expect an assault so soon? Did his fa, somewhere out there in the wildlands of Minaria, witness this massive movement of men and arms? Did he despair knowing he would return to find his home once again taken from him?

Khoti backed away from the ledge. His fingers methodically checked the girth straps on his saddle then quickly stroked the horse's legs for signs of strain before he mounted. He turned back, allowing the gelding to pick his way through the rough terrain. For an instant, he let the sheer enormity of it overwhelm him, his legs trembling against the horse's sides as nausea rose in his throat, his hands shaking as heat rushed his face. He smashed his fist into his palm, forcing himself to focus. If in battle, would he let fear paralyze him like this? He breathed a vow to himself, coiling his fear into a hard knot of resolve. He could never again yield to the panic that took him outside the Staph-el mine, as it did here looking upon the massive Minarian army. The Lharans needed every single one of its people to survive. He couldn't afford to defeat himself before he ever even faced the enemy.

Khoti rode to a narrow pass that afforded a wide-ranging view to the east. In the distance, he could see where the lesser-used Lhata Road veered off just before the Staph-el Road entered a steep gorge, then turned north on toward Tasch-el and Sefresal. Minarian scouts patrolled the road's length, watching for Tawnkat tricks.

He must act. What could he do? He must act. Khoti argued with himself only a few more moments, then dug his heels into the horse's sides.

17: Closing the Staph-el Road

The calling stones echoed among the rocks ahead of him, claiming Khoti returned as if Ghyldus himself pursued him. As he neared, he saw Konner and several other Tawnkats gather outside the caves, ready for a battle.

The gelding favored a leg, his nostrils flaring and lather working from beneath the saddle, as Khoti jumped down, sweeping his gear from the horse and calling for a fresh mount. He pointed at a mare that trotted toward him as all the others shied from the commotion he'd raised. He stalked to Konner like a squall line.

"Troubles? Back so soon?" Konner drawled.

"Catapults and a host on the march. Got any plans?" Khoti countered as he gasped for breath, feeling the pinch in his side begin to burn.

"Where?" Konner's hand signal brought more sentries scurrying from their positions to Konner's side.

"Staph-el Falls," Khoti said as he downed a dipper of icy water. "They were still reinforcing the bridge when I left last night."

"You got here in a day!"

"If you saw that mass of men and machines, you'd sprout wings! There's scouts all over the Staph-el Road. They got huge towers, Konner, like for going after a city wall. I've got to warn the duke. He's evacuating his people here, right?"

"How did you know? Yes, yes, warn him. How long before they could get to Sefresal?"

"Their scouts have been there and back by now. We have maybe a week before the army arrives, unless we stop 'em."

"So, we need to warn the duke, get his extra folk up here, find a place for all of them and try to stop this madness in a week." Konner groaned. "Ah, Khoti, I wish I could'a talked your fa out of this foolishness of his. We need him here, not off on a suicide.

143

Though, I'd bet we can do a bit of damage."

Konner barked orders that sent Tawnkats for weapons and others to prepare for the evacuees. As they ran to their tasks, Konner laid a hand on Khoti's shoulder.

"I knew you'd be back, Khoti. We need you here more than running to the enemy looking for Tsevon." He paused as Ahrwesz arrived, arrow nocked in bow and face ready for battle.

"Warn Aibak," he told him. "Position your scouts on the Staph-el Road and ask him to meet us east of the Lhata fork. We're going to need to pull off the biggest raid the Tawnkats ever tried. We won't let them reach Sefresal." Konner turned to Khoti. "We're not letting them through. Hear me?"

Konner seemed to blanch at Khoti's grin, as Tre, a boy barely a year younger than Khoti brought the saddled mare and stood patiently as Khoti peeled off the stifling Minarian garb to reveal his own buckskin clothing underneath.

"If you make Sefresal in anything like the record you set getting here, we got a chance," Konner said. "We'll be stretched thin. See if you can talk Eithurdon out of his Guard in exchange for the warning. You can lead his people back here if you like, but we're going to make a stand on the Staph-el Road. If Eithurdon wants to hold up his end, he'll be there. It's his folk we'll be dying for."

"I'll be there, Konner. I'll take Tre with me and he can guide the duke's folk back. I'm riding with the duke if I have to drag him onto his horse."

Konner chuckled. "I think you're just stubborn enough to do it," he said, then laughed harder at the startled look on Tre's face.

Khoti stood almost half a head taller than the younger Taschian who had been tending sheep in a valley half a day east of Tasch-el the night it burned and lost his father in the battle to rescue the captives. Khoti knew Tre yearned to go on raids with the Tawnkats and prove himself, just as Khoti had. As Khoti settled his bags on the mare's back, Tre rushed to grab a pack and ready a mount to join him, the youth's excitement at the opportunity palpable.

In minutes, they raced toward the pass like a storm as all around the Val erupted in preparations to stop an army.

Heads turned and faces peered from the wall to see them pounding up the road to Sefresal, sod flying from their mounts'

hooves. Moments before they reached the gates, the massive doors to Sefresal opened. Khoti and Tre passed under the arch and crashed through the small brook trickling from the gods garden at the entrance, sending water splashing into the crowds of startled onlookers.

Khoti jumped down at the doors to Eithurdon's hall, no longer the frightened boy who had raced to the city in his nightshirt only a few months ago. As a groom rushed to tend the horses, Khoti stalked through the doors, Tre clinging to his heels.

The gloom of Eithurdon's halls assailed Khoti's eyes, but this time the duke's guards and servants stood back and allowed him to pass.

"Khoti!" Eithurdon sounded pleased, or perhaps alarmed, to see him. "Your father?"

"On a fool's mission to Minaria."

"You have come to serve in my Guard now?"

"In a way, Lord," Khoti admitted. "We're kind of hoping your Guard'll come and serve with us."

Eithurdon's eyebrows shot up as he glanced at Tre's dusty, sweat-stained face.

Khoti laughed. "No, Lord. With the Tawnkats. Though it wouldn't be wise to underestimate Tre any more than me." Eithurdon accepted the statement without challenge. Khoti knew Tre beamed beside him.

"You must carry an urgent message to run my horses this hard. If you ask for the Guard's help, I must take counsel," Eithurdon said, putting on his diplomat's face.

Before Khoti could protest the waste of time, Eithurdon had swept from the hall with a silencing gesture. An aide led Khoti and Tre to seats at a long, polished table in a small room off the reception hall. Light streamed in through a recessed window and gleamed off the table, smarting Khoti's eyes. A Guard apprentice brought bread, smoked fish and wine, which the youths tore into as they awaited Eithurdon's return.

A younger version of Eithurdon arrived with the duke, taking a chair to his right. Awe-filled, Tre scrunched down in his seat beside Khoti as if to hide in Khoti's shadow, one hand absently stroking the smooth finish on a table like none either of them had ever seen.

While he'd finally turned seventeen, owed a voice in his tribe, Khoti didn't expect the duke to treat him any better than an errand runner. The respect shown by this noble exceeded anything his fa would bestow on the duke's messengers. It made him squirm a little, wondering whether he witnessed deference to Tsevon's son, or to a man the duke genuinely respected, or for some amusement of his own.

"My brother, Lord Steadon Dodfrenyen," Eithurdon said, gesturing toward the younger man.

Steadon gave Khoti a stiff nod. If tempted to smile at the duke's indulgence, he didn't show it. Instead, he mirrored Eithurdon's gravity.

Eithurdon held Khoti's silence until dusty Kefta Salman arrived, having donned his Lharan Guard Captain's surcoat and insignia for an official meeting, and took a seat across from Tre. Kefta grinned at Khoti, nodded to Tre then leaned forward, his angry red beard twitching in anticipation.

"I assume you bring bad news if you request the Guard's services," Eithurdon said, staring intently at Khoti.

Khoti studied the ceiling a moment, calculating on his fingers. "I was at the Staph-el Falls about three days ago –"

"Three days!" Kefta almost dropped his wine. "You have wings now?"

Eithurdon silenced Kefta with an impatient nod. "And it required haste. What did you see?"

"An army of such size I couldn't count them, Lord. Rank upon rank of archers, swordsmen, pikemen, cavalry. And others whose purpose I, a simple Taschian, could never understand," Khoti said with his best attempt at humility and diplomacy. "And machines they had, Lord. Giant catapults cresting the pass there, so many in the spare hour I watched as could fill the entire valley at Sefresal's feet. And towers pulled by teams of oxen and horses. So many thousands couldn't all fit into that little narrow on the Ymmenay's banks. They were stopped on the road and in the pass and looked as if that's where they'd camp 'til the carpenters repaired the bridge."

"Repaired the bridge?" Kefta echoed.

Khoti allowed himself a thin smile. Tre even ventured a grin. "The bridge the Tawnkats have destroyed, what," he glanced at Tre, "Three times now?" Tre nodded. "They use the bridge to haul metals from the Staph-el and Lhata mines into Minaria, and to stage transport downriver to Ymmenay Bay. Now they reinforce it to take the weight of their machines. Scouts rode the Staph-el Road as far as I could see. I guess they guard against our traps. I figure it'll take at least a week for them to reach Sefresal once the bridge is complete. There don't appear to be scouts on the Lhata Road."

146

"That was three days ago. So, in four days they could be knocking on the gates of Sefresal," Eithurdon said.

"More like five, Lord. They couldn't have crossed the bridge at least until the next day," Khoti said. He began to feel his exhaustion and his face warmed under Eithurdon's scrutiny.

"What would you have me do? You ask for the help of my Guard when we are about to be assailed by an army?" Eithurdon asked. "Even the Lharan Guard cannot take on Minarians at the mines with anything like the effectiveness of your father's Tawnkats."

"Stand with us," Khoti said. "Tre's been up the pass a few times before and can lead your folk to shelter in the Val. Konner vows to stand to the last to stop them on the Staph-el Road and hopes the duke will uphold his promise."

Eithurdon raised an eyebrow at Kefta.

"We can ride inside an hour, Lord," Kefta said.

He looked at Steadon.

"We have to stop them somewhere, Eithur," Steadon said. "It makes more sense to risk the Guard facing them in mounted battle at a place of our choosing, than holed up behind the walls."

"One hundred Guardsmen against thousands? It commits us to war not yet sanctioned by the king," the duke cautioned. "We have no declaration of war."

"Under such circumstances, I doubt the king would expect restraint," Steadon returned. "We will not hold them long, but if we can delay them for a while we might save some lives. I can ensure young Tre here has company on his journey home. We already warned our people to be prepared to evacuate on an hour's notice. We established supply routes. Nothing need stop you. And you have made promises of mutual aid to the mountain tribes that must be honored."

Eithurdon stared into the table as if finding an answer on its surface. "Then I will keep my promise to both you and Tsevon, Khoti. I will not abandon the mountain people, and you will again ride with my house." Eithurdon smiled, but with little pleasure.

Inside, Khoti glowed.

The Tawnkats chose to make their stand at the steepest and narrowest pass, a gorge just east of where the Lhata Road veered south. The gorge forced the Minarians to close ranks to only eight abreast. Machines threatened to scrape stony walls, one wheel rolling askew in a shallow stream course. With Aibaks' forty Shiadin archers on the south rim, and some sixty Tawnkats on the north, Konner hoped an ambush would scramble the enemy, and lead them to believe the Shandeans more numerous. That, and it gave Ahrwesz time to set his trap.

The vanguard of the enemy had funneled halfway through the gorge. The air hung heavy with the collective held breath of the defenders.

"C'mon Khoti, where's your Guard!" Konner hissed to himself as he at last lowered his arm. On the signal, Aibak's archers fired. Through cupped hands, Konner watched a dozen of the enemy in the first ranks fall. In an instant, Tawnkat arrows toppled several more. More arrows found targets amid the sudden chaos of the Minarian vanguard struggling to reposition as the following ranks continued to move forward. Arrows began raining upon them from behind. With another signal from Konner, the Val's youths pelted the army below with rocks as flight after flight of arrows fell.

After several minutes, perhaps a hundred of the enemy had fallen, wounded and dead, a mere dent in an army of fifteen thousand. A Minarian cavalry captain shouted an order and his unit sped ahead, seeming impervious to arrows that bounced from their helms and mail, only a few slowed as their mounts became targets. They raced to break free of the restrictive canyon walls where they could find paths up onto the rim. Drums beat a cadence. War banners unfurled. The troops trampled over their dead and the catapults rolled on.

"Khoti!" Konner begged for a miracle he doubted would come, or be of help if it did.

The youths on the rim tossed buckets of heated grease, while others grabbed brands from the fires they'd set near the rim and tossed them into the chasm. One of the towers burst into flames, halting the ranks behind it. With the machine wedged tight against the canyon walls, none could pass. Konner let out a whoop. The archers on both rims picked away at trapped soldiers as flames rose and the youths continued to throw buckets of boiling water and hot grease at the men and their animals, the terrorized beasts running amok among the soldiers.

The first ranks of horsemen reached the canyon mouth, out of archers' range. Konner prepared to call what he knew would be a costly retreat. Some hundred mounted swordsmen had survived the gauntlet, enough to easily overwhelm Konner's force.

On the verge of signaling the order for retreat, Konner heard an unearthly screech above the din. It echoed along the canyon walls, the wail of a tawnkat, spitting mad.

He shielded his eyes against morning to see the enemy van, which had dismounted to climb up to the rim, now racing back to their mounts. The horses pranced in nervous circles as again the shriek scraped the canyon walls. Suddenly, finding organization, the Minarian van charged, swords drawn, to meet the Lharan Guard.

Konner glanced back at the flaming tower, wanting to whoop his joy. Another tower flared and burned, blocking the escape of at least another twenty ranks. Those behind turned to retreat. One by one, the archers drove the soldiers trapped between the two burning towers to the ground. The Val's youths pelted them with rocks as others flung the last of the grease and firebrands. Konner swelled with pride, certain Ahrwesz wouldn't fail him.

The long road from Sefresal had taken the Lharan Guard through the charred timbers of Tasch-el where bones settled on platforms and Tsevon's mark glared at them. They thundered through the abandoned hamlet where fresh green overgrew the pathways, hooves churning the road as their passage echoed before them. Tasch-el burned in Khoti's throat long after the Guard reached the cover of a jumble of boulders scattered in scrub pine just east of the entrance to the mouth of the gorge.

For all Khoti's confidence, he wavered when he saw the Minarian horsemen charging toward them, only to stop and begin their scramble up the slopes to seek the gorge rim. He took deep breaths, forcing himself to reject the panic that wanted to take him. Instead, he looked on each Minarian soldier as the one who had thrown the torch into the stable, shot the arrows at his brother, or dragged his mam into the night.

When Eithurdon gave the secretive signal and the Guard leaped to battle as one, Khoti leaped with them like a veteran. Though the Guard had hidden only a few hundred paces from the canyon mouth, the din and echoes of battle from within had muted their approach. Their enemy lost precious seconds racing back to skittish mounts that wheeled back toward the canyon, or sought escape up the weathered slopes. At that moment, some primal call came from Khoti's throat, a screech that leant wings to the Lharan Guard and froze the Minarian swordsmen.

As the Minarians brought their ranks to order, Khoti

screeched again, a wail that tore from him with more strength than he thought his voice could bear. Yet it only seemed to give him greater strength. Eithurdon raced at the captain and struck him down with his first thrust.

The canyon locked the two groups in battle. Horses pressed against each other, their broad sides clamping warriors' legs so even the dead could only slump forward or backward over their horses. At first, Khoti found himself crammed in among Eithurdon's men so tight he saw nothing of the Minarians. As the animals bit and kicked and squealed amid the fury of hooves, at last, the crush loosened. Guardsmen hacked at Khoti's sworn enemy. The Minarians, finding their wits, struck back. But Khoti, the fire for revenge stoked and blazing in him, felt useless. His fury had his face hot, had him trembling and twitching with the eagerness to join the battle and prove himself better than the foolish boy who had died at the Staph-el mine. Even the horse beneath him seemed to echo his urgency. The chestnut mare that had chosen him in the Val had pushed aside better rested mounts at Sefresal, and earned his appreciation as she snuffled the oats he'd offered her. Now she seemed as attuned to him and the movements of battle. Her haunches bunched, ready to leap ahead, her neck arched in eagerness to race into the fray.

Suddenly, the space around him expanded and a Minarian horseman battled to within a pace of Khoti. A Guardsman went down, blood splattering Khoti as he dodged the Minarian's follow through. He tried not to retch as the mare stumbled over the yielding body of the Guardsman.

The mare's lurch pulled Khoti beyond the reach of the Minarian's blade, which swiped within inches of Khoti's face. For an instant the panic almost took him again. He made himself remember Von's call for help, the smell of the charred remains of Tasch-el. With an alien fury, he brought his sword around to meet the blade of his attacker. He tried to remember the feel of the sword he practiced with in his alcove. This weapon was Lharan-forged, heavy, crafted of adanan with a keen stellan edge, not the lighter and more agile work of Minarians. He erased everything from his mind but the flash of the enemy sword coming at him and his own artless parries.

Something gripped Khoti, more brutal and fierier than his own keen temper. Something not him. And he saw it reflected in his foe's eyes. Khoti brought his arms up. The tender muscles in his side pinched the air from him. The Minarian blade slid against his, down to the hilts to strike the back of Khoti's hand before they separated. His attacker was stronger. The man suddenly grinned as if he looked upon a child.

That smirk flushed everything but victory from Khoti's mind. With a quick parry and thrust, Khoti had the Minarian on the defensive. The warrior tried to back his horse away from Khoti's attack. While stronger and better trained, his own particular passion was no match against the madness, or thrill, the thing that Khoti felt gripping him. Khoti pummeled the retreating Minarian with his sword like a club. Finally, he saw his opening. He lunged, striking with a strength he didn't know he had. The Minarian lost his grip on his sword, and brought his shield around too late. Khoti smashed on through to cleave his enemy's skull.

Khoti trembled with a strange pulse, some sort of calling that thrilled in him, brutal and passionate. His blood ran hot, yet his heart felt ice cold as long as he wiped his mind free of distraction, free of anything but feeling that cold warrior heartbeat.

He had barely let out a breath when another swordsman rode straight at him. Khoti had found his strength. He struck first, then swung his blade around, sending the attacker's sword flying to clatter useless among the rocks streamside. The man stared at him, open mouthed. Dispassionate, Khoti swiped at the man's head, felling him. He had no desire to game with his foes.

The surprise of the Lharan assault forced the Minarians into retreat back into the confines of the gorge, where Konner's archers picked more of the survivors from their mounts.

The day had barely advanced and it was over. Kefta gathered prisoners and searched bodies. More than half of the Minarian van lay dead in the dusty gorge.

As his passion cooled, Khoti's long illness overcame him and he slumped forward in his saddle. He stroked the lathered and blood-spattered neck of the mare. Despite her heaving sides, she continued to hold her head up proudly as if ready to race into the next battle at his call. He twisted his bloody fingers in her gray mane, clinging for the support to keep him from slipping from her back. He looked up to find the duke, sweat and dust-coated, at the mare's head.

"Perhaps I was hasty suggesting you could one day train for my Guard. You are ready now." Eithurdon narrowed his gaze on him. "You are injured." Khoti shook his head to rid it of the fog and hum in his ears. Eithurdon barely caught him as he fell.

Konner knew Ahrwesz would hear the enemy's retreat west along the Staph-el Road where he waited to set off avalanches from the steep, loose mountainsides. He wanted to crow when he heard the first taps announcing that slides along a broad stretch of the road had buried a Minarian catapult, dozens of supply wagons and not a few enemy soldiers. The road to Sefresal had closed. They had no retreat.

About to shout their victory, he saw Khoti supported by one of Eithurdon's men. Konner added his own support to keep the groggy youth from slipping to the ground. He quickly searched for a wound beneath Khoti's bloody shirt, and examined his hand to see that it remained attached to his arm.

Eithurdon stopped Konner with a shake of his head. "I suspect he left his bed too soon. There may still be lingering fever. Again, he proves himself worthy of my Guard. Tsevon's repaid his debt today, three-fold. The debt I owe will likely only grow greater. You spared Sefresal a blow we could not have withstood. You are a worthy Second. But this will not stop them. They will find another way."

As if in confirmation, Kefta joined them, his expression sour. "They took the Lhata Road, though not easy to follow. It seems the Tawnkats buried the Staph-el Road and a good measure of Minaria. At least ten thousand survived to make the muster."

"Eilime!" Eithurdon cried. "What has Eilime to defend itself? Not even walls! Better to have taken the brunt at Sefresal than to have poor Eilime defenseless."

"And if they'd gone for Sefresal they still would'a moved on Eilime," Konner countered. "We've time now, Duke, to do what we should've done all along: build an army. It'll take 'em next to forever to get through the mountains and far enough south to bypass the Dodfrenyen Marshes. From Lhata south their trail's barely a trail at all. Many moons'll pass before they reach Eilime. We gave ourselves some much needed time, not to mention a boost of confidence."

'I have to wonder what hurry, or foolishness, sent them on a route so far south when regrouping they might have beat, or dug, a way through," Eithurdon mused. "What did they know, or expect?"

Khoti stirred. "By the gods, let me go!" he gasped when he realized Konner held him up. "You'd think I was a babe!"

"You can't be making my heart stop like that," Konner

growled, letting Khoti find his legs. Khoti's hands immediately clutched his side. "I said you had some fool notions leaving the Val so soon. You've probably torn yourself again and we don't have a healer near as good as your fa." He put his arm around Khoti's shoulder and gave him a rough hug. "I wish Tsevon could'a seen you today. He'd never be prouder. You got the best stuff of your fa in you."

Two spots of red grew in Khoti's cheeks as he tried to duck under Konner's grasp and still keep his balance. "I did well?" He swaggered a bit as he grinned at the older man. Then, turning grave, he turned to the duke. "Then, Lord, I accept your offer. I want to be a Lharan Guardsman."

"Maybe after you're well," Konner cautioned. "Your fa would say no."

"Khoti should come back to Sefresal to share the people's praise. He can rest in my house, and learn his sword when mended. We bear our fallen home. Still, we must celebrate a victory of so few against so many. I do not doubt that too soon we again will see battle with Tawnkats at our side."

With a curt gesture, Eithurdon signaled the Guard's departure. Khoti pulled himself onto the light-hearted mare, appearing small and weak as battle caught up to him. The strange fury Konner had witnessed in Khoti had abated like the back of a storm when rain lingers, but the wind and thunder are only a memory and the drip of rain strangely silent.

A half dozen riderless horses stood among the milling Guard, and many Guardsmen bore the wounds of battle. No banter disturbed the ranks as they looked upon their fallen or contemplated the gravity of the first life they had taken.

"When you return to the Val, you may find a great lot of my people," Eithurdon told Konner. "Keep them there. Victory or no, all too soon an enemy will march on our gates and I cannot arm a city with children under my feet."

With a salute, the Guard trotted for home while Konner gathered his men for their return to the Val. While a victory they would celebrate with Aibak's men that night in camp, it was only one battle. Konner glanced at the shrinking figures of the Guard. He recognized Khoti riding straight-backed into the mirages of early afternoon under the heat moon, neck craned to see the road ahead. If Konner feared anything about the future, the trials to face, he stored it in his worries for Khoti, who, intuition told him, would be in the center of whatever was yet to come. It made him go cold, what he saw with healer's sight.

THE EAST

18: Overheard

Nali stared out the thick glass window of The Old Scow. He tried to ignore the way his head throbbed from the blow he'd received in his dooryard early that morning, and the way the distorted pane made everything swim through his vision. Pedr had clucked on about the assault, wanting to parade each Harbor visitor before Nali to see if any matched the shadow the derna saw moments before something struck him so hard on the head, he remained too groggy to sit up an hour later.

Nali didn't mention the medallion. Even if Pedr found the man, Nali wouldn't, couldn't, admit it. They had too much to do yet. They couldn't raise Minarian suspicions or the people's alarm. Thinking about it made his head throb harder. Someone with malicious intent had crept to within arm's reach of where his lifemate and children slept. Where else did enemies creep in unseen like pantry beetles?

The calm harbor sunset outside the window felt too peaceful for such dark thoughts. As Jan bustled about lighting lamps, Nali leaned back to regard his empty plate. Aron drew the first tentative strums from his music box and soon a round of voices joined him in song.

A meaty hand on Nali's shoulder startled him, as Jan, in his ever-grimy apron, held out an ale. Nali took a deep drink as Jan pulled up a stool, gesturing at the empty platter.

"My Cookie makes a fine venison."

Nali nodded emphatically as he wiped up the last bit of gravy with the last crust of heavy bread. Jan's guarded expression reminded Nali too much of all the troubles he wanted to forget. He rubbed the bruise on his ribs where he'd fallen with his attacker atop him. He let out a long sigh, not wanting to be troubled by anything more important than his beer, even if only casting an augury or a blessing on the ale.

"Olna says you're looking for me."

Jan jerked his head toward the boardwalk outside, leading the derna to a spot where he leaned on the railing and looked out over the darkening water.

"It's like this," Jan whispered over the lapping waves. "I know something's goin' on and that you're involved somehow."

Nali tensed, annoyed by people's obsession with his doings and about to say so but Jan held up his hand and pushed on.

"Now let me finish. I've got my eyes and ears open and you might be interested in what I've heard."

"Go on, I'm listening."

"It's them Minarians," Jan's voice had dropped so low Nali could barely hear him over the lap of waves and strains of music and laughter coming from the inn.

"And?"

"They gave Pedr a toss in the water today for trying to uphold the peace. Just tossed a royal officer in the harbor like that. They've been pushin' people around, layin' their hands on women and just takin' things without payin' and threatenin' anyone that challenges 'em on any of it. I don't want 'em in my place, but if I tossed 'em out they'd be back with friends to break the place to pieces." His voice had risen a little in indignation. He went back to a whisper, leaning close. "Half a dozen come in last night, sat by the arch in the side room. You know how the sound carries there, and I hear 'em talkin'. Something big is up, Nali, and I don't like the sound of it."

"Like what?"

"One says they had to get all spit and polish because the delegation from the consulate would be sailin' with 'em. That's nothin' really, but later one who'd had more than his portion starts talkin' like he'd be taking over this place and retire from the sea, keep on the cook maybe. That gets my head racin'. So later another asks if they've heard when the fleet's comin'. Not calm and ordinary, but kinda ominous and the other shushed him."

"Did they say when this fleet's supposed to arrive?" His tone

155

revealed more of his thoughts than he intended.

"Started to, I think. One said somethin' about the first quarter of this moon. It might have been unrelated. I wasn't thinkin' clear. I'm probably makin'more of it than I should. I got all worked up when this one shushed the other and pointed at me. I couldn't help it. I must've looked guilty, not to mention surprised. They didn't say no more. Kinda gave me a murderin' look when the left and shorted me on the bill. Scared me half to death."

Nali chewed his cheek. First quarter of the blossom moon. Depending on the winds a fleet could arrive as early as the end of the month, only two weeks from now, if the same fleet as the ships Yechan reported in Ymmenay Bay and not one departing Minaria. A fleet – how large? Carrying what? – could wait just around the point.

"Nali, what's goin' on? I'm too sharp a bird to not pick things up. That brawl had you all nervous. Olna tells me you're always gone up to the palace by royal courier. I hear a bunch of messengers flew out of the palace gates in the night at breakneck speeds, bards complainin' the king hasn't come to table and audiences simply cancelled. I haven't seen the prince in over a week and he missed a match. You're walking around cross-eyed with that knock on your head and folks turned up dead! I'm your friend. You gotta tell me what's goin' on. Foreign sailors walked through my doors with designs on my place like they already got it!"

If Jan could see it, would it be obvious to the Minarians? "How many have you told about this?"

"No one, 'cept for Cookie and my boy Jali. They were in the kitchen – thought my heart had stopped, I shook so bad after them sailors left."

"Tell Cookie and Jali to keep quiet, and you too. Might be trouble, might not. Don't need to have folk getting all excited. I can't really tell you anything, Jan, not until the king says I can." Nali narrowed his gaze on the innkeeper. Though chubby and no longer young, Jan's renown in archery and hunting might be invaluable. "But you can count on being one of the first to know."

Jan slapped the heel of his palm against the rail. "Oh, it slipped me. I meant to tell you. The day of the big brawl, a sailor comes 'round askin' questions about you, like he wanted a derna to cast an augury for his child-to-be-born. Thinkin' that, new as a derna and all, you might be lookin' for business, folk told how you're friendly with the prince and how your rank's so special.

Aron thought maybe we should ask your leave, but before we knew it, folks had pretty much given up your life's story."

"That's why!" Nali pointed at the lump and a small cut hidden by the hair falling across his forehead. "I s'pose folks were more than willing to offer up my address and cap size, too!"

Jan's mouth hung open and Nali could see the innkeeper piecing it all together.

"Then maybe a bit more makes sense," Jan said. "The fellow turns to me, says I could be a rich man for knowin' you. I thought he meant about gettin' favors from royals, not tellin' him the prince is a friend. Seems, instead, he was buyin' news of you. I'm so sorry, Nali."

Nali turned and hurried into the dark, without acknowledging Jan's goodbye. First, he'd fetch his fa to stay with Olna and the children now that he'd made them targets. Olna didn't need worry unsettling their unborn child. Then, once again, Nali would ride to Sihmad Shal. How careless he'd been, how careless they all were. What next? Would they accidentally reveal their meager defense plans? Or put the prince up against some Minarian assassin in a wrestling match? What clueless fools. Knowing it gave Nali a deep sense of dread.

19: Indefensible

Arshal had thrown himself into their skeleton of a defense plan, dispatching messengers, poring over trade accounts of the city's consumption of goods and mulling over the census used to assess regional taxes. He found population, occupation, and sometimes even crop yields, but not how many able-bodied defenders they could call up. He kept deferring one item on the list, the most awkward: asking the Consul of Otayr for help with the inconceivable. Finally, put off as long as he dared, Arshal had to make the overture despite the king's fear they would provoke war by preparing for it. Would the man laugh him out of his office?

"Oh my!" Marol, Consul of Otayr, exclaimed on finding Arshal at his door, his words accented with the heavy dialect of the eastern lands. "My sincerest welcome, Lord!" The rotund man executed a stiff bow.

Dressed opulently, from his gold belt to gleaming gold necklaces, Consul Marol appeared a colorful contradiction. His square face perched like a block on his round body. The gold brocaded tags fastening his red surcoat threatened to yield to the bright orange blouse beneath, which topped yellow stockings and black boots. Dark unkempt hair hung straight to his shoulders where it mingled in a tangled mass of full beard revealing a hint of a ruddy complexion.

"How am I of service, Lord?"

"I seek advice on a delicate matter, for which I'll ask you to observe the utmost discretion."

Marol's face puckered into seriousness as he ushered Arshal into an anteroom furnished with a narrow table, a few chairs, and little else.

"Your country has fought long against raiders from the wildlands, and I'm told you had a distinguished career as a marshal of troops," Arshal said.

Marol bobbed his head agreeably.

"Thus, we come to you." Arshal took a deep breath then blurted, "We wish recommendations on the arming and defense of Sihmad Shal." Arshal slipped into the padded chair Marol held for him as the consul's face ran a gamut of expressions, settling on incredulous.

"Defend Sihmad Shal? From what?"

"We have reason to believe we may come under attack." Arshal felt the heat rush his face as he dared to utter such a statement.

"You are serious?" Marol frowned at the polished surface of the table for a long minute. "If you are serious, I cannot give such advice without leave of the Otayran Council."

Arshal felt his mouth drop open then quickly shut it, trying to maintain his composure.

"Understand, we could become embroiled in all manner of trouble if we are perceived to be helping one side in a dispute. I certainly would help you, if I could, but on such matters even my king has no right to say so. It must go before the Council and they are not known to move with haste, nor wish to pick sides in foreign disagreements."

"What if it's a hypothetical exercise? Perhaps this is merely training, or a diversion? A way to build good will with the future king?"

Marol went to a small window facing the florid walls encircling the borough Oj. He stood in silence so long Arshal felt certain the man worked on a way to make him leave.

"Hypothetically," he said at last, shaking his head. "This city is indefensible." He held up a hand before Arshal could protest. "I have served here for a long time. I studied the construction and cried for the neglect, pondering all the things I would do if I could restore it to its glory. It is a most confounding puzzle for a strategist and worse for the tactician. In months of hard labor and great expense, you maybe can make the first couple boroughs into formidable barriers. But not this, nor the next. The wall into Yckeb, here. A battering ram, sappers," he snapped his fingers, "It tumbles in moments. That wall," he pointed to a low wall into Oj, painted in multiple hues and lined with flower boxes and windows. "Worse. It is made of a paste of sands and coral. The upper walls were the last to be built. They built them for their symmetry and beauty, to honor the gods with gardens and ponds, and to separate the functions of the palace and the residents, not for defense. By the time of their construction,

Shande was at peace and defensive walls an afterthought. Even your palace is constructed of soft materials, the towers easy for scalers. Some of the lower walls, made with granite and hardstone, will hold longer. The adanan reinforcement and plating of the wall around Dyndevas is very strong. By the time an enemy breaches it, all within would starve to death. Though, I would strip the adanan from it and use it to forge arms and reinforce gates."

"But the city was built in the wake of the Great War! Wouldn't the walls be built to hold?"

"Time and neglect made it weak. That was over a thousand years ago! And why tackle walls when gates will fail? I doubt you can close any gate in the city! You filled the interiors of the walls with offices and guest rooms separated with wooden dividers. Burn them and the heat cracks mortar, even stone. Postern doors stand open, their locks lost. You have flower boxes and benches where soldiers need to maneuver. In places stonework is loose and crumbling. Even the defenses outside the city walls are useless. You filled defensive ditches to use for irrigation and stripped their scarps of stone for barns and paddocks. Ten thousand workers could toil on this city for two decades, maybe then."

Arshal stared at Marol's back, his hands locked, white-knuckled in his lap. He shook his head as the consul turned from the window.

"Even defended, Lord, she is just too large to feed and provision. Half the people starve in only a short siege." He shrugged; his mouth twisted into an apologetic smile. "Sihmad Shal is a dream for a strategist and tactician, Lord. I admit spending many hours imagining it restored."

"So, to defend the city, we only need –"

"No, no, not only, Lord," Marol interrupted, as his excitement made his breaths quicker. "Arms. Your armorer barely knows their use, much less how to forge them. Spears? Arrowheads? Swords? Your metalworkers only know the odd hunting weapons or farm equipment, pots and pans, and filigree." Marol sat at a chair too small and teetery for his bulk. "Shande disbanded its army. I always marveled at this. Where will your soldiers come from? Who will train them? What strategy will you use? Mounted, on foot, by sea? How will you deploy? Offensive measures outside the walls or defensive measures within? How do you equip your army? How do you feed it? If you call up your army, who will grow and distribute your food? Craft and manage your supplies? Will this be an army of the nation? Who will train and do those things in the far provinces? Will some enemy merely go around you and strike the next undefended city? How will you transport your army to where the battles are? Who is in charge? How do they communicate among the different units?"

Arshal felt like he'd swallowed a hot stone that had lodged somewhere deep in his throat. "I think, first we need defense for the city – within the walls. I imagine heavy arms will take time to forge, especially if we need to repair the gates."

Marol bobbed his head. "What gates you have. May I make suggestions?" He awaited Arshal's assent. "In Otayr, our battle is in remote wildlands. We travel light, yet protected from arrows and darts with boiled leather armor." Marol produced a parchment from a drawer in the table and scratched his ideas. "Find a trustworthy smith who can make axe, arrowheads and spear heads and learn to craft a fine sword. That," he gestured at Arshal's sword of rank, "Worthless. You need craftsmen to make bows and arrows, leatherworkers to create armor and shields and tailors to make uniforms – perhaps a cloak – for your soldiers to build unity. You need stores masters and planners who gather and organize your supplies and distribute them. You will need firefighters, people to feed your army and, inevitably, people to treat the wounded. Someone must teach the soldiers how to use their weapons and follow orders. Strategists must decide where best to deploy your resources and predict your enemy's movements. Tacticians must quickly analyze and adjust your plans when it all goes awry."

Arshal felt overwhelmed imagining creating an army from merchants and farmers as Marol's bold lines shaped a plan, scratching out how, if he had unlimited funds and time, he would rebuild Sihmad Shal into a fortress and deploy her resources.

"Unfortunately, this city is indefensible above the third wall." He drew a large X across half the city, including the palace.

"But the wall into Dyndevas you said is the strongest!"

"Before that wall, seven boroughs fall, housing the entire population of the city. Better it is to strip the adanan from the wall and turn it over to the smithies." Marol sounded almost giddy.

"So, what do we do?"

"Aside from hoping you have no enemies, not much. Evacuate Shanai borough inside the walls. Send your noncombatants far from harm to make provisions last longer. Then, the first wall, strong granite. The gates may need only a little repair, but I doubt it. The wall into Fearnia is the strongest in the lower boroughs and fifteen paces thick. But you need to remove the wooden walls inside of it. Place infantry near the gates, archers here, perhaps small cavalry here and here." Marol scratched more and more diagrams with furious strokes, marking where postern doors needed reinforcement and crossing out the northwest section of the outer wall. No attacker could scale the cliff and climb the buttresses there. Marol's eagerness made Arshal wish he could feel anything but overwhelmed. How many would die in a fruitless attempt to hold the indefensible city? If, of course, they truly had an enemy. If, of course, that enemy targeted Sihmad Shal.

"Now we see armorer and smithy and perhaps look at gates, yes?" Marol turned to him, breathless, his eyes bright. Arshal followed the jubilant consul, numbed by the enormity of it all. What foolishness had he led them to?

"No, no, no, no, no! You silly boy. He just lopped off your hand! How you going to fight now?" Marol cried in disgust with the familiarity of one who has spent the last two weeks trying to mold soldiers from dandies.

Esthen grinned, victorious, as Marol grabbed the heavy wooden practice sword from Arshal's hand. Arshal's shoulder and arm ached, but he couldn't rest. If the rumor of a Minarian fleet was true, he had no time for mistakes. He wiped the sweat from his face and rubbed the bruise on his wrist where Esthen's wooden weapon had struck him. A red line rose there now. Mistakes hurt and were seldom repeated.

"What you grinning at, stupid boy?" Marol demanded of Esthen. "You should be dead, twice. He is just too silly to follow through. Arshal, you let your sword drop too low and left your arm open and undefended and didn't raise your shield! Esthen, you are off balance. One strong parry, you fall and zip," Marol ran a finger across his throat, "Off goes Esthen's head. Now try again!"

Marol proved a relentless teacher. They spent their daylight hours practicing in the gardens, fighting with Marol's wooden practice swords, facsimile daggers and even their bare hands as they tackled fighting dummies and all manner of Otayran-style training machines mimicking faux enemies, before he set them upon each other. Marol found them well-versed in bare hands and wrestling, and they took to the short daggers well. The rudiments of sword play came harder, even with eager pupils. In the evenings, bone tired and muscle-weary, they pored over diagrams Marol gave them to imagine various movements of make-believe armies. He made it into a game of strategy as they each took a side in a battle, deploying units and responding to each other's moves.

Officially, the king termed work under way on the gates and walls preventive maintenance against further decay of historic structures. The echoes from the gardens – Marol's admonitions and the princes' angry shouts when a blow made contact – they attributed to the competitive whims of the young men. Marol pretended not to hear remarks from his pupils about an actual enemy, and they phrased their questions in conjecture. Trusted craftsmen had begun their work. Only a few rumors rose, quickly squelched. Rumors of some threat to the peace proved too fanciful for anyone to believe, though, no doubt, the Minarians paid attention.

"How you going to maybe teach others if you do not learn right? Do it again!" Marol snapped, pushing Esthen for emphasis.

Again, Arshal and Esthen circled. Sweat ran from their faces as they lunged and spun away, lifted their shields and thrust their swords. The dull thunk of wood on shield and the exhausted gasps of their breathing ripped the still gardens. Finally, after a furious exchange, Esthen's sword flew from his hand and fell into a flower bed. Arshal moved in closer as Esthen reached for his boot sheath and pulled the facsimile dagger. With a kick, Esthen sent Arshal's sword flying from his hand. Before it fell Arshal had already reached for his own dagger.

"Enough!" Marol barked, and the brothers dropped to their knees, panting. "Finally, you do one thing right. I know you can fight with daggers. Put them away. Fetch your swords and do it again. Show me this was no accident."

The brothers battled in the hot sun until the wall formed long shadows over the gardens and they were sweat-drenched, bruised and bleeding. Finally, Marol called a halt. He smiled as he handed them a flagon of water.

"You do well today. Tomorrow, you do better," he said while they groaned in protest and drank deep of the tepid water. He slapped Esthen across the shoulder, evoking a wince. He winked as Esthen rubbed the sore muscles. "Maybe we make warriors of soft boys yet, like me." He patted his oversized belly. "Victory trove," he laughed. "Tomorrow, you get your swords. The smith finished them, a fine job. You must make your sword an extension of your arm. You must know its weight and learn its dimensions. You must sleep with it, eat with it. You must feel naked without it." He handed them a parchment with several new complex strategies drawn on it. "Tomorrow, you will show me your game plan for marshalling your armies on three fronts each."

Marol strode away, whistling, making an occasional jab at the air with his finger to some rhythm inside his head.

Nali approached from the garden gate.

"Nali, my friend!" Arshal called. "I'm a great swordsman, am I not?" He swished the air with his practice sword.

Nali nodded, but didn't smile, his expression unreadable. Arshal let his sword arm fall.

"What is it?"

"Before dawn this morning the Minarian delegation snuck from the city. They boarded a trade ship and set sail at first light. They must've planned this for some time because they emptied their offices and quarters of everything from furnishing to hinges. The only thing left is a drawing scrawled on the wall – you know the one. It appears painted with blood. Workers have been trying to wash it away all day."

Arshal's stomach had lurched into his throat.

"A call to arms may come soon. His Majesty's closeted himself to prepare a speech, but he wants Cree's advice." The officious tone in Nali's voice softened. "He's so agitated. I think he's planning something, Arshal."

"He's been tight. It's all too much for him. I wish Cree would wake! My father needs his guidance and we need to know what he's seen. He must have taken a tremendous dose. What if it kills him? It's been weeks!"

"We can't wait forever. This is the surest sign, what we needed. They confirm our worst fears."

Arshal could only stare after Nali as the derna paced back through the garden to the gate. They needed more time!

As night fell, Arshal went to the darkened room where Cree slept, unchanged, as he had since he'd taken the elixir the day Yechan arrived. He searched the Visionary's features for any hint of waking, but the ancient's face remained smooth and pale, eyes open, gaze on the ceiling. The prince set a cup of cold broth to his tutor's lips. Cree swallowed mechanically. The single drop of osfothye Arshal had consumed took him into dreams for three days. Arshal tried to imagine the seer wandering through a host of visions for the rest of eternity. He set aside the broth and blew out the small bedside candle. If only he felt the confidence Esthen had. He couldn't escape the sense of something stealing his breath, undoing his certainty, like some internal judge reining in his every decision. He needed Cree's assurances.

The clatter of hooves on the mosaic path from the gate and a shouted objection drew him to the small window in Cree's chamber. In the courtyard below a groom hurried to grab a riderless horse as a messenger ran for the palace steps. Arshal recognized the courier sent to Sefresal. The man could never have reached Sefresal and returned so quickly.

Arshal found the king in the empty reception hall, the echoes of his feet chasing the hall's length. Dark but for a single lamp lit near the dais, Arshal noted first only how the king's head bowed in sadness, or perhaps defeat. As Arshal neared, he noticed the messenger standing in the shadows before the dais, wringing his hands. Clothing mud-splattered, each movement sent puffs of dust swirling toward the light.

King Ebon looked up at Arshal's approach. "I'm glad you've come," he said. He nodded to the messenger. "Please, repeat for the benefit of my son."

In words heavy with exhaustion, the messenger relayed how he met an errand rider from Sefresal at an exchange station and traded messages. He unrolled a scroll for Arshal's inspection.

The familiar script of Arshal's cousin, the Duke of Lharan, echoed Yechan's words, detailing scenes of armament along the Ymmenay River. Arshal's eyes widened as he read of caravans hauling arms, of villages destroyed, dozens of Shandeans killed or captive, of mines lost. Arshal dropped the paper, stunned. It re-rolled itself with a snap.

"The first of the blossom moon would coincide with the overheard departure date of a Minarian fleet," Arshal mused. "With favorable winds it could be any day now. What's aboard it? Armed warriors? Besieging towers and catapults like Marol described? Certainly, these are acts of war. Will you be announcing a call to arms?"

King Ebon shook his head. "We have time yet, in a few weeks. Many preparations must be made. I want our smiths able to handle the call. They've only just begun."

"We may not have weeks. And we still need to train those we call up!"

The messenger stared at them wide eyed.

"Have you words for this worthy courier?"

Arshal stammered his assent then ordered the messenger to Sefresal with a call to arms that likely wouldn't arrive for weeks. As the messenger left that odd sensation returned, a sense of doubt, inadequacy. Arshal's message had sounded crass in the face of his father's decorum, accusatory and undiplomatic, the shrill cries of the defensive. Why did he think these things, doubt himself when he'd always felt such certainty?

An oppressive silence weighted the huge hall. Each drip of candle wax brought them closer to a confrontation for which they remained unprepared.

"I wish I could speak with Cree," the king said.

Arshal straightened. "We can't wait for him. We need to send messengers to all the provinces or people won't be ready. We have no idea where the first blow will fall. We only assume Sihmad Shal is the target. Look at Sefresal and their troubles."

The king nodded. "As you think best."

"We must warn those Cree suggested they'd target: shawnsi, Visionaries, derna, royal employees."

"As you see fit."

Arshal's hands rose and fell. "Why don't you speak in your own name?"

"I grow old," the king began, a gesture silencing Arshal's protest. "Certainly, I should live decades yet, but I won't. I age before my time. That's my fate. I'm a ruler of peace. I can't change that. The people need the guidance of a strong leader, not an old clerk. You must make these decisions. Tradition cripples me. This is your destiny. Your name in the old language means, Defender of the People. I never placed much in the choice of names, merely took what the seers gave. Now it frightens me, for you, your brothers and especially Resala. The auguries for Ebon's children gave no comfort."

"What do their names mean? Certainly, Resala is from Daughter of Sala."

Ebon looked away. "Perhaps Cree will tell you one day. Or if he doesn't wake, perhaps Nali will find it in the Lierye. Resala has another name, one you don't need to know. A name can be a secret used to harm, or even to usurp destiny. Certainly, Cree told you this. Be satisfied with your fate. It's a noble role." King Ebon emitted a long sigh. "Dispatch your messengers in my name. Invoke it for any order you see fit. At last, I must trust your judgment. You've proved me wrong." Ebon rose and placed a hand on Arshal's shoulder. "I have faith you won't err."

166

The king turned and left, Arshal too stunned to reply.

A soft step and rustle made the prince crouch inside, as if he expected something to come at him from his dreams. He turned, hoping to find Cree. Nali emerged from the shadows.

"I didn't hear you come in."

"Because I arrived before you," Nali said. "I was speaking with the king when the messenger arrived."

"About what?"

"You, me, him," Nali said with the off-handed manner of a fisher discussing fair weather. He settled himself on a step, re-arranging his derna robes about his knees. "He wanted to discuss a decision he's considering."

"He could have spoken with me."

"It involves you." Nali gave him a sidelong glance.

"What is it?"

Nali's eyebrows shot up. "Compromise a confidence, Arshal? You know better."

Arshal took a step back. He heard a counselor, not a fisher. "Forgive me, but my father's mood has me worried. He's planning something, isn't he?"

Nali gave a slight nod.

"Why not tell me?"

"Just as I won't betray your confidence and trust in me, I can't betray the confidence of the King of Shande by the oaths I took when I became a derna. You'll know what we discussed when he calls the nation to arms. That's all I'll say." Nali stood, closing the discussion. "I must go home. Poor Olna, with child, the extra work I left her, and the burden of my fa in the house: she'll understand my secrets too well, too soon." He clasped Arshal's arm, then strode from the hall, his footsteps echoing long after.

The prince stood alone, absorbing the sense of impending tragedy, needing to feel the authority and command his father had given him. Like never before, he felt unworthy of it, as if some doubt wiggled like a worm into his core. Right now, the fleet could be out there. And they still hadn't called the people to arms.

20: To Arms

Horns blared as heralds spread the word throughout Sihmad Shal that King Ebon would give a special address, only the second since he'd announced the birth of his successor. The other had come the year Kedtair decimated the nation's crops. Markets buzzed with speculation, from Prince Arshal taking a bride to a financial emergency. Some recounted rumors of ports closed and letters of credit no longer sound. One woman dared suggest war, but jeers and laugher silenced her.

Long Day had dawned hot, the sun baking the city like pottery in a kiln. Clouds of dust rose around and coated the hundreds of stalls that had turned the Fearnia market into a hubbub of bartering and gossip. A tense undertone grew as the more observant tried to draw connections to the so-called restoration work that had removed flower boxes, gods' gardens, benches and office walls, and the oddity of adanan reinforcements being removed from the Dyndevas wall to be affixed over doors and gates. A dozen forges, normally silent on market day, sent out a metallic heartbeat and messengers raced through crowds of shoppers with alarming recklessness. Craftsmen refused to discuss their work, only adding to that sense of impatience as the people awaited the evening's address.

At the city's heart, Arshal paced his chambers, sweating his anxiety as he tried to imagine how people would receive his father's address. Would they panic? Would people comprehend the gravity of it? He only assumed he planned a call to arms. What would that mean to people so long removed from the kinds of turmoil other countries had faced?

He had the sudden, unreasonable fear the king might recommend capitulation, though to what he couldn't imagine as they still hadn't heard a word from the Minarians. Thus far, Minarians in Sihmad Shal had only stolen a few furnishings on their way out of the country and threatened their relationship with trading partners. No evidence linked the murder in the exchequer, death of Azuth, and the attack on Nali to Minarians. Would the people even care about an assault on distant mountains in such a vast country? What if no one answered the call?

He couldn't even talk to his own counselor. Nali stayed with the king, who would permit no disturbance during what seemed an endless night before the pending address. Nali had left at dawn to fetch his family to market day and the address in Oj to follow, still refusing to discuss what advice he offered the troubled sovereign. Arshal knew history would record this day. Yet here he was left out of the proceedings he'd initiated and unsure of what the king intended to do.

Arshal paused in his pacing to stare at the heavy sword he'd hung in brackets beside his chamber door. He ran his fingers over the engraving on the blade close to the hilt: an eagle clinging to the back of a snarling wildcat that trampled flames. The image had simply come to the smith and neither he nor the prince knew what it meant, but Arshal felt more confident practicing with this special weapon in his hand.

He yanked the scabbard from its hook beneath the sword and strapped it on. He sheathed the weapon, which felt oddly comfortable at his side. He snarled in his best imitation of a warrior cry Marol had taught him. He swiftly drew the sword from the scabbard, slightly crouching as if an enemy reared up from beneath his bed. He swiped at the air, then, with a flourish, stabbed a table, skewering parchment detailing the city's supply of salt. He held up the paper in triumph.

Startled by a chuckle behind him, he whirled, sword raised, to discover Zopher don Saran, the man's hands pantomiming applause.

"A battle of words, Arshal?" Zopher reached up to pluck the parchment from the sword, giving it a cursory glance before letting it flutter onto the divan.

Resala's pompous suitor had shed his finery for the hunting attire Arshal remembered fondly from their long friendship. Not the fine clothing of the mounted hunter, he wore the weather-stained protection of a tracker in the wildlands: hide shirt, dark cloak, leather footgear that reached to his calf and hide breeches tied at the knee. The hilt of a dagger peeked from a boot sheath and he had slung a short hunting bow at his back.

"You looked idiotic. I had to laugh," Zopher said, his speech missing the feigned stuffiness courtiers imitated. But he hadn't completely shed the twin self that thrived on the biting wit of the arrogant. "Fine looking weapon. And just what purpose does it serve?"

"Surprised to see you without my little sister here to drape you in matching ribbons." Arshal said as he sheathed the sword. "And what new fashion trend is this?" Arshal plucked at the rain-stained cloak. "Certainly, more appropriate for the dark moon than the light."

The two men stared at one another. At last, Zopher sighed and turned as if to leave. Instead, he shut the door and stood a moment, his back to Arshal before he pivoted to face him.

"Can we put it aside?" he asked finally. "I've been a fool. I tried to become something I'm not to gain Resala's favor. It was so easy to do! I ended up losing myself, and what endeared me to her in the first place. I tried to be the aristocrat and failed miserably, and angered my friends. I, the son of an insignificant western baron, sought the hand of a princess. What arrogance! As if by acting the part I could elevate my station! Your father could see her joined with the prince of another kingdom! Forgive me, Arshal. I neglected you and became false to win a woman who preferred the original to the forgery."

Arshal shrugged and at last cracked a smile. "I've never stopped being your friend, Zopher. I just couldn't stomach the sight of you. You're always forgiven. So, what opened your eyes? Has Resala's mean streak finally driven you away?"

"I remain devoted to her. But we reached an understanding. I think she found something exciting in being courted by a social misfit." Zopher shrugged. "My father will be disappointed. I think he thought I might one day become a respectable noble."

"So why the clothes? Are you going to the mountains? Saran? You must be unbearably hot."

"Why the sword?" Zopher countered with a hint of sneer. He sighed then at his own lingering insolence and pressed his hands away, as if pushing away that side of himself. "I thought to go home to Saran for a time, but thought it best to consult you first."

"Why get my leave to go anywhere? If you've broken your suit with Resala, that's your business –"

"It's not about Resala. I was thinking it might be a bad time to leave."

"Bad time?"

"I'm a fool, not blind. Since when do restoration projects

involve tearing out gods' gardens in place for centuries and reinforcing gates? Errand riders are riding horses into the ground. To where?" He gestured at the sword. "You skip matches and carousing in the Harbor for sword games with Esthen. Your father hasn't been at table and barely speaks to Resala. And now there's this address in the midst of Long Day festivities. All this, and yet there's no gossip to be had, unless you listen to mariners ranting about closed ports. As a betting man, I'd wager there's trouble brewing."

Arshal pulled on his lip as he studied Zopher. Gray eyes beneath bushy dark brows, his unkempt brown hair – cleansed of powder and mostly concealing the starburst birthmark on his temple – lanky build, and weathered clothing all gave Zopher that scruffy look Arshal had missed.

"And if there's trouble?" he asked softly.

"I offer my skills as bowman and tracker. I did apprentice with the Lharan Guard. I'm bound to serve my king as he requires."

"You sound as if you expect some sort of conflict."

"What else can I think? I know fortifications when I see them."

Arshal shook his head. Soon everyone would know and likely a good number of them had figured it out. With a sigh, he quickly shared what they'd learned from Shiad and Sefresal, and the recent actions of the Minarian delegation. As Arshal spoke, Zopher fell into a chair, staring at the prince as if the reality was too much to keep his legs locked beneath him.

"So, it's real," Zopher said at last. "I guess I'd hoped you'd tell me I'm wrong. I offer my service to the best of my ability." He pulled the dagger from his boot, stood and offered the weapon to Arshal with both hands. "Will you accept me?"

"I wouldn't have told you if I hadn't already accepted it. But your service is first owed to the king. I'm still learning all this ridiculous protocol. As if we don't have enough to think about without worrying about silly rules. We do need your talents, Zopher. In all of Sihmad Shal maybe a handful have your knowledge, and your experience in the Lharan Guard will be critical. You'll be busy."

"Then I take my leave to sharpen my knives, and perhaps some rusty skills." He grasped Arshal's arm. "Thank you for trusting me. We've been asleep so long. Maybe a little excitement will be good for us."

If what Arshal dreamt came to pass, they would see more excitement than any deserved.

Arshal thought the hours until dusk could drag no slower.

When at last King Ebon, followed by his family, approached the platform erected in the vast plaza of the borough Oj, a hush fell over a sea of faces. Tens of thousands gathered as torches sputtered and smoked, sending their fumes into the darkening sky where stars wavered in the haze still clinging to the city. The king scanned the crowd. After a last glance toward the tower where Cree still slept, he turned and raised his arms for silence. Whispers died away and an eerie quiet grew, broken only by the snap of pennants on the towers.

"Shandeans hear and heed me, your king," he began in a voice that boomed from buildings and walls, unlike the weakness of age he'd claimed. "I bear sad news. We are a peaceful land threatened by the specter of war."

A uniform gasp, then a hum of voices rose toward a crescendo, tapering off as King Ebon again raised his arms.

"Lives have already been lost," he continued. "Murders, kidnappings, burned villages, and broken trade agreements. These acts preceded war throughout history in other lands, while Shande remained at peace, complacent. We trusted our generous treaties, vast reaches and great plenty. Now, a foe arms for war against us, with resources stolen from Shande by force. Misguided souls turn from One to a power with an ancient grudge. A being so destructive One banished him from this world seeks revenge through the arts of his emissary, the Enchanter, Ghyldus."

The crowd gasped. Mothers pulled children to them. Hands covered faces and small cries of disbelief escaped. Arshal recognized Nali's hand in the speech. He would know what would move the people.

"King Mol Azezial of Minaria fell under the Enchanter's spell and ascended to his throne on promises of vengeance. Against us. He spreads the lie that we, Shandeans, stole Minaria's birthright: Shande. With the Enchanter's guile behind them, they aim to destroy everything the gods made here: these lands, their offspring, and the faithful tribes of Shande." The king's voice rose with the indignant tone of the wronged. "Our kingdom is threatened. Our people have become targets. Two thousand eight hundred and seventeen years have passed since the gods' Great War with this same evil when a generation died in its youth. Since then, we have known only a few isolated and internal skirmishes. Our differences made us stronger, our leadership benevolent, our treaties generous, our people prosperous and partners in their leadership. Shande never preyed upon its people the way Minarians do upon the lowland Pladde, making of them expendable servants to their lord's demands. Our peace made us complacent. We disbanded our defenses and failed to remain vigilant. Now, the greatest request a leader can ask of his people, I ask of you: to defend Shande, its peoples, cultures and souls. For our children and those to come."

The city had fallen so silent Arshal heard the low growl of distant surf and the appeals of a roaming cat in the next borough wailed at the hot night. It seemed all life stood still and no one dared breathe. What if the people rejected the call? As he went on, King Ebon's voice held the weight of the decision he had debated all these weeks.

"I'm the ruler of a land of peace, yet I call my people to arms," he said, holding hands out, open, to his subjects. "I can't accept the death of my countrymen on my hands. I won't lead them to war. It's not my destiny to do so. That is for the young and strong." He paused for a long moment. "Yet I live. I can't lead you nor can I abandon you. Thus, I abdicate my sovereign authority to my son, Crown Prince Arshaldon Dyndevas, destined to defend us." King Ebon gestured to Arshal, his last words almost lost in the buzz of exclamation and uncertainty from the packed square. Arshal could only stare at his father. "I remain king until I die," he continued as the crowd quieted. "But my son shall rule in my name as regent. That's his destiny."

The king motioned for Arshal to step forward. The prince scanned the gathering, seeing familiar faces gazing back, people for whom he'd ducked a day of lessons to share an ale or bet on a race. He spied Nali standing to the side with his stunned family, the derna's encouraging nod like a prod that forced words from his mouth.

"I accept my father's charge," Arshal said, his voice barely carrying. "I hope I'm worthy."

A roar of approval from the crowd stunned him. Something surged through him, an emotion untapped.

"All is not lost!" he shouted, words rushing from him, his voice ringing with a strength and resonance that felt alien, deeper and more powerful than he'd ever before delved. "We must be strong. We will be strong! We're called to arms! Arm to defend this land. Arm to protect our people. Arm to oppose evil. Arm for our future!" Tens of thousands of voices rose in a roar of approval. "To arms then! To Arms!" he shouted, strengthened by their support.

"To arms!" they echoed, their voices shaking the foundations of the city named for a hope for peace. The fervor even seemed to grip his brothers. He looked upon a sea of torch-lit faces, their arms thrust upward in their appeal for leadership. "To arms!" they shouted.

Arshal's glance fell on a face that remained conspicuously unmoved. The man returned his stare defiantly, then reached inside his tunic and held up an object shining fiery red in the torchlight. Two ruby eyes glinted from the medallion, like embers that burned into the prince's heart to leave behind a charred ring, like a cinder hole in fine tapestry. Doubt leapt at him from the medallion's eyes like the creature from his dreams. Or had it been real? Gasping, he forced himself to remember where he stood and looked quickly for an officer to detain the man, but in a breath the man had disappeared into the press of people while Arshal's heart continued to flutter in fear. He jumped down from the platform and strode from the din, confused and alone among thousands of cheers of support.

It took hours for Oj to empty. People lingered to read the calls for volunteers that officials posted throughout the city. Families and friends hesitated to part from each other's comfort. Some took up torches and paraded through the streets followed by crowds chanting and singing with patriotic fervor of the glories of the past, dusting off the old songs of Dynfearn's time as they struggled to remember ancient words. Young men scrapped and wrestled, boasting their fitness for service. Some rushed home to dig through larders and pantries to find some small weapon, others took measure of their supplies and some wondered which cousins in the countryside would take in their children.

Arshal returned to the palace and climbed to the high Window of the Sun, feeling sick from merely glimpsing a medallion. Looking out, he marked the flickering torchlight snaking along the Sijway, a ghostly yellow glow moving along the eaves and shimmering from walls as parading torch bearers wound their way down to the lower boroughs. The still night lifted the voices up to him. He heard a step on the stair then sensed someone beside him. He found Nali staring out the window at the city below.

"Everything's so small!" Nali exclaimed. He gazed out, gingerly, as if fearing to fall if he came too close. Sihma Harbor glistened in the distance, radiant in the light of the full moon high overhead, moored ships like toy boats in a small pond. "I can see so far!" he gasped.

"It's most beautiful when the moon is full. I like to come here to think. I feel like I see things clearer, like I'm seeing the world as the stars see it."

"Everyone's gathered as you asked. They wait in the king's study," Nali said, turning from the view.

"My father burdens me, Nali. I wonder if I'm ready for this responsibility." That alien surge of doubt surfaced again. Fear welled up in him, a strange paralysis he couldn't understand.

"It's your destiny. The king knows that. It was still hard for him to do. You're young, and it admits the future and all its omens to pass along the leadership. But you've already made decisions in his name. He's relied on your guidance."

"I confess I'm afraid, Nali. We know so little! The visions leave so much room for error. Cree said our gods decreed that the rulers of Shande honor peace and be as siblings to our neighbor. What if the visions meant to warn us against the path we're taking? What if we're dooming ourselves? What if it's the Enchanter weaving these spells in our minds? Think of exacting revenge by dooming us to the disfavor of the gods. Cree should be here guiding us. I know our path must be clear before him. His fingers twitch and his eyes jump. He's seeing great things, Nali. What if we're wrong?"

Nali studied him a long moment, as if he saw through to the core of Arshal's fear. "I've had doubts, too. But gods who lost so much defending Shande wouldn't give up now." Nali paced to the east window and gazed out on the squared walls marching into the distance. The hills beyond rolled east until they met a vast plateau, glowing incandescent as the moon shone upon wisps of drifting fog. "I think we've never understood Kedtair. Folks call it Demonstar, but that's not just for the effects we see. It's also to remind us to look to Kedtair for guidance against evil. Kedtair doesn't just show us what we're protected from. It shows us what protects us. Those visions we share? Kedtair gave us this. Without them, a fleet would arrive without warning. You must believe it was Terremar who came to you. Evil couldn't create him in your mind."

Arshal nodded, trying to press down the urge to flee. "Right or wrong, it's done. The people have been called to arms." Arshal put a hand on Nali's shoulder, feeling knots of tension. "We shouldn't keep them waiting."

Within his mind's prison, Cree knew what passed in Oj. His chest rose in a deep gasp. Tears streamed from unseeing eyes.

He looked upon desolation, felt deeply the pain his siblings had wrought in the world. The prince's name chanted through the streets reached his ears as a prayer that he awake. Instead, he remained locked in a world where the musing of subconscious memory took threads of reality, spun from the collective psyche of the gods, then bound him with symbols seen but not remembered, taunting him with the half-heard voices of his brethren calling to him.

In one semi-lucid moment he saw an intricate web built as fine and complex as any spider's, stinking of evil and deceit, spread out across existence to capture all in its sticky cords. Such was the image, a trap in itself, that soon he lost it in the shifting visions in his head like the world spinning by the over-imbibed reveler who prays for the movement to stop. Of the host of images, he would remember only a few, and not the most important.

21: The Black Pennant

A somber group gathered in the king's study late that night. Resala and Queen Sala sat in silent shock. High color in Resala's cheeks hinted at annoyance, which sparked Esthen and Peshal to speculate on her reactions loudly enough for her to hear. Zopher leaned in the corner, his dark attire wrapping him in shadow. The king again sat at the table, his head resting in his hands in a posture most unlike the sovereign.

Arshal gestured for Nali to read from the list of duties the prince had drawn up, tasks none of them felt competent to carry out.

Esthen and Arshal, by virtue of training with Marol, would share command of their defenses. Zopher would lead and train archers and scouts. Peshal would assign volunteers, and evacuate noncombatants to a safe region and plan an escape from the city in event of siege. Sala and Resala would manage provisions and oversee the able-bodied noncombantants remaining to sew, smith, fight fires and nurse the wounded, and the king would order the packing and hiding of royal treasures and records.

Nali faltered as he read the last item on the list, giving him command of Harbor defenses, evacuation and provisioning. Nali let the paper fall and looked up, confused.

"I have no idea where to begin."

"None of us do," said the king.

"It'll be difficult, Nali," Arshal said. "The Harbor will receive the first blow of any attack on Sihmad Shal. It's your job to make that landing costly."

"Peshal," Arshal turned to his brother. "You have perhaps the most difficult task. The refuge you choose for noncombatants must be unquestionably safe. We can't spare one soul to guard them. As for the escape route, government employees, shawnsi, and derna are most endangered. If besieged, with no hope for victory, these people must escape."

Resala gasped. "Leave the people leaderless? How dare you!"

"If we must surrender it's safer for everyone if we're gone. They'll direct their energies to our capture. It'll go hard on anyone helping us. If conquered, we'll be killed. If we escape, at least we could lead from exile. I'm not even sure if we'd have a way to escape a siege. Let's hope this is merely an exercise and they find us too strong."

"I need the city's construction plans," Peshal said.

"You'll have them."

"I need a decree granting me authority to do as I will in the Harbor," Nali said, stroking his beard.

"Done," Arshal stated, pacing the room.

"You have a plan, wise one?" Zopher asked, detaching himself from the wall in a fluid motion.

Nali continued pulling his beard, his gaze narrowing. "I've a few ideas. I'll call on Jan, whose knowledge goes a lot deeper than it appears, and naturally Aron Keeper and Reve Pedr. You can't do a thing in the Harbor without Aron, and Pedr's got folks' respect. I'll need every vessel, thus a royal decree. And a decree will calm Aron when I take his lighthouse and commandeer his pilot boat. I'll do my best, but what do we know of defense tactics? We won't hold long."

"Is Sihmad Shal truly in danger?" Resala asked, eliciting exasperated sighs from her brothers. "I mean," she said, her tone prickly. "Perhaps they aim elsewhere? Did they sail north to the Aziaris Sea, or south to the Sea of Simiriel? If south, perhaps Shela's their destination."

"A valid point," Arshal returned. "We've heard references made about Sihma Harbor, and ships reported in Ymmenay Bay. We considered other targets and have warned those provinces, but Sihmad Shal remains the most likely. Mol Azezial expects to surprise us. He'll thrust for the leadership. At least, that's the best tactical move. By cutting the nation off here he'd cripple the country and shatter morale."

"How," Resala pressed, drawing a private smile from the queen, "Do we know when they'll arrive? How will Peshal know when to evacuate. How will we know when to bar the gates?"

Nali was nodding. "We could set a watch on Mania Point."

"With a good wind behind them a fleet would arrive about the same time as a watch rider," Peshal said.

"Why use a rider?" Nali asked, forming his idea as he spoke. "We don't need a long message. Simply, they're here. What if we take a lesson from Aron's lighthouse? Aron can see both the west shore and city from Lone Rock. From the cliffs a watcher on the west can see a warning fire on Mania Point."

"Yes, good idea!" said Arshal. "Not just to warn the city but the entire countryside. We'll need bells in the lowlands, or riders in distant reaches. The first warning can signal sighting. A second when they enter the Harbor. See to it."

They hashed out rudimentary plans late into the night until the stuffy air in the study felt like it would suffocate and the yawns climbed upon each other until they yielded nothing but nonsense as Arshal gazed out over the quiet of pre-dawn over the city. Long Day night should have been raucous with a carnival atmosphere. Games, fest fires and the spirit of young love usually ruled until dawn when revelers finally retired with the rising sun. Instead, an eerie quiet had fallen as Sihmad Shal tossed in a restless sleep troubled by the echoes of the call to arms.

"I wish Cree would wake," Arshal said as he turned from the window. "We have a very long day today," he stated, signaling the end of the meeting. "And possibly for many to come."

Only a few sleepless hours later he found himself trying to carve some order out of the chaos of a city called to war. As he passed the armory in search of a messenger, he stuck his head in a window to see a line of volunteers stretched out the door and around the building as Peshal recorded the name of each volunteer and assigned them to Arshal, Esthen or Zopher. He had turned away young children and the elderly, but directed a number of skilled women to Zopher's unit. Others Peshal sent to Resala to staff hospitals or fire brigades. The sun had barely broken the horizon and it seemed every resident of the city had passed through the armory. In the Harbor, Arshal knew Nali and Jan performed a similar, onerous chore.

The gods' gardens around the palace had never seen such a deluge. Would-be troops dodged ponds or hopped over rows of mid-summer flowers. They fumbled with the clasps of basted cloaks and swapped ill-fitting boiled leather armor. Only the first-comers received daggers, swords, leather armor or bow. Despite the weeks to prepare, the smiths couldn't equip so many so quickly and the racket of the forges struck a backbeat to the chaos.

Recruits fetched decorative swords from over the mantle, hunting bows from behind the door, or raced home to grab kitchen knives from their mothers' hands. To most the armorers issued sticks, or nothing when they ran out of sticks. The handful of volunteers with hunting, fencing or horsemanship skills soon held rank above their fellows and immediately became lost in the mayhem of inexperience training no experience.

"This is ludicrous!" Arshal shouted in frustration as Zopher strode by searching for a wayward group of archers, while Arshal struggled to keep his companies together. "How can we create an army in a day?"

"Told you, cannot be done."

Arshal turned to find Marol appraising the scruffy columns of blank-eyed soldiers. "Oh Marol, help me with this hopeless mess!"

Marol shook his head as he shuffled his bulk from foot to foot. He glanced up at Arshal from the corner of his eye. "I am sorry, Arshal. I like you and Esthen – you learn quick, good boys. But the hypothetical ends. We sail for Otayr today." Marol ignored the way Arshal's mouth had fallen open. "Your city arms openly now. My king sends no word on your request for aid. I know he will not be blind to your troubles, but we can no longer remain on soil arming for war. The consuls from Shiad, Arenh and Shikora depart today as well. I am so sorry, my friend."

"I need your counsel, Marol."

"I know, but I cannot give it. You remain my friend. Maybe a suggestion or two between friends?" Arshal nodded eagerly. "Gardens are fine for two boys playing soldier, but thousands? Take them outside the walls. It matters no more who sees them. Take them into the fields around Shanai. Do not fret over crops. If you do not organize these people, you will see no harvest." Marol pulled Arshal farther from the ears of his soldiers. "Do you remember what I said? Evacuate people who cannot fight or be otherwise useful? You must find safe refuge for them, out of harm's way, yes?" Marol gave him a calculating stare. "I am your friend, yes? I tell you where I live. Maybe someday you come visit?"

Arshal's eyes widened.

"I live near border to Shande, near the small hills north of the Sea of Iyrafael. It is in a great forest of tall pine, only a short ride from Shande. You can smell pine on the wind a day away. It will lead you. I like visitors. My house holds many guests." He gestured at Arshal's sword arm. "You have new strength. Use it wisely. I await your visit greatly." Marol turned, and soon disappeared among the milling soldiers of Shande's fledgling army.

The long day spent trying, mostly failing, to organize an army became a blur as they moved out onto the plow-furrowed plain. There, at least, Arshal could take to Booty's back and better direct the mayhem.

His day didn't end at dusk even as he returned to the palace. He still had training plans to devise and recruits to sort. Late into the night he still worked at his cluttered desk. He stared bleary-eyed at a servant who shook him awake, a stack of parchment slipping from beneath his elbow to the floor.

"What is it?"

"Dawn, Lord. His Majesty summons you to the Long Hall. A Minarian demands an audience."

Arshal quickly slipped on a cloak over his dusty clothes as he hurried to the hall.

Arshal recognized the Minarian who caught his eye in the crowd during the king's address, whose medallion could make the prince's heart pound just to recall it. Though the only Minarian in the city, he stood as if backed up by a thousand armed men. Arshal stood beside his father on the dais, neither taking the throne, nor yielding it.

The Minarian removed a sealed scroll from his leather pouch, turned to Arshal and ignored the king. "Congratulations Prince Regent. His Majesty will be most interested to learn of the temporary change in rule here. I bear the grievance of King Mol Azezial." He broke the seal and unfurled and read from his scroll. "The shawnsi rulers of Shande have oppressed Ea's people, hoarded the world's riches for their personal gain, and falsely claimed divinity. Shals, made of these soils, molded and given this world by their Maker, deserve these lands and destiny. Through deceit you convinced the people that false gods gave you the right to rule. The God of Ea is Ghyldus and Minaria is the true inheritor of Ghyldus' favor. We declare Shande a Minarian Protectorate and demand the shawnsi yield now for the glory of a shal-led governance guided by Minaria. You have until sunset to surrender and turn yourselves in for arrest and trial. We will crush with prejudice any attempt to resist this liberation. These are the words of my lord His Majesty, Mol Azezial, King in Minaria with the guidance of the mighty Ghyldus, God of Ea."

The messenger snapped the scroll, letting it re-roll and threw it on the dais at King Ebon's feet with a scornful smile. The Minarian turned to depart.

"Wait," King Ebon called. He scooped up the scroll and bent over the lamp on the top step of the dais. He unrolled the scroll, as if reaffirming the truth of the messenger's words. Arshal's heart lurched in his chest with fear his father would yield.

The Minarian's sneer quickly turned to surprise. The scroll, dipped into the lamp's flame, ignited and fell away to ash in the still hall.

"Your terms are unacceptable," the king stated, extending a hand toward the door. "Leave, ingrate. One's wrath will be yours." His voice boomed in the empty hall and echoed throughout the palace, falling on the stunned ears of servants and household.

"You make a grave mistake. The peoples of Shande will curse you for the suffering you bring upon them. You will die a cold death!"

Unbidden, Arshal saw a hand in the snow.

"In the name of His Majesty, Mol Azezial, and the Great God of Ea, Ghyldus, we declare war without peace until no shawnsi remains in this land. Shande will be ours, or it will be nothing!" The messenger pulled a strip of black cloth, red gems glittering on it, and flung it at Arshal's feet. He flicked the medallion on his chest so that a spark of red struck Arshal's eyes, then strode from the hall.

Arshal exhaled. It had finally come. He tried to erase the flutter of indecision that rushed him. Could he have averted the declaration of war? He shook his head to silence his mind's complaint and ordered the herald to raise the pennants long buried among the royal clutter.

Thus, an hour after dawn, not quite two days after the call to arms, Sihmad Shal raised beneath its royal blue pennants the black flags, mark of a country challenged to war.

Throughout the city, people fell silent and gathered, weeping as the black pennants unfurled into the cool morning. The quiet of uniform regret, maybe fear, held the city spell-bound while the wind snapped the flags as if in a tempest.

Offices of trade and government shuttered windows and locked doors. Only the forges and the hammers of carpenters broke the dreadful silence. Officials bustled about with records hastily stuffed into undersized casks and hidden away in long-unused niches, while monetary officers loaded carts to overflowing with metals and world currency to spirit them away.

In the Long Hall, Arshal affixed the king's seal, signing his name as Prince Regent, to dozens of scrolls that messengers, bearing black standards, would carry to distant provinces.

On Lone Rock, the lighthouse shone white against the black stone and dark waters. At the top of the narrow tower, Aron Keeper raised a flag. Beneath the royal blue pennant and above the Harbor flag, a black strip of cloth unfurled to twice the others' length.

As the flag crept up the pole, four ships maneuvered to escape the safety of the breakwater. Foreign colors and insignia of the consulates flapped wildly as captains bypassed the pilot boat and soon headed out to sea. Ships awaiting entry came about. Dozens of vessels inside the sea wall prepared to depart, including the lone and conspicuous ship flying the Minarian flag.

In the Harbor, the waterfront fell silent as a mob of fishers, merchants and Shandean sailors gathered on the boardwalk. Some stared after the departing ships and livelihood. Others beat clubs in open palms as they eyed the path to the tender for the Minarian courier ship. As the mob fell upon the returning Minarian messenger, a cheer carried through the village.

On this day, so much darker than any in so many hundreds of years, an odd desperation gripped the city and Harbor. From an unseen source, a flaming arrow struck the rigging of the Minarian ship. A moment's gasp rippled through the crowd, then a cheer as the fire spread, which died away to chilling silence as all realized what they had done, with what bold step they had plunged into their violent and uncertain future. The ship burned to the water line, where the charred timbers hissed their last gasps, her crew leaping into the water, some striking out for The Beach Head, in hope of escaping the dangerous mob on the boardwalk. Solemn now, the people stared at the distant line of open sea in grim anticipation. Only the lap of waves and screech of gulls disrupted the silence. Somewhere out there a fleet drew near.

22: In the Shadow of War

In the narrow crawlspace inside the Fearnia wall, a man welcomed nightfall. He cranked open a vent, gulping in the night, which, though warm and damp with the heat moon, freshened the tepid crawlspace. The racket of war preparations yielded to darkness as he eased free of his confinement. This night he wouldn't slink through the city to gather its news. The sentries grew alert and afraid of shadows and darkness. Soon he would have other duties and shed the imposing wall, no longer taunted by the scents wafting from the markets, bakeries, and kitchens, when he survived on strips of jerky and stale water from the fire bucket.

He stretched, a silent shadow unfolding in the wall's recesses. Echoes chased, but he knew no one strayed near. These rooms once housed guests. Guests had left the sparkling city.

He grasped for the comfort of the triangular medallion he wore on his chest. Only elite Eidhalt warriors who served King Mol Azezial and the Great One wore medallions like this. Though no Eidhalt, nor swordsman, only a humble and honored Pladde servant, he felt blessed to serve. His accomplice wore this very medallion the day he leaped from the upper wall. He felt an unspeakable honor to stroke the hot metal, the burning red stones, mumbling words he'd learned under pain of Verdred's loving lash, though they remained senseless gibberish to him. Verdred, devoted Champion of the God of Ea – a mute of His making – taught him the words. When Verdred had beaten all the truth from him, even his own name, and he, but a lowly Pladde, had ordered the words as he must, Verdred praised him and the power of his god pulsed from the medallion Verdred bestowed, the medallion now branded on him.

Now, as the cadence of words became his lifebeat, the gems beneath his fingers burned and sparked. He stood rigid, the

184

presence of the God of Ea flooding him, entering through his fingertips, racing up his arm to smash into his skull where the humble servant stored all that he had seen that day. Long minutes later praise resounded behind his eyes. He sank to his knees. Tears streaked his face as blistered fingers gripped the cooling medallion, the imprint of which scarred his palm. As he gasped, hot face falling against cool stone, he felt the happiness, the reassurance, that he served as the eyes and ears of the Great God of Ea in the enemy camp.

In the northeastern highlands a few days' hard ride from Sihmad Shal a small campfire went unnoted by neighbors in the empty range. A half-dozen Eidhalt warriors stood motionless as they looked upon a medallion. In their minds, black-gloved fingers shaped orders. The Eidhalt observers knew how to read those fingers and call forth those images of Verdred. Whether far from their commander – the signs projected across the vastness of Ea – or in person complemented by Verdred's silent and shadowy countenance, the Eidhalt would stand riveted by those fingers. They knew the consequences of failure.

The warriors shifted as the dream in their minds, the searing gem-like eyes, faded into a red mist.

"So, we have our orders," a man stated.

Though the vastness of Shande and all of Minaria lay between them and their commander, they kept their voices low. If mute Verdred could make words appear in his hands by staring into the glow of a gem, perhaps he could see into their most private thoughts. The elite Eidhalt kept no thoughts but their service to god and king.

With a wicked grin, a man tossed the contents of his cup into the fire to send up a spume of ash and smoke. "Verdred throws us a bone," he said. "To thank us for unsurpassed service. Kill the upstart prince? That child runs to his nurse for a breast when it thunders."

A round of chuckles concurred. "But if they fear attack now, will he be guarded?" another asked as they stowed their cooking gear: a knife, cup and pouch of osfothye leaves.

"Their eyes are on the sea!" He drew his dagger with a flourish and slowly ran its length a breath from his neck. "And what protection will he find but more milksops who do not know the sharp end of a sword. Why Lagdche worries about this lamb is not for me to ponder. But I, for one, can already taste the juicy substitute for mutton."

Their laughter rose into the night as they kicked out their cook fire and took to mounts heavy with the trappings of Minaria's elite warriors. Their horses' hooves beat Shande's northeastern uplands as if already conquerors.

In the sweltering humidity of the heat moon, Peshal and Arshal pored over a crude map of Ea spread across a table in the high tower of the Window of the Sun. Arshal gave his youngest brother the impossible task to find safe refuges for the government in exile, if it came to it, and for noncombatants. Arshal tapped the map with a terse rhythm as they leaned over the table.

"I don't see it, Pesh. This is the best you can do? Lharan?"

Peshal glared at him then shrugged. "You're asking the impossible: to move hundreds of people unseen to some safe haven where no one will notice them? We need a large and fortified settlement in a region otherwise sparsely populated to not draw attention to ourselves. They won't expect that direction, a world away and near on top of them. Eithur has a military structure in place. The route appears passable, and the countryside has plenty of resources to feed us. The only other option is east toward Iyrafael, far more populated and where they will look first."

"It assumes the region isn't already lost and that there's some means of travel. You need to come up with a better plan." Arshal said as he looked through Peshal's notes. "This tunnel, though, that's a fantastic discovery. After all these years!"

"It must have been a construction tunnel. Or maybe always intended as an escape. I didn't have time to explore all of it, but I think there's room to hide stores there without risk, or even use it as a route to flank an enemy."

Arshal nodded, his attention already on the last pile of notes. "And the other trek."

"Eight thousand people provisioned for, I'm guessing, three weeks to cross rivers, marsh, and forest. Did Marol expect so many guests? How many old and ill will survive? And what will they live on when they get there? It's a grueling journey to expect of them, Arshal."

"Believe me, I don't want this. They'll be safer. Here they're a burden, depleting supplies and easy prey. But eight thousand. There must be more than that! I see children everywhere! How can we feed so many with disrupted supplies or even a siege?"

"Many sent their young to relatives in the country. They're all pretty sure the battle will stay in the city and Harbor. Others volunteered for needed tasks. Besides," Peshal held Arshal's gaze. "Lead even more on such a journey? It's a disaster to lead any, insanity."

"Perhaps idle merchant ships?"

"There's no idle merchant ships. They defend the Harbor. Besides, you'd need an armada to transport so many. We'd be refused by all ports and it's not like we can just beach a fleet of ships on some shore and expect people to go scrambling off through the surf. If Marol can offer a refuge without Otayran government approval, then they'll be safe as long as the Minarians have their war only with us. East is the only direction and that by land."

"Could we go to Otayr instead of Lharan?"

"Everyone knows we're evacuating noncombatants and that route will leave a trail an infant could follow. Otayr's safe because those folks don't threaten invaders. But the royal household and its officers? We need a route unexpected and untraceable."

"How long do you need?"

"A week."

"You have until tomorrow. Convince more to go. Order them if you must!"

"Tomorrow! I promise nothing. Why did you give me these responsibilities? I'm too soft-hearted to force people from their homes and rip children from their parents. Esthen should be doing this. He has the more brutal nature." Peshal's teasing drew only a thin smile.

Arshal turned to stare out the window in dismissal, leaving Peshal to gather his notes and slip out.

In the cold of the next day's gloaming, glum, tear-stained faces lined the Sijway. Hands reached for one last touch as family and friends trudged by with carts piled high. Peshal led a column near ten thousand strong out of the gates into Shanai, his prancing bay oblivious to the somber mood of the day. The sun broke the horizon as they turned east, the morning promising another hot day as summer slipped into the second week of the heat moon.

Infants wailed, cart wheels squealed, hounds bayed and a

donkey brayed, yet the silence of a death rite clung to the glum procession. Tearful gazes fixed on the rutted road flanked by farm fields and small hamlets that would grow more sparse as they trudged east.

Peshal fretted over a mental checklist, certain he'd forgotten something vital in the rush to depart. Milk-cows and fowl protested the forced march. Cured hams, dried fish, grain sacks, bags full of produce and sow skins full of water hung from carts stuffed with blankets, tools, hunting and fishing gear, cook pans, tinder and fuel. Fisher's tarpaulins protected dry goods and doubled as shelter. Enterprising elders had loaded bags and pouches of seed, roots, and bulbs into nooks and crannies against the unthinkable possibility their absence might take them through a growing season. Peshal reviewed it all, but couldn't imagine anything he'd forgotten as the city faded into the distance.

Caught up in his inventory, he startled at the pound of hooves from behind. He recognized Arshal's figure, new blue military cape flying behind him as Booty labored up the long slope they had just climbed. Peshal urged the bay to canter the length of the column, hoping Arshal would halt this impossible trek.

"You forgot something," Arshal said as he reined in. Peshal felt his face go red. "First, if you don't return in time, where's the tunnel, how do we travel and where do we meet?"

"Wait for me in the storerooms. I'll be there," Peshal said, not wanting to admit that aside from a hazy destination he had yet to figure the rest out. The evacuation had taken priority, and he expected the city would still await its nebulous attack, or even be standing down, on his return. Even if a siege, they had time to plan.

Arshal frowned but didn't challenge him. Instead, he pulled a blue cloth from inside his shirt. "They should have this." Arshal held a royal blue pennant with the Dyndevas coat of arms embroidered on it. "It's my vow: I'll lead them home myself." Arshal grasped his brother's arm in parting then turned Booty's head back to the west.

Without another word, Peshal trotted to the head of the column to fasten the blue pennant to a protruding stave on the lead cart, vowing to himself he'd stop at nothing to return home in time. Peshal couldn't think about anything more pressing than finding Marol's lodge among the pines.

The blue pennant heartened the travelers and the pace picked up as someone began to hum a song, soon joined by the voices of thousands with Peshal's clear baritone leading them east.

As the days of the heat moon fled, the people of Sihmad Shal buried their fears in labor. Garden earth filled sacks that reinforced barricades made from idled delivery wagons. Pond water filled wash tubs commandeered by fire brigades. Cattle and horses herded into the upper levels of the city fed on the gardens as cooks guessed the beasts' weight against the size of their pots. Government offices served as shelters and kitchens as Shanai evacuated inside the walls. The kitchens made jerky and hardtack, dried berries and fruits, and filled barrels with pickled eggs and vegetables to feed the defenders and support a siege.

Beyond the outermost wall, trampled fields hosted drilling troops and sported small tent cities for those recruits trickling in from the countryside to heed the call to arms. Though three weeks had passed since the call, grocers, artisans and clerks still didn't resemble an army. Those recruits suited to soldiering soon became squad leaders, but Marol's lessons in theory defied becoming practice. Minaria had kept a standing army for more than a thousand years, prided in its military history, weaned its children on soldiering and revered the traditions of war. Most of the recruits still practiced with sticks and pitchforks.

In a trampled and dusty field outside the city walls, Esthen threw back his head and laughed from his belly, arms reaching around himself as if he could hold the laughter in. Instead. it escaped in louder and louder guffaws as Zopher pulled himself to his feet, dusted himself off, and grinned sheepishly at the audience of chuckling soldiers.

Esthen wiped his eyes, leaving behind streaks of grime. "Oh, don Saran, a wonderful demonstration, but I don't think we got it. Would you please repeat it?"

"You like that, Esthen? You thought that amusing?" Zopher returned with a laugh. Esthen nodded as dusty Zopher rubbed his seat for the ring of laughing soldiers.

"I believe you were demonstrating the proper way to seat a horse?" Esthen's attempts to sober his expression merely contorted it.

Zopher gave him a wry smile. "Let me put a burr in your girth and see how long you stay on," Zopher challenged, holding up the offending sharp sticker for all to see.

More laughter erupted with a round of oh-hos as the trick came unmasked. A few more chuckles greeted Zopher as he checked for burrs with exaggerated care.

The prank broke the tension, as the captains intended. No one could guess Esthen's next move, and this, and the way he remained familiar with his soldiers, endeared him to them. The arrogant prince who had clung to his aristocratic clique seemed to find a niche as the commander of troops in a land known for peace.

Unlike Arshal, whose duties brought him back inside the city each night, Esthen and Zopher pitched tents beside farmers, coopers and teamsters, joined their games and boasts, or helped to cart a barrel of ale into the camps amidst hushes and giggles. Encouraging competition against each other felt more real than some nebulous enemy. That's where the exchange of pranks began. The rivalry brought pride to those boasting they had signed on with Esthen or Zopher.

As Zopher mounted his horse and the laughter faded, instruction continued as the tension built and the black pennants flapped in the west wind.

Within the city walls no lesser tension surrounded the preparations. In a shady courtyard in a quiet borough, weavers, dyers, and tailors performed their tasks with ever more precision, the youths, women and elders working in a silence punctuated by the ominous racket of the smithies.

Among them, Resala massaged a lotion into burning, chapped hands. A light stain of blue dye clung to her nails and outlined the spirals of her fingertips. The small cuts and needle pricks remained dark. Beside her, lines of cloth dripped blue puddles.

She tilted her head back at the sound of someone behind her. The queen regarded her with an austere expression, then gathered Resala's hair and began to pin it.

"You let yourself fall ragged," Queen Sala whispered.

Resala shrugged, working the lotion up to her wrists. "For whom do I dress? My vanity shouldn't come before my work." She blew on her hands a moment before picking up her shears to continue the almost endless task of cutting bandages and cloaks.

"I do not speak of vanity. You must set an example for others when they feel most hopeless." Queen Sala said into her daughter's ear while pinning long, fair locks out of Resala's face.

Resala stole a glance at others working nearby, noticing how some looked her way, as if judging their own work and composure against hers. She tilted her head again to look at her mother.

"Do you really think it makes a difference?"

The queen gave her a sage nod. "If the people see despair in your eyes, your clothing disheveled or your hair mussed as if you no longer care," Sala plucked a wavy strand from Resala's face and tucked it into the pin, "Then they think the situation bad indeed if the princess looks so hopeless. We must wear a cheerful face and work harder than anyone. Perhaps people will find strength through us, and trust your brother's decisions." Sala twisted the last loose strand of hair around the rest and gathered it with a scrap of blue cloth. "There. See? We have our own uniform."

The queen turned and her daughter laughed to see her mother's salt and pepper hair pulled back and held by a blue ribbon.

Resala noted another woman study the hairstyle then bind her own hair with a strip of blue fabric. It became a game as they worked: to chastise others who arrived out of uniform and soon even the errand boys bound back their hair or wore blue head bands.

Resala studied the queen from the corner of her eye as she cut and folded and gathered some more. Queen Sala gave her a private smile as they took in the change the little strip of cloth made. Hands worked faster. Chatter and teasing came from some who had worked silently. Resala paused to suck a cut finger. She promised herself she would remember the queen's lesson as she joined the gossip and soon giggled with the others, enjoying a camaraderie unlike any she had known. For a time, she forgot the purpose of the cloth she cut.

At the city's heart, the king labored with no less dedication, now that the responsibility of war planning fell to others.

In an anteroom of the reception hall, King Ebon's hands brushed smooth satin as he tucked his formal jeweled headpiece into a casket. Sapphires glinted from the end of long strands of stellan that hung like hair from the crown. A stellan circlet arched upward at the brow, nestling a giant blue gemstone set in a star-like design that recalled the shape of shawnsi birthmarks. The whole gleamed as bright as its crafting day. He stroked the fine cloth, remembering his coronation day. It stood out fresh: the carriage, the cheering subjects, the royal officers bedecked in their formal attire; the pageantry of horses and escorts trotting apace with bard and trumpeter as he rode to the doors of the palace where Cree recited the words binding Ebon Dyndevas to this land.

King Ebon shook his head, looking around the room where bare spaces on walls and floors clashed with his memories of the palace's warmth and comfort, fullness, richness. The palace became a stranger as he emptied it of its furnishing. He remembered Cree describing the palace as it first emerged on a hill overlooking the plain, at the time not knowing the Visionary spoke from memory. It seemed they travelled backward in time. As they emptied the palace, it again became a barren place in the shadow of war.

He sighed and closed the casket. The drab box captured and concealed the last bit of brightness from the room. He took a last glance around before hefting the casket to his shoulder and locking the door behind.

Only a shout distant from the King of Shande, within the city's walls, near the city's heart, he performed the God of Ea's will. A medallion cooled to the touch against his chest as he took a deep breath to calm his rapid heartbeat. About him he'd gathered documents filched before the Shandeans could stow them, as well as other notes of his own on the city's strengths and weaknesses, not the least this wall he'd made his home, and the keys to enter it. He knew too well those least-guarded entries, the ones by which Eidhalt could enter the city and destroy her leaders. He smiled to himself, knowing he assured his place in the God of Ea's heart. Eidhalt had no need to fear Shandean defenses.

He knew, too, that beyond the city walls, pounding hooves would beat the night. Dark-clad horsemen, red and orange tails streaming from dark helms, raced across the uplands of Kalilia on their way to the city. He knew, because he called them, could see the image of them in his head, just as his god placed it there.

They raced down a slope and crashed into little rivulets feeding the Whittea River, sparkles of water rushing upward to greet the light of a hazy moon. The figures remained in shadow as they continued their race, heedless of the terrain. He knew red and orange warming blankets muffled the jangle of brass trappings beneath, because he should remember that. The finest of Minaria's steeds raced against the darkness, arched tails like pennants unfurled, curved necks stretched, they seemed held back from their true potential as riders leaned over braided manes and their spare mounts followed without the need of leads.

The Shandean king and his sons feared ships and an assault from the west. Even as the youngest prince marched eastward at the head of a straggling exodus of old, ill, young and weak, he followed the churned trail of Eidhalt sent to annihilate the sons of Ebon.

23: Prophecy

As each day passed, uncertainty mounted atop deepening dread. Then it all came crashing in. Scanning the city's preparations from the Window of the Sun, Arshal glimpsed a barely discernible spark of light on the distant shore beneath the bluffs of Mania Point.

"Gods above, we're not ready!" he gasped, raising his gaze to where he imagined the gods dwelled. "Give us time!" He closed his eyes, begging for some miracle to delay the inevitable, bending his thoughts in an appeal to stop the wind.

The sound of footfalls on the stone steps of the tower disturbed him. Then came an urgent knocking on the tower door. Throwing a last glance toward the harbor where the red lighthouse lamp now blazed, he saw a sign of hope. The black pennants on the towers fell limp. For just the barest moment, the blue pennants still flapped wildly in the turbulent west wind, then lay still, concealing the black pennants beneath them.

"Thank you," he whispered, almost weeping as the wind whistling in the towers fell silent. An odd exhaustion crept into his limbs, as if his fear and urgency had drained him like some match with a superior opponent.

He yanked the door open to find an agitated servant pacing. "My Lord, Cree awakes!" The man dared grasp his prince by the arm and lead him to the Visionary's rooms, where Cree sat upright in bed, face pinched and tired.

"An eventful day," Cree said in a rumbling voice Arshal had missed.

"What did you learn, Cree? What will happen to us?" Arshal demanded without preamble as he knelt beside the Visionary's bed.

"I learned much, and nothing. I did not see all and do not remember all I saw. I was not meant to," Cree said, pausing for so long Arshal feared he had fallen back into his osfothye dreams. "I wish I had not sought these visions," he continued at last. "War will never end; peace will never endure, until the world we stand upon is destroyed." Arshal sat back on his heels, his mouth falling open. "It is the legacy of Fyraer and Terremar. Envy and ambition will always challenge peaceful stability, each skirmish a passion that builds into a consumptive thing that feeds upon itself. Ea's tribes will fracture, each as certain of its principles as it is evil in its methods. For there can never be one truth when both have done wrong against the other. A paradox. In the end, ego and greed will conquer the apathy and ignorance that sustains peace. The portent of the future smells of death."

"So hopeless and pointless? Should we just give up to avert some paradox? It's ludicrous. It's wrong!"

"I never said do anything." He held the prince's gaze. "I only report what I think it means, what I think I saw. You must fight the battles because our beliefs require it and you cannot abandon the people who need your leadership. Each generation fights its battles and, in their wake, leaves more dismay, more anger, and more hate to carry to the next generation. It is why other lands still fight their wars and now why one comes for us. Needing to find answers for the pain it has inflicted upon itself it seeks others to blame. Know this: you cannot turn back, and you will find no glory as Esthen perceives it. The lessons of history are there for us to avoid the same mistakes. And yet, it is that history that people turn to when they seek a scapegoat for their troubles. You must defend Shande, but you cannot defeat Fyraer, ever. He, too, is part of the fabric of Ea. To do so would throw all that Is out of balance. Yet, you must try. Thus, the paradox, the futility of the effort, the wrongness." He rested a pale hand on Arshal's arm, his veins like dark ridges at sunset. "Your future remains concealed. Perhaps I saw what could be if you fail. One can assume one sees the inevitable when viewing only the possible. I saw what I saw: a world torn by war and petty rivalry. Hopeless people crippled by apathy. Perhaps you will prevent this future. I sought answers but found only futility. All these days you awaited my guidance and on the day sails crest the horizon I am worthless to you."

Cree again fell silent, his eyes closed. Arshal moved to rise, thinking the Visionary slept. The seer's hand gripped his arm.

"You remain a dark page, a place into which I cannot see. Always remember that each action you take, every decision, is like a pebble in a pond. It will bear upon the future, even if it takes centuries for the ripple to reach them."

Arshal could only nod as he took his leave. The despair he heard in Cree's prophecy sapped the strength from his limbs. No matter what he did, he was doomed. And this, the day watchers on the western coasts at last sighted an enemy fleet.

After a week of fitful winds left the distant fleet mostly becalmed, a great moist gasp had again filled the sails, pulling it swiftly over the horizon hidden by Mania Point – the headland more than a day's journey north and west of the Harbor. Nali needed every moment of that delay. Yet, he was still performing some of those tasks deemed most important two days after the fleet regained the wind, slight as it was. Any moment it could round the point. A month had sped by since the declaration of war, and still preparations were incomplete as the last week of the heat moon approached. Nali almost looked forward to the day he would finally see them; at least the terrible waiting would end. Each night he thought it was the night they would finally arrive under cover of darkness. Each day dawned with still seas.

In the near calm of the sheltered harbor, Nali tugged on the oars of his little boat, fatigued muscles straining as he helped haul a raft out toward the dead reef leading to the lighthouse. With every pull against the rope's slack, he felt the wrench of his arms as his little boat crawled farther. From the corner of his eye, he could see the two other craft where oarsmen labored against groaning oarlocks to pull the bulky raft.

The guide on the raft, Jan's son Jali, lost bottom and could no longer help steer the ungainly floats. He made inept efforts to use his pole as a rudder as the raft limped ahead.

To their right, the lighthouse reached up starkly white from its black base. The warning fire atop it extinguished, only the black flag flew from it now. Nali pulled, a swell of blisters sprouting in his palms.

Aron waited in the shoaling waters ahead to help anchor the float to the dead reef, a submerged bar that acted like a bridge to the lighthouse during low tide. Small swells rose to pass over the shallows, slapping Aron, who stood with an impatient scowl on his face, feet braced apart and arms akimbo. And all the effort would be worthless if the Minarians didn't arrive in darkness. Nali counted on the night to hide Aron's lighthouse, leading ships to the dead reef where a false light Aron made for the raft would be lit. Aron thought him a fool to make assumptions about a fleet that could arrive during the day and they with no better ideas for Harbor defense. But with Aron's every protest at the waste of Harbor resources, the cost of labor, or viability of any idea Aron hadn't personally had a hand in, Nali held up the decree signed in Arshal's bold hand. If they failed, it would be on Nali.

Jali again found bottom as they neared the eroding reef. Nali sighed with utter exhaustion when they dropped the four anchor lines onto the porous bar, Aron diving into the cold water to set the hooks in the jagged coral.

Nali caught his breath looking back at his town. The empty piers stood a stark reminder of the state of war. Ant-sized figures coated the bridge across the Rigannon River with grease and pitch, while others did the same with the docks. Merchants shuttered storefronts and hauled goods away. He thought he recognized Jan directing the saturation of the wooden boardwalk with grease and oil. If Shande held, Nali couldn't imagine the mess they'd have to clean up.

Nali maneuvered his boat closer to the little raft where young Jali tightened the slack in the anchor lines and double-checked the pillar of wood surrounded by red glass. Nali hoped the deceptive light would lead the enemy to believe they headed for the channel until too late to avoid running aground.

"Now you know to fire this as soon as you see a light on the west shore?" Nali asked as he released the stern line he'd used to pull the raft. "Whatever happens, once you light this you hop in that little rowboat and get to shore as fast as you can. You're like a white gull on a black rock out here, 'bout as open a target as anything."

Jali swallowed hard, blue eyes wide against a shock of red hair and scatter of freckles his mam gave him. At fourteen, he had claimed himself the man to tackle the job, refusing Jan's attempts to send him away with Peshal, just as Nali's father insisted the family Drulson stay together in hiding in the country. Now the youth wore his doubts as he gauged the distance he'd have to row, swim or wade to reach safety.

Nali chucked the boy on the arm before heading for shore while Aron paddled out to supervise a steady migration of boats waiting to tie on to their fellows in a line across the dredged channel. Fishers and sailors said their last goodbyes to their crafts, prepared to scuttle the vessels the moment the false harbor light flared. Large merchant vessels maneuvered to block the deepest section, while smaller boats trailed off toward the shallows and shore.

Aron fought the plan even to its execution, certain they would stop the enemy on the reef itself. Sihma Harbor would have to repay all the merchants for their lost vessels, for essentially no return, not to mention, the cost and effort of dredging the harbor and replacing fishing boats that were folks' livelihood. Most of Aron's argument echoed resentment that a younger and less experienced man new to his robes suddenly had authority over the Harbor's senior officials who should control the Harbor's defenses. Yet, Nali, king's confidante, had earned his First Degree. He admitted sinking the ships might be a futile gesture. They hoped to make it a hard landing. They all knew the Harbor's recruits could not stop trained soldiers once ashore.

As he neared shore, Nali saw that Olna and Cookie had supervised well some of the last preparations: black cloth hung in the windows of still-occupied buildings, and a stream of Harbor residents moved toward the countryside with family treasures, food, and anything they could consider weapons strapped to hand carts or livestock. The village's silence felt ominous. Nali took a deep draw off the wineskin stowed in his boat, hoping the drink would unbind his throat and let him again find his breath. What fools to hope the Harbor would be anything but a minor annoyance to the Minarians?

As night deepened over the high cliffs beneath the north wall of Sihmad Shal, a cluster of shadows detached from the wall to meet the hesitant silhouette approaching through the darkness like a hare tiptoeing around a fox's lair.

The dark figures huddled around the Pladde man, who shrank from them as if he faced pestilence. He handed them the keys, maps of the city and its passageways and in a low voice detailed all the niches he had discovered in many months of ferreting out the city's secrets: from the stairway to the tower the prince inhabited, to directions to caches and hiding places he found, the city oblivious and ignorant of its spies.

Hoping for the recognition his due – some sort of honorary membership in the Eidhalt or appointment to some plum post – instead His humble servant gained martyrdom. The Eidhalt repaid his months of service in the city with the swiftness and surprise of his death. As they rolled his body from the cliff into the sea below, the Eidhalt slipped under the cover of Sihmad Shal's buttressed sea-facing wall to wait. If the princes died too soon, the people would take new leaders. When the people despaired, they would strike. With laughter drowned by the surf of a freshened sea wind, unheard from unguarded walls, they snapped at Shande's defense, victory in sight.

24: A Fog in the Harbor

The half moon lit Sihma Harbor's waterfront with unusual intensity and sent moonbeams bounding off the water as a clear night settled over Shande. A slight figure rowed a slow path across the harbor toward the dark silhouette of a raft reaching just above the horizon of gleaming water. Short arms barely lifted the oars far enough from the water to clear, nor pushed them deeply enough to pull. Instead, he swished along, loudly. As the boat neared the raft, a low whistle and laugh carried over the distance.

"I can tell my supper's a comin' now!" a voice called from the darkness. "Sounds like you're bringin' a whole fleet there, Bert."

Bertal Nalison yanked the oars, flinging water out in front of him as he zigzagged closer. "Shut yer mouth, Jali, or I'll jus' turn 'round and you can eat floaters for supper!" Bertal plucked a small dead fish from the water and lobbed it at the older boy. He giggled as Jali's silhouette dodged the rotting carcass.

"Boy, don't you know I'm workin' hard out here?" Jali grumbled as Bertal stowed the oars to pull out a basket giving off the aroma of the chowder Jali's mother made. Bertal lingered over it a moment before handing it over.

"I don't think they'll ever come." Bertal hid a yawn behind his hand. "The watchers' must'a seen wrong. It can't take two days to get 'round Mania Point."

The novelty wearing thin, Bertal wanted to move on to better adventures. He even looked forward to running south along the river to Cousin Tel's to join his mam and sisters, as soon as the enemy arrived.

The moonlit waters to the west darkened, the deep shadows of the western bluffs reaching toward them as the moon descended.

"Think a me, will ya!" Jali said. "Been out here on this stupid wood pile with nothin' to do but sit for hours listenin' to the sailors in them boats." He waved an arm toward the shadowy line of craft spanning the harbor. "All they do is carouse all night, that and the waves. It's terrible –"

"Hist!"

"Don't hiss at me."

"Look there!" Bertal pointed toward the sea. Against the dark wall of the western bluffs a small lamp shone near the mouth of the harbor. "Quick! Light that thing an' let's get out of here!" Bertal shrieked, pulling the oars out and tossing the chowder-filled basket into the bottom of the boat. Frightened glances noted the brightness of the moon silvering the shore and ships. The false lighthouse wouldn't work if the enemy could see the shining white pillar of the real lighthouse many yards to the east.

Jali fumbled with the tinderbox, clumsy fingers trying to light the oil-soaked logs and bracken, forgetting in his haste the woodcraft his father had taught him. When the logs caught, smoking at first as the oil burned with a greasy smell, Bertal untied two of the raft's anchor lines so it would swing and bob with the waves to mimic the turning wheel of the lighthouse light. Jali eased a grate over the top that kept the flames from rising above the glowing red glass.

"Hope the fuel lasts," Jali said as he jumped into the boat with a loud thump and took the oars to row with a fury. Half heard at first above the swell of water over the reef, but growing in volume, they heard the splintering wood and gushing water as one-by-one silent sailors scuttled their boats across the harbor. In all the noise, an eerie silence fell.

In his bed, Arshal rolled over in the dark and sighed. "What is it, Nali?" No answer came.

He sat up. He could swear he had heard Nali call. Groping for his slippers, the prince wrapped a robe about him and went to the window, expecting, as usual, to see nothing of concern. This time the view made his heart skip. From this angle he couldn't see the false harbor light. In the distance he saw the small watch light at the base of the headland and thought he discerned clusters of suspended light, no doubt attached to ships. His breath locked up. He didn't feel the dread he thought he would, more of a calm. No more nagging doubt. No more debates about the rights and wrongs. At last, he confronted his fate sailing around the point.

Then he realized he could see the top of the lighthouse on

Lone Rock: a silhouette in the sparkle of moonlit harbor. If he saw a silhouette, those looking east would see the white tower pushing upward to its dark lamp. Closing his eyes and tilting his head back, he gripped the sill with frustration. They counted on crippling the enemy before ever it gained the shore.

He froze to discover Cree stood at his elbow.

"You forget all your lessons," Cree admonished.

"It's hopeless. Look at the moonlight! All Nali's plans!"

"Child!" Cree turned from him. "You surrender before the fight. What kind of leader are you? King Ebon would not throw his hands up in defeat –"

"What can I do about it? Should I fly out the window and cover the moon?"

"Yes! Did you attend any of your lessons? You are descended from Terremar. His daughter rules the moon, yes? It is a family thing."

Arshal stared at Cree, wondering if the games Cree played with his mind under the guise of training really had any bearing here.

"Go inside. Think. Concentrate. Feel the thing you desire and make it come to life!" Cree's voice was like the rumble of surf in his ear. "Think. Call upon your strength. Conjure up what you want to see. Find the spot: the world inside that rules the outside."

"Do you think I can do it?"

Cree inclined his head.

Arshal cinched his robe about his waist as he ran from the room, his slippered feet slapping the flagstone corridors as he dodged crates and stores piled in the passageways. When at last he reached the Window of the Sun, he stood breathless, staring out on the vista below. From this vantage, he spied the snaking line of scuttled boats he hadn't seen before, the false harbor light, and the barren waterfront aglow in the moon's spare light. He concentrated on the moon, but it wouldn't darken. His prayers had stopped the west wind. Why wouldn't the moon cloak herself?

Instead, he found himself picturing a concealing fog. He concentrated until his temples pounded and his breath came in short gasps. Remembering Cree's lessons, so abstract in the giving, he stepped into his mind-fog, craning his neck to see above it where stars winked and the upper layers of fog took on an eerie opalescent glow. He reached his hand out in front of him and studied it, watching it flit in and out of the strange vision.

Damp mist curled about his fingers, leaving them clammy and chilled. Blowing at the clinging wisps, he watched them float by and part to reveal things he needed to see. He pulled the fog close to him, wrapping himself in fine mist, then like a cloak, spread it upon the water at his feet, leaving the shore clear and sharp in contrast. A light breeze threatened to enter and blow the wisps to sea, but he pushed his hands from his body, palms wide to hold back the wind, and watched the fog settle in thicker.

With disarming facility, he stepped outside his mind and imagination to view the strange sight below. This thing he created from within, this thing even Cree didn't know he could do, had made a thick cloud layer on the water, ending short of the Harbor bluffs. The false light glowed a misty red to the west, the lighthouse hidden. At the mouth of the harbor, the fleet of lights lay becalmed, the sails falling limp and gray in the moonlight. They moved forward yet from momentum, and Arshal sensed, more than saw, oar ports open now that the vessels left the heavy swell of open sea. The fleet formed up and marched into the thick white bank. He barely felt Cree or servants tending him, or the mantle draped over his shoulders to ward off the damp of fog that seemed to swirl about his legs as he stood in the high tower. He didn't know how many hours the tips of the enemy's masts loomed through the top pearly layer of fog in their steady march along the western shore of the harbor, marked only by the lonely lamp topping each veiled mast.

The moon had fallen low and dawn lay only a few hours off when the mast tips closed on the red-tinged bank. As his vision narrowed to just the ships themselves, the fog fell away behind them, dissolving into snaking white tendrils along the waves, an island of mist moving along the water with them. Then, as he studied their line of progress, he saw the first mast light stop short and waver, then tilt to the side. He half fancied he heard the shouts, the splinter and crunch of wood, and the frenzied warning cries as several more masts stopped and tilted toward the first or spun wildly away. The ships behind milled like leaderless sheep awaiting a direction.

Tentatively, the remaining upright masts moved parallel to the shoal toward the line of scuttled ships. As the fog bank followed, it cleared around the grounded war ships where Arshal sensed scurrying warriors clambering through the surf, their equipment already rusting in the surging brine. A swirling patch of mist detached itself from the fogbank and crept toward shore, where it lurked around the bridge over the Rigannon River.

A thrill of victory coursed through him when he saw the remaining masts falter and run aground on the scuttled ships. The fog dispersed, wafting toward shore as the moon's last light, glowing orange as it neared the horizon, revealed fires being set to burn the scuttled vessels to the waterline. He knew enemy warriors piled into tenders that would pass over the shoal as soon as the scuttled craft burned.

Hearing footsteps and the squeak of the door behind him, Arshal turned from the view, the fog clearing. The servant looked from Arshal to the distant Harbor and back, his awe-filled expression bordering fear. Arshal gave him an impatient gesture.

"My Lord, the Visionary said you have orders?"

Arshal rubbed aching muscles in his neck. "Yes, I suppose I should," he said, his voice barely audible. He tried to shake off a sudden, terrible fatigue as he turned his back on the servant and stared out the window, studying the picture for any changes since his attention turned. "Send word to Esthen and Zopher, and give the order to bar the gates when their troops are within. And fire the final warning beacons," he said as he rebuilt the fog bank in his mind, shaping and molding its misty walls as a barricade upon which to fall back.

Nali's overwhelming sense of smallness at the sight of the false harbor light grew to awe when a thick fog rolled in. It came, he sensed, in answer to his plea for help. Instead of thinking of the gods he would thank, he turned toward Sihmad Shal with his gesture of thanks, not altogether sure why he did so. With a terse word, he ordered the Harbor's barricades readied and sent all but the hardiest and most skilled fighters to the city, and the last noncombatants to flee, including his own son now running for Cousin Tel's. What remained to be done by those few hundreds left required stoicism, not numbers.

The hours it took for the ships to grope through the fog passed like days. Despite his impatience for an end to the waiting, when he heard the cries of sailors close at hand and amplified by the foggy silence, then the splinter of ship hulls grounding on the reef, he thought he might never breathe again.

As they huddled behind a barricade of wagons, casks and crates while Menarian soldiers floundered through the tide on their way to shore, frightened faces turned to Nali, awaiting his cue. Those nearest pressed closer, as if the derna, dressed in his drab, pitch-stained fisherman's gear, could protect them. His unit crouched behind an overturned dung wagon thrown up to block the road and common at the end of the boardwalk. Behind them, the road curved along the banks of the Rigannon to the bridge, crossing near the barge docks. Another barricade, at the bridge, would aid their retreat up the scarp to the fields outside the city.

Nali glanced up at a sharp laugh. Jan stood atop the roof of his inn, nocking an arrow. Aron lit it. Jan released the arrow, which reached for the wounded ships on the reef. Falling short, dark waves snuffed it. He nocked another and with a greater pull, adjusting his trajectory, shot. Aron clapped Jan across the back as fire broke out on a ship.

Aron and Jan scurried to another building, joined by Pedr as arrows thunked onto the roof they had abandoned. Pedr and Jan ignited their arrows from the same spark, firing another ship, and then another. Nali smiled, tight-lipped. Any dent in the enemy forces mattered. Every machine, soldier or supply destroyed or damaged meant one less that could assail Sihmad Shal. At least some of his defenders didn't stand frozen in fear.

He felt a grip on his arm and turned to follow the gaze of his companion. Having reached shore, the first enemy ranks spread out along the boardwalk. They flitted in and out of the fog as they stumbled into barricades. Nali took a tighter hold on his club and reached for the reassurance of the dagger tucked in his belt. He tapped a young man next to him and pointed to a torch readied just beyond the barricade. The frightened defender scurried out and crouched, awaiting the signal. As the enemy gathered in ranks on the boardwalk, Nali surveyed the number still fighting the surf and the tenders skimming across the harbor, closing too fast. If he held this position, the enemy would cut them off from the bridge with nowhere but the bluffs to go. They had to retreat.

The fires on the ships, scuttled boats and raft created a ring of light silhouetting the enemy, making targets for archers who had joined Jan, Pedr and Aron on the roof of the stables at the end of the boardwalk. The sing of bow strings above joined the chunk of arrows returning.

"Fall back to the bridge," Nali told those nearest him. A knot of men behind drifted back, staying low and dodging arrows. It only took one man to throw the torch and in the dim light, he noted that man's eyes grow wider and wider. At last, discovering the source of the arrows, the Minarians raced down the boardwalk toward them, passing boarded buildings where archers lurked to harass them. Other Harbor men darted out to pull down the unwary few from behind, club them and leave them sprawled senseless on the oiled timbers. Archers still fired from the roof of the stable.

As the attackers neared Nali's position, the occasional enemy dropped, clutching at throat or chest to tumble into the fire-lit water. The surreality of this battle in Nali's sleepy village left him frozen for only a moment. The last of the archers retreated along the rooftops. As they drew near, and Nali knew they could escape before him, he tensed, ready to run.

"Now!" he called. The torch bearer struck flint to the torch, and when the spark erupted into flame, he lobbed it down the boardwalk. The first Minarian rank faltered only a moment, barely giving Nali and his unit time to scurry around the curve of the road and out of sight. Archers scrambled down from the stable roof to drop in the hay below, the last one, Aron, setting the hay afire as he stumbled away out to the road on his way to the bridge.

The enemy had taken chase, undaunted by a measly torch sputtering on the boardwalk. Suddenly, the torch flared, and with it the aged wood of the oil-soaked boardwalk. It erupted. In an instant fire raced the length of the boardwalk and built skyward with billows of thick smoke. Those still approaching from the sea stayed oars in confusion, unable to beach their craft, or come near the spitting fire. Inns and shops blazed as the fuel stacked inside their doorways caught with a poof.

Nali scrambled to a barricade on the other side of the bridge. He craned his neck to see into the confusion. Nerves fluttered in his stomach; his breaths filled with acrid smoke. The cool dark of the river below offered a small respite from the red-gold blaze on the other shore, each ripple on the river's surface as the tide churned into the mouth picked up the highlights of the growing blaze. Black oil-smoke blocked the stars and hung heavy in the air. Some soldiers dived into the water to escape the inferno, which threatened to engulf the entire village as flames boiled up into the night. Others stumbled and fell in the flames and didn't rise again.

Jan reached him, gasping in the thick, fog-heavy air. "I'm too old for this. I'm not built to climb roofs no more." He patted his paunch for emphasis.

Nali grinned. "You done just fine, Jan, just fine. In a few more weeks you'll be looking twenty years thinner."

"And twenty years older. Uh-oh, look there." He pointed at the orange-tinted water where light flickered from the helms and mail of warriors in long, red boats with at least thirty men to a craft, six sets of oars speeding them over the water unlike the ungainly tenders. "Looks like they found us."

"No." Nali scanned his men. It served nothing holding any barricade against the superior experience of an army. Nali considered all the lore of war he'd absorbed. Dynfearn's stand at Shela had been similar. Likely their only defense would be in surprise and nibbling at enemy ranks.

"They'll try to land on the barge docks, or, worse yet, on the near shore if they can," Nali thought aloud. "They might tie on to the bridge piles." Nali scanned the high cliff behind them. "Jan, take half your archers and spread them along the road, at all the bends where they can pick off the enemy. Post the rest atop the cliff to guard our retreat. Some folk will need to hold on the banks here. Don't wait for them. They'll have orders to lay low. The rest will work up the road to the plateau in relay with your men." They conferred a few minutes more before Jan hurried away, leading his archers. Nali called his remaining unit in closer.

"I need a volunteer to set fire to the barge docks and loose the barges. Don't try to cross back. Whoever it is, likely won't get to Sihmad Shal before the enemy." The Harbor men looked around, gauging each other's bravery. Finally, a young man raised his hand.

"Aye, sir, me people got a place up near Mania Point. I'll hie up there." Before Nali could agree, the soldier grabbed an unlit torch, raced across the grease-slicked bridge and scampered across the steep rocks to the barges.

"It's gotta be everyone for himself down here. Aron, I need your squad ready to grab from behind or sabotage whatever you can. You have to be quiet. Don't let them know you're here. Then if you can get up to the city, fine. If not, well, best of luck. Head out to Whittea or wait here-abouts in hiding 'til we call you in. Someone will need to fire the bridge."

The first of the enemy boats negotiated the shifting sand bars near the river's mouth as he spoke. The village still burned, new fire springing up here and there from the heat emanating from the glowing waterfront. Figures bobbed in the deep water of the dredged harbor. Some struggled to swim, but their equipment made them slow and sluggish. By the time many managed to peel away the weight of helms, mail, gauntlets and weapons, they merely floated in the steaming water. As each wave splashed against the burning pilings, it sent smoke and ash sputtering into the late night, concealing the stars and the first streaks of dawn.

"All set?" Nali whispered into the dark.

Aron led his squad to wait along the shoreline. The rest Nali led up the winding road cut into the scarp, its chest-high stone curb partially concealing them from the river below. Puffing, they spun around each of the nine loops to the top, greeted by silent archers waiting in the shadows of each curve, eyeing the sky lest dawn come too soon and reveal them. Halfway up Nali signaled a halt. Many sagged against the wall in search of breath.

Nali watched with a mix of fear, elation and regret as Aron lobbed the torch onto the bridge. Flames roared upward, raining burning ash on the boats tied onto the piles below it or trying to pass beneath it to reach the barges. He heard the enemy yelp in pain as burning timbers sparked into the water with a hiss while the boats tried to cast off. The flames gnawed at the ancient bridge that had linked the village and city for almost three thousand years. Though repaired now and then, the original timbers and braces on the oft-replaced piles were ancient trunks that had towered hundreds of years before they fell. To Nali, the flaming bridge seemed a more final separation than the burning village beyond, an abrupt breach with their peaceful past. His men stared at him. He blushed in the first light of the gloaming and turned away to trudge on toward what, he didn't know.

25: Fire on the Prairie

As dawn widened, Nali looked back to find the outer harbor swarming with dozens of ships lowering red thirty-man boats. The damaged vessels that ran aground or burned amounted to only a small percentage of the fleet. Some barges carrying horses and equipment maneuvererd to tie onto the still smoking piles to serve as a temporary bridge.

It happened so fast! Nali pushed his unit to run up the scarp, their fear beating down their exhaustion, the effort drawing gasps that pulled in acrid smoke to choke their lungs. For whatever reason, the man sent to the barge docks failed to light them. Not that it would have stopped the enemy from landing. Nali imagined the Minarians would have piled their own dead to make a bridge if they needed it.

Dawn illuminated targets on both sides and soon Minarian arrows fell among them. Nali felt an arrow tug his tunic just beneath his arm pit. He twisted as he ran, seeing a tear in the fabric and a faint scratch beneath. Somehow, he thought arrows would never touch him.

As he crested the scarp, he paused for breath, hands on knees, struck numb by the view. Smoke hung gray and thick along the waterfront, broken periodically by licks of flame. Few standing landmarks remained along the boardwalk. Surviving buildings stood soot-blackened and singed, the rest smoking skeletons or still burning. While his little house high on the bluff had escaped fire, it wouldn't escape the ravening of enemy soldiers roaming the alleys and yards in search of booty and those few stubborn residents remaining.

Nali turned away, seeing his own expression in the vacant and stunned eyes of his men. Then he noted the odd look of an archer behind him. Repulsed, he saw death in the wide eyes and the arrow protruding from the man's chest as he slowly collapsed. Arrows dropped all around them. He could kick himself for letting them all stand so open a silhouette against the dawn. Nali pushed along a young soldier scooping up the arrows as they fell, prodding his men to hurry along the road.

They descended for a moment into deep grass at a marshy spot where irrigation ditches had channeled a stream that disappeared into the earth here to surface farther down the scarp wall through a culvert under the road. Nali studied the water a moment, then the green line leading to a farmer's field where a dam created a sluiceway and trough for livestock. From that same trough, brick culverts led to a network of ditches. Only a trickle reached the cliff wall. He nodded to himself, recalling the heavy machines gathering at the river mouth.

He shouted for Jan, who stood among the last group of archers acting rearguard for the retreating Harbor detachment. Jan staggered to Nali's side, face pale, eyes like ice as he wrapped a strip of his tunic around a bloody bulge in his calf. "I'm already a wounded hero," he said without humor.

"Got a few you can spare?"

Jan eyed him a moment, then at the dwindling resources of his remaining four dozen archers. They all shot enemy arrows now, their features sweaty, sooty and exhausted.

"All fresh as today's catch."

Nali pointed at the marshy ground where the rutted road needed repair and the green line stretching away toward the distant farm.

"Do you think it'll do any good at all?" Jan asked as the sound of massive wheels on crushed shell echoed from below and Pedr called out a warning. "Well, aren't you a bright one!" he crowed, slapping Nali on the back. Jan detached three of his men to follow the line to the farm and open wide the impoundment gates. "Water won't stop an army but it might slow its machines!" Jan beamed as he listed the small victories they had so far, marking them on grimy fingers. "We're the gnats, here to devil a giant. The insects send their giant runnin' away. Maybe we can send these jokers back to sea!" He limped off to supervise his men, chuckling to himself as he went.

As he shooed his troops before him, Nali wished he felt Jan's confidence. Cutting off a long loop in the road, they trotted through head-high prairie grass at the top of the scarp. Chaff and pollen adhered to sweaty bodies as their legs fought the tangle of untended rangeland, men coughing and sneezing as they gasped in the choking dust raised by those before them. The land began to rise, almost imperceptibly at first then leveled onto large fields dotted with farms, patches of prairie, abandoned crops, and pasture. The city stood out as a far-flung silhouette against the morning sun, still better than half an hour distant at this pace.

He prodded his unit to hurry as his own breaths ripped out in gasps and his heart pounded in his chest. His calves knotted as he forced one leg before the other. On reaching the plateau, Nali called a pause, the fast-warming morning burning in his face. Down the long slope behind, he discerned the broken path where Jan's men followed and the tangent of those sent to release the impoundment. The first enemy wagon crested the lip of the scarp, led by enemy troops.

Now the city filled Nali's vision, the walls reaching to either horizon. Distance on the plateau deceived. Neglected fields choked with brambles hid the ruts of plows and even when they reached the road again they still would have a long hike with the better-rested army behind them. Even after reaching the walls, they would need to follow the long loop to pass through Shanai to the south-facing gates.

"Gotta go," he said. "Sorry, boys."

As they trudged on, faint at first, then growing louder, they heard a jangling racket from behind. Nali slowed and turned, peering through tall grass, his men crouched, clubs ready, faces tight and resigned as a sound like the rattling gear of an army raced at them. Nali concealed himself behind a screen of thicket off the trail they'd beaten. Each man, eyes wide, prepared to bolt in a different direction as a shape loomed up through the veil of grass. As the shape emerged, Nali pounced, throwing the shadow to the ground.

"Cram it, Nali!" Jan yelled.

"Where do you get off sneaking up on us like that? We could've killed you!" Nali shouted, fists balled at his sides in frustration.

"We weren't exactly sneaking!" Jan shot back, leaping up to face the derna.

Pedr shoved his way between them.

"You're supposed to be farther back," Nali returned.

"You go back! They've fired the prairie!"

Nali craned his head to look, but didn't need to reach far. He could already see the rising columns of gray smoke, fanned by a strong west wind.

"Go! Go! Go!" Nali shouted, herding his men in front of him.

At last, they reached the road and the cooler shadows thrown by the western walls, their pace faster on easier ground. Calls of encouragement showered them from the battlements as they finally made their way through vacated Shanai to the city's gates.

Footsore, some bloody, they sagged in relief when the gates slammed shut and a mob of helpers greeted them with cool water and care for the injured. Nali leaned against the cold metal of the gates, letting his gaze drift up to the towers, wondering if Arshal watched. The haze of smoke gave the morning a reddish cast. He rubbed his tired, soot-filled eyes. He longed for fresh air but the air hung thick with ash from the burning Harbor and prairie.

"Got any ideas, Nali? I don't have people here. Mine are out in the country." Jan gazed at the gates as if he could see the rolling farmland beyond where Cookie and Jali hid at the family farmstead. "I don't know where to go," he whispered. "You'd think we fell from the sky today." He jabbed a thumb toward the crowd of curious gathering around them.

Nali grinned and rubbed his sooty beard. "They've never seen an honest-to-goodness real live wounded warrior, Jan. You're quite the novelty."

Jan's eyebrows arched. "Well, yes, I guess I am!" He puffed himself up for the crowd.

"Get your glory now. Heroes and wounded warriors'll be common as carp pretty quick," Nali warned, already feeling the sanctuary of the walls wearing thin. He motioned for Jan and the bedraggled Harbor men to follow him up on the walls where the rest of the Harbor recruits sent to the city the day before waited, fresh and rested, and hungry for the tales of the battle. "Might as well stay in the middle of things as wait for the middle to come lookin' for us."

"But we could use an ale now, and a rest, Nali." Jan lowered his voice. "If you're hoping to be a good commander and show up Aron for all his griping, you gotta keep up the morale. We deserve a little something for our labor, a pick-me-up and a pat on the back. They see your face like that and they'll see no reason to fight. You got defeat written all over it."

Nali shrugged. "I can't fight the inevitable." He waved away Jan's protest. "I know, I know."

When they reached the battlement and looked west over the plain, he could see nothing of the enemy beyond the smoke of the fire feeding on the prairie and the little farmsteads dotting it. He signaled his men to take up positions, grab a bite and rest as he joined Jan and Pedr to peer out at the fire through crenellations in the battlement. At first the wind raced out of the west as if driven by a gale, but as noon passed, the fires slowed, the smoke thickening.

"It's looking out there, not knowing," Nali said dismally. "What do you think's behind that smoke? Why would they set it afire knowing they can't come on until it's spent? Is it to hide the size of their force? Or their machines? To keep us from using fire against them again? The way they just kept coming on in the Harbor – They're so organized, and experienced, and how do I keep up such a great lie? These men know they'll either die here or surrender here –"

It happened so fast Nali was already sitting on the worn stone rubbing his stinging jaw before he could register that Jan had put him there. He looked up to find Jan standing over him, arms akimbo and a murderous look on his face. Pedr didn't lift a toe to stop the confrontation, even though Jan clearly struck his commander without provocation.

"Go ahead, Commander, I dare you to say you didn't deserve that. A lot fewer'll survive a battle if they think there's no reason to fight it. Yes? Makes sense, don't it. But Minaria wants a fight, so the battle's comin' no matter what. If all's lost then hang out your flags of surrender. Take down the black rag and run up the yellow."

Nali stared up at Jan from the corner of his eye as the older man put out a hand to help him up.

"I'm sorry, Nali. It's bad enough we've all lost everything, without havin' to fight your friends." Nali glanced at Pedr, who had slumped down against the parapet, mouth hanging open in a snore. "You can't just be goin' 'round like this, Nali. You're our commander. We look to you for inspiration. You'll get us all killed if you start burying us before our time."

"Look there!" a man cried, pointing west.

"Ha! See? It isn't all on their side now, is it?" Jan slapped Nali hard on the back.

Nali peered out through the smoky haze. The fires only crawled ahead now and the smoke flattened out along the ground. Then, as a small gust swirled the smoke, he glimpsed the army forming up along the burned fields. At first, he saw nothing at which Jan could crow. The enemy spread rank upon rank at the edge of the blackened, steaming prairie. Then Nali noticed a bottleneck of wagons and catapults tilting toward the marshy dip filling with water, a swarm of soldiers laboring to free them.

"See how the gnats devil the giant?" Jan exclaimed as men

around them laughed at the enemy's predicament, replacing the fear and exhaustion of moments before. Jan sped along the battlement, slapping men on the back and pointing to their victory, shoring up morale as a good commander should. As Nali should.

Nali tried to shed the fatigue and empty his mind as he leaned against the parapet beside Pedr. It appeared so stark with the flower boxes gone, only an occasional dead blossom swirling in drafts giving any sign of the color that had been. Unlit torches and piles of fuel under cauldrons of oil and water and grease looked out of place on the windy upper walls.

"Nali?"

He turned to find Griag, a young Harbor neighbor sent to the city before the invasion. The young man shifted from foot to foot, staring into the stones at his feet, his dark hair hanging in his eyes.

"It really ain't none of my business, but someone told me I really oughta let you know." Nali waited, brow raised. "It's about Drul."

Nali straightened. "What about my fa? Spit it out. Did that fool stay in the Harbor against my orders?"

"No. No. He ain't in the Harbor. Just thought you should know, gave Olna the slip, he did. He's here in the city. Said there's no way he's goin' to hide himself away like a child. He's gonna fight like a man. No matter what his fool boy has to say about it. His words, not mine."

Nali gave him a wry grimace. "As if I don't have enough problems, now I need to worry about him doddering around a war. Should've tied him to a cart and shipped him off with Peshal." Nali sized up the young man. "Think you can drag that old badger up here? Tell him it's an order, and if he disobeys, it'll be to the prince he answers," Nali warned. "Not to mention what I'll do to him!"

As Griag hurried off, Nali shook his head, too frustrated and angry to admit he should have expected it. The man had never accepted the limitations of the back injury that forced him to turn over his fishing boat to his son. Did his father realize just what his pig head had gotten him into this time? Nali stared up at the Window of the Sun and the dwarfed towers beside it, all gleaming in an odd milky glow of smoke-stained sunlight. He tried to think of nothing and not let himself brood over what he felt certain would come as snippets of his dreams tried to force their way into his thoughts. A squall rolled in off the sea to stanch the fires as the enemy crept closer, burning farmsteads and, at last, as dusk closed on them, Shanai burned. It felt familiar, like a version of a vision proved true. But which version? Arshal had shared with him Cree's prophecies. Was the future his dream memory of flocks of carrion birds descending upon fields of twisted-limbed bodies and a world gone mad?

Nali's head banged against the corner of a merlon as someone shook him awake. His grimy hand shot out to grab the shaker. The stars hid behind the haze of smoke, but he instantly recognized the silhouette of the bent figure rousing him.

"Well, Fa, what do you have to say for yourself?"

Drul offered a hand and pulled Nali to his feet. They looked down over the smoking fields below. Faint light from the burning watch fires and smoldering Shanai and the still burning Harbor in the distance glowed off the haze, casting a yellow pallor on Drul's face. Nali felt naked, as he had from the cliff looking over the Harbor that morning.

"Fa, we make a target here."

Drul looked at him with watery sea-blue eyes gone red with the grime in the air. "Aye, son, I s'pose we do." He held out his hand to see the thin shadow it threw.

Nali shook his head, memorizing the wrinkled shadows of his father's sea-beaten face. A salt and pepper tangle, Drul's hair twisted like seaweed. Work-roughened, strong hands grasped the stone. He was nowhere near as ancient as a life of hard labor and good drink made him appear.

"Fa, they don't have to stay by the fires and they can see our silhouettes looking out at 'em." He tugged his father's elbow and led him to the inner lip of the wall, where the warmth of the city exhaled at them with each pause of the breeze.

Drul shook his arm free. "Don't talk to me in that tone." He walked stiff-legged in the direction Nali propelled him.

"And don't you treat me like a schoolboy, Fa. You defied me a-pupose. Like it or not I'm Commander of the Harbor recruits. I counted on you to defend your grandchildren. We don't have enough stores in the city as it is. You're not trained. You're not armed. What were you thinkin'?" Nali turned away, fists clenched, feeling guilty for yelling at his father. He tried not to imagine Olna alone, facing an enemy invasion with her children clinging to her.

Drul sighed as he leaned against the inner parapet. "You're a different man, Nali. A commander. The day you was born we heard 'em trumpetin' through the streets, sayin' the crown prince was born, an' of all the omens and such. An' I looked at the Demonstar burning that night as it rose, an' your mam said: 'he's part of some other design.' An' before she died, she said, 'there's something in store for Nali. Take note an' see what it is so you can tell me when you come.' See, I gotta watch, 'cuz I gotta answer to your mam wherever she's gone. If she ain't satisfied, I might pay for eternity." One watery eye winked.

"Fa, being here you'll go to Mam a lot sooner. You'll put a burden on me if something happens to you."

"I won't be in the way. I already volunteered to do some things as need to be done." Drul cleared his throat and stared into Nali's eyes. "Wish I could tell your mam she's wrong, you're just a normal boy. I know it won't be that way."

Drul dropped his hand on Nali's shoulder and squeezed hard, then made off, a last backward wave before hurrying down the ramp to the borough below. Nali watched until the figure disappeared into a Dlan alley, then again found his attention drawn to the shadowy towers of the palace in the distance. As he stared, he felt sure some battle took place there as well. He imagined eyes staring from the Window of the Sun. It didn't comfort him. If anything, he felt as if he held vigil for something he wasn't sure would come.

An expectant pause reigned as the enemy neared, a squall squelching the prairie fire and the wind switching back on itself. Now the enemy covered the plain below, beyond the range of any weapon the city possessed, except Arshal himself.

The strange sense of power he'd felt building the fog still gave him a thrill to contemplate, even though by morning he fainted with exhaustion. As servants carried him to his bed, Cree's words of strength in his ears bore none of his usual disdain. Arshal rubbed the back of his head where he had hit the floor and pulled his heavy mantle tight about his shoulders, cold despite the heat that hadn't dissipated with the rain. The strange ability sapped his strength and stamina and only seemed to heighten his feelings of doubt for his every decision.

The enemy spread out as they reached the plain, some units deployed to the east and west, as the the main body approached the gates from the south. Here and there a flash of orange and red standards among black banners and trappings identified units as they moved in cadence to throbbing drumbeats. The whole Minarian army moved as one, like some hungry monster stalking its prey, first one group then another, shifting as it positioned itself to pounce.

Arshal tried to shake off the way the drum beats added to his uneasiness. The enemy would soon surround them but for the cliffs to the north. As the troops approached, they set fire to the houses and barns yet standing, black smoke boiling from the windows. With each new blaze, Arshal's muscles knotted tighter, his heart pounding as the monster's maw began to close, the sword glint of teeth paralyzing, chilling as once again he felt that alien sense of inadequacy and failure. What could he do? He needed to escape, to hide.

He whirled for the door, almost bowling over the Visionary at the top of the stairs. Arshal lurched away, seeing a nightmare image from his dream. How long had Cree watched? Cree grabbed Arshal's arm with a talon-like grip and forced him to turn and look out the window.

"It's a test." Cree's words felt softer than his grip. "You cannot abandon them. They feel the same fears as you."

As darkness loomed, the enemy pitched tents and set watch fires. Another ring of fires flickered on the bluffs above the Rigannon where troops struggled to free mired wagons or bring others through. A few crept along the Sijway as small flickers of lurching torchlight. How could he feel so suddenly hopeless who had boasted of righteous strength? He felt sick to the heart of himself, emptied, used, and shamed. His enemy had come, so much greater than him. And he had no weapon to match it.

Cree peered at the prince he had once despaired of training. Dark smudges beneath Arshal's eyes wrapped themselves in shadows, his cheeks pinched and face pale despite long days in the sun among the troops. What had they wrought? What had he wrought?

"I'm not strong enough Cree. The powers just don't respond."

"Do you plan to defend the country with powers? Then you are a fool. The power to project these things draws from your strength and morale. The shawnsi powers of old were much stronger, and still they needed armies to raise their swords in battle. If you try to fight a war with powers there will be nothing left of you to face Ghyldus. Do you think he will accept one victory and go home? He will send more troops and more until by sheer numbers they overwhelm you. For what? A moment's glory because you have powers? You surprise me. You would waste your resources when you can have alternate plans."

"If you think it's stupid to waste my strength, then why did you encourage me?"

"To teach you. There are times, like last night, when it will be advisable to deploy these gifts. Now you know what it takes and will develop greater strength and control. Besides, I did not know you would try something so strenuous. Remember, we only suspected, we did not know if you had these abilities." Cree turned, afraid Arshal might read the fear on his face. "I thought you had killed yourself. It is possible. We discussed measure in your studies. You apparently were not listening that day."

"I can't use them. I can't even think."

Cree peered at him. "You will need to develop these powers to use them efficiently. You will die if you attempt anything so foolish again. I am surprised you are out of your bed, already."

"Cree, I – I can't face it. There isn't enough left in me."

Cree turned from the cityscape to find Arshal leaning against the sill, head bowed and eyes shut. Cree hesitated. Could the prince recover if he collapsed again?

Arshal sank to the floor, back against the stone. He buried his head in arms wrapped around his knees. "I'm so tired. Help me?"

Cree grasped the prince by the chin and forced his head up. "You must seek your strength." Arshal tried to shake free but Cree held him hard. "Go inside yourself, to that resting place we spoke of. Go there and seek guidance."

Arshal tried to protest that he couldn't desert his people on the eve of battle. Cree's gaze pulled him in, forcing silence as the Visionary drew him into the trance state that would allow the prince to recover. Cree tucked the heavy cloak around his charge. "You must turn inward to find strength."

Arshal didn't respond, only emitted the briefest gasp of terror as he fell into the emptiness Cree had created for him. The prince sagged a little and Cree at last relaxed the grip he'd had over his own emotions. He didn't even know if he gave sound counsel. So much of the future had changed!

The Visionary stood guard over the prince where he lay on the flagstone floor. He refused to acknowledge servants' calls. Every so often he set a finger against the prince's neck in search of a lifebeat before returning to the window. The moon dodged in and out of wind-driven clouds, briefly lighting the enemy troops creeping closer to the city walls. A few archers aimed for the dim targets as the enemy shot flaming arrows at Shanai's dry thatched roofs.

Fire once again lit the Shandean night, the enemy coming on with more purpose than Cree remembered, less ably resisted. Which future would they follow? One in which they held and defeated the invasion? Or the one where they must flee the burning city, leaving behind their dead and dying? And where in the future was Peshal?

26: Touchstone

The first wave struck as the fires of Shanai still smoldered just before dawn. Their machinery still mired, the Minarians instead sent mounted archers wheeling in to fling flaming arrows over the wall and flee before the defenders could find a mark. A rampart erected from the burned ruins of Shanai gave cover to other archers who picked off any Shandeans who showed themselves to fire back. Other enemy troops dashed to reach the base of the wall to cast grappling hooks upon the wall faster than they could be cut down.

At sunrise, attempting to make a show of strength as much for those within the walls as without, Esthen led hundreds of cavalry out an eastern sally port, his pennants flanking him as the sun blazed off raised spears and swords. The fields here had largely escaped the fires and enemy troops still organized their defensive lines. The Shandeans' horses tore the ground like the rumors of Dynfearn returned to the world. But instead of disrupting the enemy's work they ground to a halt on the swords of Minaria's elite Eidhalt who raced from hiding near the northern walls. Esthen's warriors rallied to his marker in the melee, but could do no more than retreat back to the walls for safety as the enemy gathered around the smirking Eidhalt who regarded the city as if sizing up a slab of pie.

The din of battle heightened as day broadened, only to be overwhelmed by the constant beat of Minarian marching drums as the weary Harbor contingent held the first wall against scalers.

"Over here! Over here!" Shandeans shouted as youths raced to supply arrows to archers. They collected the enemy's arrows by the hundreds, plucking them from walls or chasing them across the stonework. Medical teams climbed the ramps to retrieve wounded and dead on litters made from planks torn from buldings.

A moment's lull let Nali wonder when he had last slept more than an hour or two, certainly not since before the Minarians rounded Mania Point almost three days ago. He shook himself alert as he scanned for breaches along his stretch of battlement. As he shouted encouragement to a ragged trio of soldiers, a shout drew his attention and he felt his pulse quicken. A swarm of scalers had breached the wall. Weariness forgotten, he wielded his club two-handed to batter heads and hands that crested the wall. Scaling hooks dropped around him and he sidestepped arrows, rallying his men in a voice gone hoarse.

Something struck his leg and in the same instant pulled it from beneath him. The three-pronged grappling hook had pinned his calf to the parapet, its rope cutting across his chest with the weight of a scaler. He peeked behind him over the breastwork to see how fast the scaler climbed, ducking back from a hail of arrows. A few paces distant he saw a burly warrior hacking ropes with a sword, back to Nali's predicament. Nali struggled to pull the rope and loosen the hook's grip but he didn't have enough leverage. The hook had wedged into a deep crevice in the stonework and Nali couldn't yank hard enough to release it nor pull himself free of the weight of the rope.

"Got a moment?" he forced out with what little breath he could pull as the burly warrior turned. Through the growing buzz in his ears and the dizziness weighing his movements, the situation seemed morbidly humorous, if the scaler didn't reach the top first. If only he wasn't so light-headed. He needed to concentrate. Daring another peek, he turned back to be greeted by Esthen.

"All the time for you, Nali," Esthen called as he flung a severed hook into the face of a man attempting to get a leg over the edge. "Glad to see you in one piece."

Sweat ran in rivulets down Nali's face and into his beard. He assumed fatigue made him feel so oddly giddy. "I seem to be stuck here," he gestured at the hook. "Climber's near the top. Can you cut it? I can't reach." The humming in his ears drowned his words as a faint tried to overtake him. If he could just take a deep breath –

Esthen leaned out to slash the stone. He darted back from arrows that slapped at the stonework around him. He tried to find a place to slip his sword beneath the rope crossing Nali's body without cutting the derna. Esthen called for help, to be joined by Pedr who pulled slack into the rope as Esthen tried to loosen the grip of the hook.

One of the Minarian's hands reached for an axe at his belt, the other grasping the rope only a hand's breadth from the lip. Just then Nali felt a tug and a ripping pain in his leg. Something whipped by his head. Nali sagged, stunned. Esthen grabbed him in time to keep him from toppling over the breastwork. The pain crawled up his leg and smashed into his hip as Esthen and Pedr helped him to the inside parapet.

"Sorry," Esthen said as he eased Nali to the ground. "No way to go at that but to yank as hard as I could."

Nali stared at his calf where blood welled from a jagged hole, startling him and bringing his stomach into his mouth. He hadn't realized the hook gripped his leg until the prince pulled it free. It already swelled as the blood began to pool on the stonework, looking like it might be a while before he could walk. He looked up to find Esthen and Pedr had already turned back to the battle.

He felt a hand on his elbow and realized his fa guided him toward the ramp down from the battlement. "Looks like the fish got their evens," Drul said.

"Now I know how they feel," Nali said through clenched teeth. He shook off his father's grip as they reached the ramp. The borough below swam in and out of focus as he clung to the wobbly rail while Drul shouted from the top for him to have a care. As he neared the bottom, an old woman dressed in the garb of the medical teams tasked him for his hurry. He'd barely cleared the ramp before she had pushed him down onto a crate and ripped his trouser leg away.

Twisting his head from side to side, Nali tried to see around the woman to where the battlement had grown quiet, protesting that others in worse shape needed her attention. He needed to see what was happening. Arrows no longer whistled overhead. The quiet made him uneasy. Did they lull them into a rest to catch them off guard? Dynfearn had used that ploy in his siege of Sefresal. Nali wanted to find Jan and Pedr and ask their thoughts. Instead, he had to wait for the woman tending him to finish her work, sometime in the next moon if she moved a little faster, Nali figured.

The woman appeared ignorant of his frustration as she bled the puncture, applied a burning salve and bandaged the leg with a slow method that barely kept up with the blood soaking the bandage. She added a shivered lath as a splint to the last few wraps to the bandage and gave him a nearly toothless smile. Nali pulled himself up to leave, but she pushed him back down.

"Now you wait 'til I tell you, Commander. You'll have plenty of time yet to get yourself killed."

How had Peshal fared if this woman wasn't too old to stay behind? As if sensing his thoughts, her smile faded to a frown. She forced him to take a measure of spirits and a dipper of cold medicinal tea. His nausea returned as he tried to keep the bitter mix down, but it took a bit of the edge off the way his leg throbbed as it swelled against the splint. A weary-eyed girl toting a water bucket and a basket handed him a hard biscuit and a ladle of water that soothed his nausea. He couldn't even recall the last time he'd eaten. Before he could offer his thanks around the dry biscuit, the old woman and girl had already moved on to another wounded defender who grumbled his need for no help.

Pulling up his bloody club for a cane, Nali stood, leaning against the wall until he could support himself. Habit made him pivot on his injured leg. He would have fallen if he hadn't clutched a torch bracket until the dizzying pain passed. It rankled. A commander couldn't be slowed by so small a wound. Others, like Jan, fought on with their wounds and so should he. He scanned the battlement, finding a familiar silhouette against the sky swimming against the flashes of light in front of his eyes.

"Nali!" Jan shouted down at thim. "There's folk riding in from the northeast, chased close!"

Nali scanned the ward before the gates for Esthen, who he last saw overseeing efforts to lower a secondary portcullis that had become stuck. Nali's heart pounded in his ears, certain Peshal tried to make it through.

Jan called down again. "There's an enemy unit riding tangent to block them! They won't make it!"

Using his club as a cane, he limped toward the gates, his steps coming more easily as he grew accustomed to the pain and stiffness in his leg. He called out to the prince as he neared. Before he could finish explaining, Esthen dashed to the top of the wall. Nali waited as the prince's silhouette, trailed by his standard, hurried along the battlement and disappeared behind the barbican and rooftops as he circled toward the east. Moments later he returned with Jan and several others running behind, calling for horses as he made for the gates.

Nali tried to decide if he should return to his unit or get a few minutes rest. He imagined Arshal would call for him when Peshal arrived. Yet if he rested too long, his leg would stiffen. As he pondered his options he startled at cold metal against his arm. He turned to find Jan, grim-faced, holding out a sword. Nali took it by the hilts.

"The prince says he needs thirty archers and twenty swordsmen. Most of his men are engaged on the west wall," Jan said.

"So why are you handing me a sword?"

"Well, he'd like the more experienced fighters to ride with him. That's us Harbor fellows."

"I'd hardly call myself an experienced swordsman, Jan!"

"Can't be no different than a club, just a sharper edge," Pedr offered as he chewed his cheek. "Really, Nali, we need you. As commander, it's only right you should."

"I – I can't ride –"

"You probably can ride better than you walk," Jan said, as Esthen's call silenced Nali's protest.

After a few brief instructions, Esthen signaled them to mount up. Nali swallowed hard as Jan helped him onto a twitching gelding. They gathered in the short tunnel between the half-lowered portcullis and the main gate as Esthen gave the order to open the gate.

Nali's horse leaped forward without command as a rain of arrows from the defenders above gave them cover from the enemy. Nali gripped the reins and held onto the mane in desperation as his mount labored to keep pace with the others. Esthen took the lead, standard bearer on his heels with his blue pennant flapping behind.

After a few moments, Nali found his balance and stared ahead through the whip of mane. The dark spots of three dozen horses grew against the eastern wheat fields, the enemy hard on their heels. A sudden break in stride and a hard lurch almost unseated Nali. He glanced back to find a body sprawled in the field. Around him other horses vaulted other bodies and finally the ditch they had taken cover in at the outermost range of Shandean archers.

As Nali's horse leaped the ditch, a pikeman jumped up. Nali felt a chill when two red glints on a medallion flashed in the westering sun. He swung the sword like he would his club, the horse's momentum giving him a powerful blow. The pike clattered between the horse's legs as the man crumpled to the ground.

Beside him, Jan nocked an arrow in his familiar short bow while the string still quivered from the shot before. Knotted reins lay loose on the horse's withers, leaving Jan free to fling arrows at the enemy popping up from the tall growth near the ditch, while the horse kept pace with the lead.

Without a cue, Nali's mount changed gaits, hind end bunching up as it slowed to cut away with the familiarity of its role as a herd pony, just as Nali realized they had reached the struggling riders.

The newcomers rode ahead, Esthen's sortie falling in as rearguard. Nali scanned the horsemen. No figure seemed to match Peshal's. The men lay low over their horses, cloaks whipping about them.

As he turned with the rest of the sortie to face the oncoming Minarians, Nali felt naked, an easy target. Archers swung into an outer moving ring around the swordsmen, shooting at the two groups of Minarian pursuers. Several of the pursuing enemy fell and many turned back as the fresh unit came on, led by an Eidhalt, bright horsetails streaming from his helm, the trappings of his horse's gear emitting a brash jangle that unnerved the Shandean mounts.

The Eidhalt plowed through the ring of archers and rode at Esthen, who made an easy mark with his standard behind him. The Minarian swung. The prince ducked and parried, immediately pressed by the better-trained warrior. Another attacker thrust his way through the melee so he too could engage the prince. Esthen fell back beneath combined blows, his shield severed and useless. As their horses sidestepped and reared, shying, Nali drew close enough to stab at the sleeve hole of the second attacker. His blow split open the man's leather armor as with both hands Nali drove the sword into the Minarian's side. The man fell at his mount's feet.

Nali's gelding stumbled over the bloody body lying in the wheat, wall-eyed, its nostrils flaring. As Nali tried to regain control of his mount, he saw with dismay Esthen's sword lying on the ground, being smashed into the churn of turf beneath the horses' hooves.

The press of animals thwarted Esthen's attempt to escape, his dagger useless. The Eidhalt grinned and swung. Esthen raised his left arm in defense, trying to reach the sword his standard bearer held out to him with his right, but couldn't grasp the blade in time as the Minarian blow fell. Esthen bellowed. The sword might have shattered bone and still driven on into Esthen's stunned face, but at that moment Jan's arrow struck the Eidhalt in the eye. Esthen lurched back as momentum from the blow sent the dying man forward, his sword peeling away the muscle from the bone of Esthen's arm. As the Minarian toppled from his horse to be trampled by his own mount, Esthen slumped, cradling his arm and trying to hold the flesh together.

"Nali!" Esthen choked, motioning with his head toward the city as Nali took the reins and led the prince's horse behind him, screaming a retreat. The standard bearer raced to keep astride Esthen to defend him and hold his balance while Nali and the others lay low over their mounts' necks. Ahead the gate opened briefly for the newcomers, then closed to a slit as the sortie approached.

Suddenly, Jan cut away. Deftly he plucked a select arrow from his nearly empty quiver and swept it through an enemy campfire. It burst into flame. He sent the arrow into a supply wagon piled high with bundled arrows and spears. It sputtered for a moment, then began to smoke and burn as soldiers rushed to put out the flames, opening themselves to archers on the walls.

The gates clanged shut behind Nali as he, the standard bearer and Esthen brought up the rear, ducking beneath the half-lowered portcullis as arrows skittered among their horses' legs. None of the newcomers was Peshal. He heard growing expressions of outrage as soldiers saw the prince cradling his bloody arm. In moments, Esthen had been whisked away to healers before Nali could even dismount.

Silence fell again as the Minarians retreated out of range and Nali eased himself from the saddle, shaky and sickened by the blood spattered over him. As it caught up with him, he thought only to take a moment to catch his wind, using the sword for support as he aimed for the shadows of an overgrown courtyard a short way up the Sijway. Hazy sunlight shone on a pond circling an artesian well, bright against the vines and fruit trees lining the yard, the sounds of battle muted. As dappled sunlight climbed the eastern walls of the encircling buildings, Nali sank onto a stoop. Sword handy beside him, he closed his eyes, thinking only to rest a moment before finding a bite and returning to his command. Within moments, he dreamt of his family gathered again in their cozy cottage.

Nali awoke to a choking cough. His eyes burned from smoke and ash in the air and rubbing the sleep from them only made it worse. He struggled to straighten his leg and rub the kinks from protesting muscles, startled to discover dawn painting the roofs gray and the too-familiar hue of orange tingeing the sky behind him. An occasional rain of sparks drifted into the courtyard. He shook the fog of sleep and fever from his head and listened hard, hearing the shouts of firefighters calling for water and the crackle of flames. Smoke rose all around him.

Where were his troops? Did Jan lead them through the night, their commander unaccounted for? An echoing boom shook the ground beneath him, at last rousing him. It repeated, rhythmic, insistent, like the war drums directing the enemy army. Nali stumbled from the steps. At the last moment he reached back for the sword. He limped through the narrow alleys to the Sijway where lines of sweaty firefighters fought flames raging across thatched roofs. They stumbled beneath the weight of buckets as brigades could only tackle the worst blazes.

Flaming arrows arched over the wall, leaving a trail of sparks and catapults rained debris on the defenders. The machinery had finally arrived. A battering ram boomed against the gates. Defenders on the wall faced siege towers. He limped into an eerie nightmare world of fire, smoke and battle, knowing he'd find Jan in the thick of things, bringing the machines down in flames.

He wondered if he'd been missed and if any of the chaos was his fault. A few dozen defenders huddled behind the barricade at the gates, twitching with each resounding strike of the ram that, if it could break gates of adanan, would make short work of the barricade. He didn't know what became of Arshal, doubted Esthen could return to battle and felt certain Peshal wouldn't find a way into the city. Only Zopher remained of Sihmad Shal's top leadership, if still unharmed. Last accounts placed Zopher on the eastern walls. A woman, her head bandaged with a bloody rag, brushed by him, shouting for her unit to gather to her, her quiver empty and her bowstring frayed. Nali felt the nag of hopelessness again as he reached the ramp to the battlement. A man fell from above, hitting the ground at Nali's feet with a thud that made the derna gag. The body rested, vacant eyes staring at the growing light of day. Clinging hard to the wobbly rail, Nali forced himself to climb.

He had barely reached the top when a hail of catapult-flung rocks and debris clattered against the stonework. He yanked his hand back with a yelp, too late to avert the sting of a rock bouncing against the railing to smash onto the flagstone below. He rubbed his stinging fingers a moment before venturing to raise his head above the lip of the parapct.

Injured huddled against the inside of the battlement, more than the harried medical teams could aid, with only enough hands to take the living. He noted several from his own unit, but didn't see Jan among them. He recognized his father running at one end of a litter further along the wall. Most of the defenders lay where they fell, slumped over the parapet or crumpled behind the protection of the breastwork.

Nali scrambled for the protection of a merlon in the barbican overlooking the gates. As he peeked through a narrow arrow loop, he gasped at the change the night had wrought. The ghostly glow of dawn lit figures that swarmed across the blackened fields. Torches clustered around the creaking wooden wheels of siege towers creeping to the walls. Vats of hot oil and water dumped on the batterers had stained and blackened the ground around the gates and the serpentine ram bristled with arrows intended for the batterers, and others meant to set the thing afire.

As night gave way, Nali realized no fire would light the ram. Whether from an unscheduled dip in the sea, or by intention, the ram's mammoth trunk swelled with water. Nali touched the arm of an archer aiming at the ram, warning her not to waste her precious arrows, and instead to aim for the towers that crept into range. She gave him a weary nod and adjusted her aim.

Nali scurried along the battlement in search of Jan, finding him in a bartizan on the other side of the gates. The innkeeper directed two youths heating oil and water, both liquids near gone. Nali peered through the slit as, with Jan's help, the boys hefted a massive pot, a quarter full with the last of the oil and rested it on the parapet. They paused to spit and blow on their hands before giving the soot-blackened pot a final push. With a resounding clang it struck the battering ram and bounced away, knocking attackers to the ground and splattering oil everywhere.

"Now!" Jan yelled.

One boy swept up a flaming brand from the fire and tossed it at the ram. The hot oil, near flash point, flared, sparking and spitting the length of the ram, reducing the batterers to howls as they rolled in the dust to extinguish the sparks. The boys rolled the empty water pot to the edge and it, too, went over, smashing into two captains ordering their men back to work. They crumpled like wounded spiders and didn't move again.

Jan turned to give Nali a triumphant grin. "Now see boys," he said, not looking at the boys who tried to soothe their burned hands. "This is how the weaker man wins a battle: brains. We know how to improvise."

As morning broadened, revealing the movements on the plain, Nali's breath caught in his throat. Siege towers crowded the walls, their tops and ladders crammed with warriors, more ready to replace those who fell to the dwindling Shandean arrows. Nali glanced at the two boys who stood agape, wide eyes fixed on the plain.

"You two," Nali ordered, his command calling him back from despair. "Back to the second wall. Warn them we're going to retreat. Set the pots on the fire and be ready to oil the Sijway and fire it." The boys scrambled past the dead and dying in search of the stairs. "Jan, prepare for retreat. We can't hold Dlan, not with these machines."

"Give up?!"

"We're not giving up. As soon as those machines gain the wall we'll be overrun. We need to get the wounded moved back and we have more and fresher men on the Fearnia wall. Besides, Dlan's burning out of control. If we wait too long, we'll be trapped. There's no point in wasting firefighters and soldiers on something we know we can't hold."

"But we've held –" Jan's defense came weak and half-hearted. "What about Zopher?"

"We need to send a messenger around anyway. Wounded first, dead if there's time. Hold for a signal. We'll need to find a herald who can trumpet over this din."

"Aye, Nali. We'll make a commander of you yet."

Nali gave him a weak smile he didn't feel and slapped him on the back, hard. "And I'll make a warrior of you, Jan."

Only Jan's red eyes showed any sign of the fatigue he must feel as he grinned. "Yessir, you surely will. But it's us Harbor Gnats as will hurt these devils most."

"Careful, Jan, that name might just stick." Nali grinned then. Just accept, don't think about what's happening, don't rationalize his action; live minute by minute. That's what he had to do. Nali gave Jan's shoulder a squeeze as they limped away together to give their orders.

As morning advanced, the retreat began with the wounded. Heralds took word around Sihmad Shal's far-flung walls, while Nali and Jan struggled to hold back a flood of advancing Minarians.

"It's a hit!" Nali shrieked, slapping Jan's arm with a jubilance born from the need for something to cheer. Jan replaced in his quiver the arrow he had already knocked as he took a moment to enjoy his success, rubbing fingers that had blistered beneath his finger guard as fire sputtered on a siege tower a stone's throw from the walls. Warriors clambered down ladders or jumped to escape the fast-spreading flames as a cluster of flaming arrows fed on dry wood.

Turning at the last second, Nali swiped at a Minarian warrior behind him. Nali's follow-through almost sent him to the ground as he pivoted on his wounded leg. The warrior ducked the swipe, lunging at Nali's unprotected mid-section with a dagger. Nali hopped back, losing balance and nearly stumbling on the blood-slicked stone. The man stiffened, grabbing for his neck. He fell face forward to reveal waxen-faced Esthen behind, the prince's arm wound thick with blood-stained bandages.

"You owe me again, Drulson," Esthen said as he retrieved his dagger.

"Should you be here?"

"Where else should I be but with my troops? It's where Dynfearn would be. We can't leave our soldiers leaderless! I heard you called a retreat. I needed to see if it's warranted."

"And?"

"Zopher's already in retreat. Pedr's moved his squad to rearguard on the gates. Didn't you hear the heralds?"

Nali scanned his scant forces trying to hold back an army, then shouted for retreat in a voice that tore his smoke-dry throat.

"Where's Arshal?" Nali asked as he hobbled to the ramp, glancing about in search of danger.

Esthen's brows met. "They say Cree has him locked in the tower and no one can see him. And I'm worried about Peshal. It's moving so quickly. What if he's too late? What if he's trapped outside? He never gave us his entire plan."

Esthen's questions hung between them as they reached the top of the ramp, waiting as their men scrambled to precede them.

"He'll be here," Nali assured the prince, placing his hand on Esthen's shoulder with unaccustomed boldness. Nali could see how soldiers brightened when Esthen moved among them. Their fatigue seemed to fall away with just his reassuring nod or a pat on the back. It was leadership Nali wanted to emulate.

As they descended behind the retreating Shandean defenders, Nali spied a rush of enemy warriors crossing to the wall from a siege tower, unchecked. He shouted a warning. Esthen and Jan dashed behind the barricade as Nali tried to fend off his attackers while retreating backward down the ramp. His leg buckled beneath him and he lurched to one side to sprawl on the Sijway. Half scrambling, Jan dragging him, he at last rolled to cover as arrows chunked into the barricade.

Nali gasped as he broke the shaft of an arrow embedded in the muscle of his shoulder. Jan tugged his sleeve. As he turned to look, the blood rushed the derna's temples, his wound forgotten in the instant he looked upon the prince. Esthen had fallen just behind the barrier, a spear protruding from his neck. Nali scrambled to Esthen's side and grasped the fallen prince's hand.

Esthen gazed back, resigned, as life pulsed from him, face going slack and the fire in his eyes fading as each pulse poured his blood onto the Sijway. All around them, stricken soldiers stared, battle seeming forgotten, their hearts torn and determination stolen. It was too much, this last blow. Nali motioned for two soldiers to carry the prince away. While all around rose chaos and din, Nali heard only his own gasps like a stiff wind in his ears.

"You're injured, Nali. Let me look" Jan began, tugging at his tunic.

Nali jerked away. "Don't worry about it, Jan. It's not my time yet." He peeked over the barricade then scanned the remaining soldiers. "Have them pull back, Jan. See to it, will you?"

A sense of uneasiness grew in those around him. Silence pummeled them as a red glow grew above the barbican. The crawling sensation of intense scrutiny made the hairs lift from Nali's skin. Suddenly an explosion ripped through the gates, knocking soldiers from their feet and sending others cowering for cover. The red light flared bright through a breach before fading to a small device: a medallion held by an Eidhalt.

"They've taken the gates!" someone shouted.

Nali roared retreat as soldiers scurried along the curving Sijway trying to reach the Fearnia gate. A glance had shown him adanan gates twisted against the half-lowered portcullis, blocking the advance of whatever power backed up the Eidhalt. Nali limped at the rear of the retreat, driving the defenders before him with a scowl as he wondered what tool of evil had been turned against them, for which Shande had no defense.

Jan paced beside him, glancing over his shoulder at the pursuit. "Someone needs to look at that wound there, Nali." He jabbed a thumb at the stump of arrow in Nali's shoulder. "A litter could run you to safety faster."

Nali glared at him and didn't reply. The blaze of light – What would be conjured to challenge them next? And with Esthen lost, where would their army find its heart?

Jan said no more, only now and then taking Nali's elbow to keep him from straying from the road and warning the derna that the enemy closed on them as retreating firefighters dumped oil on the Sijway behind them. The borough had become a roaring inferno around them as they dodged swirls of embers and falling timbers.

They plopped down just inside the Fearnia gate.

Nali fell against Jan, too exhausted to do more than gasp in lungsful of sooty air. The market square loomed large and empty in front of them. Only an occasional group of soldiers dashed across it. On the walls above, silence reigned, the troops studying the enemy movements with a universal numbness. They had lost perhaps three thousand already. And it had only begun. As his body slowed, Nali finally felt the wound in his shoulder. His leg throbbed. Each heartbeat sent stabs of pain up his entire side. His eyes closed as the familiar nausea gripped him again.

"Let me get a medical team."

Nali brushed Jan's helping hand away. "No. I've a problem with blood. It passes. Don't worry. I need to get used to it." Nali struggled against the desire to faint, wishing away the swirling light behind his lids.

Hearing Jan's sudden hiss of breath, Nali opened his eyes to find his father's blood-soaked body on a litter held between two Harbor men. Nali couldn't find his breath as he stared at the seafarer's blistered hands and darkened face.

"On the wall, from behind," one of the men said softly as Nali touched Drul's cool hand.

"Fool, you just wouldn't listen. You'll have quite a story to tell Mam." He dropped his head on his knees and pulled his cloak about himself. "Glory, they said. Rows of shining spears and colored standards in the wind."

The litter bearers moved on, leaving Jan stiff and stunned beside the silent derna.

Weariness and injury at last overcame grief and Nali slept, Jan soon drifting off beside him.

When Jan opened eyes stuck shut with soot, he found Arshal crouched before him, pale and oddly skeletal. The prince glanced at the bloody derna beside him, but didn't appear to recognize the cloak-covered shape.

"It's about time you showed up," Jan said, stretching legs gone stiff.

"I – was delayed. I'll tell you later. I've missed a lot. What's happening? Where's –"

Jan gripped Arshal's arm. "Esthen's dead."

Arshal choked on a gasp then stumbled forward to support himself against the wall.

"Before the gates. A rallying point. Nali said it's the meanin' of his name, to be a touchstone, a standard validatin' the mettle of Shandeans."

The prince's shoulders shook a moment while Jan still grasped his arm. Then Arshal nodded, looking up. His teeth bared with his last struggle to hold his grief in check.

"You saw him?"

Jan nodded.

"Fearnia will fall," Arshal stated after a long moment as Jan sucked in a breath. "Where's Peshal?" Arshal stared at the east wall as if he could see his brother racing home from Otayr.

What hopes had they placed on one young prince's shoulders?

27: Eidhalt

Late sun baked the hills and wooded valleys an hour's ride outside of Sihmad Shal. Peshal peered from the cover of a thicket, too stunned to move. Carrion birds rose from fields like smoke curling up from campfires. Minarian troops dotted plains that sported slashes of fresh green among charred ruins and soot-blackened trees. Wagons full of purloined supplies rolled away from what had once been sleepy farmsteads toward the besieging army.

He'd come too late. Sihmad Shal spread out before him, too distant to discern whether faces lined the walls, but he could see the smoke rising from within. Arshal knew war would come, dreamt it. What more had he known? That Peshal would fail this task and prevent his family from escaping? He tried to picture Arshal, his parents, Esthen and Resala, meeting over maps and plans, trying to plot new strategies because Peshal hadn't come. In their imaginings did they worry he'd lost, too, the thousands whisked into the forest of Otayr by Marol's friends? What fears and heartache did his failure cost them?

He could try to work his way west, sneaking through the night to reach the Rigannon then enter the city through the tunnel he had found. His every step would place his mission in jeopardy. That journey would take him through the bulk of the forces arrayed outside the city, and across the broad and treeless stretch of the Kalilian countryside where nothing like the small wood he hid in could conceal him.

Hooves beat the road behind him, closing.

Peshal crouched lower, hoping the Minarian wouldn't note the horse tied among the trees. As the Minarian neared, Peshal saw that the man wore a uniform unlike the others. An officer? Orange and red threaded fine trappings on the horse. A streamer of orange and red blew back from a helm gleaming dull black.

Peshal couldn't pass among these people, notable, if not by the birthmark on his temple, by his clothing and speech. Did this Minarian rank high enough to avoid scrutiny, or was he merely some messenger?

Peshal drew his sword. The road dipped as it passed through the small wood. The thicket Peshal hid in crowded the road where a trickle of stream crossed it, leaving a marshy, muddy mess rutted by wagon wheels and horse hooves.

Peshal swallowed hard. Arshal needed him. His family needed him. Hundreds relied on him for a safe refuge. He could lead sorties through the tunnel if only he could get to the city walls undiscovered.

Peshal slipped down into the dip. He rode up on the balls of his feet with impatience as the Minarian slowed to negotiatie the muddy banks of the stream. Peshal couldn't miss. His timing had to be as perfect as Arshal's lunges in wrestling, more so.

Just as the horse splashed through, Peshal jumped out and pulled the man from his horse and fell on him before the Minarian could reach for the sword scabbard dangling from his saddle. Air oomphed from the Minarian's lungs as Peshal dropped on the man's chest. The Minarian arched his back to throw Peshal aside as Peshal tried to wedge his sword against the man's neck, the weapon too long for him to maneuver easily.

Stupid, he should have grabbed his dagger.

The Minarian grabbed Peshal by the wrist, forcing the prince's own weapon back at him. Any moment the bone would snap.

The Minarian laughed a strained chuckle that crept around the pressure of Peshal's knees on his chest. "Demon, you are a gift of Ghyldus!" he said. "I will enjoy removing your head from your body." His breath smelled fat with the scent of some meal taken at a Shandean table. "You dare trouble an Eidhalt with your childish struggle?"

"You'll have the honor, then, of dying at the hands of one most purely of Terremar's house," Peshal said, his words more bold than his struggle as the Minarian threw him aside and yanked a dagger from a sheath at his side. Yet, merely uttering Terremar's name gave Peshal confidence. He yanked his wrist free of the Eidhalt's grip. The Minarian swiped at him with the dagger. Peshal darted aside too late to avoid the bite of the weapon in his upper arm. Peshal had to survive. Too many relied on him. He couldn't fail.

He raised his sword, sidling in the mud of the stream bed as the Minarian's horse nibbled nervously at the undergrowth, the sword in its saddle scabbard beyond the Eidhalt's reach. The thicket hummed with insects and gasped summer heat at them. It all seemed so clear so intensely alive as Peshal's lungs sucked in the dampness of the muddy earth and the floral notes of a flowering vine whose tendrils threatened to trip him.

The dagger flashed out at him again, but Peshal swung his sword with all his desperation behind it. The weapon met the Eidhalt's dagger as if it were but a bundle of rushes and smashed on into the man's chest. The Minarian emitted a gasp as Peshal's sword drove mail mesh into flesh. Before the Eidhalt could gather his breath, Peshal thrust. The sword parted the mail, through the flesh, to bone.

The Eidhalt fell from Peshal's sword. He let his weapon drop as he sucked in deep breaths of the thicket's sweet aroma. Swiftly, he dragged the body from the road, even as the man struggled feebly in his last moments of life. Peshal rolled him so that he lay face down in the stream then led the Eidhalt's horse into the underbrush. He transferred the tack and trappings to his own reliable mount, and his horse's bridle to the Eidhalt's horse.

As he returned to the dead man in the stream, he felt an urgency that made his hands tremble. He stripped the uniform from the Eidhalt and tore off his own clothing. After ripping a strip of cloth from his blouse and wrapping it around his bloody arm, he donned his enemy's belted tunic and the mail coat that went over it. He swallowed away the revulsion at the feel of blood soaking the black material. The Eidhalt helm reached low enough to cover the shawnsi birthmark on his temple and mostly concealed the distinctive facial features of one more purely shawnsi. Boots, arm guards, dagger sheath and a long black cloak completed his attire. Though a little larger than Peshal, the man's clothing made a good fit, if a bit coarse and warm.

Peshal stared at the man, so much less frightening as he lay naked in the thicket. Something about the very look of the huge medallion on the man's chest assured Peshal he didn't want to touch it, much less wear it. His fingers still tingled as if something crawled over them where he'd handled it to pull the clothing from his victim.

"Hey there, sir," a voice called from the top of the rise toward Sihmad Shal. He stared up at the man who stood silhouetted against the westering sun. Did he dare look to see if the dead man's body remained visible? Peshal inclined his head and adjusted his clothing to imply he'd stopped to relieve himself.

Shifting slightly, his leg pushed a branch over the man. Did he dare try to imitate their accent?

"What luck to meet you," the Minarian continued. "We took captives in the ruins of a barn just over this rise. My captain would be honored if you would join us."

Peshal swallowed hard. What could he do? He inclined his head and after retrieving the horses let the Minarian lead him from the dead man he had made.

They reached the deep shadow of the remaining wall of a burned barn just as dusk gave way to darkness. A wagon had been filled with booty from the farmstead. A torch sputtered to life behind him, sucking at the night with the gasps Peshal wished he could release. Sooty, bloody, weariness ringing their eyes, the captives – a family – stared back at him with a palpable hatred.

He couldn't reveal his dismay. Thousands waited on him.

An old woman on her knees, her lips moving soundlessly, regarded some private horror, her face blackened on a side and her hands gripping the fragment of some blanket or cloth stained dark. A younger woman and girl huddled together, their clothes torn and soiled, the girl's gaze wild, her mother's so hateful Peshal thought he could feel it knife through him. A younger man, probably the girl's father stood a step ahead of them, bloody, his nose broken, his eyes swollen, yet defiant as he stood with broad stance to face his enemies. It was the young boy at the man's side that made Peshal's heart stop, made the breath lock up in the prince's throat.

The boy, maybe ten or twelve, stared at Peshal as if he knew him, eyes wide, mouth opening as if to call his prince's name. Did the child know him as the man who begged his parents to send the old woman and children to Otayr? Or had this been a boy among the thousands who came to Long Day or Evenday races and witnessed the princes compete with the best gamers of the provinces?

Peshal regarded the ten-man Minarian contingent that followed him into the barn, they fawning and attentive to whichever way he looked. Maybe he could take out three or four before they realized their error. They'd reveal him. They'd kill him. And so close he could see the towers of Sihmad Shal reaching into the smoky sky, he would leave hundreds of shawnsi and officers to be rounded up and killed. What vain promise had he made?

"Master? Sir Eidhalt?" The man who had found him tugged at

his cloak. Peshal made a dismissing gesture and the man released his cloak as if he touched a hot coal. "Do you wish to offer these demon lovers in tribute to the God of Ea?"

The boy knew him. Mournful eyes pinned him. The boy would die because of him. He could see it in the child's gaze, in his hope eroding to disappointment, fear, hatred.

"These are of no import to the God of Ea," he said softly in his best approximation of a Minarian accent. "They are not ... demons and unworthy of tribute. I have no time for shal prisoners who are more useful to us as labor."

"Certainly, sir, they are hardly worthy tribute. We cannot spare the men to guard prisoners until the city is secure. We are too busy gathering provisions for the army."

"And why should I assist you in your work? You waste resources that could be providing for our soldiers who so valiantly battle in the name of the great God of Ea."

Peshal turned his back, hoping they would read his motion as disinterest and disdain as he headed for his horse. Instead of carrying off the prisoners to serve the army, as he had hoped, he heard behind him a club strike something soft. A cry ripped from one of the women, then a scream. He couldn't look. He had to. He made himself turn and look at the child who stood over his fallen father as the Minarians yanked grandmother, mother and sister to their feet. The child's gaze burned into him. What leader placed his family before his people?

"Sir, our captain would sup with you," a Minarian called to him.

"I would not sup with him," Peshal returned, escaping into the night as the shrieks of the prisoners howled in his ears, no matter how far he raced from the torchlit barn.

THE WEST

28: Lagdche

Amhese dropped down beside Tsevon in brittle weeds, raising a puff of dust. He rested on the outside slope retaining a massive impoundment high above and on the outskirts of Lagdche, the king's seat in Minaria. Despite a cap she'd woven from weed fibers to keep the sun out of her eyes, weeks of trekking through hot barren lands, more unbearable each day, had burned Amhese's face to the hue of leather. They left the Val several weeks into the light moon. Now the heat moon gave way to the ripening moon. It would be the warmest month in the mountains, but never so hot as here. Tsevon kept to himself his worries of what passed so many weeks distant. Had Konner sent their son to the spirits? Or did the boy simmer with anger at his abandonment? Had the Val fallen without some of its best to defend it?

"We'll never pass for Minarians here, the way we look," Tsevon told Amhese, his voice cracking from the dry heat that parched all their throats.

"Maybe not you, with that northman's red face and sun-white hair," she teased. She jerked her head, tossing Staphian-dark braids over her shoulder to snap his cheek and raise an almost smile.

Long before Segan's head appeared at the lip of the reservoir, they heard his return in the rattle of dry weeds.

"You'd think at least near water this place might find a spot of green. Not a tree, not a bush, nothing but scrub," Segan said as he handed Amhese a waterskin, her lips curling as she swallowed. The water in this land made them sick at first, tasting bitter and salty, even though the sweet waters of the Lharans fed the river. Below them, a slash of green taunted with the promise of watered lands. There, the marshy lowlands of river delta emptied into the Sea of Tebez. The city straddled the river and crowded against the foothills. They had watched clouds boil up and rain out their cool relief below, not a drop reaching the uplands. As far as they could see north and south, the hills marked a brown line that kept the people and their farms crowded against the coast.

"So now what, Tsevon?" Teckhan asked through lips burned and peeled to dry scabs.

Teckhan struck the root of Tsevon's worries. Who knew if Shande remained, the Val, Sefresal, or even Sihmad Shal? They saw an army of thousands pass them heading into the Lharans. Nothing could have withstood it. Tsevon had faith in Konner, maybe even Eithurdon, not so the king.

"We need a good look at Lagdche to start with," Tsevon said, weary with some malady that had haunted him since the night he'd rescued the captives, compounded when he called his son home from the spirits. The barren lands of Minaria seemed to draw his strength from him. "There's got to be a way without being noticed," he said. "We need to find Mol Azezial's hall, and its weaknesses. We need an escape route and diversions to stop pursuit." Tsevon stroked the grimy tangle of his beard, squinting as he studied the western horizon where the reservoir sent a steady stream of water tumbling down into the river bed, along with several small canals that channeled water toward different parts of the city.

Halieri, who sat cross-legged in the weeds, glanced up at Tsevon with dark eyes, then back to the small whetstone upon which he honed his knife. He pulled his words out between strokes. "If thinkin' 'bout takin' this city, here, what's a good place to start, in this land?"

Tsevon frowned, he wished Halieri could just straight out say things. Tsevon often found his ponderous and hard to decipher counsel sound.

"I can't figure what you're saying, Hali. The sun here's dimmed my wits," Tsevon hedged. Cornering Halieri would get Tsevon nowhere; the man closed up. He wasn't sure whether Halieri's pick had always struck a different rhythm, or if days buried alive among Lhata's dead had left him a little odd. Tsevon chose the Lhatan for his cunning, not his conversation skills.

Halieri stared into the sky, drawing a few of the others to follow his gaze. "Well, who's got most to gain, most to lose?"

Tsevon sighed. "Minarians got the most to gain, Shandeans the most to lose."

"No," Amhese said as Halieri turned away with the expression of a disgusted mentor. "The Pladde have the most to gain, the Hogde the most to lose."

With the ghost of a nod Halieri worked his whetstone.

"We're talking here," Amhese continued. "If we're to take Mol Azezial, Tsevon, who'd have the most to gain? The Pladde. The most abused people on Ea are the ones we should count on. If we win their help, we may gain access to the city, or even Mol Azezial."

"How can we trust –" Tsevon began.

"We have to," Gelter said as Halieri honed his knife, sprouting a hint of a smile. "The Pladde can't be happy with their lot. And Aibak said they have refused to abandon One."

"If they're so unhappy and oppressed then why haven't they risen up?" Tsevon asked.

"Did you see the same army I did?" Pician asked from behind Tsevon.

"Yes! And I saw Pladde driving the supply wagons and tending the livestock."

"But maybe they just need to know it's possible," Amhese mused. "If their lives have been directed by others for so long, they may not know how to begin. Certainly, they would oppose everything the Hogde are, and support everything they aren't."

Halieri rewarded them with a broad smile as he stood sheathing his knife. "And all that's weak in the city," he said.

"They'd know the city's weaknesses," Tsevon admitted. "With most of Minaria headed for Shande, maybe there are a few more weak spots than usual. So, it's Pladde we need to find, who aren't too scared to help us and have nothing to lose."

It only took a few hours to find the run-down shacks of a Pladde enclave just outside of the city, and only a few more to arrange a meeting with a local headman. Several days later a nervous Pladde man finally led them to a tiny cottage. Only easygoing Velder joined Tsevon, the rest keeping watch from a distance in the event of betrayal.

Tsevon succinctly laid out his needs to the headman who had risked death to meet with Minaria's sworn enemy. Tsevon was no diplomat. The dark cottage stank with the tension. A candle burned low, barely illuminating the men sitting on stools around the cottage's rough-hewn table. As the candle sputtered in a hot wind that poured through chinks in the shack's wall, a hand reached out of the shack's shadows to replace it.

Tsevon, intent on reading the reaction of the Pladde headman, barely registered the disruption. The elder's face appeared chopped from a block of wood. Circular scars on both cheeks from some rite formed deep shadows on his face, giving him an almost skeletal appearance.

The man, who refused to name himself, finally shook his head. His gray braids, bound in a black thread, were so heavy they barely shifted. Coiled like thick rope, he secured them through a twine loop tied to an eyelet in the short sleeveless tunic he wore. At last, the man turned from Tsevon's gaze to look into the shadows behind the Tawnkats.

"There is much we risk," he said in a dialect so thick Tsevon barely understood it. The man's hands, twisted by hard work, lay on the table in front of him, open. "What promises can you make that you bring the Pladde anything but more grief."

"I can't make promises." Tsevon's tone was unyielding. "Your king preaches destruction of anyone who isn't a servant of his personal god. That means your people, my people, all of Ea."

"It is not our concern to fight for Ea."

"Not for your people? To not fight's to deliver your own folk over to demons."

"We have lived under Hogde rule since before my father and his. We have endured and our beliefs have endured with us. This will be no different."

"But it is different this time," Velder said, leaning forward, his voice the kind that compelled others to listen. "Pladde already die on battlefields, not of their choosing, and with nothing to be gained for them if the Hogde win. We're told your people are forced to make sacrifices to this god, to yield up your children to Mol Azezial as slaves to honor a creature that would erase your beliefs, and tear apart your families."

"To resist is to be killed."

"If it isn't stopped, we'll all be killed," Tsevon returned. "They beat, rape, and kill your people to please a false god. You're forced to labor for people who treat their livestock better than you. If freed of this, wouldn't your life be better, even if a few of you die?"

"It is not my right to decide that some should be put at risk to save others!" The man's jaw tilted upward; his lips pursed in a half sneer as he regarded Tsevon. "That is the choice of the individual. What you propose denies their choice."

"No," Velder said, laying his hands palms up in front of the Pladde headman's. "You have the choice to listen to us and help us, or not. We warn you of what we aim to do. If you choose to help us, how will that hurt others? We'll do it anyway. If you warn your people, they won't be killed."

"What exactly would you have us do?" another voice demanded. A shadow detached itself from the wall behind Tsevon and joined the thin light thrown by the candle. The man's stature hadn't bent with labor like the headman's. His hair remained jet in tight braids. Though his voice carried urgency, his features revealed nothing, though the circular scars stood out stark and fresh on his cheeks, as one who has only recently passed through some rite.

"My son Jeret speaks out of turn, when it is not his right to do so," the older man said, glaring at the younger. "That is the way of the young."

"It is the way of the old to curl up like a desert rat, afraid to face a challenge," Jeret returned. "'It will blow by,' you say. 'It will not hurt us,' you say." Jeret leaned on the table to peer at his father, one braid slipping from its loop to touch the table. "These men speak truth. We will all suffer, greater and greater trials each day, if we do not stop this madness. What good is it to us if Mol Azezial grows stronger by conquering our neighbors? Who was it who suffered most in the wars with Arenh and Shiad? Who was it who labored for a Hogde army for none of the spoils? When their power is complete, and they no longer need Pladde to wash their bottoms and suckle their spawn, the Hogde will wipe us from Ea. Father, of that I am certain."

A long silence followed, in which only the slight whistle of the wind through the building's walls could be heard. Tsevon clenched his fists beneath the table. From all he had learned, he knew his ten – stout-hearted as they were – could not accomplish their goal without the Pladde. His hopes rested on Jeret, who had arranged the meeting and had the fire in him. But Tsevon must win Jeret's father.

"And you think it will help us?" the older man asked Jeret. An emphatic nod from Jeret led the man to sigh, stand and stretch. "I warn you, Tsevon of Tasch-el, what you do, it will be hard on all if you fail." He cast a dark glance at Jeret. "And, hear me, son. Once you have called the Pladde to rise, you will never again know peace."

"There is no peace now. It is a falsehood," Jeret returned.

"Then we live a lie." He turned to Tsevon, his intense gaze belying the doubts his words had expressed. "What would you have us do?"

Tsevon smiled. This was the easy part: action. His entire squad knew, as did Tsevon, they would have one opportunity. They could not fail.

29: Mol Azezial

As the ripening moon advanced, Tsevon's squad immersed itself in divining the secrets of Lagdche. At last, near the end of the moon, a lull came to their frantic scheming and preparations. An eerie quiet settled over Lagdche as the moon hesitated to sink beneath the horizon, marking the onset of their assault.

Halieri crouched among the shadows thrown by the aged gates of the dam retaining Lagdche's reservoir, joined by a handful of Pladde accomplices. Watching the moon's descent, a smile broadened on his scarred face. The dam's attendants dispatched, he turned control of the flow of water over to Pladde whose revenge for decades of oppression verged on fruition.

Southwest of the impoundment, Gelter, Davin and their complement of Pladde separated a dozen horses from the herd milling about the king's stables and led them to a hilltop overlooking the city. They nudged the remaining horses from corrals to wander far from their keepers, whose blood seeped into the cracked earth from slit throats.

Meanwhile, Segan and Pician slipped into the cold brine of Lagdche's harbor. They swam to anchored ships and cut holes below the waterline. Minarian soldiers slept soundly in their narrow racks below decks, waking too late as water slowly rose within.

Near the center of the city, Dagon and Velder slipped along the top of a battlement securing Mol Azezial's stone palace, cutting the throats of its few guards. Dashing across the moonlit patches and clinging to the dark, with ease they overcame sentries standing inattentive at their posts. After all, who would dare attack the king in his halls?

At the base of the high stone wall, Teckhan kept watch as

Tsevon and Amhese climbed a rope attached to a hook wedged in the stonework of the wall. When Tsevon and Amhese had disappeared behind the parapet, Techkan scaled the wall, pulling the rope up behind him. Only a pace away, a sentry sprawled, a few bubbles still popping in the blood welling from the gash in his throat.

Amhese followed her lifemate and young Teckhan, ignoring the sentry's body. She had hardened against such sights. Hurrying down the steps to the gardens below, she held in her heart the pride of acceptance. She touched the new tattoo at the base of her neck where men wore the markings of their manhood ceremony. There she bore the lazy W of Tsevon's mark, like all the others who had proven themselves worthy of the Tawnkats. She held her head high: a Tawnkat, a warrior now.

The late sounds of partiers drifted from palace windows as their Pladde spies had promised. The Minarians celebrated their certain conquest of Shande, the long-awaited party delayed when a rival poisoned Mol Azezial's favorite concubine. A lamp went out in the rooms above. They needed to work quickly. Whether their plans held or not, when the heralds called the first hour after midnight, shortly after moonset, the reservoir gates would open.

Amhese tensed when Techkan tossed the hook at a stone window ledge some twenty paces up. A soft clank brought Tsevon's breath through his teeth with a hiss. The rope dangled from the ledge above rooms said to be Mol Azezial's.

The Tawnkats counted on a raucous celebration to cover their furtive sounds. Pladde servants had toted barrels of wine and a bale of osfothye into the palace and delivered summons to hundreds of the city's elite. Mol Azezial did not take his wine well, the Pladde told them, and likely would retire long before the fete ended. If only a Pladde servant could just slip poison in the king's wine, or slit his throat in his sleep, or at least help the Tawnkats enter. But Mol Azezial allowed no Pladde to serve his food, nor suffered them in his halls at night unattended.

The Tawnkats just hoped that by striking the head from the beast it would end the war, or at least give Shande time to defend herself. If their actions fed a Pladde uprising that diverted soldiers from Shande all the better.

Amhese took a deep breath and rubbed her hands on her charcoal-blackened hide leggings. Teckhan tugged on the rope to secure it as she stared up at the small dark window left open to the cool wind off the ocean, a window too small for any but

Amhese to fit through.

She grasped the rope to still her shaking hands. So much depended on her. Her thoughts briefly reached for the many who would succumb to a wall of water when Halieri heard the herald's call. So many innocents. Warned, most of the Pladde waited on high ground or had prepared their escapes. She couldn't help but think of the Hogde children who had no say in the evil their parents wrought in Ea.

Dark shrouded Tsevon's features as the moon fell too low to reach over the wall. His hand brushed her cheek before he disappeared into deeper shadows. Only the tiny sounds of scuffing feet and gasps of breath told her Dagon and Velder continued their grisly march around the palace walls.

Amhese wrapped the rope around her hands and walked up the palace wall, the abraded stone, dissolved by decades of salt wind, scuffed with each step. Pausing just below a sill carved with the representations of a multitude of gods, she waited for the moon to duck behind a cloud before blocking the window to climb inside. She held her breath. Certainly, he would wake to the sound of her heart drumming inside her chest.

The room stood empty. Spare light from the window revealed a turned-down bed of fine linen, the curtained and tapestried walls and fur-lined stools of a royal's suite. A robe lay across the bed, giving off a satiny sheen. Wine and a platter of pungent cheese and cured fish waited bedside. She saw no sign of Mol Azezial.

A moment's panic seized her. The wall of water would come and swallow them all, the Pladde lose hope and give up. All their efforts, all their plans, would amount to nothing. In his tower, Mol Azezial would survive a mere annoyance like all the other Tawnkat raids that couldn't stop an army. His soldiers would continue to maul Shande. She stared at the empty bed, frozen. She came with no alternative.

A door opened in another room of the suite and yellow candle light from the hall rushed in. Amhese slipped behind the curtain fronting the bed. How long would it take him to fall asleep? When his eyes grew accustomed to the dark, would he see her shape behind the cloth? What if he lit a candle?

A voice pleaded for mercy. It carried the distinct pattern of the Pladde dialect. A woman's voice. No, a girl's, Amhese realized as Mol Azezial's bulk crowded the room, the girl towed behind him by the wrist. The girl tried to twist away, and planted her feet on the rough stone floor. He finally yanked her to the bed and fell atop her with his bulk.

Amhese froze. Could she stand idle and witness the assault of a child? Likely Mol Azezial would sleep after if she let him have his will. The stench of wine came in a great gasp of his breath and curled Amhese's lip with its sourness. If she acted now, she risked the girl crying out or the king seeing her movements.

He clamped one hand on the girl's mouth, ripping at her skirts. Amhese stepped from behind the curtain while Mol Azezial concentrated on loosening his own robes as the girl squirmed beneath him. She cried out her fear. That instant, Amhese leapt upon Mol Azezial's back, yanked his startled head back and dragged her dagger across his exposed throat. As blood spurted from his neck, she held a hand over his mouth to muffle gagging gasps, while the blood-spattered girl stared up at Amhese in horror, squirming from beneath her assailant's death throes.

As the girl tried to retie the torn wrap skirt Pladde women wore, Amhese finished the job she had come to perform. Her knife was sharp, and a blood-soaked pillowcase served her well. Amhese scanned the yard below. She sensed Tsevon staring out of the dark, not seeing her, fearful, tensing, impatient as Dagon and Velder joined him, their work done. The moon had set. She only had minutes before the herald would call the first hour of the morning. If they fled now, they still might not make it. She shouldn't have hesitated.

Amhese took the girl's arm and gestured for her to hang onto her back. She quickly donned her archer's wrist and finger guards, hoping they would help her support the additional weight as the two of them awkwardly squirmed out of the window and she slowly walked down the wall.

"What on Ea," Tsevon whispered as Amhese reached the ground. The girl dropped from her back, the two darting to the protective shadows of the wall. Tsevon glanced from the blood on the girl's clothing and the way she had clumsily knotted her skirt and met Amhese's gaze. She had no words for him yet, all breath locked tight in her throat. Teckhan motioned for them to follow him up onto the wall. Amhese held out the pillowcase she'd tucked in her belt. She saw Tsevon judge its shape and weight. He gagged and gave her a wide-eyed look that made her heart sink. Shock. Wasn't this what he wanted? Tsevon prodded Teckhan, who led the way at a run, slowing only long enough for them to slide down a rope to the dark streets outside the palace.

The herald's horn sounded the first hour.

They barely noted it as they dashed through the dark alleys of sleeping Lagdche, too late to save the Minarian children.

Amhese gripped the Pladde girl – who had named herself Teshet – by the arm as they ran, pulling the girl along on legs that stumbled and buckled beneath her. Certainly, the slap of their feet on the stone and packed-dirt pathways would bring light sleepers to their windows, or the gasps of their breath, or Teshet's cry when she fell to her knees. No alarm rose.

A distant rumble shook the earth beneath their feet. Is that the way the wave would sound? They couldn't see above the roofs to know how far away lay the hilltop where Gelter and Davin waited with horses. If luck held, Segan, Pician and Halieri had already joined them.

Tsevon looked back over his shoulder at her with his expressionless face that said so much about what went on his head. He wanted this, didn't he? He had vowed this as his vengeance. He hadn't tossed it away. The bloody thing bobbed against his thigh as he ran, the pillowcase corners tied around his belt. Her stomach churned as she thought of the grisly thing she did. The bile rose in her throat. Dagon gripped her arm a moment and she turned her thoughts away. First, she must reach the hilltop.

She heard the flood now: waters long locked into submission at last freed and the sound of the Pladde's first lurch at rebellion. She pumped her legs harder. She thought she could go no farther. Her legs weighed heavier, her calves knotting. Then, desperate, she looked up from her feet to realize they climbed a long slope.

They would make it. Teshet stumbled, but Amhese dragged her on, heedless of the girl's sobs as she yanked her to her feet. Amhese didn't slow her pace. They hadn't gone high enough. They still had to reach Gelter. Would the flood do enough damage? Would someone pursue them? What if Segan and Pician had triggered an alarm, or Gelter and Davin? Maybe someone had already stumbled, retching, from Mol Azezial's room to report the gruesome scene.

They left the last few stone houses behind and the alley broadened into a track that opened onto dry field. The track grew harder to see in the moonless dark and they still had to descend again before climbing the next hill to escape the flood. A shallow pool spread below them already as backed up flood water rose out of reach of the destructive wave.

They splashed through, finding the once parched ground still hard beneath their feet. And at last Gelter and Davin's silhouettes holding the reins of several horses, emerged on a hilltop. From their vantage they could see the full destruction of Halieri's work.

Amhese fell to her knees on reaching the hilltop. Teshet broke from her grip to stumble to the comfort of one of Gelter's companions. The man, Jeret, groaned dismay as he named his niece.

Tsevon leaned on Gelter, panting. Segan and Pician had only just returned in time, their lungs still gasping for breath.

"Hali?" Tsevon asked between breaths.

Gelter pointed at the wreckage where the reservoir had once stood. The force of the release had completely collapsed the entire retaining wall on either side of the gates. "There's no way they could escape it," Gelter said.

Though dark without the moon, the light of stars hinted at the path of destruction. They'd lost the last Lhatan, and with him his Pladde companions.

Jeret, clasping Teshet to him, expressed no grief for the loss of his comrades. Heroes, he named them. Their stories would be told among the Pladde for generations, he vowed. As Jeret and his companions relived their victory and speculated on their next acts, Amhese heard in the voices the rebirth of pride. Jeret gushed his thanks as Tsevon's Tawnkats mounted the waiting horses and bade Lagdche farewell.

They came for this and now they departed, as swiftly as it began. Start an uprising and flee. Somehow it felt wrong to Amhese. What would happen to the Pladde when the Hogde unmasked the Pladde role? What if the uprising sputtered to a halt without Tsevon to goad it on? What if all this loss of life, all the dead, meant nothing?

Amhese didn't look back until they slowed to cool the horses. Her heart ached with grief not only for Halieri and the Pladde lost with him, but for the innocents. They shouldn't have come. The Tawnkats wanted to deal a blow to Minaria and start an uprising. Wouldn't Mol Azezial simply be replaced with some other tool? The bundle secured by Tsevon's saddle ties drew her gaze. Nausea rose in her throat and a shiver took her with such violence she barely held the reins.

Segan reached across the gap between them to touch her arm. "Amhese, don't let it torment you."

Tsevon turned in his saddle to stare back at them, but said nothing, his expression lost in the dark.

"But was it our right?" And has it truly helped? If all this did nothing –"

"It was right. It helped. It wasn't for nothing," Segan said, releasing her arm as Tsevon urged his horse to a trot toward occupied Shande.

30: Magic

It didn't take long for Khoti's skills to make him the ideal link between Sefresal and the Val. He served his abbreviated Guard apprenticeship mapping the safest routes up the pass to the Val, marking each cave and cleft that might be used to store goods, shelter soldiers or ambush the enemy. Long days in the pass made his shortened Guard training more intense, the din of the city more offensive.

While many noncombatants had evacuated to the Val, most trades and services continued, as did noisy preparations to defend the city. Carpenters and stone masons beat together a rampart at the mouth of the pass to stand as a last defense against any besieging army. With sheer mountain walls at its sides and the pass behind, the rampart could be supplied from caves in the pass. The rampart blocked the only trail leading to the pass and only a narrow, fortified path ran from it to Sefresal. No matter how sturdy they built it, or how long a respite they had to fortify it, all knew that in the end the rampart would never stand against an army as determined as that marching south along the Lhata Road.

In advance of the Minarians rounding the Dodfrenyen marshes to march on Eilime from the south, noncombatants from Eilime, too, sought shelter in the Val, much to Konner's dismay. The Second grumbled that Tawnkats should be harassing the Minarians, not playing nursemaid to exiles. Instead, Guard scouts now employed Tawnkat tactics: setting off avalanches, flinging exploding pottery jars, and whittling away at the enemy army's scouts.

Around the rising of the ripening moon – the warmest month in the mountains and worse here on the edge of the plains – Kefta at last began Khoti's specialized instruction in weapons and the ways of service in the Lharan Guard, the last steps before his full membership in the cadre. Khoti had already learned more than he thought he could absorb in a lifetime: from protocol among nobles and the colors of the royal houses, to outfitting for an expedition, hand signals and care of his weaponry. Now Kefta drilled him from dawn to dusk until Khoti could barely lift his sword arm for his aching shoulder, nor do more than drop into bed each night, asleep instantly.

If Tasch-el still stood, by now Khoti would have endured rites that culminated in Konner making three small cuts on Khoti's neck to be stained dark with a burning dye so all would recognize a man of Tasch-el. Rites every man of Tasch-el dreamed of from his first steps as a boy seemed unimportant now. Riding beneath crossed swords and biting praise into the role of man-of-arms in the Lharan Guard made the fasting and dancing of voicing day seem trite and childish.

Khoti belonged to Eithurdon now: He wore Eithurdon's buff and pewter colors, bore a sword imprinted with Eithurdon's insignia, and slept in a tiny room in Eithurdon's Halls as an honor bestowed upon the son of an ally. Here, Khoti of Tasch-el stood a seasoned warrior. It brought out a swagger in his walk. When messenger duties brought Khoti's young friend Tre to Sefresal, the youth's awe only added to the cockiness in Khoti's grin.

Yet it wasn't home. The tiny room in the servant's wing of Eithurdon's Halls hemmed him in a way the alcoves of the Val, or his old loft room with Von never did. His straw-stuffed mattress rested on a frame above the floor, and he had his own washstand and even a window. But it was a lonely place without family and neighbors. Even rooms in the armory, where other single Guardsmen stayed, would have at least distracted him from the strange moods that gripped when in his idle hours he pondered all that his people had lost and yearned for the smell of pine and a cool wind off the snowpack.

As Khoti sat on the edge of his bed working his sword belt with an oil cloth, he found his thoughts turning to their darkest place: the uncertainty of his parents' fate. Did their bones lay in some desolate place far from home, picked at by carrion birds, forever bound to that nightmare?

The door to his room smashed open. Khoti lurched to his feet, hand already reaching for his dagger.

"Dust your brains out, boy!" Kefta pushed his bulk into the tiny room. "You kept me waiting!" Kefta came at him, sword upraised, angry red beard twitching.

Khoti shrugged him off, sat again on his bed and retrieved his belt and rag. "Oh, it's you," he said. "I thought someone important had come. If you're not here to tell me all of Minaria is at the gates, go away."

"Such gratitude," Kefta said with a laugh as he sheathed his sword. "I teach you everything I know and you discard me like a child's toy."

Khoti gave Kefta one of his most wicked tawnkat hisses that ended in a menacing growl.

"It's like that, is it?" Kefta said. "You owe your Guard brothers a few things: respect, trust and camaraderie. None of which you show when you act like that. Whatever's chewing at you, do you think your troubles are greater than the man who sends his lifemate, heavy with child, on a hard trek to the Val, to maybe never see her again because he's likely to die in some fool war?"

Khoti mumbled an apology, knowing how Kefta hungered for news, or even a visit with his lifemate. "I just can't stand sitting here! If I'm a man of the Guard and not just playing at the job, I need to prove it. There's got to be something, anything, I could be doing!"

"Soon you'll be wishing you had the time to sit and brood. And I don't want to hear this ridiculous talk of proof. You earned the right to wear the duke's colors. I have it on the best gossip there's not a man in the Guard who'd say a word against you. They respect you. You proved your mettle on the Staph-el Road. You're a man-of-arms now."

"I want to scout, Kefta. I need to do something with purpose, to use everything the Tawnkats learned to put fear in those wicked Minarian hearts. Let me go, Kefta. I'm ready."

Kefta leaned against the door frame. "It's no wonder your folks ran off. You must've been a trial to raise."

"I'll do you proud, Kefta. That's one thing you can count on."

"I don't doubt it."

A commotion drew them to the small window to see a horse on its side in the courtyard. Khoti recognized its trappings as the royal blue of the House of Dyndevas. A black banner fluttered from a staff in the hands of the messenger hurrying to the doors of Eithurdon's Hall. Kefta motioned for Khoti to follow as he hurried to the hall.

Eithurdon looked up from the messenger's scroll when Khoti and Kefta arrived, their riding boots loud on the rough floor. Eithurdon appeared pale in the dim hall.

"Minaria declared war," the duke said. "A fleet of ships, no doubt armed with Lharan metals, sails on Sihmad Shal. Prince Arshaldon directs our defense and I recognize his mark on the orders. I don't know what that means, when it should be from the king. The province of Kishma is to prepare for war."

"As if we haven't known all along," Khoti said to Kefta, not meaning for his voice to carry.

"Granted," Eithurdon said, peering at him over the scroll. "But this is a call to arms, at last. There is more. We must prepare for possible refugees from Sihmad Shal in the event the city falls."

"What madness is this?" Kefta protested. "Retreat here? Lord, they can't be serious."

Eithurdon shrugged. "Shawnsi, officers, derna. It echoes the earlier warnings. We must assume they know what they propose."

"Well, Khoti," Kefta said. "On your way to join Ytri's scouts, you may as well warn Konner he'll need to make more room." Kefta's red beard quivered. "How do they hope to get here? By ship? By river? And if all the land's lost, what good will it do? What they need's fighting men in that city. Lharan Guardsmen. Like as not they expect to fight a battle with a host of treasury officials." Kefta's tone rang as sour as the taste in Khoti's mouth. The Guard captain gave Khoti a push toward the door.

Khoti glanced back as he prepared to leave. Eithurdon sat still and erect in the chair at the head of his hall. Light from the doors revealed tapestries on the walls behind him, the cloth detailing the history of his house, including the symbols representing the gods counted among shawnsi ancestors. Standing before the duke, the messenger supported himself on the standard from which the war banner hung limp, darker than shadow. Kefta, his red beard like an angry slash, nodded for Khoti to hurry. Khoti swallowed hard. Something about the scene seemed like a mote of distant memory. Certainly, he had never experienced anything like this. He shook himself and turned from the darkness in Eithurdon's Hall.

On a bright morning in the Val a few days later, Khoti sighed his relief that his messenger boy days had finally ended and he could join Ytri's squad of scouts. He should have already joined his scout friends Geleg and Tuban, and Kefta's younger brother Mitte, harassing the Minarian army. Anyone could have carried Eithurdon's orders, but then Konner's anger would have fallen on them instead.

Konner went red in the face, decrying the way refugees smothered them already. And now Tawnkats would need to make caves on the other side of the valley habitable instead of fighting. And wouldn't so many refugees finally lead the Minarians in on top of them? And what would Khoti's fa say to learn they'd done nothing but babysit lowlanders, especially when he found out his son joined the Lharan Guard, something Tsevon had already forbidden? Konner had sputtered to an end likely where his heart really lived: they needed Tsevon's son more than the Guard did.

Khoti realized he wore a scowl as he strode from the caverns to whistle over the din for the mare who had served him so well during the battle for the Staph-el Road. He had dubbed her Fidra, Shiadin for 'faithful.' An uncanny mount, she learned his cues and moods, and refused other riders. Fidra trotted to the gate and blew in his face, then pressed her nose into his chest, bringing a smile back to his lips.

When he finally nudged Fidra toward the pass, he suddenly had to rein in to avoid running over a woman blocking his path. Her dark hair, barely restrained by a scarf, blew out around her like a cape. Though dressed more plain than usual, and no attendant waited on her, he instantly recognized Eithurdon's only offspring, Asteria.

Khoti gave her a curt bow – he'd learned at least that from Kefta – and excused himself to pass. She reached out and grabbed Fidra's bridle, eliciting an instinctive snarl from Khoti as Fidra tried to toss her head, trembling.

"Please, take me with you. I must go to Sefresal." She held him with a dark gaze that had always made him feel as if her eyes might swallow him.

He looked away. "No," he said, as he tried to extricate Fidra's head from the woman's grasp. Asteria moved beyond his reach, maintaining her grip on the bridle. It wouldn't be right to insult the duke's daughter, but she irritated an already annoyed warrior. "I'm not going to Sefresal, Lady, only part of the way. Besides, your fa insists you remain here. I serve him." He meant the last as a rebuke, but she ignored it.

"There is nothing for me to do here. I feel burdensome. I am not trained to do such work as there is and I horribly ruin what they give me." Her stange dark gaze implored him. Burden, he figured, likely an apt description. Doubtless, she wouldn't want to do the labor common mountain folk would. "I can be helpful with a few things from Sefresal."

He hesitated. Here stood a woman of power. When her mother

died young, Asteria grew to take on the role of matriarch, running the duke's household, despite being only a year Khoti's elder. She gave orders with the assumption she wouldn't be refused. How could he delicately insist that his no meant no?

"Lady, I can't be defying the duke. I've done enough of that to my own fa and I don't like the results. There's no need for fancy things here, and I'm sure our simple life's boring for a woman of your position –"

"I want my loom," she said, tone indignant. "We need blankets. If we must expand these caves, we need wall coverings and mats to warm them. We will need warmer clothing soon. This valley cannot supply all the needs of so many people. We do not have enough hides to tan, nor cloth to sew. I can weave, but your few looms here do not need extra hands. I can stitch, but we have no cloth to sew."

"I'm sorry, Lady. It's a worthy request. I still can't take you there. I'll send word of your needs. But I don't see how anyone could haul a loom –"

"It came in a crate from Otayr and is easy enough to take apart and haul by sledge," she said. "But we need other things. The derna need materials to teach the young, and we run low on elixirs and medicines the healers need. We need needles and shears, and so much more that I cannot list. My father and officers have no time to find those things, much less pack and –"

"No, I won't guide you," Khoti said finally. "I have to answer to the duke, and I haven't the time to go all the way to Sefresal, much less be slowed –"

"Then I will find my own way!" She released the bridle and strode off toward a stand of aspen, her arms swinging with balled fists at their ends.

Khoti grinned to himself, unsure why, chuckling as he set off at a trot for the pass.

It wasn't long before she made her presence known. Khoti knew the pass too well to miss the sound of hooves echoing behind him, or to sense her when she crept near his fire that first night, just beyond the circle of light. He ignored her.

He really thought she'd tire and turn back. Though ripening moon days grew hot, mountain nights remained cool, filled with howls and soft growls. He moved slowly, compared to many of his wild rides up or down the pass, not wanting to risk laming Fidra and having to turn aside. Besides, he wanted to just enjoy his time away from the press of people and duties in Sefresal and the Val. He worked his way down the deserted pass for two days, careful to pick new paths as he did with every trip to avoid creating a trail that might lead the enemy to them. Still, she followed. He hoped she knew enough to keep going when he turned aside for Lhata. Yet he had to admit grudging admiration for her. Stubbornly she paced him, always out of sight, and her defiance reminded him of his own.

In the afternoon of the second day, Khoti walked Fidra along a stream course, enjoying the lazy heat of the sun on his back. The path he took ran along the edge of the treeline, the pines sighing below, muting the cool airs deviling the rocky slopes above. Only a short distance ahead, another stream joined this, one Khoti planned to follow along the mountains' feet toward Lhata.

A gasp and clatter of stones came from behind. He whipped around, knowing he'd see Asteria. Her mount had shied at a sunning snake and thrown her from his bare back. The horse lurched up a loose slope, its reins trailing.

"Look out!" Khoti shouted, too late.

As Asteria's mount unlocked the stones, the slope shifted. Asteria knelt in its path, stunned from the fall and unmoving as she stared up at the mountainside. Too late, she struggled to gain her feet, but the onslaught of stone bowled her over. In moments, the slide spent itself. The horse labored up the slope a few more paces, loosing more rock, before it trotted to firmer ground in search of Fidra.

Khoti ran for the spot where he had last seen her. Not a large slide, like those closing the Staph-el Road, it could still kill a man. Khoti cursed her stubbornness as he dug through shale and gravel, seeking the solid floor of the pass where she should be if the stone hadn't rolled her along with it. He couldn't find the spongy turf. The slide filled a section of the pass neck high with gravel, dirt and thin rock slabs the size of washtubs.

Khoti stopped digging to listen, hearing nothing but a light shift of stone a pace away. Trickles of pebbles filled some pocket. Gingerly, he pushed away the rubble.

He only needed to dig a little way down to find her leg wedged between two sharp chunks of stone. Brushing away more debris, he pulled aside several slabs before he could free her. Already, bruises marked her face, but her chest rose slightly with each shallow breath. As he bent to lift her, she let out a moan of pain, though her eyes remained shut.

He could see her injury, sensed it almost as if he could see deeper than the purpling bruises to the flesh beneath. Not for the first time, he wondered if all people saw wounds thus or if his fa's healing arts had been passed to him. Hesitant fingers probed for broken bones, but he found none. Internal ruptures, a common injury in treacherous mountains, often hid beneath bruises like hers. The look, the feel, left him certain that inside she bled.

After securing the lead of her horse, he led Fidra to a spot where he could use a rock ledge to mount while cradling Asteria before him. He urged Fidra toward Sefresal as fast as he dared, Asteria's mount trotting behind. As they passed, he glanced longingly toward the flower-dappled glades of the valley leading away south toward Lhata.

Khoti rode several more hours down the pass, chewing on his ill humor before he sensed her gaze on him. He had just negotiated one of the most hazardous descents, a steep rock face he could have avoided by a longer more circuitous route if he felt he had the time.

"I am dying," she said around a gasp.

"Don't be ridiculous," Khoti said as he guided Fidra down a fall of stone. Asteria's mount balked, jerking Fidra off balance on the treacherous slope. "You'll feel better soon."

"No, everything is falling away."

Khoti stared down at her. Once he felt as if he "fell away." He had called it loneliness, that feeling when the carrion birds had settled around him –

"Just stay with me, Lady. It won't be long now," he soothed, ignoring her shaking head.

Did he have his fa's medicine? The sticks his father had made for him to replace those lost in Tasch-el were deep in his pack, untried, though Tsevon had seemed so confident Khoti would one day wield them. Healers belonged to a cadre of lorists about which other mountain folk knew little. They trained, his father told him, and that's all he would say. Was it only a learned skill? He'd seen it performed enough. Gods, he could see it in her, something ruptured and bleeding inside. He couldn't help feeling a little responsible. If he'd just acted as guide as she'd asked, or forced her to return to the Val and put under guard, or at least ensured her mount was properly equipped, this wouldn't have happened. And now, what if she died because Sefresal had no medicine to heal such a wound? The duke's grief would be Khoti's burden. Her people relied only on herbs and bleedings, ignorant of the blood spirits and he sensed they thought of mountain medicine as some backward ritual like naming and voicing days. If he tried to use his fa's medicine, it couldn't be in

Sefresal where so many would gawk, or laugh, or touch their monuments to the gods for protection from such strangeness, and destroy his concentration on an uncertain task.

He needed a safe shelter where he could light a fire and rest when the medicine wore him. What if his skills, if any, fell far short of his fa's, like Konner's? Khoti struggled to remember the images that had come to him in his weeks of fever, the words he'd heard his father mumble. What foolishness did he contemplate?

He made for the rampart at the mouth of the pass, a vacant place now as night descended. Now and then, Asteria gazed up at him, unseeing. He found a spot on the Sefresal side of the barrier sheltered from the wind and carefully tucked his cloak under Asteria's head before dashing back to collect his pack and gather dryer pieces of wood and shavings from trees cut during rampart construction. Soon he had a warm blaze going, and at last turned to her, trying to still trembling hands. He could do it; he must.

"I – I must touch you, to mark the injury," he told her, reaching to pull her tunic above the waist of the hide trousers she'd donned.

"What difference? I will be dead," she gasped. "I am such a fool. Is this what my mother felt –"

"Quiet! I need to think," he said. He found the spot. He could see it, feel it. The heat swelled up at him at the mere outline of a bruise. When he gently pressed, she cried out, her eyes closing as a small shiver took her.

He set his knife in the fire, awkwardly gripped the sticks in shaking hands and chanted his fa's song to the spirits, his voice so low it barely rose above the wind. As the rite took him, the sticks found a rhythm, faster and faster, tapping the sounds of earth and tree, rock and water, wind and sky.

A deep cool breath rushed him, familiar. The spirits who sent him home to Tsevon's call danced on his breath, made the sticks sing in his hands. The sticks whistled like wind through branch and stone as they clacked and rattled in their hollow pitch. His task absorbed him; the memories of a lore thousands of years old filled him, fresh and young.

As he concentrated on the tera sticks, entranced by the wonder of what he called into himself, he barely noticed the expression on Asteria's bruised face soften, pain giving way to comfort. On the edge of his heightened perception – a euphoria of spirits touching, soothing, joining with him – he glimpsed Kefta watching from just outside the circle of light. But Khoti couldn't look away from the blur of sticks and fire.

Khoti continued his music as he dropped one stick in the fire to smolder. After a moment, the beat of the other two slowed in his hands then stopped. He retrieved the burning tera stick and smothered the flame with fingers that felt only the cool of mossy stone where the sting of heat should be. Crouching beside Asteria, eyes closed, he traced her injury with the stick, leaving a streak of ash, the coal, the stuff of the earth, remaining behind over the invisible wound. He took up his fire-purified knife and waited a long moment as the blade cooled, his eyes pressed shut. He couldn't let himself think about what he did, just repeat what he'd seen, feel the spirits flowing in him, pouring through his veins, throbbing in his temples, pulsing in his blood. What made them in him? Was this the secret of his fa's medicine? He couldn't think about it, couldn't think about anything, especially not of how he intended to bring blood from the flesh of the duke's daughter. Eyes still closed against the night, he at last reached out and pulled easily along the ash marked line on her skin.

He might have heard a gasp on the wind, somewhere beyond his circle of fire, the shift of feet on stone. He opened his eyes. Asteria's expression remained comforted. He'd made the cut just deep enough to allow the blood to bead up and spread over her skin. Hesitating only long enough to take a deep breath, Khoti slashed the knife across the palm of his left hand, leaving a deep cut the same length as Asteria's. Blood oozed up and ran down his arm. So absorbed in the medicine, he barely wondered at the absence of pain, nor feared whether he could handle such powers as healers held. He pressed his hand against her, so the blood of the two wounds met. She sucked in a breath, not one of pain or fear. A smile tugged her lips.

A sudden heat and pain throbbed in his hand and side, a phantom pain. Khoti swallowed hard, feeling an instant's panic that he'd done something wrong, before he sensed the spirits within him, absorbing the poison, whisking it out of him so that her injury only briefly touched him, the pang almost lost to memory as soon as he felt it. He squinted at Asteria, concentrating, trying to remember every motion his fa had made. He set the bloody knife in the fire. As the blood burned away into flakes, the pain she gave him faded and the sweat slicking his face dried. His hand still bled furiously. He had cut it too deep. After only a moment's hesitation, he took the knife from the fire and pressed it against his palm. The pain lasted only the breath of an instant, bringing the sweat to his forehead again, a sickening, sinking feeling like he'd felt when he found the dagger in his side. Swiftly, the ache faded as the cut congealed in the burn.

He gave Asteria a cursory glance. Her bleeding had already stopped. He wrapped a rag around his hand then poured a splash of spirits on Asteria's small wound before covering it with a patch of fabric he tore from her tunic, and gently resettled her clothing. He felt so lethargic, so heavy in the limbs. He had things he should do now. Absently, he tugged his blanket from his pack and tucked it around her. At last, he sat back to wait, feeling wearier than any time he could ever remember, more than battle weary, healing weary. He had been home to the spirits!

Kefta stepped into the light of the fire. His confusion screwed his face into a questioning scowl. Khoti barely acknowledged him, though he stared at his captain with the bright fire of the spirits burning strongly, still, in his heart.

"Lady Asteria?" Kefta asked, squatting by the fire.

"She'll mend. Rock slide broke her inside. She'll rest now." Khoti's words came slow. His fa's medicine, a powerful thing, wore hard on him.

"What – What was that you did? At first, my instinct called me to defend her from you. My heart felt the power of what you did. I couldn't move, speak. Ah, but this is some strange magic!"

"Medicine."

"This is the medicine in Tsevon you spoke of?"

Khoti didn't answer. He'd forgotten something. He picked up the tera sticks and tapped his tribute to the spirits for their help. He felt them leave as he did, each tap draining a little more of the fire that had filled him, taking a touch of him back into the wind the pine and the stone.

Kefta knelt and stared at Khoti, his expression soft as the rhythm carried their hearts into the peaks of the mountains. When Khoti set the sticks aside, Kefta gestured at Khoti's wrapped hand. Khoti pulled away the bandage, revealing an ugly burn over the darkened cut.

"It must hurt –"

"It's nothing." Khoti felt only the desire for sleep now that the spirits had abandoned him.

"You're a strange man, Khoti. A magic –"

"It's the spirits. Their doing. It's Fa's blood. His gift to me in life and when he healed me."

"Such power! You could heal our armies. No one need die –"

"No!" Khoti tried to sit up but his limbs refused to respond. "It only helps. It mends in measure only what the spirits will allow. It's why my fa couldn't heal me all at once. It took him and Konner weeks and they still weren't sure I'd live. You can't bring a person back to life, or replace a severed limb, or take away all the pain, or heal all the ills in a body. It does only what the spirits want. Most, it gives the injured enough strength to mend, takes away the poisons of fever and speeds the natural healing." Khoti paused, his eyes closed. He spoke again just as Kefta began to rise. "I didn't know I could do this, Kefta. Trying, I could've killed her. If I hadn't tried, she would be dead. I could've killed myself – to take the poison into one's self, the weariness – it's killed healers in the past. I'm glad you're here. Now I can rest without worry."

With his last words fading to a whisper, Khoti drifted into sleep, slumping down beside Asteria, barely aware of Kefta readjusting the blanket to cover them both as he settled down to watch the fire die.

Khoti awoke to the sensation of being watched. He tried to jump up, falling back when the blood rushed from his head. He found Asteria studying him.

"You saved my life. You will always have my debt." She touched his arm.

Khoti brushed aside her words and squirmed from her touch, realizing they had shared a blanket. He scooted away, nearer the coals of the fire. He heard Kefta chuckling, but couldn't wrest himself from Asteria's gaze, her dark eyes wide on him.

"That's not what I want," he stammered. "I did what I thought I should."

"You are blessed with gifts. You save our city, heal –"

"Just leave it," he said, his ears growing hot. "I mean, Lady, please, it wasn't important."

"To me it was!" She frowned.

Kefta's chuckle became laughter as he pulled Khoti to his feet and gave him a conspiratorial nudge. He laughed harder at Khoti's glare.

Still bruised and weak from the injury that had taken her so close to death, Asteria couldn't steady herself. Kefta had walked to the rampart, and now strode away sniggering, leaving Khoti to support Asteria before him on Fidra as he led her horse. Though she sat upright now, and clung to Fidra's mane, he thought she pressed needlessly hard against his chest.

"The duke'll have my head," he grumbled.

Astera leaned back and stared up at him with shining eyes that made his mouth go dry. She seemed to snuggle against his chest as she pulled the edges of the cloak he wore around her own shoulders despite early morning heat wafting up at them from the plains. How should he to react to a woman of her rank who behaved toward him in a way her people would condemn?

"The gods are in you, Khoti of Tasch-el," she said, gazing at him. "Such power I have never seen, or felt."

Kefta's laughter at Khoti's discomfort echoed against the rampart. He could only scowl as Asteria smiled up at him, her eyes expressing gratitude and, perhaps, something more. It was nothing a warrior needed. Warrior. Would he deal both life and death with his sword hand?

PART 3: THE FALL – THE EAST

31: Peshal's Tunnel

The hot days of the ripening moon piled upon each other as the siege of Sihmad Shal wore on. The Shandeans, jammed into tight quarters and unable to seek the cooler air on the walls, held on, encouraged by heavy Minarian losses. While thousands of Minarians had fallen, mostly at the hands of the Harbor Gnats, there always seemed to be more ready to take their place

As Arshal had warned, the Fearnia wall soon fell. The enemy made a raucous ceremony of defiling the monument to Terrmar in the market's center. As hope of holding out much longer dimmed, Arshal ordered the release of horses into the borough Dyn, even his dear Booty, where they grazed in courtyards, in many cases their days numbered. Older beasts had gone the way of fowl, swine, hares, cattle and saltmeats. Milk cows, too, dwindled. Provisioners stretched the grains and legumes, moldy cheese and anything else they could find to keep the army on its feet, the gristle and gruel almost as noxious as the mordant odors that wafted over the wall from the desolation beyond.

With a growling belly, Arshal leaned against the stonework of their outermost defenses, studying the slate roofs and dormers of Dyn, listening with weary distraction as Nali reported on defensive positions and supplies in a voice gone hoarse. They knew they couldn't hold long. And when they fell, Arshal knew the streets would run with the blood of shawnsi and government officers. Peshal likely had turned back to Otayr when he saw

Sihmad Shal besieged. Daily the Minarians executed captured shawnsi in displays that varied only in their viciousness to wear the fraying Shandean morale. The grisly displays became routine, blending together until they meant no more than any other horrific act. Except they were friends, neighbors, and in the pit of his stomach Arshal feared one day family.

Arshal refocused on Nali as the derna's tone changed. A fleet with reinforcements approached the harbor including a ship flying the colors of the Minarian king's office overprinted with the crossed bars of a protectorate. They meant to stay.

Nali's face contorted with the effort of repeating Zopher's plans for a retreat to the Thaila wall, with many pauses and stumbles over details, as if he struggled to concentrate. For days now, Nali had fought fevers festering in his wounds. Smudges of sleeplessness under his eyes stood out deep and stark against the beard that had grown wild and snarled into unkempt hair. And how long would Arshal himself be much use, his mind wandering off with each tangent that crossed it?

Nali's words trailed away, his point forgotten, as Jan trotted along the wall to reach them.

"They're unloading the ships," he said when he reached them. "By the thousands. At least as many as in the initial invasion."

Arshal swallowed hard before he could regain his breath. "Nali, order the palace to prepare for evacuation –" he glanced at Jan, then shrugged. "Order them to knock down walls if they must to find that tunnel. Jan, be sure unit leaders are briefed on the surrender plan. The siege will end when those troops arrive. Understand?"

The two Harbor men nodded and turned away. Arshal restrained Nali with one hand. "Nali, you have to evacuate with us." Arshal silenced Nali's objections with a curt gesture like his own impatience. "It's too dangerous. You've been privy to counsels, are a known derna, and by Jan's account, already marked. The enemy will want revenge for such losses and will blame the commander of the Harbor Gnats, and will assume a royal counsel knows where we've gone. Confide in Jan and make him your link to the Harbor contingent. Once you're out with us, find your family and go into hiding. I wish you could come with us, but you're needed here, not swinging from the enemy's gallows." He waited a moment before he released Nali's arm. "We'll either find it, or die in a last stand in the king's halls. I want you in the countryside nearby where, if we make it, I can get word to you. Perhaps we can begin to re-arm against the day

_"

"You make it so final," Nali said, shaking his head.

"It is final, Nali. Didn't you see visions of us battling on open plains, not inside walls? Of attacking, not defending?"

"Remember, visions show just one possible outcome. Otherwise, to believe Cree's would be to live without hope. We've proven some false; Esthen didn't die in our dreams. Look, we've already held out longer than we thought possible. Our losses are heavy, but nothing compared to theirs. If we've held two weeks, why not longer? We can weaken them so they can't overtake the rest of the country!"

"You aren't thinking, Nali! What are we supposed to feed these people? We knew we couldn't survive a determined siege."

Nali scowled. "Then why did we try?"

"We can do more good out there, covertly, than in here, trapped. If we can escape at all."

"Two weeks, going on nothing but anger," Nali said, his gaze darting as if seeing the enemy in each shadow. "I'm driven to destroy these people. They've made me into a soldier. Me the fisher, me the scholar, me the fa: a soldier. They've hurt me and filled my eyes with things – The memories of this battle, what we learned from it, will haunt us forever. How can we ever live in true peace after finding joy in another man's death and suffering?" Nali's tone took a savage twist. "Arshal, I do want them to suffer for what they've done. You want us to retreat, to run and cower? You think they'll go easy on us just because the shawnsi are gone? It's us as much as shawnsi killing their soldiers."

"I had no idea –"

Nali made a dismissing gesture. "I know you're right. It just tears me apart. You can't move without hope. So, you build false hope that maybe a bunch of fishers and farmers and dandy shawnsi can stand up to a trained army. A few victories and you start to believe. That's the problem, believin'. The reality comes along in the shape of warships in the harbor."

Arshal put an arm around Nali's shoulders. "You're ill and exhausted. It's too much for everyone. The only one who seems to thrive is Jan. He looks twenty years younger."

Nali snorted. "Aye, and he's lost a span around his middle if he's lost a pound. He's everywhere."

"Trust him. Stay in touch with him. We'll get our revenge."

Nali nodded, his haunted gaze stabbing up at Arshal before the derna hurried away, swaying with a stiff-legged limp as he rubbed his soot-reddened eyes furiously. Arshal sighed and turned to study the grazing animals in the yards below as the city's cooks stalked the dwindling herd. He turned his back as a cook caught an old mare by the halter. He weaved his way along the battlement, dodging the sprawl of defenders. Some slept, some tended weaponry, one small group tried to guess the most offensive thing that might be in their stew to justify how horrible it smelled and tasted while another cluster compared battle injuries as if comparing medals. All hung on by a will that felt stronger than Arshal's. He could barely remember a time when he felt confident.

Arshal sensed someone at his side and startled to find Zopher.

"I took a prisoner while I was scouting," Zopher said. "I brought him for you to interrogate."

Arshal turned to find a Minarian. He had bowed his head so Arshal saw only the leather nose guard of his helm and multi-colored horsetails of the Eidhalt trailing from the crown. He hoped Zopher had discarded the medallion. Even thinking of it gave him a crawling feeling.

"We don't need prisoners and there's really nothing we can't see for ourselves," Arshal said at last.

Arshal stood agape when Zopher leaned against the wall and held his stomach with the heartiest laughter Arshal had heard since before Esthen fell. The prisoner tugged the helm from his head, revealing Peshal's tousled fair hair and sunburned face. Arshal threw his arms around his brother, letting his worries loose in a hug that forced the wind from the younger man's lungs.

"You make a convincing Minarian!" Arshal said as he released his brother to survey him.

"More so than Zopher!" Peshal said. "He sat so tall and stiff in that uniform I knew it was no Minarian, and I could be pretty sure it was Zopher."

"I didn't like the idea that the man who warmed the clothing for me was dead," Zopher returned, stroking a gold chain he wore around his neck, one Arshal had given his sister some naming day long past.

"The Eidhalt wearing this outfit didn't volunteer!" Peshal laughed, but it sounded humorless. "I'm not as convincing as you might think. I couldn't wear the medallion. I killed a few as answer questions. It got a bit tense. I wanted to come in through the tunnel to ensure the other end is open, but I couldn't get around. I had so many captains and unit leaders asking me to carry this message and that, I was sure I'd be discovered. Last time I pick up the uniform of an Eidhalt. Those poor slobs have a lot of demands on them." Peshal paused for breath, more confident and animated than Arshal had ever seen him as he shed the gauntlets and mail, until he wore only a tunic and leggings. "Everyone's well? The family?"

Zopher and Arshal's gazes met over Peshal's shoulder. "We lost Esthen when Dlan fell, eleven days ago."

Peshal took a sharp breath, staring at Arshal a frozen moment before turning his back on them to stare into the borough Dyn. His fingers gripped the stonework until his knuckles whitened. A long minute passed before he turned back, in control, eyes blazing, so much stronger than Arshal remembered, along with a new leanness and muscle. He'd wound a blood-stained strip of cloth around his upper arm and every so often he reached for his knife, as if to be sure it remained at his side. Arshal felt a sudden deep loss for the quiet, big-hearted youth who led so many to Otayr. That man was gone.

"Have you avenged him?" Peshal demanded, hazel eyes boring into Arshal as cold as autum ice on a dark lake.

"I don't have the heart of a warrior." Arshal looked at his feet, unable to withstand that gaze. "I don't think I could kill with malice and I've been fortunate I haven't been faced with the option."

"I guess I already have."

Arshal thought he heard a hint of disgust in Peshal's tone. For him? "But you made it to Marol's?"

"Everyone's fine. All settled safe as they can be, little farms by the creek already taking shape." Arshal looked up to find Peshal gazing across the battlement to the open fields where the enemy prepared for the arrival of reinforcements. His voice had cracked. "How can you not hate them, Arshal, not feel malice? There's a ... thrill. Yes, that's the word: a thrill you can only get by repaying them for an unforgivable injustice."

Zopher was studying his feet and said nothing as Arshal's mouth opened and closed before he said, "You sound like you've been talking with Nali. It's the evil of their god driving this, making us think these things."

"I hold no malice for the Pladde manning machines and ships against their will. Only the Hogde who lead them."

"What's made you so brutish!"

Peshal kicked the pile of Minarian gear at his feet. "What hasn't?" He kicked the pile harder, the helm skidding a pace across the battlement. "I had to act the part. They take few prisoners, kill those fools who opted to stay on their farms. They burn, torture, rape, and sacrifice their prisoners, claiming to be cleansing Shande and honoring their god. Any tribe will do. Shawnsi are best. I witnessed –" he stammered to a halt, swallowing hard and gazing skyward. "I could do nothing. I know the boy thought it was as much my fault as the enemy's."

"How can you think you have fault?"

"How can you say I don't! I did nothing! And he pinned me with these accusing eyes. I'm at fault because I wanted to save my own skin so I could help my family escape and leave the people to fend for themselves. I can't forgive it! Never!" Peshal's fists were clenched at his sides, the veins on his arm bulging. "There were less than a dozen, so caught up in the massacre of innocents I could have taken half before they knew it. I could've made an effort! I didn't. That boy's hatred will follow me to my grave." He shook his head as if to dislodge the horrible memory. "This enemy will make us slaves by crippling us with their sheer brutality, our awe for their ability to have no mercy for people they think of as beneath even their livestock, and feel nothing but fanaticism for the glory of some imagined Minaria and its horrible god."

The three of them startled at the sound of a throat clearing. "Hold onto that anger, Peshal," Nali said, laying a bold hand on Peshal's bandaged upper arm. "They've breached the wall. We have to pull back. It'll be battle all the way."

The Dyn wall barely held an hour and soon the gates of the Thaila wall, too, crumpled before batterers as postern doors opened with ease, the enemy slipping in with keys rattling from their fingers. The swift fall of Thaila wall gave the defenders no time to retreat before the onslaught, barely gathering their weapons and few of the wounded.

As night fell on the retreat, a full moon lit the opulent white walls, colorful doorways and multi-hued flowerboxes of Thaila with a spectral light muted by the lingering smoke hanging over the city.

In the alleyways, feet slapped cobblestone as Arshal and Peshal dashed from shadow to shadow, just ahead of Eidhalt bent on their capture like arrows racing for a bull's eye. They'd come halfway from the wall through the borough, the Eidhalt chasing as if they knew their quarry, though both had long ago shed markers of their status.

Only a few more twisting, narrowing passages remained before the princes would reach Yckeb.

Arshal skidded to a stop when Peshal yelped and stumbled, the younger prince slamming onto the rough cobbles. Arshal grasped an arrow protruding from his brother's thigh and yanked it out. Peshal bared his teeth but made no sound. Arshal pulled him up and drew his sword.

He weighed the blade in his hand as he moved forward to meet the two Eidhalt shadowing them. He'd never drawn the weapon in battle. The nearest Minarian charged Arshal, the other circling to meet Peshal. Arshal parried, hesitant at first, sidling with his back to Peshal's for protection. The feel of the sword in his hand charged him. His arm tingled with anticipation.

The Eidhalt appeared confidant, their moves calculated. One slipped in Peshal's blood. Arshal thrust at his chest as the man reached to break his fall. Striking near the base of his neck, Arshal felt the odd sensation of metal through flesh to bone and the tug as the Minarian fell backward. Arshal wanted to gag.

An eerie quiet returned to the alley when, after parrying the Eidhalt's sturdy blows, Peshal dispatched his foe with a crude skill. Peshal sheathed his bloody sword, then, looking at Arshal, his mouth twisted again with disgust. Arshal stood over the body of his foe, hands trembling as the sword hung limp in his hand. Peshal gave his brother a shove to move him along.

"Don't regret it, brother. He wouldn't," Peshal said, leaning on Arshal for support.

"Not so much regret," Arshal said. "It didn't feel like me fighting." Arshal shuddered again at the stony coldness in Peshal's gaze as they made for the Yckeb wall.

"Behind you!" Jan whispered.

Nali ducked and pivoted on his bad leg. A Minarian closed from behind on the slick, light blue slate roots of Thaila. Below, Nali glimpsed the flitting shapes of defender and attacker passing from one shadow to another in a reckless chase to reach the walls of Yckeb borough.

The slick tiles beneath his feet threatened to pitch him into the bloody streets below. Nali jabbed his sword at the Minarian, who lurched and grabbed a dormer for support. Nali lunged again, his sword penetrating the flesh and striking the bone of his foe's thigh. The Minarian's leg buckled beneath him and he grabbed the dormer with both hands. Nali kicked the man's grasping arms. As he stared at Nali in terror, the man lost his grip and hung by one arm. Without hesitation, Nali brought his sword down on the man's fingers, and watched without emotion as the man slid down the roof into darkness, landing in the shadows below with a thud.

"Good work!" Jan whispered.

They raced across the roof to the next chasm. Nali jumped. As he landed, his feet slipped from beneath him on the dew-dampened roof. A hand grasped his and dragged him over the sharp tiles of the roof edge. He crawled to the peak and clung a moment, struck by a sudden giddiness at the the height as he looked at the moonlit battle below. If they could just reach the Yckeb wall, he and Jan could reach the tunnel. Both would be marked men if captured in the city. How many others struggled to reach that same goal? They had to escape, survive, retaliate. Yckeb would not hold long, its gates more decorative than functional. Retreating Shandeans already crammed within so tightly a Minarian could swing and fell three, they unable to fall back for want of space.

"Come on!" young Griag called to Nali. "They're gaining!"

Scrambling over the roof, Nali saw the wall of Yckeb only a few rooftops away. Adjoining roofs amounted to only a narrow space to cross, but the last jump to the wall dropped three paces from the last roof and had a span of perhaps ten. Below, the alley ran in a black chasm some fifteen paces deep. Griag scrambled ahead and jumped, grabbing for the hand reaching out from the battlement to grasp him. An arrow struck his helper's hand, and Griag fell.

Nali scanned the remaining silhouettes of Jan and two other Gnats crouching with him on the roof, wanting a moment to beg the spirits to let his young neighbor survive the fall, but knowing he had no time for it. Jan took a running leap. His hands grasped the edge of the battlement. Feet scrambling, he finally threw a leg over the parapet and disappeared from view. Feeling like a target again, Nali tried to crouch lower. If he fell, and survived, he'd die in battle rather than reveal the destination of the escaping shawnsi.

Jan called softly across the gap, and one of the silhouettes made the leap, clinging to Jan's arm, which shone white in the moonlight against the dark wall. The man noisily clambered up the face to be pulled out of sight. Staring down, Nali again felt giddy, too weary and feverish for this. He could see figures below, defender and attacker, scurrying through dark streets and alleys, moon-bright metal clanking as axe or sword clashed.

'Your turn," the silhouette beside him whispered.

Nali took a few steps back then ran at the chasm, trying not to think of the distance. He felt the sudden weightlessness at the apex of the jump, then the sinking sense of falling as he descended only a hand's length from the wall. He had a fleeting thought of how it would feel and sound when he struck the ground. Jan's fingers clamped on his wrist and Nali's body slapped the wall. He thought of himself falling anyway, his velocity pulling him from the clammy hand, or, worse yet, pulling Jan with him. Instead, Jan towed him upward, and climbing with bare feet clinging to the cool stone he found himself grasping the lip of the parapet and swinging his leg over to the safety beyond.

As he stuck his arm out to receive the silhouette that flew from the roof at him, certain he'd be hit by an arrow. None came, but the man leaped too early. His fingers barely brushed Nali's as Nali leaned over trying to get a piece of him. Without a word the man fell with a thud that brought the bile into Nali's throat.

After sparing only a brief thought to the man's family, Nali raced along the wall to gather other evacuees. How many wouldn't make it? How many had already been forced to surrender? He found it difficult to watch his step for the blurring in his eyes.

When at last he reached the palace, Nali's memory of it sped his feet down the short dark and hidden stairway behind the curtain backing the dais where the king had held court. In the hallway it led to, an officer pointed toward a door that matched the masonry and appeared like part of the arched vault supporting the structure.

"Are there more of your unit behind you?" the officer whispered, his voice echoing along the hall, muted by the distant sound of battle outside.

"Jan is trying to reach a few officers he saw defending on the west wall. He shouldn't be far behind me. Are you –"

"Staying? No. I'll be coming through behind the last. Unless the palace is breached, in which case I close this door. I'm going to set a fire in the courtyard." He gestured toward a small private palace courtyard that opened a few paces down the hall. "Mostly unimportant papers, to make them think we have burned documents that might give away royal servants or other folk who couldn't escape with us. You'll find a lot of people down there, hundreds. You should have no trouble catching up."

Nali nodded his thanks and ducked through the low doorway

into a narrow stairwell. Hundreds! How did Peshal imagine moving so many, so far, unseen? He counted at least one hundred winding steps down, through several more doorways and narrow passageways, a route they would never have discovered in time without Peshal and the map he had foolishly carried with him to Otayr. At the base of the steps another officer directed him to another hidden doorway into a dimly lit storeroom. There, another door hidden in the angle of a corner arch, stood ajar, opening onto darkness and a gasp of cool musty air.

Nali scanned the crates and barrels that had been hastily stacked to the ceiling with the country's treasures and documents, breathing the sweet aroma of casks of wine mixing with the greasy odor of swords, axes and armor – some of it picked from Minarian dead – packed in oil cloth. In another room, barrels of seed and metal bars stretched back until they disappeared in shadow. Nali could only hope the precious stores remained undiscovered.

For an ancient and unused tunnel, it remained in excellent repair. It felt cool and dry, its hard-packed dirt floor level beneath his bare feet, his shoes lost in his run across the rooftops. The ceiling had room to spare and three men could walk abreast. For a moment, he thought the whole city could escape this way. Tens of thousands remained. And an empty city might lead the Minarians to rip apart the palace brick by brick.

He jogged, a rocking, limping gait that sent an ache up his leg, his echoes running ahead of him. Every so often he came to a torch fluttering in crude brackets. After a few easy turns, he guessed the passage paralleled the Sijway above. He put his foot out in the spare light to find the first of several uneven stairs down. The tunnel seemed to keep an even distance below the city, which rose from the first wall to the palace some fifty paces.

He took a sharp turn and the tunnel suddenly widened into a cavernous room falling away at his feet. Damp assailed him, and he recognized the polished walls of a cavern dug by nature and water. He stood at the top of a long flight of steps. Below, torchlight touched refugees resting in quiet groups on straw mats or rugs they'd tied to their packs. Nali descended the many steps unnoted, careful on the slick stair that had been carved out of dripstone. High above, torchlight played across the stones of myriad hue hanging like icicles from the cavern's dripping ceiling.

Nali recognized Peshal first. The prince stood in the center of the cavern, dwarfed by spaciousness as he studied the strange formations. Despite the bloody rag wrapped around his thigh, the young prince stood feet apart and hands behind his back as he stared at the ceiling. He turned as Nali reached him, awestruck.

"Only a god who marvels at beauty could create this, Nali," he said. Following Peshal's gaze, Nali felt dizzy and disoriented in the vast space. "Not a god of malice. We found a marker honoring Darak, the engineer who fell into this room more than twenty-five hundred years ago, right after the Great War. King Dyn planned it for escape. I guess kings kept it so secret people forgot it even existed, or the knowledge went down with Dynfearn the Lost. When we regain the city, I want to open these caverns for the populace to view: to show them the greatness of Terremar's craftsmanship!" Peshal pointed at the dripping lifeline of the cavern, above. "The creek that runs across the prairie must flow underground here before reaching the spring. Such a wonder!"

Nali smiled a little at Peshal's strange mood. "I hope sappers haven't dug so deep as to compromise the tunnel anywhere."

"We're too far underground. The marvel of the city's construction is the planners had to know this cavern existed. I'm sure the Fearnia Market lies just above. They wouldn't want to place heavy structures over it. Too much risk of a sink hole. And Terremar's monument must be directly above us." Peshal turned to peer at Nali. "Are there others?"

"I expect Jan. We lost a lot in Thaila." Nali shook fingers that recalled the brush of – "Many missing?"

"A lot of the royal officers and a few of Zopher's folk. Maybe they'll find their way."

"The Yckeb wall won't hold. They're like apples in a barrel up there." The burning coal returned to his throat. How could he abandon his men? What would be the fate of those remaining to face the Minarian's wrath with no shawnsi or Harbor Gnat leadership to vent their anger upon?

He heard his name, and turned to find Arshal. The torchlight accentuated the way Arshal's face had thinned and he felt certain the prince's hair in several places grew in white.

"You look like an old man," Nali said, not intending to say it aloud.

"I feel like an old man! It's a relief to see you here in one piece." Arshal gave him a thin smile. "You're looking like a shaggy mountaineer, or an old salt. I can't decide which, but at least you no longer have that fishy aroma following you."

Nali gave him a crooked grin and examined his bare, scraped

feet and clothing that had gone weeks without washing, splattered with mud and blood. "I could use a bath," he ventured.

Arshal nodded emphatically and laughed aloud. "We'll all get that soon enough. Peshal expects us to swim the Rigannon! I can't believe he wants elders wading a fast river like they're school children on holiday."

Nali studied the exiles. All they had lost was reflected in delicate movements and stunned expressions. It showed in the way the queen's head sagged on the king's shoulder, and how the sovereign sat with his head bowed beside the silent, ever-watchful Visionary. All of them had packs at their feet and dressed for a long trek. Like Nali, Cree had even packed away his robes.

Yet, Resala shone as she moved among the exiles, offering slivers of dried apple, a splash of wine and encouraging words. Their grateful smiles made Nali wish she had treated his wounds instead of the toothless old midwife. What became of the woman, her young helper, and the many like them who remained until the last to pull out the wounded before each retreat? How many of them, like Drul, had fallen among the soldiers? Nali nudged Arshal and gestured with his head at the way Zopher's gaze followed Resala's movements.

"Happy to see you whole and sound, Nali," she said with concern as she offered Nali and her brothers wine and apple. It hit his stomach with sudden warmth against the cool underground air.

"So am I, Lady," Nali whispered, suddenly recalling Thaila's dark alleys and his dash across the rooftops, still feeling the sharp tiles cutting into his feet. Looking down, he saw instead the dark stone beneath him, doubting he would ever escape the haunting memories.

Arshal allowed the refugees a few more minutes' rest before he prodded all of them to their feet. They had a long march through the tunnel, with old, young and injured to slow their pace. With laden packs, they couldn't comfortably walk more than one at a time through the narrowest stretch winding from the cavern to the river.

The tunnel branched here and there, leading to small natural pockets, or rooms carved out for purposes long forgotten. The tunnel made a few more curves to match the Sijway, then struck out due southwest, according to Peshal's map, where it would meet the Rigannon River more than an hour's march south of the

Harbor.

Only torches they lit as they went guided them in their long journey through the dark, and what passed above seemed far away and unreal as they crept beneath their enemy. They rested often, sitting along the tunnel walls in the dark to nap, sip from waterskins or nibble at fruit and jerky.

At last, when it seemed they had marched for days, they reached the rotting doors Peshal had opened for the first time in generations when he first scouted the tunnel. A pile of dirt and debris that had shielded the door littered the smooth floor and roots and grasses hung like a curtain over the opening. They entered the tunnel in a moonlit night. Now late afternoon opened before them.

Arshal ducked beneath the grasping roots to stand on a rocky and wooded bank above the river.

"It must have poured all day," Peshal said as he pushed his way out to join Arshal, while Nali lingered beneath the shelting bank. They studied the river's boiling water through a veil of rain. "We can't cross this!" dismay had crept into Peshal voice.

"We have to. It's the best time. No one will see us," Arshal insisted. "It was your idea. We can't wait for them to find us."

Peshal jerked his head toward his parents, who huddled near the mouth of the tunnel, Cree's craggy visage and other faces peering out behind them. "The current's too swift!"

"It looks like the rain will stop soon."

"But the water will stay high. Who knows how much is on its way downriver from the west. We have to follow this bank south until we find a crossing. It's too deep here."

"The closer we get to the Quelica, the worse it'll get. The water will be even wilder! It has to be here, and while it still rains, we'll be concealed. They may discover the tunnel and be on us right away. We have to risk it!"

"Maybe we should leave it up to them." Peshal swung an arm toward their observers, whose expressions were growing more and more alarmed as the brothers stared at one another. A murmur grew among those further back in the tunnel.

"Jan's here," Nali said, finally stepping out into the rain as Jan pushed his way through the crowd, looking from the river to the princes' stubborn faces. He burst out laughing.

"What's so funny?" Arshal demanded.

"Well, you picked the worst place you could to cross," he began, shaking his head. Peshal grinned as Arshal scowled. "But it'll have to do." Arshal threw Peshal a smug smile. Nali hid his rare grin beneath a hand as he stroked his unkempt beard. "Now if you'll allow us," Jan continued. "Nali and me can fix this little dilemma in no time at all."

The princes turned to Nali, who merely shrugged and grinned more broadly. He studied the bluffs above, then the ones on the other side of the river, almost hidden by the driving rain.

"What are you babbling about, Jan?" Arshal demanded.

"Is this the place?" Nali asked.

Jan nodded. "I grew up on a farm just up there," Jan pointed at the top of the bluff facing them. "I'm hoping that's where Cookie and Jali are."

Nali brushed the rain from his eyes, finally recognizing a scrubby old tree clinging to the cliff opposite.

"So, your point?" Peshal prodded.

'Maybe nothin'. It's been a long time. But we'll check and be right back," Jan said. He gave Nali a sharp look. "I didn't come alone. Those with me aren't in the best way. The princess tends them back in the tunnel. It got a little ugly after you left, Nali."

"When wasn't it ugly?" Nali asked.

"The Yckeb gates opened like a tap on a fresh keg." No one spoke, the only sound the rain striking the damp shore and the water boiling through the gorge.

Jan strode off down the bank; Nali trotted after him into the pouring rain, their bare feet slipping on the muddy riverbanks or tripping over stones and roots reaching from the undergrowth. Peering up into the rain, Nali searched for the small cascade children had discovered anew for generations.

"It's been a long time. I think I remember Jali being caught slipping his lessons here, 'less that was me," Jan mused as he searched the rocky bank for the smooth stones worn by children's play for generations. "I know I played here when you were just a babe –"

"There it is!" Nali called, pointing. Memories flooded him of hot afternoons he and friends slid down the smooth stone of the cascade into a deep pool below, or dived from the cliffs above. The rain-swollen stream now thundered over the face of the scarp and crashed into the river below, nothing like the childhood rivulet that he recalled.

"You got rope?" Jan asked.

Nali pulled a hempen cord from his pack and unwound it. It still gave off the faint briny smell of his fishing boat where it had been stowed for years before it became part of a soldier's pack. "I dunno, Jan. River's pretty wild. We aren't the lads we used to be.

It might not even be there anymore."

"We'll find out soon enough. Whatever you do, don't let go!" Wrapping one end around his waist, Jan pulled the rope tight as he stepped into the cold water. He picked his way toward the deep channel then pushed off, swimming furiously, the current pulling him downstream as Nali braced himself. After the initial surge, Jan gained against the river, and finally the rope went slack as the innkeeper found bottom again and sloshed his way up the bank.

Jan looped the line over a rock and wandered among jumbled stones in search of the flat rock they remembered from childhood. With a yelp, he found it, and pushing it aside, pulled out a bundle wrapped in a tarp and held it up. Nali waved and grinned as Jan tied one end of a rope bridge he'd found to two bent trees, side by side, some four paces up the cliff, their trunks sunken from years of abuse. Jan tied the other end of the bridge to Nali's line. Nali pulled it across and secured it to a sturdy rock at the base of a path that snaked up to the top of the cascade. Jan ran across the bobbing bridge, which sagged to within a thumb's length of the river's surface.

"I remember lifting a few pieces for that bridge," Jan said with a laugh as he tested Nali's knots. "It was old when I played here. Boy did I hear about it when some of my fa's good line turned up missing and I see it's had some work on it recently."

With a wistful smile, Nali recalled secret meetings Harbor children arranged with farm children on the east bank. Early in the morning they would tie the bridge to a rope thrown across to the east bank. He'd always felt sad at sunset to pull the bridge back across. Would children ever again play here? Or were such things casualties of war?

It took several hours for all the exiles to cross as the rain continued, concealing them as they stumbled along the bank to the cascade then clung to the bridge as they shuffled over the river. Nali crossed last, having tied slip knots so he could tug the bridge free and haul it to the west shore. He half expected to see a westering sun shining on the east bank, the childhood memory tattered as he stowed the sodden bridge in its tarp and hid it in the niche beneath the stone. He turned to find Arshal beside him, Peshal waiting a few paces back as he re-wrapped the bandage on his leg.

"Fare well, Nali," Arshal said.

Nali glanced east where Sihmad Shal hid beyond the top of the bluff. "I'll be waiting for your call. I'll be there." Arshal nodded as they grasped forearms and parted.

Nali waved at Peshal and the last stragglers followed Zopher to the top of the bank. Then Nali joined Jan for their own dangerous path. Sensing Arshal's gaze on him, Nali didn't turn to look, fearing the prince would read his intent.

He and Jan only had a short way to go to reach the relative shelter of a pine woods on Cousin Tel's farm. They crept silently through the trees, bypassing Tel's house where black cloths hung over the windows and cattle peered from the lower story stable. They trotted on through the dripping shadows of pine to a small cottage on the corner of Tel's place. Nali drank deep of the pine scent, the quiet, the feel of the soft ground beneath his feet. They crept to the side of the cottage and listened beneath a burlap-covered window. Nali heard his son's high laugh as young Rena prattled. The smells of home escaped around the burlap, as did the aroma of stew.

"Hist, Bert. Open the door," Nali called through the covered window. Bertal peeked around the sack, scrubbed face pink with joy. As he opened the door, Nali and Jan slipped into the one-room shack. It still rained hard, the pine needles letting only a soft dripping fall on the cottage roof. As they shook the water from their faces, both inhaled the homey scent so unlike days of smoke, gruel and death.

Bertal's arms gripped Nali's waist. Olna dropped her sewing and rushed to her lifemate, freeing uncharacteristic tears.

"We were so worried, Nali!" she cried as she held him, a dew-on-drying-hay scent about her reminding Nali that wherever Olna stood was home.

Embarrassed, Jan took advantage of a fire in the grate as Bertal fetched a bowl of thin stew, which Jan needed no urging to take.

"Your fa –" Olna began, but Nali shook his head, lips pressed shut. She closed her eyes and took a deep breath, asking no further. He couldn't talk about it. Especially not with Jan and his children there. Too many things reared up raw and unanswered. He'd had no moments to ponder and justify with a derna's calmer senses.

"Nali! There's meat in this!" Jan said after his first taste of stew. Nali quickly joined him, the two emptying the bowl in moments.

The cold and damp fell from Nali's limbs as he let himself relish, if only for a moment, the comfort of reunion. Olna stood at his shoulder, clucking at his torn clothing and sobbing afresh when she discovered the arrow wound.

"You've been hurt! What happened? We've heard nothing."

Nali and Jan's eyes met.

"Where's Kia?" Nali demanded, looking around the small room for Bertal's twin sister.

"Picking mushrooms."

"Where? Bertal, fetch her now!" Nali ordered, his tone the sharp words of a commander. Olna stood, stunned, as Bertal rushed out. Glancing at Rena, who stared at him with wide eyes, Nali put a hand on Olna's belly. She hadn't taken the children with Peshal to Otayr because they feared she might lose their child on such a long journey that they weren't, at that time, sure they even needed. Now, that decision haunted him. "Can you travel?" Olna nodded. Nali ate a few more spoonfuls, not wanting to give up this moment of warmth. "The city's fallen. I'm not exactly a popular person with the new tenants."

Olna pulled up a stool and sat, staring into her lap as if preparing for the worst news. "What happened?" she whispered.

"We'll have time for that later. We need to leave. I'm too well known. Not that I think any of our friends would willingly betray us, but it's safer if we go. Arshal hoped I'd stay, but it's too risky. I have my family to think of. Jan'll take care of things around the Harbor. His farm's far enough out we hope they won't give him much trouble. But we need to leave. Now."

"But we need to prepare. We –"

Nali gripped her hand. Her gaze stabbed up at him, wary. "We've taken too much time already. We can't tell anyone where we're going, not even Tel. We need to travel light, and on foot. It'll be hard on the young ones, and I'm worried about you, but we'll be safer."

Without a word, Olna extracted her hand from his and pulled together what they had brought to Tel's shack. She tossed dry clothing and shoes at Nali, which he quickly donned. Staring at the leanness of his body, she bit her lip, silent, even as he rewrapped his swollen leg and applied salve to the arrow wound in his shoulder. He checked the edge of his sword before concealing it beneath his cloak.

"You've changed so," she said softly as she stuffed clothing in a satchel.

"Yes, I have. Jan'll join us as far as his farm. We'll get some supplies there and head out."

Bertal rushed in the door with Kia in tow, her hands and apron grimy as she dropped a basket overflowing with mushrooms and a few wild onions. She threw herself into her father's arms. Olna had to drag her away as Nali continued to pack up what little remained of all they owned. One more family uprooted and fleeing. Who knew where they would next encounter the enemy, if they could, indeed find any place in Shande where the soil hadn't been war charred and battle blooded.

32: Tall Grass Dark River

Dawn revealed an endless sea of waving grass, broken only by the snaking line of the Quelica River stretching west. Spongy ground sucked at Peshal's feet and spewed biting flies. The river ran between uncertain banks, filling backwaters with dark, tea-colored water. Too deep to wade, the shallows were muddy ooze. Despite the wind, the surface remained glassy, the current revealed in little eddies and in the center where debris slowly passed.

Peshal stood with his brother, just beyond the hearing of a dismal camp where exiles packed bedrolls, faces drawn from days of siege rations and hardship. They'd left the tunnel three days ago, but already appeared more weather-worn than the refugees he'd left in Otayr. He knew the high banks of the Rigannon would flatten as they neared the Quelica, but his maps said nothing of the way the river meandered at its mouth, or the vast marshes along its banks, or the squads of Eidhalt racing across the countryside with the gold victory banner snapping behind them. Unharvested fields and overgrown prairie had sheltered them several times already.

"Well?" Arshal cocked an eyebrow at Peshal.

Peshal shrugged, avoiding his brother's gaze. "Errand riders follow the river. There must be a path."

"Where? We can't leave the river, nor get close to it. And if there's a road you can be sure Eidhalt'll be on it."

"How do the Kishmans get their goods to Sihma Harbor?"

"By barge. The point?"

"I'm thinking. If you have any great ideas let me know."

"If you two would stop bickering, maybe we'd get somewhere!" Resala snapped.

Arshal jumped. Peshal caught his breath, and the hand that instinctively reached for his dagger. Her soft footfalls had gone

283

unheard in the sighing grasses.

"Do you have any bright ideas?" Arshal asked.

"One is for you to think how it looks." She waved toward the exiles watching them with doubtful gazes. "We count on your leadership but all you do is sulk at every fork. You're frightening people."

"We aren't any better qualified than anyone else. It's our role by default," Arshal said. "To tell you the truth, we still don't know what we're doing."

"Then pretend! At least put up a good face."

Arshal placed an arm around her shoulder. "Well, we can certainly see this trek brings out the best in you!"

She harrumphed and tossed her head, tousled hair whipping back. Arshal pulled a briar from the snarled curls.

"You should wind your hair, Resala, to protect it from the weather." She gave him a curious look. "We wouldn't want Zopher to lose interest. We'd have a terrible time finding another suitor to put up with you."

She slapped his hand away when he reached to pluck another twig from the strands. Peshal chuckled as she stomped away, her feet squishing in the soft turf. He laughed louder, pointing as she gathered her hair and wound it into a braid.

Peshal sobered when he looked back at the glassy river. "She's right again. It's becoming a habit with her. We have to be less stubborn or we'll be here yet come winter."

"It's your fault, Pesh. You used to let others lead where they would."

"There must be a landing somewhere." Peshal peered at his rough map. Lines had blurred from rain, parchment separating at the creases.

"What good will a landing do? People will see us –"

"There could be barges or boats –"

"We still have to get there if there is one –"

"Now look, you're arguing with me again, this is getting us nowhere!" Peshal crumpled up the map and threw it on the ground. Arshal held up his hands as Peshal gathered up the map again, flattened it against his knee and held it up to the morning light to clarify the lines. "The river bends north. There must be a crossing there, or even a messenger exchange. Maybe the terrain improves further west. We're so close to the mouth of the river here it can't hold a single channel. I don't think anyone comes this way but by barge. The main road cuts across the headlands from Sihma Harbor and maybe connects somewhere west of here. That part of my map isn't clear." He gestured at the torn crease.

"So, what do you suggest?"

"Pick a path along the bank. I don't want to leave our source of water, maybe fish and greens, and we're unlikely to meet anyone." Peshal gazed across the flats where the grass grew steadily taller away from the disrupting flow. He tried to imagine what it was like during the spring floods, but could only picture the ocean as the tide roared in.

The nightmare of the next days left complaints unuttered, tempered by the ever-present fear of discovery. Hundreds of pilgrims stumbled over uneven and marshy ground, forced hours out of their way to circle deep pools or seek dry ground for camps, all while battling clouds of biting insects. The trail they made quickly deepened, filling with a seep of water so that those who followed found themselves splashing through puddles. On the evening of the fourth day, they didn't even find dry ground.

Many openly shed tears of relief when the next day Zopher returned from scouting ahead to report a barge landing on the opposite side of the river. The two dozen barges, many with foot-operated paddlewheels to supplement poles and oars, and a few smaller rafts, designed for hauling cattle and produce, broad and sturdy, had flat bottoms. The call to arms had left the landing unattended, some of the rafts still stacked with the sacks and crates of a bountiful harvest.

When darkness fell, Zopher and several other men swam to the landing. They stacked sacks of grain and beans and crates of vegetables in the middle of the boats and attached ropes to tow the vessels across to the north shore. They only hoped news of the city's fall would keep locals from seeking the thieves, or at least have the sense to say nothing.

Tired, sick and stinking of sour mud, the exiles collapsed onto the barges, so crowded, they could barely shift positions without elbowing a neighbor. Arshal and Peshal quickly divided the strongest young men among the vessels to man the poles and paddlewheel treadles. Working upriver out of the current, the vessels took them farther in the few remaining hours of darkness than they had traveled in all their days struggling through the marshy bottomlands. Many slept through the night for the first time since Sihma Harbor fell.

With morning, they pulled up onto a long shallow spit as gathering parties fanned out in search of game, returning with a variety of young fowl, and even a wild hogger that they cooked or cured over a few small fires. When sunset arrived and they doused the flames and took to their poles again, the refugees went on with a new energy, dreaming of the safety they felt certain awaited them in Sefresal.

Countless pinpricks of light pierced a moonless and cloudless sky their second night on the river. Water purled against the bank or muttered when a pole disrupted the current or splashed with the turn of paddlewheels. The chatter of frogs and insects echoed in waves from one side of the river to another, now and then the booming 'ngunh-ngung' of giant frogs shattering the rhythm. As they neared, the chorus of night sounds faded, only to return with renewed fervor as the barges passed.

Zopher leaned into a pole, avoiding the current as he stared into the shadows of the shore, ever watchful. Somewhere the war would find them again. In this world of tall grass and dark river it seemed distant, unreal. More than three weeks had passed since the Minarian landing in Sihma Harbor. It felt like forever. He knew, deep down, his turn in the war had only begun. He scanned the sprawl of sleeping figures on his barge. Many leaned against one another, or against the supplies allotted to each vessel. His gaze lingered on Resala where she rested against her parents. He briefly touched the gold chain she had promised would always bring him back safely to her. If only she'd had more such talismans for others, like Esthen.

On the verge of being hypnotized by the murmuring waters and singing frogs, Zopher heard a soft splash, followed by a cry. He peered into the dark, unable to discern the nearest raft. They rounded a bend and he could see only the silhouetted head of the man at the pole of the barge in front. A soft call sounded loud as the frogs went silent.

"Hold on! Just hold on tight. Someone will come!" He recognized Peshal's voice, then the alarms of others. "Zopher, someone fell in!"

He peered over the black water until he saw a face glowing wet in the faint starlight. The girl clung to the north bank where the current had pulled her. Small hands grasped dry weeds, which came out by the roots. The current pulled down and under with a hidden force apparent in the child's frightened whimperings.

"Hang on there!" Zopher called as he nudged a bleary-eyed man to take the pole. The man jumped to action as the child cried out and went under, her just-wakened mother's shriek tearing the night. Briefly, the girl's head broke the surface.

Taking a deep breath, Zopher hesitated a moment, then dived into the black water, hoping he'd correctly gauged its depth from a notion of the pole's length. The shock of cool water sucked his breath and the current pulled him downstream a pace for each stroke forward. He could see the child losing strength as the river swept her down sections of bank before she made another feeble grasp at the grass. With a powerful kick he reached for her, but she was gone. Something struck his leg, soft and yielding. He floated with the current a distance, kicking in the deep water of the channel, unable to find bottom or the soft body that brushed against him.

Suddenly, he smashed into the submerged branches of some flood-borne tree set in the mud. The current strove to pull him beneath the surface to pass through an open space in the branches. He clung to slimy twigs in desperation. In a last hope, he flailed his legs, hoping to come against the trunk for leverage. His foot struck something soft, waving and curling around his leg, like the long tendrils of river weed. Clinging to a sturdy branch, he reached down to grab the weeds and pulled, feeling the resistance of weight, and the buoyancy as the child's body came free. He wrapped an arm around her torso to hold her above the surface, but the weight felt dead, the current grasping. He knew he couldn't hold. He looked at long, limp hair mercifully plastered across her face and felt again the despair he thought he'd left at the barge landing. If he hadn't hesitated to dive. If somehow shawnsi children could have escaped to Otayr –

Calls came from the north bank only paces distant. Peshal held out a pole to just a pace from him.

"Have her grab it!" Peshal shouted.

Zopher shook his head, unsure if they saw him. "It's too late," though almost a whisper, his voice carried. Silence again fell over the river. Zopher felt a familiar knot in his gut that war had stretched so far to take yet another innocent child. Who would be next, some elder or a mother needing a midwife? The dark river purled around him, more menacing, more ominous. He didn't dare forget war again, not even here.

Grass sighed around Nali, cracking underfoot or shaking chaff into his hair and clothing as the derna trudged along with his youngest on his back, Bertal and Kia following in silence, barely visible as they flitted in and out of the grass forest, with Olna ensuring the twins didn't stray. Birds piped from within the head-high grass, unseen but for an occasional flash of color as the Drulsons struggled to lift knees above the tangled roots and push aside the grassy curtain.

Nali caught a whiff of wet soil, a slightly fishy smell of dampness, stronger now than a few moments before. He stopped, listening for the river. He didn't remember Rena being so heavy, and as he tried to shift her weight up his back found her asleep. He stole a glance at Olna's lowered head, brown hair escaping her scarf and clinging to her face. She didn't complain, but days of fighting through matted undergrowth wore on her. Reaching for her stomach suddenly, she looked up. Nali looked away. He knew she didn't want him to worry. It wouldn't help. He knew Olna would never make it if they continued on foot. In just over a week she thinned to a point he knew the child she carried took more nourishment than Olna could spare.

He took another step and thought he glimpsed sunglint on water. A beat of wings erupted in the air as waterfowl darted skyward. Nali dropped Rena to her feet as Olna set down the heavy satchel and rubbed blistered fingers. Bertal tried to press forward to peer ahead, but Nali restrained him with a firm hand as he crept to the river's edge.

The recent rains had muddied and eroded the bank, though the river still ran a pace below the top of a flood-built levee. Nali pulled aside the living curtain and searched the surface of the wide and sluggish river as the fowl circled overhead a moment before flying farther west. Nali could see the river took a long curve at this point. A beaten-down path upriver had churned the bank into a hodgepodge of tracks where wildlife crossed. Nali sat back from the water's edge and motioned for his family to join him. Olna dug into the satchel for the empty waterskins and held them out for Kia to fill.

"I think –" Nali began, but stopped when a cow lowed. He silenced Bertal's question with a swift gesture. Nali swept up one of the empty waterskins and pushed it into Bertal's hands as he led the boy toward the cow's comment.

"Bag's full," Bertal whispered when they sighted the cow. She stood just outside a pasture grazed to the ground. The fence rails had been pushed down as the cow ventured into the taller grass, a calf nibbling in her shadow.

"Means she's full of milk, right?" Nali teased. The cow turned to regard them with dark, only mildly curious eyes.

"I don't think she'll run."

"Probably because her bull boyfriend is lurking around here somewhere."

"C'mon, she's movin' away."

Nali let Bertal lead him, alert to the pitch of bird calls and mouse scratching. With the sun closing on the horizon, he worried the farmer might come in search of his cattle or they come within sight of a house. As he held open the wide top of the skin while Bertal's small fingers tugged at the teats – eliciting an occasional comment from the cow – Nali constantly scanned the field. When they'd filled the skin, Nali clamped it and slung it over his shoulder. He had just pulled Bertal behind a veil of reeds and grass when two boys arrived to cluck at the errant cow and with a few prods and slaps send her and the calf home at an irritated trot. Nali let out his breath and urged his grinning son on.

To Nali, a few pieces of jerky and the last of the mushrooms, washed down with warm milk, tasted like a feast. But he wouldn't let them linger. They pressed on to find a safer place for the night, far from farmers' pastures.

They had to make it to Sefresal. Then what?

33: Aron's Gambit

"Information leading to the apprehension of rebels and fugitives will be richly rewarded," the placard read. "Rid Shande of troublemakers and thieves."

Aron Keeper stared at the placard, shoulders bent. The squeal of cart wheels and the rattle of wagons hauling away goods wrested from hiding to the coffers of the Minarian government in Shande added to the din of the occupying army celebrating its victory. Celebration had gone on for a week and a half now. They ate, drank, and flaunted their new wealth to those still starving from the siege, many suffering unhealed injuries. The Minarians forced former Shandean soldiers into work parties to cart the putrefying Shandean dead from the streets and battlements to a pit outside the walls where they also tossed the rubble of burned Dlan, city refuse and animal carcasses to be burned. Minarian dead they buried in a designated heroes' field to the west of Shanai. Not a few, starving and sick with their injuries, joined their fellows on the refuse heap they helped to build.

Aron studied the mesh sack he held: a loaf of stale bread, a few limp roots, soft tubers and a tiny chunk of slightly moldy cheese. He did well compared to others. But his ration must feed ten children, himself and a lifemate.

He chided himself for returning from the relative safety of Whittea to become embroiled in the occupation. Now they had recorded him and listed him in a census so he couldn't come or go without accounting for himself. Besides rejoining his family, he'd come seeking instructions from Nali, Jan and Pedr, but he could gather no news of any of them.

"Rich reward," Aron spat as another man stopped to read the placard. "They'll declare us liberated or some such thing. That'll be the reward for some poor idiot who empties his head."

"I hear they got bags of riches to hand out to anyone as tells 'em where the royals went," the man offered.

"The royals, eh?" Aron said. "Serves 'em right, their fancy goods used to pay people selling word of 'em. They never hesitated to leave us to fend for ourselves, hungry and homeless –"

"Wait there, Keeper," the other man blustered. "They'd be dead now. We'd be worse off for keepin' 'em. You'd rather the country's leadership be captured and killed?"

"What's that leadership gotten us?" Aron returned. He realized a Minarian soldier watched them and turned from the placard. "It ain't right to turn on Shande just for some baubles and whatnots," he said. "But I sure see the incentive. If you know big things, I bet they'd give a lot to know, too." Aron smiled at his companion, his secrets itching to escape. "Besides, they'll be in carriages, with servants, fine-dressed at the best inns. It'd take a dim Minarian to not find their trail."

It didn't surprise Aron when soldiers followed him. At first, he feared they knew he'd been a leader in the Harbor defense, or wanted him because he'd been a royal appointee. He expected it when an official wearing the insignia of the Minarian Protectorate pounded on the support of the lean-to he'd erected in the burned remains of Shanai, his home in the lighthouse lost to Minarians.

"You were keeper," the official said from the threshold of the three-walled hovel. "You resisted the liberation."

Aron inclined his head and squinted at the man. "I admit it. I defended my home and family. I'm no major cog in the Gnats."

"Gnats?" the man asked with feigned innocence.

His family's pinched and frightened faces turned toward him. He couldn't help but think others' acts had brought war to hurt them, and how convenient it was that the leaders of the so-called Harbor Gnats had escaped, Nali as bad as the royals, forgetting his people in his haste to save himself. Hadn't Aron risked his life under Nali's command? For what? Hadn't Aron thrown business Nali's way once he'd earned his robes? And here Nali disappeared with the royals, leaving Aron behind to pay for their bad decisions.

Aron rose from the little stool where he held court for his family and pushed past the official into the street, where people stared at him.

"You want me having the hatred of folk I got to rely on," he said, sweeping an arm to encompass the bones of Shanai and the scraps of color against the charred timbers where homeless Shandeans spread blankets for house walls, their privacy a few threads thick. "I've ten youngsters they'd hate on."

"What if you did not have to rely on your neighbors?" the official asked. "What if your children were accommodated? Would that free your tongue?" he asked in a whisper only Aron could hear. "Keeper, you know things," the man added when he saw Aron's hesitation.

"Maybe I do," Aron admitted. He took a long breath. He knew himself smarter than a good lot of the occupiers. Could he win a few rewards by offering some useless tidbits?

"Why the hesitation? The sooner all the demons, thieves, and troublemakers are dealt with, the sooner we will have peace." The man's words dripped a persuasion hard for Aron to bear.

His stomach growled, chasing up his insides. People in the street watched him like the sole actor on a stage at the climax of a play.

"Gather your family," the Minarian urged. "There are large, empty houses in Thaila ready to house those willing to cooperate and set an example. That, and full rations, perhaps jobs with the government. There are many roles that need filling." The man waited a long minute as Aron continued to squint at him. At last, the Minarian shrugged. "When you have decided to make the correct decision, report to the information offices in Yckeb," he ordered, leaving Aron standing alone in the street, head bowed, heart cold with fear, as his neighbors looked on.

He had so many youngsters relying on him! Though dangerous, he knew himself savvy enough to pull it off. Wisdom pointed the clear trail. While angry at the country's leadership for abandoning him, he understood why they had. It tore him up. He loved Shande, the Harbor and the city like he loved life and his family.

He would make the best choice for Shande.

When a few days later a Minarian led him into the palace reception hall, Aron recognized the governor's companions as Eidhalt, with the small constriction in his chest that would have preceded a gasp if he had one. He wanted to run, but Loch Asmodiel, Governor of the Minarian Protectorate of Shande, smiled his welcome and gestured to a padded chair at the foot of the dais. The governor called for a second chair for himself. Pladde servants quickly fetched the chair and set up a small table between them.

Adesia, Matriarch of the Protectorate, sauntered across the hall. Her measured strides drew all eyes to her lithe form as she glided to a place behind Loch Asmodiel's chair. Her thick black hair hung loose, like a cloak, almost to the floor, her bewitching eyes set in a sun-coppered face to mesmerize him.

Aron struggled to stand. The Eidhalt stepped forward, hands on weapons.

"Please, you are my guest here, do not be alarmed," Loch Asmodiel soothed, motioning for Aron to retake his seat. "We are not the horrible people your gossips make us out to be."

Aron gingerly sat, leaning toward the governor as if toward protection from the Eidhalt in the hall. A Pladde servant pressed a goblet of fine wine into his hand, its sweet scent mingling with the aroma of meats and cheese wafting from a salver placed on the table at his elbow. He took a light bread, soft in the center, its crust crisp.

"Most gracious Governor," Aron said, raising his glass, his guilty frown barely allowing the sweet liquid to cross his lips.

"It is for such wise men as you, Keeper, that we saved Shande," Loch Asmodiel replied. He appeared so regal in his red tunic, a black surcoat trimmed in orange and gold brocade, his dark wavy hair oiled and scented. "Men like us will soon see order restored. Change can be hard for people and those who have been under the sway of manipulative leaders and their lies may find it difficult to see the truth. It is hard to accept that you were misled by people you thought acted in your best interests, when they instead stole your labor and grew fat on it."

Aron felt himself a little unanchored. Loch Asmodiel smiled at him, his words not those of a vicious man. Aron briefly wondered if in the heat of battle his fellows had exaggerated the brutality, or perhaps the excesses he'd heard of came from the passions of war.

"I trust your new home is comfortable?" Loch Asmodiel continued.

"Most generous, Lord!" Aron slurred, glowing as the wine hit his empty stomach. "My children are excited to have their own rooms –"

"You have ten, I am told." The governor's smile grew wider as he leaned forward, waiting for Aron's nod. "Impressive! You may be interested in a very special program we have developed for educating the young. They have had phenomenal achievements even among the Pladde who do not usually take well to education, allowing those children to step into successful roles. Older children, however, do not do well. I understand your eldest has fifteen years. Unfortunate." He leaned back, his smile apologetic, his words dripped scorn like crystallized honey. "We find that by fourteen, they cannot be educated. Set in their ways, they have bad habits impossible to break and become rebellious. The young learn easily the skills to do well. They adjust, succeed, and are apt to be placed in the best positions."

"My daughter, the eldest, Laria, she's a good learner," Aron said, concerned the blossom of his house would miss an opportunity to gain from their conquerors what her siblings had won.

"Laria?" Loch Asmodiel maintained his smile. "Perhaps we can arrange something for the girl, as a reward for your service. She is clever, you say. Attractive? Perhaps she could serve my Lady Adesia, if she can learn proper decorum and grace for the position."

Aron downed his wine and held out his glass for more, certain he set his family up for their success. "She's a lovely girl! Of course, I've a bias," he said as he took a bite of bread. "But Laria knows her place. She's been a handmaiden to nobles since she turned twelve. Near a woman now, she's not at all gawky and could serve your lady with honor. Obedient. I trained her right there."

"Perfect!" Loch Asmodiel declared. "Send for her and I will personally see to her accommodations. Adesia will make of Laria a woman the girl could never have imagined and she will be an example for other young women to emulate!"

Aron's eyebrows rose. It sounded like a far better guarantee of position than any of Laria's earlier postings.

"And your other children," Adesia said, her voice like a cat's purr. "Even the youngest will be trained for success in the new realm. We will hold a parade to honor them and they will be an example for others to enroll their children. It is a residential program, so that they can be completely immersed in their studies without the distractions of home. When they return, they will be a cause for pride."

Aron grinned, so pleased with himself he slapped his knee and sat back comfortably in his chair as he contemplated a secure future for his children after so many months of uncertainty.

"So, tell me more about yourself," Loch Asmodiel said in an easy tone, after Aron had accepted yet another glass of wine. "You were lighthouse keeper. And I understand you served in the ... Harbor Gnats, they called them?"

Aron nodded, glowing with his fortune. "Me and Nali Drulson were best friends, confidantes, you know," he blurted. "Nali was a good friend of the royals so we heard a bit of the gossip." He figured, what harm could come from talking about people long gone.

"This Nali," the governor snapped his finger as if trying to remember an unimportant name heard in passing. "He was a derna? Seems odd for a Harbor man." He waited for the bob of Aron's head. "So, what became of him?"

"I think he probably got out of the city somehow during the surrender. He's a bright one. I don't know just how," Aron said, his tone in the pitch of a storyteller as he glowed with his importance. "I'm pretty sure he headed west with the royals, based on gossip I've heard," he mused, trying to imagine a route that might mislead the pursuit when he expected they'd joined the refugees in Otayr. "The northwestern plains up there are pretty barren, and the royals are friendly with don Saran, the baron's son lookin' to be joined to the princess. I heard as many as two thousand went with 'em, a mighty lot of folk to take on a march like that, with younger and elder, and the king and his children. So, I'm pretty sure they had to take ship. Some folk suggested they'd seen ships waiting in a bay west of Mania Point. I can't be certain of this, mind you. I was down in Whittea."

As Aron spoke, glowing with his cleverness, several Eidhalt slipped from the hall. Loch Asmodiel made a small sign as they left, continuing to attend to Aron as the keeper sold his friends for his family, unaware that in just a few minutes he unburdened himself of them, as well.

The Harbor man took gulps of sweet wine, and mouthfuls of tender bread and soft cheese, speaking as he chewed, relating small anecdotes of his friends' lives he thought unimportant. So, as he spoke of Jan the Innkeeper, Reve Pedr the Drayman, the family Drulson and others he had seen no sign of since his return, the governor smiled indulgently.

The door opened as Aron babbled on. Soldiers ushered in dazed Laria Keeper, her arm held firmly in a soldier's grip as she stared at her father with an expression Aron thought might be fear, though it seemed to express disappointment. He would need to speak to her of this and correct such a lack of discipline. She twitched, as if poised for flight, as Loch Asmodiel appraised her. She locked her gaze on the floor as a dutiful child should among her betters.

"She is so rabbit-like, Keeper," Loch Asmodiel said as he circled the girl. "I think she would probably squeal if I called 'boo'! Look at her. I bet even her frightened feet would thump like a desperately fleeing hare." He smiled at Adesia, who appeared stiff as she regarded the girl. "Knowing my Lady Adesia's needs for pampering, I shall ensure she is properly taught myself as a gift to my dear lady."

He called for servants, ordering them to have the girl dressed appropriately for her service to the Matriarch of the Minarian Protectorate. As servants led the frightened blossom of Aron Keeper's house away – her feet reluctant, her will not enough to resist – Loch Asmodiel stared after her. He licked his lips and smacked them, as if at a morsel of dessert. He glanced at Aron, whose smile faltered when he saw the look in Loch Asmodiel's eyes. His daughter threw a last desperate look at her father, and he could swear that in that expression, she judged him.

Only a few days later, the city mostly secure, Loch Admodiel at last addressed his conquest, on the very dais, he learned, the defeated King of Shande had foolishly issued his call to arms against the Great God of Ea.

He scanned the sea of faces looking up at him, solemn, sullen, some frightened. A few stared at him with open loathing. His officers took note of them. Most expressed shock as they learned how their former overlords had deceived them, or dismay to learn that they must prove themselves trustworthy subjects of the protectorate and give up their demon worship to receive the privileges afforded their Minarian benefactors.

The sounds of shouts and the occasional scream echoed through the city's alleys as soldiers rounded up those missing a speech clearly noticed as mandatory. Two weeks had passed since the city fell. The time had come for people to accept their fate. No Shandean military organized a counter offensive and no country dared challenge Minaria's superior might, especially if they wanted to continue to benefit from trade in Shandean goods. The swiftness and ease of this conquest left Loch Asmodiel stunned that this fruit had remained unplucked for so long. It reaffirmed that Minaria reaped the reward of Ghyldus' will.

Mol Azezial could have selected no better governor. Loch Asmodiel excelled at discipline and order and suppressing dissent. Hadn't he brought into line an entire province of Pladde wailing about their kindly gods? Stroking the burning pendant on his chest, he smiled at the thought of the treasures not yet gathered from this luscious land – and, of couse, servants to Ghyldus. He grasped the blazing medallion, feeling its power, and silently hoped the all watchful one didn't think he would plunder Shande without thought of tribute for his god as well.

He also knew that when rebels swung from the gallows in the square the next day things would change. Demonstration always brought the message home. He glanced at Adesia who stood beside him. The matriarch preened as she studied an invisible speck on her sleeve. A morsel trembled at Adesia's elbow, Laria Keeper the kind of demonstration he liked. No one could misunderstand Laria's role when they saw how the gown he selected from the wardrobes of Shande's former princess sculpted the girl's fresh figure. Her eyes remained downcast, her rouged cheeks the only spots of color in a pale face, her chestnut hair pulled up to reveal her neck in a manner that in Minaria marked her among the higher caste concubines.

Adesia followed his gaze. The flower of Aron Keeper's house flinched as if from a physical blow. The girl's one-time neighbors and friends glared from the assemblage, their expressions accusing as they stared at Aron, who sat in a place of honor in the gallery behind the governor.

"As you can see, trustworthy subjects gain great rewards," Loch Asmodiel continued his lengthy address, swinging an arm toward Aron and several other Shandeans who had accepted their place in the new order and sat in the gallery. "They earn fine homes with packed larders better than they have ever known before. Their children receive the best education and positions with the government. But those who do not cooperate are treasonous enemies to the peace and will be severely punished. Remember, those hiding anyone who would do harm to the Minarian Protectorate of Shande are also guilty of treason, and the punishment is death. I have no doubt you know who those enemies are. They are your neighbors who worship demons, or who break rules or take more than allotted for their service to the protectorate, or who create dissent. They are anyone who harbors the most serious criminals and enemies of the God of Ea, the shawnsi, derna and officers of the deposed rule. Those people who lived off your labor like parasites, who forced us to give our blood to save you from them, who cost you the lives of family and friends and your homes. It is their fault and theirs alone. They must be brought to justice to pay for what they have done. And anyone who helps them must die as well."

He noted a small cluster of men in the back of the crowd moving to stand defensively around two figures, who stood with heads bowed, faces hidden beneath mariner's caps. He turned to point them out to his soldiers but they had disappeared. The stunned expressions on other Shandean faces revealed they still didn't understand. They would eventually, he knew. Hunger and fear always brought them in.

"Your oppressors misled you. Their lies convinced you that they exploited you for your benefit as they ruled you in the name of false gods." Loch Asmodiel continued. "We liberate you. But those demons pose a risk. They may still lead the weak astray. As long as resistance remains, you will have no peace. Without peace, no privileges. If you are hungry, you have only your own failure to cooperate to blame." He reached out to Adesia and raised their hands above their heads. "Rejoice now! You are the keystone to a new and unified empire forged from a world of scattered and heathen tribes. One day, all Ea will know the glory of Ghyldism, and all Ea will know peace."

He scowled a little at the oppressive silence of the square. He turned his back on the crowd, which filed away in silence to return to ramshackle shelters, their conquerors' scorn in their ears. Adesia, purring, comforted him and Laria cringed as his arm went around a waist cinched into a corset that sculpted her to a woman's shape. Shande was his. He would taste its fruit like a lover, passionate, unyielding, compelling. Unless he met resistance. The very thought guided his hand beneath the bodice of the obedient servant he had made with Aron Keeper's blessing. Like Laria, soon he would mold Shande to his needs.

34: The Gorge

King Ebon pointed at a fresh tree branch sweeping by with the river's current as Arshal's raft moved upriver. Something about the branch bothered Arshal. He studied a narrow horizon mostly blocked by a ridge where the river rushed from a deep gorge. He thought he saw a flicker of lightning, but couldn't be sure as the sky brightened with dawn. A minute later he heard thunder. Scanning the skyline again, he noted the dark of predawn in the west had hidden a towering, anvil-shaped cloud rising over the hills, which now blushed pink and brilliant white with dawn. In their month on the river, they'd sat out several storms. At times the rain fell so heavy and the wind tore at them with such anger, or hail pelted with such fury, they couldn't see the other rafts huddling on the lee bank and had to shout to be heard. The sky darkened beneath the thunderhead and he only hoped cooler air would follow, ushering out the ripening moon which had passed hot and humid and thick with biting flies.

The river moved fast now, fed by the outlying foothills of the mountains they sought. Their progress slowed as the banks narrowed, impeded now by small boulders and a current harder to avoid. They would need to give up the river soon, but the memory of the desperate slog on foot from the tunnel had him pushing as far as they could.

Arshal rubbed away the chill of the sticky and humid morning as another hazy day began. From his position in the second raft, he could see the rest of the boats trailing out behind him. Some hadn't even rounded the last bend yet. Gaunt and tired faces gazed back at him, and many of the elders wheezed with deep rasping coughs that lingered in the chest. They'd lost half a dozen already to lingering wounds, accident and illness. Not for the first time he wondered if he'd been a fool to try to lead so many so far.

He picked his way around sprawled arms and legs to a small corner of the raft where a barrier of empty sacks had been strung for privacy. After relieving himself into the river he took his turn at the raft pole, working the stiffness from his limbs as the barge bucked the current and defied the work of the paddlewheel.

Weary looking exiles roused with the dawn. The trip had eroded everyone's stamina the way the river carved the banks. Other than teams of gatherers, most couldn't go ashore. They had no privacy: their family battles, their toilet, their stolen moments of intimacy or breakdown, all on display not just for the neighbors, but for every other barge in sight. Foraging led only on rare occasions to the cookfires needed to cure half a dozen wild prairie cattle that their best hunters brought down, a few hours of nervous respite, every moment fearing discovery, before again climbing aboard the rafts. Such windfalls fed them for up to a week, the thick shaggy hides becoming blankets that warmed whole families, the finery of the court giving way to the pungent musk of uncured hides.

Mostly, boredom ruled and moods grew surly. Even Resala turned her hand to fishing. She dangled her feet in the water and tied live insects to a line, then shrieked the first time a small silver fish took the bait. Arshal roared with pleasure when she hauled it in, its eyes bulging and gills sucking, reminding him of his present to her that day so long ago – only months, but forever. She'd caught many fish since then.

Lightning grew more frequent in the massing clouds ahead, the thunder louder. As they neared the narrow canyon, Arshal braked the barge against the current's pull, the paddlewheel no longer effective. Two more men grabbed poles and worked from the sides to keep the craft from turning. Together, they crept upriver, the canyon walls narrowing until the roar of rapids all around them swallowed all else. All poles barely held them as they sought quiet water, in vain. Their poles buoyed up at them from a deepening channel, except where they found themselves wedged against boulders.

A quick glance back revealed others in similar straits. Those barges farthest back struck for shore. At last, they would have to abandon the vessels for good. Arshal scanned the gorge's rocky shores in search of a landing. Suddenly, the barge tilted over a submerged boulder, threatening to turn as they struggled to push the craft toward shore.

A flash and crack of thunder snapped the sky overhead,

sending booming echoes along the canyon walls and reverberating through the rocks above. He ducked as another flash, followed by another crack of thunder, ripped across the sky. Ahead, a gray haze roared down the canyon. A squall line struck with a massive gust of wind followed by rain so heavy it obscured the rapids ahead.

"Hang on!" Arshal shouted. Hail pelted them as he tried to maneuver among the jumble of boulders. "Hold this position!" he yelled as the polers tried to wedge their levers into the uneven river bed.

A violent lurch lifted the raft and sent it spiraling to one side. Arshal heard the snap, and caught the startled look of a man holding a broken pole in his hand. The barge swung sideways and then careened toward a steep cascade. Screams surrounded Arshal, and he glimpsed a father grasping his son to his chest.

The craft lurched and up-ended then swung around to drop into churning water. Thrown from his feet into the river, Arshal only vaguely realized he still clung to the pole as the angry river smashed him into boulders and ground him against the gravel river bottom. He struggled to find the surface. Each time, the current pulled him under to again roll him along the bottom.

He clung to a rock a moment, gasping as he scanned the water for the survivors from his raft, his lungs aching. The overturned vessel crashed and splintered against a jut of rock that stood in the middle of the river, a lone, twisted pine clinging to the top. A piece of storm debris struck his fingers and he lost his grip, again at the mercy of the current.

The hesitant waters of an eddy in a pothole sought him. He struck out for it, trying to wedge the pole into the bottom to stop his momentum. As he pushed the pole down, he found no bottom. The pole bobbed back up and struck his chest, smashing the wind from his lungs. At last, he wedged one end into a split boulder on shore. It hung above him, the prince clinging to it with fast tiring arms. Scanning the river, he noted one man sprawled on a tumble of rock midstream where a raft maneuvered to pick him up. Rescuers fought driving rain to pluck others from the river's angry rush.

Struck in the back, he risked his hold on the pole to reach for the outstretched hand of a bedraggled treasury officer. He clung to the man with one arm to keep him from going under.

The squall line rumbled down into the plains, the steady rain lit only occasionally by more distant cloud lightning. The gorge grumbled with thunder and the rhythm of the rapids.

What kind of fool would attempt to pole unwieldy barges into such a chasm? How many lives had his foolishness cost them? From the corner of his eye, he saw the other rafts that had entered the canyon held to the swirls of the lee shore and found a spit on which to beach, the narrow point bar submerging in rising waters as refugees unlashed cargo to carry it above the water line.

Arshal studied the wedge of the pole. Though near shore, he could feel the current swirling about his legs, which bobbed up and down without finding bottom. Storm wrack occasionally brushed against him. What if some larger branch smashed into him? With both hands free, he might trust the strength of the pole and pull himself toward the bank. He noted the officer's eyes had glazed.

"Lorem!" Arshal shouted, trying to bring the man's eyes into focus. The gaunt, sunburned features of the shawnsi's face barely resembled the man who once sat at the king's table, flushed with sweet wine. Lorem blinked several times and stared at the prince. His gaze followed the stretch of Arshal's left arm to where it hooked around the pole.

"Let me go. Save yourself," he gasped.

"Hang on to me so I can pull us to shore. Can you do it?" Arshal demanded. Lorem shook his head. "Come on, try. Reach your hand around my waist and hang on to my belt." The man's fingers worked around the leather strap. "Hold tighter now. I still have you. Now the other, wedge the other in there," Arshal ordered, fearing the man would let go. Lorem obeyed and Arshal at last grabbed the rain slicked pole with both hands. Lorem bobbed behind him, legs following the current, face sinking beneath the water. "Keep your head up, Lorem! Don't just give up!"

The muscles in Arshal's shoulders screamed as he towed the additional weight toward shore. When his knees scraped against the side of the pothole, then gravel, hands grasped his arms and dragged him and the half-drowned Lorem to safety. Arshal coughed, rolling onto his back. He peered through soaked strands of hair to find Peshal above him, the younger prince groping Arshal's limbs for injuries. Arshal gazed upriver to where Resala guided a bedraggled Cree along the uneven shore toward them.

Arshal pushed Peshal aside to reach Lorem, fresh scrapes protesting the air, the grit of the gravel in them burning. He ignored them. Lorem's eyes remained closed in a pale face, his breathing shallow. When he reached them, Cree stooped to run his hands over the young officer's body.

'He's broken inside," Cree stated. A hush fell among the rescuers as Resala hurried back to the beached rafts to comfort Lorem's frightened family.

Arshal slammed his fist against the gravel, despite the sting of stone on skin. "So stupid! What was I thinking?" He ran a bleeding hand through wet hair as he glowered at the slate-gray sky.

Peshal put his hand on Arshal's shoulder, eliciting a wince. "You're not alone," Peshal said. "Others could have protested. Many pulled aside when they saw how difficult the stream became. We don't know this river. We can't outguess nature. Maybe it's the gods' warning that they won't think for us and we mustn't take anything for granted."

Arshal gazed long at Peshal, wondering what his brother truly believed. "How long does he have, Cree?" he asked.

"Perhaps hours."

"We need to rest, see to injuries, get everyone on the south side of the river and decide our course. Let's make Lorem as comfortable as we can, find dry fuel and a sheltered spot to re-pack for the trek ahead."

He wished he could feel the confidence of a leader. He had once. But now, he wondered if he'd doomed them all with his rash promise. Lorem brought the toll to four. Three, swept away, likely hadn't survived, the only trace of them a cap found swirling among the eddies near the mouth of the gorge.

The others from Arshal's raft had clung until rescued or found ground and the strength to wade ashore. When at last small fires caught in the shelter of the canyon wall, defeated and silent groups huddled in the damp and cheerless glows.

They had far yet to travel, and now on foot. What if Sefresal lay in ruins and they found only the enemy ravening the countryside? Soon, winter would be upon them. Snow, like the dream. The thought made the knot in Arshal's gut burn.

THE WEST

35: The Crossing

Instinct guided Khoti as he made for the last known position of the Minarian army, circling around through rockfall and gorge as he made for a position ahead of them. When he stalked his enemy, crept up to kill scouts and sentries or set traps, his warrior's heart beat in him. He relished the brief meetings with other Guardsmen, or the occasional clack of the stone language Eithurdon had insisted he teach the scouts. He dreamed of this: a man-of-arms free of walls and rules and protocol.

But when he sheltered a flame in a hidden cleft at night, or let Fidra choose the safest path among the rocks and crevices, nagging images haunted him. Sometimes he saw Von falling back in the flames, or carrion birds stalking him, or his parents, or Asteria, bruised and pale buried in the rockslide. And then Asteria's dark eyes shining with – was it admiration? – the confusion of emotion and sensation when he touched his palm to her wound.

He recalled every word she said to him, from the exchange in the Val to her glowing account to Eithurdon of Khoti's magic. She told Eithurdon she felt the spirits in him. Had he done that? Had he brought spirits even his father couldn't? Tsevon called on their aid, but they didn't infuse him. Asteria had felt no pain from his medicine. Yet Khoti remembered the feel of his father's hot knife against his flesh. Even the cut he had made in his own palm passed swiftly, bearable. Perhaps his concentration made it easier. Guilt and worry had tormented his father. But then, Ahrewsz's yelp had seemed no sign of the spirits in his fa's hands. The way they had filled Khoti, gave him breath and heart and will, calmed his fears and guided his hands: this was new. Tales spoke of gifted healers of old –

Khoti didn't want to think about it. When he thought of medicine, he thought of Asteria. Thinking of her only left him frustrated. Even if he turned his mind to Kefta's lessons, he remembered only Kefta teasing him.

"The lady has caught you in her snare," Kefta had declared, ignoring Khoti's claim that he had no need for the distraction of a woman's attentions. "But Eithurdon's daughter, that's a sweet eye any man would wish for," Kefta had returned.

Startled, Khoti had muttered that she was too old and well above a mountain boy's station. Kefta had laughed so hard he'd tipped from his stool, still chuckling long minutes after while Khoti's face grew hot with embarrassment.

No, Khoti gladly fled Sefresal and all the gossip and teasing, and from Asteria who must have cast some spell on him when he gave her his blood. He had too much to do now, too much hate in his heart. His work gave no room for distraction. For the briefest moment he wondered what the trained healers knew. How his fa decided who to heal and who to yield to the spirits. In battle, would it be the warrior or the healer that took the field? There, another thought he had no time to entertain.

As he rode along a narrow defile from yet another successful action, Khoti heard a faint tap, Ytri calling for a meeting of the scouts. He grinned as he turned Fidra's head south in anticipation of the companionship of his fellow Guardsmen. They drove away the strange loneliness that seemed to lurk on the edge of his perception.

It took two days to answer Ytri's call, Khoti numbering among the most distant. He had never traveled so far south before. He took in a new landscape with eyes wide and ears open to new sights and sounds, his breath drawing deep the scents. Instead of snow-capped mountains, crags and cracking stone, the wind sighed softly in pines fringing even the tops of the mountains. The aroma of pine saturated the air and a blanket of pine needles and mushrooms at the feet of the massive trees muffled the sound of Fidra's hooves.

He imagined meetings of great import in an arbor beneath such lofty sentinels as these trees. Instead, the calling stones directed him to a spot east of the forest at the edge of marshes marking the tentative southern shoreline of the Dodfrenyen Sea.

To make speed, Khoti descended to the spongy hillsides overlooking the marsh and followed a broad animal path free of tree root and boulder. After only a few hours, his exposed skin became a giant welt from the hordes of biting insects swarming up at him from bogs and ponds that dotted the marshes. Fidra's tail twitched, her skin quivering and swollen. He maintained their pace until Fidra stumbled in a stagnant pool that crept to the foot of the range and came up lame. He set a smoky fire while he wrapped her leg and rested her, the fire doing nothing to drive the insects away. At last, unable to even sleep among so many whining bugs, he kicked out his fire and led Fidra along the path, his sour scowl darkening the night.

At dawn, Khoti rested Fidra again as he climbed up onto a rock outcrop for his first glimpse of the southern marsh complex of the Dodfrenyen Sea. His nose scrunched. Everything stunk of the sour mud Fidra's hooves kicked up or the smoky fire he had lit. Certainly friends and enemies alike would smell his approach. Even the hunk of jerky he worked tasted like marsh mud.

As the sun rose, Khoti shielded his eyes against the glare of sunlight on patches of open water dotted with chattering waterfowl. The marshes stretched into the eastern horizon, no edge in sight, a vast distance strange to eyes used to the bounds of mountain and forest. Far south he could see where the land rose slightly as the marshes ended in soggy scrub that eventually became Tormor Wood. He wished he could ride to the hardwood forest on the edge of Mershy province, just so he could boast to Tre that he had left Kishma.

He shook his head. It made no sense why Ytri would gather the scouts so many days south of the Minarian army. It would take weeks for them to march all the way to Mershy and around to threaten Eilime. He couldn't even see a hint of the sea on their northern boundary. In the farthest distance he spied the white tips of larger mountains marching north to the Val, where those peaks disappeared in a haze.

He leaned back against the rock outcrop, the sun driving the insects away to give him a brief nap before the tapping of stones roused him. Again, he led Fidra south, already weary of this part of the world.

The mountains threw long evening shadows over the marsh before Khoti reached the meeting place, a clearing on the marsh edge where other scouts had already thrown damp branches into the fire in an unsuccessful attempt to drive off the bugs. Khoti left Fidra tied to a picket in the trees farther up the hillside where he found more than a dozen other mounts snorting into feedbags or dozing on their feet.

The Guardsmen sat on logs ringing the smoky fire. The aroma of roasting venison reached above the smoke to make Khoti's stomach growl. He grinned broadly as several men bade him join them and someone pressed a hunk of cooked venison and a hard biscuit into his hands. Though most of those around him wore the bulky build and dark hair of Sefresal lowlanders, sitting between Toban and Geleg, he felt like he'd come home.

As night settled the last of more than two dozen scouts finally arrived and Ytri made clear why he called them.

"They're moving faster now that the most difficult passes are behind them," Ytri said to begin the meeting.

"And we've fewer tricks to use against them," Geleg agreed from his place beside Khoti.

Ytri gestured to Kefta's red-headed brother, Mitte, who held a courier's pouch. "And we got promises from the Tachi of Tormor Wood. Minarians will find no easy passage around the southern end of the marshes. But I don't think they intend to go any farther south than right here."

"Here?" Khoti echoed, looking out over the dark expanse where the wind sighed over reeds. Something felt wrong about the idea, about this whole meeting. Something in the air made his skin tingle with a hint of the warrior instinct in him.

"How would they get through this mess?" Toban scoffed.

"They've lost a lot of time," Ytri said. "It'd take weeks to reach Tormor Wood and come around to the east and then back north. History says the Minarians are known for military ingenuity. Those trees they're dropping and hauling, the ones their carpenters cut? I expect they'll lay a bridge across the marsh."

"Take an awful long bridge," Khoti grumbled to Geleg.

"It can be done," Ytri said, hearing Khoti's aside. "You lay a seven-pace-or longer halved log over this tussocky stuff and you can roll over it without sinking. As soon as the wheels touch the next log, you lift the one behind and move it forward. The trees they've felled are plenty more than seven paces. The marshes are narrow here with fewer pools. I'm guessing it might take them three days to cross. If they circle south, they have more like three weeks' travel to get back to this point on the east side. That, and there are more bogs south of here, nowhere for them to lay their bridge. This is the only place they can cross." Ytri shook his head a moment to drive away a swarm of insects encircling it. "We saw signs their scouts went to Tormor Wood and back. They spent a lot of energy in this area. We need to make this the worst passage they ever had. Once they find firm ground, they'll move on Eilime like a storm on the plains."

"Marshes surround Eilime on the south and east. They'd still have to go around, and cross the river to make the approach," Khoti said.

"There's a dike built back when the sea level was higher. It's about the same width as that canyon on the Staph-el Road. There's no way to stop them on the dike like we stopped them on the road. Just a handful of us can't do it without the advantage of high ground."

"So, what can we do?" Geleg asked, passing Khoti the wine.

"That's why I called you. I don't have any ideas. I hoped we'd come up with something." His expression reflected a certainty that they had reached the end of their usefulness, having barely scratched the Minarian army.

The scouts sat late into the night, the wine helping them ignore the feeding frenzy of insects settling on them in giant clouds like gulls descending upon an Eilime fishing boat. But late into the night, they still had no answers. Khoti didn't want to give up and go home.

A horse whickered in the trees behind them, but Khoti ignored it as the fire took his wine-sotted attention. The beast whickered again, a low greeting to another animal. Khoti tensed, instinct telling him something his mind hadn't grasped yet.

"Hist," he said thickly through lips that tasted like wine, slashing his hand downward to silence a question as all eyes turned to look back at the forest. It was silent.

"Ah, Khoti, the drink's playing tricks on you. Give it a few years and you'll better handle the stuff," Geleg said.

Khoti's glare made the chuckle die on Geleg's lips.

"Don't you hear it?" the Taschian whispered.

"I don't hear anything," Toban replied, his head cocked toward the forest.

"You don't hear anything because someone's out there. The frogs, the insects, the owl, they're all silent. I heard horses greeting. Since they all are picketed together, who do you s'pose they're calling to?"

The silence pressed at him from the hillside. Frogs chirped farther south, east and north. No sound came from the woods and hillside. Beginning to work himself backward, Khoti drew his sword as he escaped the ring of firelight. The other men followed suit as the euphoria of the wine faded.

Suddenly, Khoti heard the whoosh of arrows. Geleg fell face first into the fire with an arrow in his chest. More arrows fell among them, but Khoti couldn't tell if they found targets as he rolled behind a log.

A faint gleam moved among the trees as distant firelight lit a weapon. He thought he detected movement among the horses. Then he heard the thud of hooves as someone released them from the picket and frightened them away. The scouts had fallen into a trap. How stupid: all of them gathered like this. He didn't think the Minarians could decipher calling stones. But it wouldn't take much to see that all the trails led here, the smoky fire, the racket of their chatter. How stupid. And if the Minarians planned to cross here, certainly they'd watch the place.

The air shifted as Ytri leaped up and dashed into the shadows of the pines. Metal clanked. Then silence again, with no sign of Ytri.

Khoti thought he heard soft footfalls and peered around the edge of the log. A man crept toward him. Khoti glanced back, no one but Geleg remained, the Guardsman now laying beside the fire. The other scouts had melted into the darkness, perhaps dead, scattered in the ambush, seeking their mounts or battling somewhere up on the hillside.

The Minarian stopped a few paces away and drew a dagger from his boot sheath. He gripped it in his left hand, sword poised in the right. Khoti took a firmer grip on his own sword and shifted to free his arm to strike. He lay on his back, head to the side to watch his enemy's approach.

The Minarian leaped and fell on Khoti. The Taschian struggled to roll away, but his enemy held him in an iron grip. The Minarian dropped the sword to grip Khoti's arm, then tried to smash his dagger into Khoti's throat. Khoti ducked beneath him, the knife barely missing. The weight of the man atop him pinned Khoti's weapon between them, useless. The Taschian's fingers tried to reach the Minarian's fallen sword. Sensing Khoti's move, the Minarian shifted and pinned Khoti's forearm to the ground with his knee, struggling to keep the wiry Lharan scout from wriggling free.

Khoti wrenched to the side and the Minarian stabbed at him again. The dagger bit soft turf instead. In the brief instant it took the man to pull his dagger from the dirt, his weight shifted from Khoti's forearm. Khoti grasped the Minarian's sword. Though too long to twist around and stab, Khoti brought its sharp edge down on the unprotected backs of the Minarian's legs. The dagger came at him again. Just then, Khoti squirmed nearly free. He winced as the knife sank into his left shoulder.

As the Minarian shifted again to get in postion to finish Khoti off, Khoti wedged the Minarian sword between them, the tip resting against his enemy's mailed chest. He drove upward with all the strength he could put in his arms toward the unprotected space between the man's collarbones. The sword sank in, the man arching backward an instant before he heaved forward, the force of the sword hilt smashing Khoti's ribs and driving the breath from his lungs.

Khoti lay beneath the Minarian many minutes as the man's life bled from him and Khoti found his breath. He pushed the dead weight away then tried to stand. A tight ache warned him he'd bruised his ribs, if not fractured them. On his chest grew a hard lump and a bruise the same size as the sword hilt that had driven into him with the Minarian's weight behind it. He shook out his left shoulder. The edges of cut flesh burned. They weren't life-threatening injuries, but he couldn't heal himself and they would slow him, especially if fever set in his wounds.

The chorus of frogs and insects in the forest had resumed. Had only one Minarian done this? Where had all the scouts gone? He noted Geleg, sprawled beside the fire, and remembered Ytri running at the attackers. Almost two dozen more had just disappeared.

He needed his pack to survive in the wilds. Yet, he hesitated to make himself a target in the firelight. He crept toward Geleg. The burns on the scout's face and hands appeared mild, but already seeped. Blood dribbled from his mouth and Khoti could see that the arrow likely pierced a lung. His gaze followed Khoti's approach.

"Help me," Geleg begged, a spray of blood chasing his words.

Khoti leaned back on his haunches. "I can't, Geleg. Forgive me. I think it would kill me."

"How could you not help a brother in need?"

The words stung like no other curse. The odor of smoke and scorched hair struck his senses. For an instant he heard Von shouting his name, horses squealing in terror. Khoti told himself it would do no good. Instead of fleeing as the others had, he pulled the tera sticks from his pack to perform his fa's medicine.

Any moment more Minarians might come. He moved Geleg farther from the fire, hunched over as he worked, feeling like a target against the night. Had the other scouts drawn the enemy away? Geleg's wound glared at him; Khoti could feel how the arrow had ripped into him. The spirits came to him slower than before, yet his sticks again danced in the firelight, the cloud of insects a distant memory. He tugged the arrow from Geleg's chest, hearing no protest. What did he wield in his blood that could so ease the injured? Spirits trickled through him, hesitant, caressing his injuries as if confused by their mission. A cool scent of wilderness filled his lungs as at last his blood passed its spirit-healing into Geleg. For only a moment, the comfort of the spirits made Khoti feel less vulnerable and alone.

Khoti leaned against the log to tap his tribue. The pain in his chest and shoulder had abated when he called on the spirits. Now it returned, more intense than before. His lungs burned with each breath he took. His arm hung numb from his wounded shoulder. He could move it, but his hands tingled as if asleep. His hopes of returning to Sefresal faded. He should know better than to so foolishly ignore what little lore he knew. Yet, Geleg, his brother in arms if not his blood brother, lived now, when certainly he would have died.

The blood in the corners of Geleg's mouth went unreplenished as the man tested the still-tender burns on his face. They couldn't remain here. Despite Khoti's own desire for sleep and something to quench his dry mouth, he forced Geleg to rise.

"Must find horses, the others," Khoti muttered as they supported each other, making for the eaves of the wood where Ytri had disappeared. The smoky light of predawn glowed behind them by the time they found Ytri, his face coated with a light sheen of sweat, beneath a dead Minarian.

"Khoti, I couldn't call out. I didn't know if there were more. Help me?" Ytri gasped as Khoti struggled to roll the bulk of the dead man aside.

Khoti could immediately see the damage. He sagged, wanting only to rest as he examined Ytri's lower leg, seeing the way the bone had snapped, tendon and muscle torn. Anywhere else they might simply splint it and hope for the best. But not here.

"I – I'm too worn," Khoti whispered, feeling again the sense that he owed his brother Ytri, the first Guardsman to treat him like a man. Ytri tried to struggle to his feet, but Khoti shook his head. "You can't walk on that. It's broken."

"Help him, Khoti."

Khoti sank to his knees. His hands knew where to press, an inborn thing his father had given him. He could see the injury, but he needed Geleg's help to set it. He gasped for breath, both of them sweating in the chill of a foggy dawn, Ytri gripping him with an iron grasp as the Taschian splinted the leg with two of the pickets left behind when the horses scattered.

Geleg went in search of fuel for a fire, returning only a few minutes later. "Toban, he's on the other side of the knoll. He managed to stop them before they scattered all the horses. There's two. Toban needs you. He took a sword in the belly."

"You're killing me!" Khoti cried, looking from Geleg to Ytri. How many more injured scouts would they find? They would use him up and he would again walk among the spirits on the edge of that quiet place he had seen. He shuddered.

"You're a magic, Khoti. How can you just leave him to die?" Geleg asked. "The gods come through you! They give you the power to save your brothers in arms –"

"Fire," Khoti whispered, his words barely audible.

Geleg quickly set about making a fire near Toban, then as gently as possible Khoti and Geleg moved Ytri beside the other Guardsman.

The rhythm of the sticks came slow. Khoti felt as if he – 'falling away' Asteria had called it. He remembered elders' tales about the healers during the Great War. The tribes had many healers then. They had faded, fallen away, died from expending their strength to heal armies. Healers formed their guilds to stop such a waste of medicine. Khoti knew so little of his gift. What right did he have to withhold it? He knew he overextended himself. But how could he refuse?

The music dragged as the sticks barely swept the air, the call faint. A spirit touched his hands and the tera sticks leaped to life. He felt them in his blood, his breath. His fingers moved for him, finding the cadence and whispering their song.

Asteria called it a gift from the gods. She said she could feel them touch her. Who touched him so gently now? Who soothed him, sang to him, filled him with that cool breath of home?

His hand traced both scouts' injuries with the charred end of the tera stick, no work of his. His body, his motions, moved at the spirits' command. His mind wandered far away, trying to escape the pain filling his lungs with great gasps, sending sparks shooting from his shoulder down into the old wound on his side. He heard Geleg speaking, urgent words that fought to find him and beg him to stop if it did him such harm –

Had the spirits abandoned him? No, cool breath entered his lungs. He slashed his right hand with his left, the left still bloody from the wound that took Geleg's poison. He lay one hand on Ytri, one on Toban. Burns and cuts on his own hands, those on Geleg's face, Ytri's leg, Toban's torn abdomen, he felt each as a fresh wound, tormenting, aching, filling him with pain and grief. As he receieved their poison his throat opened in a bellow and he fell forward in a faint.

36: A Sacrifice

As Konner left Eithurdon's halls, already irritated by too many lowlanders and their demands on the Val, he noted a gathering of gawkers watching the approach of two horses and their burdens entering the city gates. Blood and mud caked every crevice of the men's bodies, almost concealing the Lharan Guard's colors in their gear. He recognized in an instant Geleg in front, a body wrapped in a Guard's cloak slumped in front of him. Toban and Ytri, their heads bowed, shared the other mount.

Kefta rushed from Eithurdon's halls behind him, the duke and Asteria on his heels.

"We killed him," Geleg stammered when Kefta looked up at the scout with a deadly glint in his eye. "His wounds aren't mortal, yet he dies. He said we were killing him, but we didn't understand."

"What are you talking about?" Kefta demanded.

"His medicine," Ytri said as he and Toban dismounted.

Konner pushed through the crowd. "How could you?" He demanded. "You used him in a way even his own people wouldn't." Fingers of fear and grief wrenched through him. He had failed Tsevon, the boy, and now another mountain life gone.

"Your people have a medicine. We rode as hard as we dared, five days, in hopes you'd mend this strange sickness –" Geleg began.

"I don't have half the medicine Tsevon does," Konner returned. "And it's little Tsevon could do at this point. He poured his life into you. He knew it. The spirits have him now."

"Would not the spirits protect him? I felt them in him," Asteria said. "I saw them! The sticks sang of waterfalls and forest glades and valleys of stone. Would such spirits let him die for helping his fellows?"

Geleg, Ytri and Toban nodded. "As Lady Asteria said," Ytri

said. "It was music, and comfort."

Konner brushed his hand against Khoti's forehead, searching for the spark he should sense if the youth remained among the living. He sensed only a faint hint of life. What made these lowlanders so ignorant? How did they survive? He should never have let Khoti live among such people.

"Then his medicine far exceeds mine and his fa's," Konner said. He could read the grief and brush with death in the long faces of the three scouts. "The healer pays a price with every wound or illness he mends. Some of that poison stays behind, only slowly fading. But if already healing weary and injured it's more than a man can take. And what remains behind, well that can grow more lethal, in his body instead of yours." He took Khoti's hot hand. "The spirits protect him from the war of poison in his body. Bringing him back could be fatal."

"But you must try," Kefta insisted.

Konner shook his head.

"If he knew, why did he do it?" Geleg asked, stricken.

"Because you asked him. If you had the power to save lives, could you refuse?" Before they could protest, Konner pulled Khoti from the horse and hefted him to his shoulder.

"Where are you going?" Eithurdon demanded.

"Home, so he can die among his people, set out on a proper platform for his release to the spirits, not tombed in the dirt among strangers." Konner's voice held as much expression as Khoti's vacant gaze as he turned toward the stables.

Eithurdon made a gesture. In an instant, Guardsmen surrounded Konner, swords drawn.

"You will take him to his rooms here. If there is a healer among you, we will find him. We will not let you sacrifice him!"

Asteria placed a restraining hand on her father's arm.

"Sacrifice! You think so low of us who shelter your people?"

"It is a sacrifice if you give up on a life that can be saved," Eithurdon said more gently. "If the gods bestowed such a gift, it was not to be wasted. If you cannot minister him, then we will search the mountains for someone who can." Eithurdon turned on his heel and stalked into his halls.

Konner suffered the Guardsmen to lead him to Khoti's room, his shuffling steps his only sign of his certainty Eithurdon's order would kill him. It went against all he knew, all that healers had learned in thousands of years. The spirits wanted Khoti.

Kefta placed a small firepot on the washstand then perched on a stool beside Eithurdon and Asteria, the room so small the duke sat partly in the hallway. They scrutinized Konner as if trying to follow a carnival illusionist's moves to unmask the trick. At least they could allow him more space. Konner could barely squeeze between the bed and wall. He studied Khoti for a long moment. He would try. The mountain folk would find other leaders if it killed them both and Tsevon never returned, but he feared he'd only make Khoti's last breath one filled with pain.

When he unlaced Khoti's tunic he found the muscles and build of a man, no longer the thin frame of a youth. A light coat of sand-colored hair had sprouted. Only the absent tattoo – something Konner would remedy if Khoti survived, those rites long overdue – suggested the body of a youth. Konner traced the hard bruise on Khoti's ribs with rough fingers sensitive to the wound beneath. A fractured rib had begun to heal. The gash on his shoulder, though, had soured. The deep wound inflamed Khoti's entire shoulder. After cleansing the wound and applying a special salve from a little tin in his pack, Konner at last pulled out tera sticks worn and blackened with use. Konner's hands trembled as if he performed his first healing.

Asteria stirred as the sticks began their cadence. "Kefta, there is no music in Konner's medicine," she whispered.

Konner grimaced. To comment on his medicine now? They didn't even recognize the sanctity of such a rite. He forced himself to ignore them as first he took the poison from Khoti's shoulder. Then, though healing weary, he beat a different cadence, an urgent call. He leaned close, calling Khoti's name as he made a small cut in the center of the young man's forehead and laid his bloody hand there.

Khoti squirmed beneath his hand, trying to jerk his head from Konner's touch. Konner gripped him by the jaw and pressed hard against the cut as sweat sprouted on Khoti's face and soon saturated his clothing and bedding until it could have been wrung.

"No!" Khoti shouted, his eyes flying open for a moment as his denial flung against the walls. He fell back in a faint.

Konner grit his teeth. "He won't let me heal him," Konner said.

"What? Why?" Asteria breathed.

"Because it'll kill me." Konner again turned to his sticks, ignoring the duke's protest. Hand again pressed on Khoti's forehead, he called, insistently. A sudden rush of poison and pain slammed into Konner. He fell back against the wall and sank to the floor, clutching his chest with his bloody hand and gasping for breath. Kefta rushed to help him to his feet.

Konner gasped, the pain stabbing through him as he shook free of Kefta's grip. "All that on himself. Would'a killed Tsevon." He took heaving gasps through clenched teeth, tears of pain running freely down his cheeks.

Konner turned to glare at Asteria. "It's your fault," he said. "You had to crow to the world that he was everyone's savior. He doesn't even understand it yet."

Kefta stepped between Konner and Asteria, his hand on his dagger.

"He told us it could not be used often. Certainly gossip –"

"But you put the idea in his head!" Konner shouted. Asteria stood her ground, her dark eyes beginning to flare at him. It still raged in him. The spirits couldn't take it all. He took a step toward her as Kefta drew his dagger.

"Konner," Khoti whispered. "Leave her be. I'm the fool."

Konner sagged at Khoti's side, so weary. He wiped the blood from Khoti's forehead with his sleeve. He could still see fever. "Ah, Khoti, I thought we'd lost you again."

"Why risk it, Konner?" Khoti said from far away. "I was happy –"

"Because we're selfish. Rest now. I'll take you home to stay among your own kind. Folk won't use you so hard."

"A gift given should be used," Khoti returned.

"But it nearly killed you!" Konner protested.

"But it nearly killed you," Khoti echoed. "I didn't ask you to do this. You could've refused." Asteria wiped the sweat and blood from his face. He didn't seem to see her. "I made the choice, Konner." His voice grew more distant as his eyes closed and Konner slowly tapped out his tribute, feeling more drained than he had ever felt before.

"Amazing, where does it come from?" Eithurdon mused as Konner tucked his tera sticks in his pack.

"From the heart," Konner said.

"From the gods," Asteria said, chin thrust out and clearly still smarting from Konner's accusation. "I felt it when he tended me. I sensed their touch. But Khoti made music. You did not."

Konner shrugged, too weary to think. "Maybe the spirits have a plan for him. The last of the great healers died in the aftermath of the Great War. One man can't cure an army. Khoti's strong – I knew – but so strong! It near stopped my heart and I know he didn't let me take it all." Konner's head dropped onto his forearm and he slumped so that his head rested on the edge of the bed.

Eithurdon motioned for Kefta to cover Tsevon's Second with a blanket before slipping out in the hall to hear Ytri's report, Asteria and Kefta remaining.

"What could be its purpose?" Kefta asked, echoing Konner's unspoken question.

Khoti stared at the ceiling, flickering candlelight shifting the shadows. How much time had passed? "We've lost Eilime."

"Yes, Eilime will fall."

Khoti turned at Kefta's voice, taking in the captain's unkempt appearance. Konner slept on a mat on the floor, his hand wrapped in a bandage. Asteria pried herself awake on a stool beside Kefta.

"Then it's all for nothing. We're so stupid."

"I heard Ytri's report. It wasn't for nothing. The scouts harried them, whittled them down. A demoralized army crosses the marshes. We hear reports of deserters trying to slip back to Minaria. Yes, it was stupid for Ytri to call you together where he did. He knew better. Ytri says you were alert enough to call the alarm –"

"I was drunk," Khoti shot back, reddening when Asteria covered her mouth to hide a smile.

Kefta grinned. "Yet aware enough. You saved yourself. Most of the scouts escaped unharmed and regrouped to continue their work. It allowed Ytri to give the order to scatter."

"But the army crossed, unchecked."

"Is crossing. You couldn't have stopped them."

Khoti tried to sit up, but fell back, exhausted. Did Konner know that somehow he held back some of the storm of poison roiling within him that would have killed the older man? It hadn't left him completely yet. The spirits had been so strong! They had guided Khoti's hands when he could no longer move them. He remembered waking in his alcove in the Val to their healing chatter and song. This time they held him, soothed him with song, caressed him when the pain seemed unbearable.

A groan escaped when he shifted and the ache found his shoulder. Konner hadn't taken close to all of it. He glanced at Asteria with the unreasonable thought that he wanted to appear impervious to pain. Suddenly realizing his nakedness beneath sheepskin blanket, he yanked it up to his chin, to Kefta's amusement.

Asteria brought him a dipper of water, holding his head so he could drink. He looked away when he saw her gazing back at him.

"Your injuries still trouble you?" Kefta asked in a whisper as Asteria returned the dipper to a pitcher on the washstand.

"Konner?" Khoti asked instead.

Kefta leaned back and narrowed his gaze on him. "Resting, as you should. A trio of scouts wearing their guilt wait on you. They'll be in debt to you for life."

Khoti shook his head, emphatic. "I don't want that. I don't deserve it. If they brought me here, I owe them."

"You look at life so oddly, Khoti. You nearly died to save them when they had no more entitlement to life than you."

Khoti frowned and turned his gaze to the ceiling. They just didn't understand. He couldn't explain it to himself. The spirits chose him. He merely served as their honored vessel. Khoti blushed as Asteria tucked an extra blanket around him. He gave her the half smile of gratitude his mother always told him looked coy. Why did he think of such things? He tried to ignore Asteria's attention, but couldn't pretend not to like it as she again dabbed a damp cloth at the cut on his forehead.

Konner stirred, then grasped Khoti's left hand and sighed to find a strong lifebeat. Konner eyed him in a way Khoti knew read his remaining illness.

"As I thought," Konner said. "You're such a stubborn cuss you've mastered the haunts of the spirits. I feel the fever in you yet. I don't know how you did it."

Khoti gave Konner a crooked smile as the older man turned Khoti's hand and studied the palm with its ragged burn marks and cuts. He held up his own palm and its thick thatch of scars.

"You're looking more like an elder than a youth," Konner said. "It gets harder to find the blood through all that scar."

Khoti held up his right palm to show the cut there. It stretched so far across his palm it almost met the sword scar on the back side.

Konner's expression soured. "You've let them use you. So bad you still hurt."

Khoti shook his head still smiling.

"My father ordered that no one ask him for healing," Asteria volunteered. Khoti grabbed Konner's arm as the Second tensed. They walked among a strange people. Such a declaration wouldn't hold in the Val, far from the halls Eithurdon ruled. Asteria bent over Khoti, her long hair falling from behind her shoulders to encircle his face. "I think he takes to you as a father. You have given so much to us. He does not want you 'used.'"

"Save yourself, Khoti, a man with three fas." Kefta said around a chuckle. "Tsevon, Konner and now the duke. You'll be driven to death by the advice – and whose takes precedence?"

"At least among lowlanders, his advice is sound," Konner said. He suddenly slapped the heel of his hand against his forehead. "Speaking of fas, Kefta, your lifemate's given you a daughter. I s'pose now you'll be looking for a son."

Kefta's whoop drowned Konner's last remark, a shout that brought Geleg bursting through the door, sword drawn.

"I'm a fa, Geleg!" Kefta crowed. "And I'll be teaching her to stay away from ruffians like you!"

Geleg grinned and slapped Kefta on the back as he pushed into the tiny room. He seemed oblivious to all others as he drew his dagger and offered it to Khoti. Stunned, Khoti remembered to ask for his own dagger to offer it to Geleg in return. They made a powerful pledge of mutual defense – only a battle-blooded knife worthy – a strange tradition for a land of peace.

Khoti frowned. "Now I'll need another dagger so I'm not forced to give yours away."

"At least ones for Ytri and Toban," Kefta said.

Konner sprouted that slashing grin that so seldom split his face of late. "Khoti's got a whole chest full of bloody knives. Take your pick."

Konner fell silent as the Guardsmen teased. Khoti knew Konner watched him, his expression guarded as he studied whatever thing he saw in his mending patient. Just the attention of friends made Khoti feel stronger, sent the posions fleeing from him, left him feeling washed and fresh and warm. As the banter built, a part of Khoti realized what troubled Konner. Khoti might have the stronger medicine, but he wasn't his fa. He doubted he could refuse a friend's plea for help. That Khoti could feel such compassion for his fellows, yet in the same breath be a ruthless soldier, was a paradox stamped on him like the hot knife that cauterized a wound. It burned in Khoti like the warrior heart he discovered. What would he do in battle when his comrades fell beside him? Avenge them, or heal them?

37: Eilime

In the cold of early dawn, Fidra stomped and twitched, sending up plumes of breath with each nervous snort. The mare and several other scattered mounts had found their way back to Sefresal some days after Khoti. Skittish and shy, she let no one near her until Khoti brought her an apple and warming blanket and led her to her own stall.

The threat in the air of the first autumn snowfall muted the creak of leather and clank of weaponry as the full Lharan Guard – grown to more than two thousand with the call to arms – waited in the square before Sefresal's gates. Khoti tried to remain unnoticed in the ranks to avoid Kefta's scrutiny. He'd only returned to duty a week ago, spending long days helping to train recruits and outfit and train his attendant, Tre. If Kefta knew Khoti's ribs and shoulder remained tender he'd order him to stay behind to defend the city. Eilime would come under attack any day and Khoti intended to ride to battle in Eithurdon's buff and pewter as one of the elite original Guardsmen. A few other mountain folk, men less accustomed to the sword but certainly ready for battle, sat their shaggy mountain ponies at the edge of the Guard ranks, armed with Shiadin swords, bows and axes. Behind them, gathered many of the new recruits on foot, armed with axe and spear. Somewhere in the rear near their supply wagons, lowland and mountain boys who attended the Guardsmen nervously held spare mounts packed with their Guardsmen's gear. Those not riding to battle hauled the last of the city's treasures and goods to the Val. When the Guard lost Eilime, as they knew they would, the enemy would have nothing to stop them from sweeping right on to Sefresal.

A hand brushed his leg and Khoti startled. He looked down to find Asteria looking up at him. The first shafts of morning sunlight glittered in her dark eyes, the cold glowing in her cheeks. Or maybe he saw something else. Khoti caught his breath and gave her an unabashed grin. He had to overcome his embarrassment around her as she tended his injuries. Even after he returned to duty, she often left him some gift: a sweet, a flagon of wine. This morning, he found outside his door a new buckskin shirt, made in the Tasch-el style with fine sinew laces and hunter's pockets, which he wore beneath his cloak.

At first, he thought Asteria's attentions came from pity, gratitude, even guilt. Why else would a duke's daughter risk showing attention to a miner's son? He decided to just enjoy her attention and not question it. Otherwise, he might read more into her gift of wine last eve. Impulsively, he invited her to join him in a cup, knowing they broke some rule among her people. Again, she had shattered all of his assumptions about her as she spoke wistfully of the Val and the wild vistas of the pass.

Now she caressed Fidra's neck as she looked up at him.

"I must thank you for the shirt," he said, touching her wrist as he spoke, and instantly yanking his hand back when he realized he'd again broken a social more among her people. Something had burned in that touch. Had she addled his senses with some herb in the wine? He continued to smile at her. "I'll wear it with pride." His face grew hot.

"I admit I had the help of your kinswoman, Latra. She is so wise."

"You're leaving for the Val soon," he said when the silence grew awkward, suddenly unable to find words. They freely poured out of him over the wine. He had even admitted his fear of dying far from mountain people who would know how to release him to the spirits, not left, like his brother, to be picked at for eternity by scavengers. Did the eve of battle have him speaking of fears he hadn't even shared with those closest to him? The heat deepened in his cheeks.

"I wanted to give you a gift." She held up a pendant that she drew from a pocket at her belt.

"You have given me so many gifts already, Lady Asteria!"

"This you must return. Let it give you strength and protect you in battle." She dropped it in his open hand, turned and fled.

A deep blue gem set in a plain stellan setting gleamed in his palm. The white light of morning fired the depths of the stone to reveal a white starburst within, not unlike the shawnsi birthmark. He quickly tucked it in his breast pocket, too late to escape Geleg's notice.

"You're a lucky one!" Geleg said with a lecherous grin.

Khoti met his grin with a nonchalance he didn't feel. "What on Ea are you blathering about, Geleg?"

"You'll see," Geleg said. "And a whole world will dawn for you." He guffawed as he moved out of reach of Khoti's balled fist, held up to accompany a grin.

Eithurdon made a motion and Kefta called the ranks to order as the last pack horses and evacuees, Asteria among them, followed the narrow path to the rampart and pass beyond.

With a horn blast that split the morning and reverberated against the mountain sides, the Lharan Guard trotted out of the gates of Sefresal.

Several days' journey east brought them to the low hills northwest of Eilime. The last of Eilime's wagons had passed, headed to Sefresal, long ago. A few farmers from the hills and valleys above town, too stubborn to leave, lounged beside the road that ran down the long treeless slope into town. They gripped pitchforks and shovels as they shouted their greetings, but Khoti could read their doubts about Guard success in their faces.

"As if they think fork and shovel will stop them if the Guard can't," Ytri said from his position alongside Khoti.

Khoti nodded, fearing what would become of such people when Eilime inevitably fell. Eithurdon had already mapped their retreat. No one expected victory against the more numerous, better-trained and better-equipped Minarians. Not here.

Khoti reached for the gemstone pendant in his breast pocket. Sleep came slow on this march, when instead of the dark side of his eyelids, he saw Asteria looking up at him.

"We'll be just fine if we can keep this love-sick cub's mind on his business," Toban teased.

Khoti reddened, unable to even entertain a private thought in the company of his volunteer body guards. Geleg, Ytri and Toban feared Khoti would find himself unequal to the dilemma of both healer and soldier. Even the duke expounded on protecting godly gifts, but also the futility of idling a good sword arm. Like his father, like Konner, they all seemed to think he couldn't think for himself. He vowed to prove them wrong.

Geleg rode in front, Ytri to one side, Toban behind and Kefta on the other side as part of the vanguard, where Eithurdon placed his greatest trust. Instead of relishing the honor, Khoti felt hemmed in by prying, lecherous minds. In a particularly sour train of thought he hoped they didn't want to keep him safe just so he could repair the damage. He knew that once he loosed the warrior within, they couldn't hold him back.

"Eh, look out for that one, he's primed for battle," Toban teased, gesturing at Khoti.

"At least he's on our side," Kefta said as Khoti glared at them.

When they reached the town, the Eilime Guard joined them in throwing up a hasty redoubt of wagons and barrels across the road as the morning broadened and scouts raced in with word of the enemy's progress. The Minarian army moved along a dike that held back the Dodfrenyen Sea in years of high water. It ended at the bridge over the Eilime River just east of where the village spread along the seashore and river outlet.

The army marched only eight abreast on the dike, but closed fast, Khoti shaking his head at lost opportunity. Tawnkats would have destroyed the bridge, or undermined the dike, even if just delaying the inevitable. He knew Eilime's mud-walled and thatch-roofed cottages on the edge of the sea would fall like pine before a fire, a mere point to mark the battle's progress. Without walls or high ground, Eilime served no strategic purpose. Instead, the Guard waited on higher ground on the village's southeastern edge, a place where none of Khoti's Tawnkat tricks would work. He scanned the men behind the redoubt, certain they'd come to a slaughter.

As if to confirm his fears, the Minarians quickly crossed the bridge and spread out on the low plain leading to town. If they couldn't assail them on the dike, at least they could have erected a redoubt at one end of the bridge and bottled them up, though they would have sacrificed holding the long slope down which the Guard cavalry could charge. And, to Khoti's annoyance, the Guard followed other rules. A flag of parlay unfurled and a small knot of Minarians rode forward.

Eithurdon, his face an unreadable mask, signed for Khoti to follow as he rode along the redoubt. Khoti ran to collect Fidra from Tre and jogged after the duke.

"I'm sorry to do this to you, Khoti," Eithurdon said when Kefta, the captain of the Eilime Guard, and the mayor of Eilime had joined them. "I expect you to speak in Tsevon's stead. You are the ranking Lharan tribesman among us."

"What's there to speak to?" Khoti asked. "They want to take over our country and we're not going to let 'em."

"Perhaps. The mountain tribes have retained some independence from the House of Lharan. I recognize your father and the Tawnkats as representing those tribes. Thus, you must answer their offer in Tsevon's absence."

Khoti grinned. "Let me at 'em."

An undignified snort of amusement escaped the duke before the serious expression returned. "I hope Kefta taught you some protocol. In the years since the tragedies of the Great War, civilized lands adopted rules to conflict. For one, you never attack someone holding a flag of parlay. We have to hear their piece. They have to hear ours. So, keep a check on yourself!" Eithurdon punctuated his last with a tight grin as his horse sidestepped beneath him.

With Eithurdon's herald bearing the flags of Shande and the duke's colors, they rode onto the field to meet the enemy. In addition to skin red and welted from insect bites, the Minarian army's leader wore a wrinkled scar across half his face, a souvenir from one of Konner's pottery jars. When Khoti quietly shared this news with Kefta and Eithurdon, Kefta laughed in derision. The duke maintained his stony façade.

Scar-Face barely looked at Eithurdon. He directed his words to the rest of the party. "We come to take Eilime," he stated.

"We come to defend Eilime," Eithurdon returned.

The Minarian pretended not to hear. "It can be a bloodless exchange of power, or we can raze the town. This is your decision. Our terms: shawnsi have wronged the God of Ea and oppressed the people of Shande and are to be turned over to us, immediately, and are sentenced to death. Visionaries and derna teach falsehoods and incite rebellion and are sentenced to death. Officers of the shawnsi cannot be trusted, as they are in thrall to these false leaders. They must be turned over for sentencing. Meet these terms and we will leave Eilime standing. You will hardly note the change in rule."

Khoti barely kept his mouth from falling open, finally understanding the instructions the duke had received from Sihmad Shal. Eithurdon fumed, as did Kefta beside him.

"And why should we believe nobles and officers of the government will sate you?" the Mayor of Eilime asked, his tone measured, though his features remained a scowl as he tensed forward. Though portly and old, he sat his horse an imposing figure.

"You must trust us." The Minarian smiled a broken-toothed grin. "You have no choice." He turned to Kefta. "You are of shal stock what have you to say?" he asked.

Kefta straightened, his red face darkening. "There's many of 'shal stock' as you put it. Shawnsi are 'shal stock.' Shande is shal stock. For whom do I speak?"

"Who do you represent?"

"The Lharan Guard finds your terms unacceptable."

The captain of Eilime's thousand-man volunteer guard nodded his concurrence, as did the mayor.

"And you?" He looked at Khoti with that mocking grin Khoti wanted to wipe from his face. "Certainly, a young man sees the wisdom of accepting change and cooperating for the greater good?"

The whole thing felt like some Long Day performace, Khoti just one small bit part in a play. So, he screwed up his features as if he considered the idea, savoring Scar-Face's anticipation of at least a partial victory. Kefta and Eithurdon stared at him, their posture stiff with their dedication to protocol when they should certainly see this exchange went well beyond any need for manners.

"I speak for Tawnkats," Khoti said at last, "Who are responsible for that lovely mark on your face." Khoti employed Konner's most disarming grin.

"What is a Tawnkat?" the burn scar flushed a bloody red.

"A cat that feeds on vengeance more than other game and finds Minarians to be a sweet meat. As we speak, Tawnkats are likely feeding on your king. Your terms are unacceptable. In fact, I look forward to your blood on my sword." Khoti smiled a tight, clench-toothed expression that made a few Minarians blanch.

Eithurdon and Kefta puffed out at his words. So maybe he wasn't a good spokesman and he had a bit too much of his fa in him. Khoti didn't care. He'd said his piece. He turned Fidra so his back faced the Minarians.

"Then you will burn," the Minarian hissed. "And I will have this young Tawnkat hide on my standard."

"You have not heard my response to your terms, or my offer," Eithurdon said.

"Your kind are not long of this world. I will hear nothing you have to say." The Minarian spat at the feet of Eithurdon's mount, turned and galloped back to his men.

"Thank you, Khoti," Eithurdon said as the Shandeans reached their own line, the duke leaning over Fidra's neck to regard Khoti with a calculating gaze. "You said what we all felt, but tradition runs too deep in our veins."

"It'll be his hide I'll have." Khoti said as he handed off Fidra to Tre and stalked to his spot by Geleg, Ytri and Toban. "Why didn't we smash them before he could open his mouth?"

Before anyone could respond, the Minarian drums rolled.

Flags and pennants unfurled and standards rose. Winding his horn, Eithurdon sent a clear note into the morning. Shandean banners stretched to the sky in the royal blue of the king's house, and the buff and pewter of the House of Lharan, Eithurdon's insignia flashing from crystals sewn upon the standards.

Khoti nodded over his shoulder at Tre, who hurried to serve him, still grinning with pride at Khoti's words to the Minarian captain. Unlike other attendants, Tre appeared undaunted by the array of enemy warriors. Khoti again broke with tradition, convincing a few others to follow suit, when he outfitted his attendant with sword, dagger and bow. If Khoti fell in battle, Tre could fill his gap in the line. Other attendants would have to ransack the bodies of the dead to defend themselves. Unlike the lowland boys who served most of the Guardsmen, the few mountain youths like Tre grew up with a bow in hand and a knife at their belt. And they knew how to use them.

Khoti scanned the field as the enemy archers moved forward. Shande had the better position. The Minarians had no time to fortify, and the ambush on the Staph-el road had diminished the cavalry that might have overrun their line.

On cue, enemy archers released a volley of arrows at the Shandean line, the first flight falling short until they adjusted for the slope. Shandean archers returned fire from behind the front lines, where marksmen like Khoti also returned fire, picking targets more carefully. With each volley, more Minarians appeared to fall than Shandeans, but the Shandeans had fewer to lose.

Khoti reached a hand back, knowing Tre would set the arrow in his palm precisely as he wished, so intent he barely noticed when he began shooting undamaged Minarian arrows Tre had scavenged.

When the duke's horn called the signal, Khoti motioned for Tre to take his place, as did his fellow scouts, as he hurried to collect Fidra. Moving up to the vacated positions the boys filled the gap in the line, but with no attendants to gather arrows for them.

Mounted, more than ninety strong, they formed up to charge the Minarian ranks. A few catapult-flung stones fell among them, but they knew it couldn't last long. They couldn't have hauled enough shot across the marshes, unless they planned to sling mud and the stick houses of water rats, or the bones of their dwindling supply stock.

"Out and back is all I ask," Kefta told them. "I can't afford to lose one of you. We're aiming for the headquarters, though we're not likely to make it that far. The goal is to create disarray." Kefta grinned at Khoti as they turned toward a small space in the redoubt the defenders cleared. "Khoti, here's your shot at getting Scar-Face's hide!"

Fidra surged ahead, reacting to Khoti's slightest pressure and mood shift. As they raced at the enemy line, Khoti reached for Asteria's pendant at his breast. The feel of the gem in his pocket gave him confidence. He felt stronger and sharper than ever.

As they neared the Minarian line, they drew their swords on cue. The Minarian cavalry raced from their camp to face them. As the two units met, Khoti's exuberance escaped in a Tawnkat screech that had accompanied many a successful assault on the Minarian army. It had the desired effect. The Minarian ranks wavered only a moment, but long enough to give the Guard an edge.

They struck the line, but his friends hemmed him in a protective circle that kept him from battle. With a growl of frustration and the slightest of cues to Fidra, Khoti sent her darting between them into the worst of the fray as if she raced around boulders in a mountain pass.

Khoti didn't look back, even though he heard, faintly, Kefta's call to form up on him. The pent-up beast within tried to escape with every breath. His sword arm twitched in anticipation as he raced ahead. He didn't have long to wait. A charger came at him, the Minarian on its back red with his fever for blood. Khoti faced him with his own brand of fervor. He let the tied reins fall, guiding Fidra with his knees. Wielding his sword two-handed, he drove his foe back until the soldier spilled from his mount. As the man struggled to his feet, he pulled up his sword too late. Khoti struck, driving the man's own weapon into his face.

Khoti had no opportunity to feel fear at the press of soldiers or the frightening power he felt running through him. Minarian horsemen surrounded him. He had become the point of a wedge, driving forward, directing Fidra on toward the Minarian headquarters marked by its picket of standards. Moved to follow him, driven into his wake, the Guard advanced with a vengeance to push the Minarians back.

Khoti's arms ached, his shoulder, his ribs, the old wound in his side that never ceased troubling him. But the thing impelling him seemed to burst, pouring strength into him like nothing he had ever known. It frightened him a little, a presence in him but not him. He couldn't think about it now, could only recognize it.

Something, perhaps the spirits, infused his limbs with strength and stamina and leant accuracy to his blows. It made him giddy, an emotional power greater than any he'd experienced on the Staph-el Road. Tawnkat cries tore through the battle as he hammered through the press, goading Fidra ever harder, drunk on this strange possession. He saw now that some of the enemy avoided him, bypassing him to strike those Guardsmen trailing behind him as Khoti pounded straight into the circle of men directing the battle.

Eyes flew wide when Khoti charged in, bearing down on Scar-Face with an awesome, alien, will behind him. Scar-Face lifted a sword to block Khoti's assault but seemed to freeze when Khoti's gaze fell on him. As Khoti tore by, the man's body lay in the dust, head nearly severed from the neck.

Finally, realizing he battled alone in a hostile camp, a brief instant of fear struck him like the wings of scavengers beating his face. Several men came at him armed with axe and spear aiming to attack Fidra and force Khoti to the ground. She sprang by them, as if she heard Khoti's thoughts before his knees could cue her. She winged back to the wedge Khoti had beaten into the lines.

Once again amid the fighting, Khoti swiftly forgot his moment of vulnerability as the emotion overtook him again, stronger, more potent. Like a whirlpool, Khoti sucked them in. One after the other Minarian warriors came at him. His friends again fought beside him, strengthened by Khoti's fury.

Dimly, Khoti heard a horn blast calling for them to return and regroup. He didn't want to answer the command. But Fidra responded to his cue, instinctively given.

When Fidra again pranced among the weary and in some cases bleeding beasts beyond the redoubt, as unscathed as Khoti and seemingly unphased by her labors, Khoti finally let out his breath like the first taken in hours. His ribs protested as his lungs sought air.

"What on Ea have we unleashed?" Kefta asked at his shoulder. Khoti peered at his captain. It still burned in him. Everything quivered before his vision, vibrant, brilliant. Kefta took a step back, sweat soaked and splashed with blood, as Khoti discovered himself to be.

"Why were we called back?" Khoti demanded. "We could've blown right through –"

"Right through to Mershy with you leading the way," Geleg returned from behind. "Maybe you can topple an army, Khoti, but the rest of us were feeling a bit pressed."

Khoti finally looked around him. Of more than ninety men, eighty-five had returned, most bloody and exhausted. He had led a wedge, they feeling his call to follow, but whatever protected him, served him alone.

Eithurdon pushed into the circle of Guardsmen tethering their mounts and glared at Khoti. "Are you injured?" he demanded, waiting for Khoti's shake of the head. "Fool!" he yelled, his fists gathering at his sides, the sinew of his arms rising through the skin in angry ridges. "What good are you dead? This is not a one-man exhibition! You abandoned your position and risked others' lives. Perhaps I erred thinking you were mature enough for my Guard." Eithurdon whirled and strode back into the mayhem, barking orders.

The fire in him quenched, Khoti's mouth hung open, staring after the duke like a fledgling thrown from the nest.

"Close your mouth and back to business," Ytri said. "There's a wave rolling in and they're here to get their evens for Scar Face." Ytri gave him a push back toward where Tre flung arrows as fast as he could find them.

Khoti couldn't shake Eithurdon's rebuke. It festered in him. After the battle would the duke ship him home like so much baggage up the pass? Had everything he'd done, risked, meant nothing? Scowling his bitterness, he let Tre hold his position, gathering arrows for the youth as if he were the attendant. Each breath burned like shame in his throat. As Khoti bent to grab an arrow from the turf, a boot pressed it into the dirt and a rough hand on his arm forced him to turn.

"What are you doing?" Kefta demanded, crouching to avoid becoming a target. Khoti held up the arrow. "Is this some game?"

"Tre's as good a shot as me. Let him have his moment –"

"It's demeaning to act this way, Khoti, demoralizing –"

"Nor for Tre. Is it better to be reprimanded in front of your fellows for following orders? 'Go for the headquarters,' you said. I killed the demon!" He tried to push by Kefta.

"I don't have time for childishness." Kefta stepped back from Khoti's glare. Even Khoti sensed something dangerous about his mood. "You're reckless –"

"Are you certain you're not just worried you'll lose your healer –"

"Next time I call an order in the field you follow it or don't take the field. I'm the Captain of the Guard, not you." Kefta turned and strode away, already calling for reinforcements to fill a gap in the defense.

Khoti retrieved another arrow then returned to Tre, letting the youth shoot half of what he'd gathered before taking his place. As he picked his targets mechanically, he tried to settle a battle between his passion and reason. Was that alien fervor he'd felt on the field a reckless danger to his Guard family? He had to admit it even frightened him.

While the enemy had stumbled in the aftermath of Khoti's assault, they regrouped and returned to the fray with a vengeance, their sheer numbers overwhelming. Khoti barely noticed the advance. Despite wrist and finger guards, his hands had gone numb. After each release of the string, he put out a hand; he'd feel an arrow pressed against his palm and he'd shoot again, mechanical, acting on instinct, seldom sure if he'd found a mark before he nocked his next arrow. An arrow dropped into his hand backward. He discovered the duke arranging the arrows while Tre scrambled among bodies and archers in search of more.

Khoti picked his target and released. Was he supposed to apologize for a possession he couldn't control?

"If you've become my attendant, Lord, please pass me the arrows as I like. Feathers to the right."

Eithurdon's eyebrow cocked above stony features as he shifted the arrow direction.

"I cannot afford a breakdown in command," the duke stated. He quickly barked an order at an aide as he noted something he didn't like in the line. "Your actions were just that. You broke ranks. You may have achieved your goal, through luck, taking one enemy captain among many is not worth risking my best Guardsmen. Neither can I afford to lose you –"

"Because if you're injured –"

"Because of your potential to be my best," the duke returned. "You defied orders to hold on your captain. Be man enough to admit it."

Khoti grimaced as Eithurdon passed the arrows back to Tre. Khoti loosed another arrow. A man fell in the van of the approaching army. By the time Khoti turned, the duke was already deep in conference with an Eilime Guard captain a few paces down the line, oblivious to just another soldier's fears.

Khoti had no time to weigh the duke's words against Konner's negative assessment of lowlanders and royals. He shot his last arrow. He looked around in search of Tre. That moment, a shout rose as the Minarian army surged ahead, overwhelming the redoubt in many places. As Guardsmen beside him fell back, Khoti stumbled in the press of bodies. Unable to use his bow, he drew his blood-stained sword.

Then he caught a glimpse of Tre, the youth's features determined, dodging the enemy press as he struggled to reach Khoti. Suddenly Tre stumbled. Eyes wide, Tre's gaze met Khoti's as the youth grasped a spear in his side.

Khoti cried out inside. He tried to check sudden rage, afraid of it, knowing the harm it brought him. He couldn't act with abandon, must think –

But not Tre. Not this friend he'd urged to serve him, his only true confidante since Von.

Khoti struck with mighty blows, alien strength, barely registering the fear in his enemy's eyes as they avoided him. A demon inside pushed his limbs beyond their limits, blinded him.

A temporary lull fell over the battlefield as the Minarians regrouped for another charge. Rushing to Tre, Khoti searched for a lifebeat. The youth still breathed; his teeth clenched in pain. Khoti could help yet, but he needed time, a fire and the sticks in his pack.

The Minarians poured at the Shandean line again.

"Time, a fire," he breathed, a cadence to keep his limbs moving.

And if he helped Tre, how could he not help every other injured warrior? He stood guard over Tre. His sword rose and fell against the enemy rushing the redoubt. Did he let a member of his dwindling tribe die because if he helped one, he could kill himself? His arms had gone numb as the press of the enemy flowed at him like a river.

The call for retreat sounded over the din.

"Khoti! Fall back!" Geleg shouted, close at hand, yanking him by the arm so that Khoti fell sprawling over the bodies of those he had defeated. He scrambled back, reaching for Tre. He couldn't leave him on the battlefield. Could he minister him in secret? He hefted Tre in his arms, stumbling as he tried to carry the attendant who had grown in stature under Khoti's tutelage. Geleg muscled Khoti aside with a snarl and hefted Tre over his shoulder.

"You watch my back," Geleg said. "That's all you're good for right now." He sped his pace to match the retreat, Khoti racing after him.

As they retreated, Khoti stopped now and then to fling an arrow, or bring his sword down, but constantly moved uphill and north. A Minarian dived for Geleg. Khoti sprang, his sword meeting the Minarian's. Forced to his knees by Khoti's blow, the man swiped at Khoti's legs. Khoti tried to jump free, but stumbled and fell. Geleg stopped, ready to set Tre aside and come to Khoti's aid.

"Get out of here, Geleg!" Khoti shouted as he rolled away from his attacker. The strange fervor had faded. Geleg hesitated then ran on, cursing as he went.

Khoti froze, ready to pounce. He'd twisted his ankle and a cut burned on his leg where the tip of the Minarian's sword made contact. Though mild injuries, his edge had dulled. No one could help him. The familiar fear lurked on the edge of his concentration. The Minarian leaped for him, as if not trusting Khoti's apparent helplessness and hoping to take his advantage through surprise. As the Minarian reached the apex of his leap, Khoti rolled, driving his sword deep into the Minarian's chest. He yanked away. The sharp edge of the Minarian's sword glanced off Khoti as the man fell, leaving a cut from Khoti's ear to his collarbone. Though minor, it bled freely, and stung. Limping away, cursing, Khoti tried to catch up to the retreat. All around him, Minarian troops overwhelmed the line. They didn't need to hurry. All knew, in time they would force the Shandeans to give way.

Khoti caught up to Geleg as he reached the horses, which had been driven back behind a second redoubt long before the retreat. Khoti fell against the Guardsman, reaching for Tre.

"He'll live without you," Geleg growled, shoving Khoti away as a medical team eased Tre into a wagon. "We both know you can't heal an army. So, if you help Tre, who will live without your help, how can you let some brother Guardsman or other mountain attendant die?" Geleg's scar-puckered face frowned, sympathetic. "Konner's right. We did use you, not on purpose, but because you couldn't refuse a friend. Tre didn't ask for your help."

The wagon lurched away.

Geleg pushed Khoti's head to the side to view the long cut. "Gotta see how many scars you can wear before you're even a man?"

"A scratch I barely feel. I twisted my ankle. Now that hurts. Who're you to say who's a man?"

"The ladies'll know." Geleg let out a sour chuckle as Khoti took a swing at him, which Geleg easily ducked. "I know you don't want to hit me. I don't think you could miss unless you tried."

Khoti felt a helpless loss as the wain hauling the worst of the wounded the three-day journey to Sefresal disappeared among the disarray of the supply line. Gone, like Von. With a last silent plea to the spirits to give strength to Tre, Khoti limped in search of Fidra, both angry, and relieved, that Geleg kept him from his friend.

Eithurdon's horn sounded again. Khoti mounted Fidra at the order, relieved to be off his ankle. He turned to find the duke, flanked by Kefta, staring at him. Eithurdon merely nodded as they formed up. Kefta didn't look at him. Khoti didn't know what to think. He felt the shame of his own recklessness hot on his face. He knew they were right.

The Shandean horses plowed over churned ground dotted with the wreckage of the fallen. The Minarian lines wavered again as Khoti, Geleg beside him, took the forefront of the assault. This time, Eithurdon rode onto the field under his banner, some thousand of the Guard beside him.

Back and forth the lines shifted as the day grew old, both sides taking heavy losses. Konner's nephew Chati, a shepherd friend of Tre's, had lost his Guardsman to a wound and now attended Khoti. But Chati could do little as the Guardsmen charged. The mountain youth knew bow and knife, but had no other training. He waited on the edge of battle, chewing his lip as he watched Khoti. Khoti had lost his grip on his sword, hands bloody with open blisters, his arms numb and heavy. The Minarian he faced suddenly knocked the sword from Khoti's grasp to fall among the churning hooves.

Khoti sucked in a breath, with nothing but a dagger in the midst of the fray. He struggled to maneuver Fidra beyond his foe's reach. Then he caught a glimpse of Chati, who rode straight for the battle on Khoti's spare horse, holding out a sheathed sword. Khoti kicked his opponent's horse in the face. The beast reared back, fouling his opponent's swing as Chati tossed the weapon over the back of another Minarian's mount. The youth raced back to the Shandean line, chased by spears, as in one motion Khoti unsheathed the sword and stabbed his opponent with Fidra's momentum behind him. The finely honed edge pierced the man's mail shirt and drove into his chest.

As darkness fell, marking the change from summer to autumn, the last skirmishes ended with the light, the lines retreating for a few hours' sleep and a meal within sight of mortal enemies. It galled many that the Minarian army camped just over there, on Shandean soil watered by Shandean blood.

Chati had squeezed Khoti's tiny tent in beside Eithurdon's.

Khoti hadn't seen the duke since afternoon, but expected the duke would call a meeting to discuss strategy and Khoti planned to nab Kefta and pump him for all he could, or at least stretch his ears to listen through the tent walls.

But as the dark night brought the cold of the first hard freeze, no meeting occurred, though a firepot glowed within Eithurdon's tent.

Khoti cleansed his wounds and salved his blisters, wanting only his bedroll for a few hours. Instead, Chati hovered over him. The youth repacked Khoti's gear, repeatedly checked to ensure Khoti's bedroll didn't touch the tent sides where it might collect dew, examined their food stores, cleaned their weaponry, throughout crawling back and forth over and around Khoti.

At last, Khoti growled and set down the tin of salve. "Out with it, Chati."

"Kefta ordered me, mind you, ordered me not to tell you." Chati set aside the buff and pewter cloak he mended.

Only a year younger than Khoti, Chati didn't fawn over the Guardsman he served like so many other attendants. Instead, he had that typical Taschian boldness and Khoti even recognized a little of Chati's uncle Konner in the youth's smile. Like Tre, who might be quiet and awed by Khoti at times, Chati clearly had his own mind.

"Tre?" Khoti asked, his heart sinking at the thought.

Chati shook his head. "He'll mend. Unlike others."

Khoti's gaze narrowed on the youth. He turned to stare at the blank tent wall where the glow of the firepot in Eithurdon's tent sent flickering shadows into the night.

"The duke's been injured," Khoti said softly. "And it's a fatal wound. And Kefta set guards to keep me out." Chati was nodding. "And you, you little schemer, have an idea."

"A minor diversion."

"That's why you pitched my tent here, crammed in like mice in a kitty." Khoti shook his head. "Can I justify offering medicine to the duke and no one else?"

"The seriously injured were moved back to Sefresal. The duke won't leave his troops," Chati countered in a whisper.

Sefresal would be lost without Eithurdon's heart to hold them. Steadon, who remained in Sefresal and had never even ridden with the Guard, would be no substitute. Would the duke refuse Khoti's medicine? Certainly, someone would hear Khoti's sticks, if they hadn't already been stolen from his gear. They needed this duke to whom he'd pledged his life when he donned the buff and pewter.

As if reading Khoti's thoughts, Chati grinned and produced Khoti's tera sticks from beneath his pallet with a flourish. "Just trust me," he said before slipping out.

Khoti listened by the tent flap. Soon he heard a loud ruckus near the middle of the camp. The guards in front of Eithurdon's tent hesitated, wondering aloud if Minarians had devised some devilry. After a few words of argument, the two men drew their swords and ran for what sounded like battle. Khoti rushed from his tent and ducked into Eithurdon's.

A sword had ripped through the duke's middle. When Khoti pulled aside the drenched bandages, the pink of the duke's insides peeked out through the terrible rip in the flesh. Could he even mend such damage? Guards would return any moment. The duke needed to live or they'd all be lost. He had no time to waste. Swiftly, he called on the spirits, sticks singing over the small fire.

Concentrating harder than ever before, Khoti took little notice of how the duke's eyes flickered open with alarm, then how the duke's mouth set with resignation for whatever justification he found for hoarding Khoti's skills to himself. Soon, the hot knife pressed against Eithurdon's wound, sealing Khoti's blood inside. Eithurdon appeared to not even feel the knife sear his skin. The duke's pain, passing through Khoti, lasted only for a breath that made Khoti's heart flutter, before it fled.

Khoti gazed at the duke as he tapped his tribute and weariness stole into his limbs. Eithurdon's survival screamed Khoti's name. Kefta would kill him for again defying orders.

Eithurdon watched as Khoti wearily rose to leave. "You're no good to us dead, Lord, and I wouldn't want to answer to your daughter." Khoti said. He slipped back to his own tent where he fell to his pallet, asleep almost before he touched it.

Exhausted, Kefta tried to stop the brawl. What on Ea could have set off the camp's attendants? Certainly they, too, must be weary. As Ytri joined him, his suspicions grew to certainty. The fight remained remarkably injury free. Kefta glanced at Ytri, one eyebrow hooked in a question mark.

"Isn't that Khoti's boy? In the middle, egging the whole thing on?" Ytri's words sent Kefta's mouth gaping.

"I'll kill that little brat Chati," he said as he and Ytri dashed for Eithurdon's unguarded tent.

"I could not stop him," Eithurdon said, struggling to one elbow, pale from the great loss of blood.

"I thought Geleg was supposed to pilfer those sticks," Kefta growled. "I ordered Chati to keep his mouth shut. We're already short of warriors! He defied your orders, again!"

Ytri knelt beside Eithurdon. "But you'll live now, Duke," Ytri said. "I know what the rules say, and he deserves it, but you can't kick Khoti out of the Guard. We need him."

"How could I?" Eithurdon asked with a weary sigh. "He is stronger than me. I – I have never known anything like this." He sank back and closed his eyes. "He cannot refuse his friends. A virtue. And he is correct: I am of no use dead." Eithurdon waved them away as his guards sheepishly returned to their posts.

Kefta led the way to Khoti's tiny tent, prepared to give him a lecture like none he'd ever heard. But when he yanked open the tent flap, he found Khoti asleep, the healer's features smoothed and unthreatening. Clearly the brawl had ended suddenly. Chati had already applied a bandage to Khoti's hand, which seeped through the cloth, as did his battle wounds. The unlaced and open neck of the Taschian's tunic revealed a swollen and greenish-purple circle over his ribs, remaining from his battle in the marshes.

"I didn't tell him, he guessed," Chati blurted, chin jutting out. "We'll all be lost if the duke dies."

Ytri nodded with a wry twist to his mouth as Chati's shoulders sagged and he took a deep breath of his guilt.

Kefta crawled into the tiny tent to examine the bruise on Khoti's chest, the bandaged hand. Kefta pressed on the bruise. Khoti's eyes flew open, then instantly narrowed into cat slits on recognizing his captain.

"Ytri," Kefta turned from Khoti's unsettling stare. "Look at this." Ytri pushed further into the tent as Kefta pointed at the bruise. Khoti rolled to lean on his elbow. "Do you recall me ordering this man to remain behind if not fully mended?"

Khoti shook his head. "You can't force me to go back. I'm not injured."

"You're wrong there. I can and I will." Kefta's tone was softer than his words. "I can't trust you to obey orders and we need warriors, not healers. Besides, how'll you grip a sword with that hand? You're worthless."

Chati was shaking his head, eyes wide. "You can't send him back among all those wounded!"

"The boy is right." They all turned toward Eithurdon's voice.

He crouched to peer in, unsteady as he held back the tent flap. "Any way you look at it, Khoti, unless you learn from your father, you will pass like the old healers Konner spoke of, waste the gifts the gods intended for some purpose larger than you. Konner claims you cannot refuse the plea of a friend. In war friends die. Can you look upon a friend, a brother in arms, and withhold your medicine?"

Khoti sat up, scooting back from Kefta. He hugged his knees to his chest. "I don't know," he admitted. "Why did the spirits give me this curse? Fa brought me home from my death walk. It's such a lonely place, to think of people I care about wandering there –" He shook his head. "Do you know what a burden this is?"

Eithurdon nodded. "In fact, I do. Decisions leaders make have consequences, like your choice at the Staph-el Mine. Men died on my orders today! Those are the consequences. We could have stayed in Sefresal and awaited them. But either way, we will die. I will die, Ytri, Geleg, Toban, even my Asteria, and you. You heal people but they will still die. Even the gods cannot make us immortal. You claim you fear some lonely death. Yet you court it! Perhaps it is something else you fear. You need to shelter this gift and use it only when its importance is clear, as in the case of a leader responsible for the success of an army. Can you accept that friends must die in war and there are times when you could save them, but should not?"

Khoti was silent a long moment, then gave the duke a slight nod, his emerald eyes glazing with his fatigue.

"Then you will ride beside me in battle come dawn. You gave that to me. We will share it." Eithurdon dropped the flap, leaving behind a heavy silence no one broke.

The next day's battle began uneven and they knew the day would be lost. Each charge pushed the Shandeans further back. Khoti remained beside Eithurdon, bound by a promise to protect the duke and rein in the reckless warrior and his desire to rush to friends when they fell. Besides, healing wore heavier on a healer fighting battle wounds and fatigue, much less the cut in his palm, which bled and made his blows fall too lightly. As well, he feared for his duke who remained unsteady in his saddle.

But not even Khoti's zeal could save the day. Though the Shandeans fought for their lives, they faced Minarians better equipped, better trained and still more numerous. By mid-day the Shandeans had been pushed north. Eilime, down a long slope, became the point of every charge. They needed three thousand Khotis and Keftas, Gelegs, Tobans and Ytris. Instead, artisans, merchants and farmers outnumbered the original Guard. Though they had been training since the call to arms, they weren't soldiers at heart.

By afternoon, Minarian flags rose over Eilime. As the Guard retreated to Sefresal, all knew that only a few days and a well-worn road separated Sefresal from an enemy that would certainly overrun it.

38: Night Meeting

When the Drulsons reached the top of the long slope they had climbed through the night, they found a high plateau edged by mountains resolving into dawn. The sight of mountains still gave him a moment's wonderment, though they first defined themselves from the blue haze of horizon some days back. Behind, the river ran east down a long fall of cascades, shallow and rapid now, icy. Here, Nali discovered the taste of a fish more delicate and wilier than he'd known. He had a distant memory of his arrogant claim that catching such fish would be easy.

From this vantage, Nali fancied he might see the walls of Sihmad Shal and its flapping blue flags, or at least the high cliffs of the Harbor peeking from the eastern haze. Or perhaps he should spy the dark Eidhalt he knew hunted them through the deep prairie, his foe speeding along the river banks like hounds on a scent, eyeing a footprint here, a scrap of thread there.

He knew Olna and their unborn child would never have survived the journey if he hadn't swallowed his moral misgivings and stolen two horses from an isolated Kishman farm. He'd studied the farm for hours, trying to rationalize the harm to a fellow Shandean. Someday, he vowed, he would make it up to them. Or, perhaps the service he gave the king absolved him of this one transgression?

The Drulsons had traveled for what seemed forever, though little more than a month. The prairie and river remained so unchanging that no matter how many hours they rode, it always seemed as if they stood still, as if around the next bend they would again spy the red and orange tassels streaming from a dark helm.

On the plateau, the grasslands gave way to weathered scrub, dry and browning with the first frost of autumn about to begin.

Ahead, the land rolled into a smoky haze before the mountains where Nali thought he distinguished the green line of the marshes around the Dodfrenyen Sea. They aimed for that vast inland sea where Eilime sat on its eastern shore, figuring Nali could at least ply his fishing skills to fit in. Peshal's maps claimed that up a small river to the northwest Sefresal nestled in the lap of the Lharan foothills. If the green line marked those marshes, they were closer than he'd hoped. He tried to recall the maps, certain the Quelica River they traveled beside must lie much farther north of the Eilime River tributaries. At last, with regret, they left the river that had fed them for so long.

He marveled at the family he'd shooed into the unknown the eve of Sihmad Shal's fall. Face weathered and peeling from sunburns, Olna appeared older, her girth seeming much larger than it should for the length of her term. He knew it was only an illusion as the rest of her body lost its healthy fleshiness and hardened in their travel. Nali's children, too, stood straighter and leaner, muscles more sinewy than a child's should be. He swallowed a sense of guilt each time he looked on them, though they'd have fared no better if he stayed in the east. The near brushes with the Eidhalt assured him his arrest would have come swiftly. While young Rena flourished, recalling no other life, for Kia and Bertal, what began as an adventure had them surly and whining for home. They might see their parents' terror when Eidhalt searched the damp banks of the Quelica only paces from where they hid, but the children couldn't understand why they all couldn't simply go back home where they felt safe.

The sun burned away the crisp morning air. Harfestide stretched before him. It was a time to celebrate summer's bounty, visit friends and family in the country, bring home ripe fruit from the market or find wild fowl swinging beside sausages in butcher stalls. Bakeries spilled the aroma of fruit pies and golden harvest breads stacked in baskets reaching for ceilings, and fresh melons, gourds or fatted grains smeared children's faces. He missed the festfires that followed a day of haying with Cousin Tel, the dusty fresh smell seeming to ride the wind from afar. Around the fire, storytellers bewitched the children huddled against parents as they spoke of distant places where animals were dangerous and forests treacherous.

A vision of his father weaving the tale of a mariner stranded on a wild shore came to mind. He could see the merry glow of the man's eyes as he whispered above the crackle of dry cedar, telling tales of night creatures with glowing eyes to the gasps of rapt children. Late, after the children slept, adults would pass the cider and sing songs of harvest, or even later dance with the spirit of the cool night.

Perhaps his children's longing flowed from him to them.

One afternoon, twelve days southwest from the banks of the Quelica River, they discovered the glitter of the Dodfrenyen Sea and the green marshes of its shifting shores before them. The sun sank behind snow-capped mountains. The last day of the waning moon, the moon of the autumn Evenday, closed as they completed their trek across the seemingly endless, waterless flats. If they didn't find Eilime soon they would never make it, their waterskins almost empty now.

Nali squinted in search of Eilime on the shores. He turned to Olna in despair. "Smoke, Eilime's burning. Where now?"

As the children groaned their dismay, Olna's jaw set in that stubborn way she had. "We can't get much farther before winter. I hear it comes early in these parts. And I'll be wantin' a midwife before the long night comes."

"So, we came all this way to exchange one occupied city for another? We'll be worse off, knowin' no one and having nothin'."

"We're better off, Nali Drulson. That's an unpopular name in the east. There, even if you changed names your face is known. Here, your face isn't known so change your name. Maybe they'll take us to heart, thinkin' we fled before the war."

"So, what should I call myself?" he asked with a resigned smile. "Nali Fisher? Likely an odd name here. And any mention of derna would be fatal."

"Take my name. It's and honorable one."

"What, call myself Olna?"

"Rebertal, silly. Or, well Bertal's daughter is just as bad, I suppose. Why not Bertalson. Nali Bertalson doesn't sound that terrible."

"Does that mean I have to be Bertal Bertalson?" Bertal groaned. "People'll tease me for repeating myself."

Nali ruffled Bertal's hair grown so shaggy on their trek. "Well, if that's the worst you ever have to face, I'd say you're pretty lucky! But you're still my son, so why wouldn't you be Nalison?" Nali studied the deepening shadows over the plain below. "Well Olna, should we just ride up to the gates? Or find a farm somewhere and see what we can learn?"

"I vote for the farm," she stated. "In a city, folk will notice if we're too ignorant, or break some rule."

"Can we trust the farmer?"

Olna sighed. "You're the derna. You think it out. It's just, if we've got to trust someone, I'd say the farmer is the better choice. In a city your rumor goes before you. In the country sometimes you can get there first."

It was several hours after sunset before they spied the silhouette of a barn. An eerie silence closed around them as they walked the horses up a tree-lined lane. The sour smell of Eilime smoldering settled into the valley they had entered. Nali took Kia with him to investigate, hoping if he greeted someone with a little girl in tow he might appear less threatening.

Only the rustle of livestock in the barn disturbed the quiet farm. It gave him a nervous sense of guilt. He figured "horse thief" would be written all over his face when the farmer answered the door. He had just entered the shadow thrown by a large pine beside a lighted window, almost to where he could peek in, when he heard a twig snap behind him. He froze. Kia's hand gripped his. The familiar soft sound of a sword drawn from a leather scabbard sounded loud in the dark. Nali shoved Kia to the ground and whipped around, drawing the short sword he'd carried concealed beneath his cloak since riding with Esthen.

A darker silhouette stood against the night shadows of the valley walls. Only the man's sword showed, reflecting the subtle light from the farmhouse window. A small whimpered 'fa-fa' escaped Kia as she crouched in the darkness. Nali's instinct to defend his child rushed his veins. Was it a farmer protecting his home? A Minarian? Or a Shandean allied with them?

"What do you want here?" The voice trembled.

Was it fear? Anger? Nali heard the lilting dialect of the far west of Shande.

"I seek only a place to sleep, the barn perhaps. My lifemate's with child and I've young ones. The night looks cold." Nali answered as evenly as he could.

The man's stance softened, but the blade remained poised. "Your words are eastern. What purpose have you? Who are you?"

Nali lowered his sword to his side, though he didn't sheath it. The other weapon dipped. "We're fleeing trouble," Nali said.

"There's trouble here, too, son. That isn't a good excuse."

"Bad? Has Eilime fallen? We saw the smoke, but hoped –"

"Everything's gone, son. Nothing'll hold 'em. I hear they sent a host to Sefresal, be there in a few days. I don't know how the rest of the land fares. Maybe we're the first. What kind of trouble you fleeing? I won't hold with ruffians. I've heard about them wild mariners back east." The last allowed a return of the wariness in his tone.

Nali smiled. "And we've heard of the lawless mountain men. As for the rest of Ea, I don't know. All I can tell you is Sihma Harbor fell the twenty-eighth day of the heat moon, and Sihmad Shal fell the thirteenth day of the ripening moon. It's the day we left. I don't know what's become of that city." Sorrow and weariness weighted his words.

Nali let his breath out as the man sheathed his blade. The derna tucked his cloak about his own sword again.

"Come here, child. Let me see what y'are." The man gestured to Kia with a kindly voice.

Nali nodded at the shadows. Kia rushed to hide behind Nali, looking on the farmer's silhouette with frightened eyes.

"Why, you're just a little sprite, and hungry, I'll bet. I might find an egg for you if you tell me your name." Kia shook her head. "I've a daughter with a one your age, and he'd never turn down an egg the way my lifemate makes them, fried up in a little saltmeat with a bit of biscuit."

Kia hestated, looking up at Nali, who shook his head. "There's three others in my family. I'll not make you hungry. We've dried fish, though we'd welcome water."

"I can spare the water, and maybe I can squeeze my chickens for a few more eggs. This little one looks famished." He smiled down at Kia. "Why don't you fetch your family in, son."

Nali chuckled as he walked up the lane. Kia trotted beside him, capering as she imagined the feast they were about to taste. He'd make their home here, he decided, a short ride from Sefresal where he hoped Arshal and his exiles had already found shelter. After all, a few Eidhalt couldn't slow so many. Yet, the king and princes sought a place an entire army marched upon. Had they just given up one occupation for another? Would Arshal turn aside for Saran or Shela? The allure of eggs and shelter after so many weeks without made even that uncertainty hard to ponder. Though fleeting, he couldn't wipe from his mind a sense of urgency in the air, a crackling thing as if a search was on for him, pursuit closing, and the hopes of all Ea were hanging from a frayed rope.

39: The Fall of Sefresal

Khoti again sat at the polished table in the duke's hall, Kefta across from him, Steadon at Eithurdon's side, and Konner in the place once occupied by Tre.

"We must coordinate our defenses," Eithurdon began.

Konner sat back and folded his arms across his chest, as if to appear comfortable with meetings at polished tables. At least the duke granted the Tawnkats a voice.

Khoti shifted in the hard chair, noting how Konner watched him from the corner of his eye. By now, the Second had heard tales of Khoti's actions through Tre, and later Chati, both youths lauding the exploits of a Taschian to the eager ears of the Val. Neither would Chati have kept to himself his doubts about the duke's motives in selecting Khoti as his personal aide and lieutenant. Was Khoti's prowess in battle the sole motivation for the duke's interest? Was it his leadership? Khoti hadn't proved himself particularly adept at following orders without question. Or did Eithurdon instead seek to keep close to him a personal healer?

"I am strengthening both walls and the rampart. We will keep both manned, but yield the city before the rampart," the duke said, jerking Khoti's attention from Konner. "We can also deploy cavalry. The enemy will still be short there, and we have done a great deal of damage that way in the past."

"And who will you send against them, Lord?" Khoti asked.

"The original Guard is still our best as a tactical unit, Khoti," Eithurdon said. "And I will lead you myself."

"No," Khoti leaned back in his chair as the lowlanders straightened in theirs. "With all due respect, Lord, you have to go up the pass along with the original Guard."

"Boy, I think your fever's back," Kefta said. "Get a little glory and your head's gone and outgrown you."

Khoti ignored him. "You heard them, Duke. Their fight's with the shawnsi and royal officers. Remaining in Sefresal, that's you, Lord Steadon, and the Guard."

"I understand your point, but who would defend the city?" Eithurdon said.

"The city won't be undefended. I'm talking about the original Guard who would be considered under the influence of the shawnsi. Our future in Minarian eyes is nil. Those who responded to a call to arms they'll treat differently."

"The records are all gone, Khoti. If they occupy us, they will never know," Steadon said.

"If pressed, if tortured, if a man's family's at stake, he might remember Kefta Salman as Captain of the Guard, or Ytri or Geleg and –"

"Treason? Never," Eithurdon snapped.

"Not treason. Everyone has a breaking point." Khoti remained steady and patient. Tsevon would be fuming by now. Khoti glanced at Konner. "With Ahrwesz, it's snakes." Khoti waited for Konner's agreement. "Me, I've a distaste for scavengers," Khoti admitted with a slight shiver, ignoring Konner's sharp glance. "With some men it's any threat to family. There's always a point when a thing's too much to bear. We've all got our worst nightmares."

"To cower in the Val? The Guard would never stand for it. I would never stand for it," Eithurdon protested in a tone that almost closed the subject.

"Lord, listen to him. We all know the Val's plenty full, but he's making sense," Konner pleaded.

"But to cower –"

"I didn't say cower, Duke," Khoti returned. "Defend the pass! Not at the rampart, but the deeper reaches. We don't have enough Tawnkats to keep it open. Not to mention what it'll take to guard the Val if we aren't revealed by some poor captive trying to save himself. When they take the city and find nothin' but soldiers, they'll look to the mountains. We'll need scouts, spies, if you will." Khoti took a deep breath, realizing the liberty a miner's second son took speaking to his duke this way, and the indulgence he'd been granted.

"It would leave Sefresal vulnerable," Steadon protested.

"So, we lose Sefresal. We know it'll happen anyway and a few dozen men can't stop it," Khoti said. "There's more at stake than Sefresal. My people lost their homes, their livelihoods, but our bonds are with our people. I know your people see importance in different things, but don't put the value on a pile of rock. In the end, it's the people who count. It's the people they'll kill. The land'll be there to retake, but not without people and the kinds of skills the original Guard can teach."

Konner appeared about to crow with pride. But Steadon remained unmoved, his jaw working as if he chewed sticky candy.

Eithurdon studied Khoti a minute, then nodded and averted his gaze. "I have looked at it that way, as if holding this pile of rock is all it was about. Perhaps I erred. Who better than the Guard to hold the pass?" Eithurdon studied Khoti from the corner of his eye, a measuring gaze, covert, one Khoti realized he wasn't supposed to notice. Did the duke regret his appointment?

"I will stay in Sefresal," Steadon said. "The principle: I will not retreat. If Sefresal falls, I fall."

Eithurdon turned a glare on his brother. "I will follow Khoti's advice. These mountain folk keep astounding me: their resilience, their medicine, their fighting skills, and clearly a measure of wisdom. This counsel is sound. My responsibilities to my people are too important for me to waste my life, Steadon. You are free to waste yours as you wish."

Steadon held the duke's gaze, unmoved.

Eithurdon looked to Kefta. "Would the Guard honor my decision?"

"The Guard always honors your decisions, Duke!"

"But freely?"

Kefta glanced at Khoti before nodding. "There's enough of us who understand this reasoning. I won't force them to go."

Eithurdon gave Khoti such a warm smile Khoti had to force himself to not yield to a foolish grin. He might be Eithurdon's aide for now, but he could easily be replaced. Von always teased that Khoti had none of their fa's aptitude for leadership. Perhaps his fa passed on just a little. He'd become a man whose voice mattered in a room full of his betters. He had more ideas. He envisioned a network of spies and scouts, of soldiers hidden among the occupied peoples. He'd take one small victory at a time.

In a moment the meeting turned to other matters, Eithurdon no longer noting him. Konner continued to glow with pride, and something else.

Though the river and marshes had been grueling, in

retrospect, Arshal thought of that part of their journey with near nostalgia, punctuated by those dark days following the loss of Arshal's barge. The grief of exiles grown close in their travels, and the injured, slowed their march.

The climb from the gorge and long days on foot in a barren land left them almost desperate. Always a pressing sensation of being observed clung. Once, sentries reported a horseman paced them in the distance. On another occasion, a flash of orange in rocks overhead convinced Arshal that enemy scouts lurked nearby. His companions doubted him. An army would seek them, not stealthy shadows. His counselors urged him to keep a light heart and think of nothing so dour. After Zopher killed a lone Eidhalt he encountered while scouting ahead, the strange sightings ceased.

When it came to lightening hearts, Resala proved their secret weapon. She tirelessly urged the most hopeless to continue on each day. Barge "families" tended to stick together as traveling companions that Resala moved among, inventing competitive challenges between the different "families" to occupy children and adults alike. Often it helped. On the cooler, crisper days of early autumn, groups competed for the quickest count of a flock of birds, or the most bird calls identified, or to gather the items for scavenger hunts. She challenged their providers to bring in the most game or gather the larger share of food while others tried to clean hides the best and fastest or children aimed at quietest and quickest to hide from an imaginary enemy. The winners won favors. Perhaps their fellows waited on them, or they won a day free of chores. It heartened many for a time, and the days felt shorter as they walked ever westward. The mountains grew upon the horizon, rising higher each day.

Then, in the harvest moon, when the valleys back home burned orange and fruit smelled sweet and remained firm in the cellar, the weather turned cold and wintry. A mountain-bred blizzard pounded the plains. Slush dribbled from the sky driven by a sharp wind and followed by snow that obliterated the horizon and at times the refugees only a few paces ahead of them. A dozen elders succumbed to the cold and wet, their illnesses lingering and holding up the march for days. Morale dived. After conferring with Resala, Arshal at last sent a party in search of fuel for several fires, risking discovery to bring strength to his people. That evening, Cree wove for them tales of the Making, chanting late into the night as he revealed himself a Visionary of One's line. Through the cold night he spoke of the

Kedtair and Terremar he had known, the golden land of Shande's past, and the hope in the gods' designs for Arshal.

They trudged on the next morning, not necessarily hopeful, but with resignation.

The harvest moon passed in bitter cold, and early winter set into the plains, then the barren hills beyond that. They began to look at the trees in the occasional stream valley as refuges from the blowing snow, a break from the unbearable whiteness of clouds overhead melting into snowdrifts on the horizon. The wind howled about them as they fought frostbite, pneumonia and fever.

Then Zopher returned with the news that Eilime had fallen, and with that news, the need to take care as they now wandered through occupied lands. Despite their grouping by what they considered their barge family, they couldn't conceal so many and were at last forced to travel only at night, walking only two abreast to leave the narrowest trail and a forced silence. In the darkness, lost in their thoughts, the sense of loss only deepened. The barren hills above the northern edge of the Dodfrenyen Sea became the final resting place of several more travelers – yet another solemn pause in their endless trek.

The novelty of snow disturbed Arshal more than most. With the hesitant shapes of half-fancied pursuit, visions that hadn't troubled the deep sleep of an exhausted exile now taunted him. Soon, he sought his father during their rests, speaking in a low voice long after others had fallen into a fitful sleep, finally welcoming his father's wisdom. He feared King Ebon might question his son's sudden interest in history or protocol or the finer points of international relations. The thought dug into Arshal like a poison thorn. He would notice Cree watching them from beneath his tattered hood as if weighing each question the prince asked. Arshal couldn't remember if he'd related his dream about his father, or if the one-time god could read his mind.

Finally, one snowy dawn, Peshal called a halt. The exiles fell in their tracks to rub sore feet and cramped calves.

Arshal peered back into the dawn in search of the watchful eyes he sensed behind him. He had heard feet crunching snow as he marched rearguard behind the stragglers. Nothing. An echo? As he turned away, did he glimpse a shadow detaching itself from a tumble of boulders? Again, nothing. Arshal hurried to the head of the column to join Peshal, and wait for Zopher whose signal had led to their rest.

He recognized Resala ahead of him, dressed much like Zopher, in hide hunting attire and braids, not the fine gowns of a princess. Arshal watched her greet children who held special smiles for her. She had changed much.

Arshal reached Peshal, adjusting the furlined hide cloak he wore, which had grown stiff around the neck from his breath, brittle and unyielding. It felt like it took Zopher ages to reach them across the featureless expanse.

"Good news or bad?" Zopher asked with a grimace.

"I could use good news," Resala said as she joined them. Peshal and Arshal glanced at each other, smirking as Zopher and Resala gazed at one another.

Zopher cleared his throat and broke from her gaze. "Well, we're almost on top of Sefresal, and it hasn't fallen," he said. Peshal and Arshal both peered ahead into the gloom on the shoulders of the mountains as if they could see the city, as Zopher's attention again went to Resala.

"I thought Sefresal was in the mountains," Peshal said.

"It is," Zopher said, turning from Resala as if with an effort. "We're on a plateau. There's a drop onto a rolling plain before we reach the foothills. The city backs up against the base of a mountain. At our current pace we can reach it in a day."

"Did you speak to anyone?" Arshal asked breathlessly, his hopes rising to a point they hadn't reached for months. "Do they expect us? Is Eithurdon's hall open for refuge?"

Zopher shook his head and Arshal's heart sank. "The city's besieged. A man anxious to retreat apparently expected us. Months ago, much of Sefresal took to hiding up a mountain pass. Only a few soldiers are holding a rampart at the mouth of the pass. We're to find our way as best we can and they'll try to hold the rampart until we reach them, then somehow conceal our passage. The Minarians have been bringing in reinforcements and the defenders aren't even sure they can hold another day, much less the hours it'll take us to get there."

"If the city's besieged, how did you find a messenger? Could it be a trick?" Resala asked.

He smiled at her. "He's a cousin, risking a lot to wait for us at the duke's behest. The city's been prepared for attack, much longer than the Minarians anticipated, longer even than we were. The independent Lharan tribes have provided aid and refuge. This siege began more than a month ago, yet the mountain people have kept a supply route open to the defenders, mostly because they've been waiting for us. We're promised refuge among these mountain people, a crude but dedicated lot, they say. My cousin refused to disclose any more information about the location, not even to a messenger of the king." Zopher jerked his head toward where King Ebon remained among other waiting refugees, haggard, thin, and leaning on Cree, not even coming forward to hear word of their fate.

"What course do you recommend?" Arshal asked after a long moment in which only the wind howled as sunlight found the mountain tops above them.

"Wait until late afternoon, before sunset, earlier if overcast," Zopher said. "Aim to arrive at the rampart from the north. It means some extra hours, but scouts report no Minarians on that route. My cousin promised to alert someone on his way up the pass."

The way even such bad news brought the marchers to their feet marked how long it had been since they had any hope. The promise of refuge after so many months sped their pace into the night.

Many imagined they'd soon find warm hearths in some secluded hamlet, a fat fowl on the fire and ale in hand. With such hopes to urge them, they reached the rampart hours before Zopher expected. At times, they passed a barn's width from enemy watch fires as they slipped through the dark in snow seeming to deepen with each step.

With great care, the defending lowland and Eilimean soldiers who had survived on the rampart on siege rations for almost six weeks, led Arshal's weary exiles to the lee of the rampart to await dawn and their next trek up the pass.

Hundreds of paces north of Sefresal's walls, Arshal peered down from the rough rampart onto a shadowy plain poised for dawn. He stomped his feet and blew on his hands a moment before flapping his arms against his sides to drive away the chill. How would soft nobles from temperate Sihmad Shal survive such an inhospitable place? They knew nothing of winter, the last weeks of snow and wind almost the death of many. The way they sank to the ground, weary and grateful for the thin broth the defenders shared, he wondered whether they would survive even another day without refuge.

The last shades of night still clung to the edges of a semi-circle of enemy watch fires. Dawn would arrive any moment and they would at last embark on the final leg of this awful journey. Yawning his exhaustion, Arshal relished the almost warmth here in the shelter of the rampart, the winds racing down from the peaks finding other routes. He wished he could just curl up in a corner and sleep away the months of hardship.

He scanned the darkness, searching the faces of the soldiers, strangers. On Sihmad Shal's walls he'd felt camaraderie. He belonged there. Here, an outsider, he represented a burden that could cost those helping him their lives.

The man closest to him sprouted a shy smile in the gloom of predawn, then nodded toward the dark expanse below. "Reinforcements arrived, Lord. Your folk better get out quick as it's light. We won't be able to hold 'em this time. All we got's what they been shootin' at us."

"You couldn't use a few seasoned warriors?" Something more than half of my people fought at Sihmad Shal." Arshal's offer sounded lame to his own ears, though he swelled with pride.

"Nothin' 'gainst your folk, Lord, but they don't look up to much now. Looks like you picked the roughest road to get here."

Arshal had thought it often enough. They should have gone for Otayr or Shela or maybe even hopped a ship somewhere. But who knew what those routes might have brought? The only enemy they'd faced thus far was Ea itself.

Arshal again scanned the plain, finding a familiarity in the scene that made his stomach flop. He'd seen it in a dream; it plucked his memory like he'd lived it.

Gray clouds rolled away from the eastern horizon, allowing the first rays of the morning sun to shaft through the boiling mists and acrid smoke from the hundreds of fires sputtering below. His belly constricted at the sight of silhouettes stirring on the field. An occasional flash of the sun's orange rays fired sword and spear raised against him. He imagined he could see the glint of the medallion glowing red on mailed chests, the tassels of Eidhalt fluttering in the wind. Rude taunts filtered up at him as the freshening wind swirled about the mountains' feet.

Behind him the mountains loomed, clouds coiling about their peaks, hiding the snowy crests and filling the valleys with fog, the sun's rays giving the misty sky a spectral glow as a squall brewed over the pass. He heard, before he saw, the first assault against the rampart, an angry yell rolling and echoing around them. Men struggled to cut down grappling hooks and ladders. For every thrown down, more replaced it. Siege towers rumbled, catapults on top flinging flaming shot.

"No way to hold, prepare to retreat!"

The echoes came from his dreams, but the plain below surged to that memory. He lived it again as he had before. Backing from the parapet, he felt faint a moment at the sound of arrows whining and sticking in the earthwork beneath him.

"Lord! Please, it's dawn. We can't hold. You must retreat. We can't defend you. If you're discovered we'll all be lost!"

Arshal touched the sword hilt at his side as a horn's blast signaled retreat. Arshal shouted his own alarm, herding his exiles before him. Lharan soldiers directed them to winding stone paths that faced into a now gusting wind and the driving force of sleet filling the still dark valleys as the defending Eilime and Lharan soldiers began their retreat toward the city walls.

Heart pounding in his chest, Arshal lumbered up snowy paths and climbed the steep sides of a narrow valley, pushing his people before him. Arshal looked over his shoulder at dark figures of pursuit. Medallions glittered against chests as the enemy hewed the Sefresal defenders as snow swirled and blew with a fury. He climbed the sharp face of a scarp, slipping in the beaten snow of those before him. Pushing upward with one hand, he sent the kicking, supportless foot above him over the ledge, and then reached as the climber turned to pull him over the lip. Below, the enemy beat back the Sefresal defenders as the Minarian flag rose over the rampart, the city's towers already topped by the dark pennant. He stared up the long slope where his exiles struggled through hip-deep snows, dragging their children and elders, in search of pathways to the mountains' depths. Where in all this was safety? If the rampart had fallen, wouldn't they merely lead the enemy right to that refuge soldiers on the rampart simply termed 'the Val'?

40: The Pass

Huddled in a tiny cave far up the pass near the Val, Khoti tended a small fire. Weeks had passed since he'd had the luxury of his feather-stuffed bed in the Val, a place made cozy by the sheer number of people and the hubbub of daily living, of communal cookfires and children's chatter, of soldiers training, of sentries calling out their reports as they passed the common room on their way to their beds.

Now, duty kept him away from the lifebeat of his people as he guarded the pass against enemy scouts and patrols with the same ruthless edge as marked his scouting duty in the southern Lharans. Whiling away a browning moon blizzard, he worked a sheath for the dagger lying beside him. He had engraved the leather with Eithurdon's coat of arms and finished it with a thin strand of stellan he wrapped up its length. He let himself relax, to think and rest. Nothing would move for days in such weather. The icy wind sent occasional blasts around Fidra's steaming flanks where she stood near the narrow mouth of the cave working a flake of hay. The cave's low ceiling and shallow back helped the fire melt the leading edge of snow drifts threatening the cave mouth.

Fidra whickered. Khoti scrambled to his feet, drawing his sword. A soft call announced Kefta. Khoti sheathed his sword as his captain pushed Fidra aside enough to stick his head in the cave.

"Asteria's with me."

"What?"

"Took off to find a child. The storm. She got turned around. I almost killed her."

Khoti pushed Kefta aside to find Asteria huddled against the wind on the back of Kefta's horse. Dressed too lightly for the weather, her teeth chattered. She shivered against him as he guided her into his shelter.

"You're all wet."

"Kefta flew at me and thew me into a brook. I broke through the ice."

"Are you hurt?" he looked closely in search of injury.

She shook her head as Khoti and Kefta's eyes met. Only yesterday a Minarian patrol ventured into this part of the pass. Kefta's reaction had been natural.

Kefta built up the fire as Khoti wrapped his blanket around Asteria and offered her the flask of spirits he kept in his saddlebags.

"It is my fault. The child wandered from my care," she said, leaning against him, still shivering. He gave her shoulders a squeeze of assurance.

"I'll look for the child," Kefta stated, staring pointedly at Khoti who merely nodded, impervious to the warning in Kefta's tone. "I would've taken her back to the Val, but you were closer. I thought she'd freeze."

Asteria continued to shiver beneath Khoti's arm. He tugged a fur closer to the fire for her, the hide softening the hard-packed sand of the cave floor. She leaned back against a large rock that had fallen from the roof, her feet stretching to the blaze. Kefta left in a swirl of snow, the draft abating as Fidra shifted to block the entrance again.

Khoti urged Asteria to move closer to the fire. They didn't speak as he unlaced her thin boots and massaged her icy feet until he felt the blood moving through them. Then he took her hands, rubbing and blowing on them without looking at her. When she at last pushed back the hood of her cloak, he looked into eyes that shone back at him bright and moist. The fresh scent of outdoors clung about her and he leaned into it. She didn't pull away. Instead, she looped an arm around his neck and let him kiss her.

His heart pounded. His skin tingled. He pushed himself gently away, blushing and trying to remember his role.

"You, Lady, are an enchantress."

"I missed you," she said, her eyes so soft and deep he thought he'd fall into them. He shook his head, trying to shake sense into himself.

"You're soaking wet." He tried to escape her gaze as he removed her cloak and set it by her boots to dry. He removed his own cloak and tucked it around her, pulling the blanket down to cover her toes. He studied the sheath and dagger he'd been working before offering them to her. Her face held a quizzical expression.

"It's not as fine as I'd like," he said. "The way you tend to find trouble, I thought maybe you'd need this. I tried to craft something fitting for a woman of your rank."

"Is this from your chest of daggers?"

"No. And I wouldn't want you to stain it in my defense." He sat beside her, hesitant, one leg stretched to the fire, the other pulled up to his chest. He struggled to keep a distance respectable among her kind, but another shiver took her and he looped his arm over her shoulder. His skin prickled as she leaned into him.

"I am so inept, Khoti. I can weave and sew, and even fish and hunt, but given charge of a child for an hour, even that I ruin."

He chided her for doubting herself as she pressed against him. He tilted her chin to look into eyes a rich earthy brown, deepened by the dim cave, yet bright with firelight. He couldn't speak at first, then, "What potion have you used to bewitch me? I don't understand."

"It is your kinswoman Latra's doing," she said. "She spoke to me of things a mother would." She put her hand on his neck and drew him to kiss her.

He took a deep breath of her and pulled back again. He glanced at her sidelong, noting how she flushed at his refusal, her own embarrassment rising to her cheeks. He wanted to hold her so close nothing could come between them but he knew better. What if he couldn't stop himself from falling under this spell? This was a duke's daughter, the only child of a man he had sworn to and could not dishonor. These lowlanders' customs felt so alien. A misstep could mean death. Had he already gone too far? The suspicions between lowlanders and mountain folk stood on a long history of ingrained mistrust, no matter what friendships war built. He had compromised the Lady Asteria already, courting scandal simply to heal her. And now, no matter that she might have died of exposure had Kefta not brought her to him, her people would instead read it as dishonor. She sat beside a warrior, unescorted. Despite it, he couldn't turn away, couldn't find a breath that didn't lock up in his throat.

"It is as Latra said," she whispered.

"And what did Latra say?"

Her head tilted and she gave him a coy smile. "I asked her how to let a man know he had my interest. A man determined to ignore me," she said, rolling her eyes before turning that inviting gaze on him again. "She said to give him gifts, refuse their return, and drive him to distraction with attention."

Khoti laughed as she spoke, pulling her closer, feeling comforted when he tucked her against his side.

"She said to make him unable to forget me no matter how hard he tried, and then, if the enchantment works, he would show his interest and present gifts of his own." She held up the dagger and sheath.

"What's a duke's daughter see in a rough-cut mountain boy that she'd play such a dangerous game?"

"I see no boy. I see a brave leader, a compassionate healer. I play no game, and feel no danger."

"It is a game. Your father would never consider me as ... suitor. If that's your aim with these tricks of Latra's. You lowlanders have different ways. Among the Lharan tribes we'd already be promised. So, if not your intent, it's a cruel game since I'd never dishonor the duke." His words tangled in her hair sprawled across his shoulder. "And you do meddle with danger. Your enchantments – You tease me 'cause you think nothing can come of this. But you know if I desire it, something will come of it."

Her expression turned serious. "No game, Khoti. I would not do that to you. And you have grown large in my father's eyes."

"You're a daughter of nobility –"

"And you are a headman's son, and an officer in the Lharan Guard."

"Isn't it the way of shawnsi to choose their daughters' suitors and pick them from peers?"

Khoti couldn't believe they spoke of such things. As if Khoti had time for such distractions. As if Eithurdon would permit it. Did she have other suitors? Men the duke dined with and saw as a means to some assured access to greater power?

"I have a right to refuse," she said, her expression reminding him of her rebellious streak.

For the briefest moment he imagined Eithurdon nodding, smiling, grasping Khoti's shoulder to welcome him.

"Ah, Asteria, what're we doing, saying? I'm no noble. The Guard's all I could aspire to. And the duke gives it to me! I can't hurt him. But now, I want you, too. Who am I to even think of desiring a duke's daughter? I don't have a rich walled city to rule. I have an alcove in a cave –"

"That is all I have now."

"But when this ends, I'll still only have a cave." He slammed his fist into his knee. "We barely know one another. And for this meeting alone your fa has grounds to banish me on suspicion alone. He'll never believe our innocence. A long as I'm your fa's man, I'll feel guilty even thinking of you as I do. As if there'd be any serious consideration. Besides, I've too much of my fa's spirit to settle for walls when the gods carved these mountains for my castle. Who am I to think I could stand beside you –"

Asteria's wounded expression cut Khoti like a knife. "As if peerage matters? What is even left of it, or Shande? Are you refusing me?" she demanded. "My father admires you. He would see our people are not so different. And I would not keep you from your castle. I want to share it with you. Please do not refuse me, Khoti, just because of an accident of birth."

Khoti tugged her to him so hard she gasped. She laid her hand on the breast pocket where he had tucked her pendant. She closed her eyes, her head falling to rest on his shoulder. Khoti let out a shaky breath. Indeed, they played a dangerous game.

Khoti sat up at a sound that had wakened Asteria as well. Like a cat, he always seemed to have one eye, and one ear, alert for danger. Asteria leaned on an elbow to watch him, drowsy yet. She ran a hand through her hair, which had tangled and now fell over a bared shoulder.

She blushed as she grew more awake and pulled the blanket up to her neck while she adjusted her shift and tunic and tightened laces that had allowed her clothing to slip out of place. How had she come to sleep here, beside him? She reached for his blanket next to her, still warm to the touch and rich with his scent. Had she dared sleep beside him? What should she read into this? Khoti took no action lightly. If anyone discovered this indiscretion, she would forfeit her honor no matter her innocence. And he might now abandon her for that very reason.

"Where are you going?" Her voice, husky with sleep, sounded loud in the cave.

Khoti put a finger to his lips then fastened his sword belt at his waist. "Something outside," he breathed as he bent to her ear, his hand warm against the skin of her neck. She shivered at his touch. The warrior had returned, emanating some alien fervor, that odd cat glint in his eyes. He handed her the dagger he had given her and crept to the entrance while she kicked aside the blanket, ready to run.

Feet scuffed against stone just outside the entrance. A soft 'snick' sound as he unsheathed his sword elicited an uneasy silence.

Kefta's soft call found them with the next gust of wind.

"You were almost dead," Khoti said, sheathing his sword as Kefta ducked in. The Guard captain pushed by Fidra to bring a swirl of cold in with him. The snow fell so fast outside he wore it like an overcoat.

Kefta's gaze went from Asteria's embarrassment, to the jumble of blankets by the fire to Khoti's cloak around her shoulders and the dagger in her hand.

"The child's safe, Lady," Kefta said.

She dropped her head to her chest in relief. She'd been so caught up in Khoti she'd barely thought of the child. No wonder Khoti feared her attentions. She acted with the abandon of a child, not a woman responsible for a duke's household.

"He wandered to the North Slope of the Val to find Eilime's children."

She nodded, thanking him as the heat burned in her cheeks. She knew he drew conclusions. She would only appear to prove them if she denied them without accusation.

Kefta turned to Khoti. "Messenger arrived. The rampart's fallen. Refugees in the pass, in this storm! And Minarian patrols await them. Eidhalt. The duke's made for their last known position. We're to join him. He wants his aide beside him." Kefta almost spat the last.

All business now, Khoti pulled his gear together, accepting his cloak from Asteria with a private smile. Then his features hardened again.

"What of Lady Asteria? It's not that safe here and she can't travel alone in this storm."

"Tre and Chati are outside. They can guard her 'til morning, then lead her back to the Val." He looked from Khoti to Asteria and back. "Speed it up, Lieutenant, the duke's waiting." Kefta's tone made Khoti's brows scrunch up momentarily, but he said nothing. Kefta turned and disappeared out into the snow.

Khoti's expression held that familiar coldness that could send an exhilarating thrill up her spine, but his gaze lingered on her. She stood mute as he brushed her neck with the back of his fingers. Then he touched his chest where her pendant remained. He smiled, something playful, inviting, but quickly gone. As he turned to leave, Tre and Chati toted in snow-covered packs stuffed with blankets and food. Asteria touched Khoti's arm, a light brush that forced him to turn back to her.

"I promise you will not always have to look after me this way. I will learn to watch after myself."

"Looking after you has been one of my greatest pleasures, Lady." He touched her hair, smiled that strange smile of his. A brief blast of snow as he led Fidra away sent sparks racing from the fire before Chati brought their mounts within.

Asteria expected to find the two boys laughing at her expense. They stared into the fire as they stirred up a blaze and warmed a pot of snow for tea. She glanced back toward the entrance and pulled the blanket closer around her. Khoti's scent locked in the fibers gave her a sense of security.

"Don't worry, Lady," Tre said, not looking up from the fire. "He'll be back safe. He's got too many folks counting on him to do anything foolish."

She smiled her gratitude at Tre, accepting a mug from Chati that warmed fingers turned to ice.

Kefta took a deep breath. "I hope you know what you're doing." He broke a silence he'd held since they left Khoti's cave, more than an hour ago.

Khoti brushed snow from his eyes. "What're you so mad about?"

"What do you think? I don't want to see you doing the service of a fool."

"To what?"

"A woman." Khoti's glare sent a shiver up Kefta's spine. That look could turn a man to stone. "Khoti, you don't know women yet. They twist you up inside, make you forget you're a man and distract you from your business."

"Is that why you got yourself a lifemate, Kefta?"

Kefta grinned. "I didn't set my sights so high as my duke's daughter. You'll bring yourself only grief. Too many people know you were alone together for most of the night. The duke won't stand for his daughter's honor to be a casualty of war."

He overrode Khoti's objections of necessity with a dismissing wave of his hand. "There's others, fine girls who would drop all suitors and fall with you in a minute if you just smiled at them. That's what you get for becoming a legend and being promoted so quick. They know you've got a future." Khoti didn't respond, merely stared ahead. "Just give yourself some time. We're in a war. You have more important things to worry about, like surviving. And you've got a lot to learn, especially about folks who aren't mountain born. If it's meant to be, then you can get moon-eyed over her when we've got our country back."

Khoti smiled, disarming Kefta. "I know what I need to." He urged Fidra to a brief canter in a small straight away. Kefta caught up to him when Khoti slowed to negotiate a narrow stream flowing too fast to freeze.

'You should know, Eithurdon already has in mind suitors for his daughter."

"She'll refuse them," Khoti stated with nonchalance, the look in his eyes holding Kefta's tongue.

Kefta stared after the Guard Lieutenant who trotted ahead, whistling under his breath a bawdy Evenday song. Kefta flinched inwardly, knowing a confrontation would come, something that could split the Guard and drive a wedge through the Val. The duke might be fond and tolerant of a fireband who earned his keep as a warrior and healer. But that indulgence had limits. A daughter to nobility, cousin to royalty, and, depending on who survived the Minarian invasion, Asteria could potentially stand in line to the throne. Her father would allow nothing to tarnish his only child's image, not even Khoti.

41: Snowfall

Sihmad Shal's exiles had struggled deep into the mountains for a week, seeming no closer to refuge. Arshal feared they wandered in circles. The promised help hadn't come. Had everyone been lost in the fall of Sefresal? Knowing no course, they took the easiest paths, trapping themselves in closed valleys and forced to backtrack. They couldn't believe they hadn't already passed their destination. Certainly, they must be almost to Minaria! With each descent the ascent seemed ever higher as they pushed west. They'd exhausted their food, and with it the energy to go on. Craggy peaks loomed overhead. Above the treeline, snow cover turned everything into indefinable lumps and drifts hid streams. Below the treeline pine boughs sagged beneath the weight of snow, the trees the only thing that gave texture to the snow-covered world.

"It's going to storm again," Zopher gazed at the sky as he walked rearguard beside Arshal.

They certainly didn't need more snow. They could barely move now.

Arshal looked down at his feet and stopped, frozen by his second sight again. The bleeding feet of hundreds of exiles marked their path, a near-dry riverbed flanked by stunted pine. Frantic, Arshal searched for King Ebon, unable to distinguish him from the dark figures ahead disappearing into the swirls of snow beginning to fall. He felt powerless to move.

Zopher stopped and stared back at him. "Are you ill?

Arshal looked up at him, stricken. "We're going to be attacked."

As he stared about in confusion, he discerned the furtive shapes of pursuit. Seeing them at the same moment, Zopher called out a warning. He ran up the slope to defend the marchers, already pulling an arrow from his quiver. Arshal stumbled after him, his breath stuck in his throat, knowing what they would find.

As soon as a volley of Shandean arrows returned, the Eidhalt pursuers retreated. It would be no trouble for them to find the exiles' trail again. Arshal fell beside one of several figures now lying in the path. He knew. Arrows protruded from the body, the snow growing pink. Only minutes had passed. Arshal dug into the snow, reliving his dreams, his waking visions, as he sought to turn over the body and recognize the face.

Beside him, Zopher urged him hurry before the Eidhalt turned. Arshal pulled the gnarled hand from where it clutched at the protruding arrow. The ring gleamed faintly in the whiteness surrounding them.

"Gods," Zopher gasped in dismay.

Arshal fell across the body, his breath ragged. The vision came true. As had the one on the rampart. Would they all be so? Could he have prevented it? "Couldn't I have done something, Father?" he cried as he tried to lift the dead weight to his shoulder. He stumbled and fell into a deep drift.

"Arshal, they return. We can't be slowed! We'll come back!" Zopher yanked Arshal's arm.

Arshal flung him aside. While Zopher untangled himself from the snow and his bow, Arshal removed the ring and circlet from King Ebon's brow, symbols the king wouldn't relinquish in life. Likely the markers sped the arrows to him. Arshal laid a hand on his father's still-warm cheek and closed his eyes.

"It's so unfair," he whispered. "You were willing to give it to me. Isn't that enough?"

Arshal fought for breath and bearings. He forced his eyes open and took Zopher's proffered hand. He looked upon a thin and tortured king, exiled and killed by an enemy that shot the aged ruler in the back. Arshal almost choked on the bile rising in his throat. The prince reached down and twisted the arrow from the body and tucked it in his sack.

"It'll be the talisman of my revenge, Father," he said, then turned and hurried up the slope without looking back.

Though snowflakes still fluttered before Khoti's eyes, the clouds had lifted some during the night. Occasional thin spots in the gray allowed a little pale light to fall on the pass as the two Guardsmen made for the duke's camp in a sheltered hollow, the duke pale despite wind-chafed cheeks. Khoti's mouth fell open in undignified shock to learn the king's people had entered the pass – easterners stumbling blindly through a blizzard – Minarians held Sihmad Shal, the nation lost. His stomach knotted. No army marched west to aid troops who had already lost Eilime and Sefresal.

Fidra pranced impatiently beneath Khoti as if feeling the warrior heart stirring in him. Eithudon smiled at him. The look held such warmth and trust, Khoti's stomach made a slow flop. How could he dishonor this man who gave so much to him?

Snow returned with a vengeance as the half-dozen Guardsmen and Eithurdon raced in search of the refugees. Their horses labored through the deep snows as if furies chased them. Late morning passed before they came upon a ten-man Minarian patrol so distracted by the scent of the exiles that before the enemy knew its danger, they had bled their lives into the snow. The Guardsmen rode on, unscathed, as if Khoti's heart fed them all. Khoti added two more enemy dead to his tally. The legend-makers of the Val would likely draw it out to twenty.

"How come we're losing when we fight like that?" Khoti demanded of Eithurdon as they herded the captured Minarian horses before them.

"We are finding our wits," Eithurdon said. "Soon we will have King Ebon, more soldiers, the scouts. We will learn and exploit the enemy's weaknesses." The duke glanced at Khoti from the corner of his eye, as if measuring Khoti against something undefeatable. Eithudon motioned for Khoti to ride closer to him, as if he hoped to feel the spirits his healer could summon.

Soon Kefta found the hard-packed and bloody trail the enemy had followed. What foolishness brought such people into a land for which they possessed no survival skills?

In the lead, Khoti rode up a trail as the fresh snow covered the stains in a deep trough. He stared at several lumps staggered along the path and galloped ahead to investigate, pretending not to hear the duke's shout for him to return to his side. As he suspected, he found the bodies of exiles who hadn't survived the trek. No force of nature felled them. He swept up an arrow and pulled his bow free in case the enemy remained nearby. The Guardsmen drew their swords as they raced to reach him, then circled him, their horses snorting clouds of steam. Kneeling in the snow by the first body, Khoti rummaged through the dead man's belongings until he pulled free a royal blue standard with blue gems sewn into it in the shape of a coat of arms. Before the duke could respond, Khoti held up his next find, a wooden seal carved with the reversed stamp of the realm, stained by years of waxes.

When Khoti uncovered the face, the duke caught his breath. "Could it be? It looks like King Ebon. Much older than I remember him. Thin. We are lost." He threw his hood over his face. "Khoti, bring him back. You must use your medicine –"

"He's cold!" Khoti broke in, stunned. This man had long passed the time when he could be revived. Was this king one of those for whom he must die to give life? This old clerk who could not save his city from defeat? Khoti might as well teach a stone to breathe.

"Alas," the duke said. "Then we are leaderless."

"The king has children," Khoti said, uncertain what to make of the duke's response. "Didn't the crown prince issue the call to arms?"

"They are so young! Little older than you. Do you feel prepared to direct a war, Khoti?"

"If it's my duty, I'll perform it."

The duke nodded. "I believe you would. May King Ebon's sons have your convictions. I would rather the king still lived, or that someone of more years and wits were the heir to the throne." The duke stared at Khoti's scarred hands holding the seal and banner then turned away, his face twisted with something Khoti felt certain was disgust that his Lieutenant failed him. Khoti tucked the standard in his belt and the heavy seal in his saddle bags, unsure whether he should feel insulted or shamed.

After gathering the bodies of the king and five other exiles, they tied them to the backs of the Minarian horses. Two soldiers led the animals back to the Val. Ahead, though the snow mostly covered the pink stains of bloody feet, the packed trail likely wouldn't melt until well into summer. How would they keep the Minarians from following it right to the Val? The remaining four Guardsmen urged their mounts up the trail.

Khoti stared ahead, seeing Asteria's flushed cheeks, feeling her cold skin against his fingers and imagining her father demanding he die to heal her. Would he do it? He must speak to the duke, end this guilt twisting up his thoughts. Kefta gave him a sharp look as if reading his intent and urged his mount closer to rip Fidra's reins from Khoti's hands.

"Are you crazed, Khoti? What're you thinking?" Kefta's words came as a hiss as Eithurdon turned in his saddle to take in the face-off with a scowl, signing for Khoti to close ranks and ride beside him.

"I won't dishonor him, Kefta. I owe him that," Khoti said, pulling Fidra's reins free and lunging ahead, the pink slices of snow rearing up behind him as they churned up the heart blood of Shande.

"Something troubles you?" Eithurdon asked as Khoti reached his side.

"I don't know much of these things, the traditions. I'd ask my fa, but since he's gone, I've got to ask you," Khoti said. "If a man wished to court a woman, what's his duty to her fa?" Khoti blurted.

Eithurdon snorted, but checked himself with effort. He glanced back at Kefta with a questionmark crinkling the star-like birthmark.

"I don't know about mountain folk, but among us, the man must ask permission of the father," Eithurdon replied softly, as if beginning to realize the direction of Khoti's inquiry.

"And if her fa refused?"

Eithurdon gave him a sharp look. "Then the man must depart."

"And if the man didn't go, despite her fa's wishes?"

Behind them, Khoti heard Kefta cursing.

"Would an honorable man defy the father's wishes?"

"Not lightly," Khoti whispered.

"There is someone so important you would risk honor earned, the debt of many peoples, the respect of the royal government?"

"Lord, I'd like to accompany Lady Asteria."

Eithurdon looked away and didn't answer for so long Khoti wondered if the duke had heard him.

"War is not enough to occupy you?" Eithurdon asked softly, at last, in a voice strained by whatever he hadn't said. "And if I should refuse?"

"Then –" Khoti's voice almost cracked as his confidence drained from him. "Why would you refuse?"

"War, Khoti. The mind of a soldier belongs to his sword. You pose a difficult question for me. Your people and mine live elbow to elbow with very different customs. The risks of hard feelings are so great. And how could I order you into harm's way knowing it would break my daughter's heart? If war takes the remaining aspirants to Shande's throne, my daughter's marriage might very well seal an alliance, a political decision, not one of the heart." The duke spoke slowly, with measured words Khoti knew he selected carefully. "You are so serious, Khoti. You have many years. Perhaps this is a temporary passion that will fade in time.

Is this your first attraction? They can feel the most confusing and intense –"

"Is this a refusal?"

"And if Asteria refused you?" Eithurdon countered.

"She wouldn't."

"You know this?"

Khoti didn't answer, less than sure himself. Eithurdon sighed. He glanced at the wary faces of the Guardsmen around them, then away.

"You tie my hands, Khoti. I owe you my life, my daughter's. You are a fine leader, if not a little impulsive. I do not want your enmity, nor divided loyalties among our peoples and the Guard. I know your strengths, your gifts, and the measure of your honor. You are so young yet! Not in action, but in years. We are at war! There are other matters that require an officer's time. I will not have her hurt. Must you do this to me, Khoti?"

"I accept the consequences of my decision," Khoti returned. "You've taught me that. I dared make my request and face your ridicule. It's your choice. I'm no son of royalty, have no wealth, not even a village. Yet I'd sooner die than see her hurt. That's all I can promise." He paused, bitterness twisting his words. "Some low-born mountain man asks the Duke of Lharan for his daughter. That you haven't struck me, or laughed me down's a wonder. Kefta certainly expects it. I'm nothing but what you've made me. You can undo me if you like."

Khoti goaded Fidra ahead, angry at the impulsive thing in him that had driven him to speak. He reached for his pocket, knowing they all watched him, including the duke, who likely thought he performed some crude mountain ritual in touching the symbol of a heart given him to keep.

He sensed Eithurdon's scrutiny. "Maintain your position, Lieutenant. I did not dismiss you," Eithurdon called. Khoti pulled Fidra up. "Be advised, there are other suitors, more appropriate. We follow a vastly different tradition that has little resemblance to mountain ways. That said, the notice must be posted a year for challenge. A promise means nothing until then. Be certain of your intent. I will speak to Asteria and inform her of the drawbacks and my reservations that a warrior who might very well die is not the best choice. If she is certain, we will see."

Khoti stared at Eithurdon with the stony gaze that turned blood to icicles, before rushing ahead, embracing defiance.

42: Rumors

Nali leaned back from his work and stretched, shaking stiff hands to relieve the cold and ache. He'd made a small fire of wood shavings in the barn's stove, but it didn't throw enough heat to do more than keep his toes from freezing. He squinted up at the old farmer silhouetted at the open barn door, where the snow-covered yard gleamed back at him.

Rathil Hostler bent his lanky frame to examine Nali's work, the old farmer as ponderous and thorough in everything he did as the night he examined the easterners who wandered into his yard.

"You do fine work," Rathil said as he examined the shovel Nali made. He'd worked the shoulderblade of a horse that had died in battle, and fitted it with a wooden handle he'd wrap with sinew, pitch and leather. "Looks to be as keen an edge as metal."

Nali snorted. "Least 'til it runs up against its first rock."

Rathil grimaced as he stood. "Still, it's fine work. And you claim to be a fisher by trade? You wasted a craftsman's talents."

"It's an excellent position now," Nali admitted. "There wasn't much call you know." He gave the farmer a wry smile, running his fingers along the smooth edge he had made. "That doesn't mean if I find a spare moment I won't try carving some hooks out of those soup bones."

"I have news," Rathil said, gazing through the open door across the snowy yard to where his lifemate, Atnil, and Olna worked together in the farmhouse great room, sewing with Nali's bone needles. Crudely carved by inexperienced hands, the tips broke and wore easily, snagging the material or separating the threads. "Don't know how they 'spect us to produce without metals, you know," the farmer said with a sigh. "Never though about all the uses 'til they hauled it all off. Can't believe they took pots, hinges and even sewing needles! How many swords can you forge from a sewing needle?"

Nali waited for the older man to get to what he'd come to say. He had grown fond of Rathil, who reminded him of Drul and even seemed to fill that place in the children's lives. It still surprised Nali the way the man had opened his house to them that first night. Rathil never probed too deeply in Nali's business, other than to glean those things Nali told willingly. He seemed to sense the deeper mystery to Nali, but kept his questions to himself, endearing himself even more to the easterners.

When the Minarians came to the farm a few days after Nali's family arrived, a suspicious distance still lay between them. Yet Rathil risked the wrath of the occupation to claim Nali a nephew helping him farm his place. It meant the Drulsons, or Bertalsons, now officially worked on Rathil Hostler's farm.

Nali's fondness for the older couple had grown ever since. He watched with wry humor when Rathil removed Nali's weapons and his own, when he didn't think Nali would notice, and buried them beneath the dung heap behind the barn. The man carefully wrapped each item, working late in the cold autumn night. Soon after, Minarian soldiers arrived, tearing the farm apart in search of weapons and metals. Later Rathil and Nali discovered several items the Minarians overlooked. Rather than risk implication in some future random search, Nali grinned and suggested they bury the items in the dung heap out behind the barn. Rathil had merely laughed and agreed it might be a good place.

Neighbors warned them when officials neared so Nali could hide his children, though the Minarians had an unnverving way of noting Olna's pregnancy, making a mark in a ledger that tallied the region's population and production. All children older than four years must report for schooling. For all folk knew, the Minarians killed them, but they could do that without the ruse. Rathil and Nali figured the Minarians planned to eliminate future resistance by erasing the young minds of their memories of home, family, or other beliefs.

As farmers, the Hostlers and Bertalsons lived better than most of their fellows. They kept most of their livestock and managed to hold a few things aside each time the Minarian wagons came to the door to collect all their produce for redistribution, what Rathil called outright looting. Some friends occasionally discovered a windfall on their doorstep and never knew the source of the stew fowl or pickled roots.

Nali found Rathil staring at him. The man came so slow to what bothered him, sometimes Nali could finish his task and clean up before Rathil got to his point.

"You think too much, Bertalson," Rathil said quietly.

"Maybe I do," Nali admitted. "There's a lot in this world to ponder."

"But you think deeply, organized and all. And you know a lot of things people don't just learn from living, like you're practiced at it."

"Man gets a lot of time to think when the fish aren't up or storms are blowing," Nali hedged.

"They got a list posted in the Eilime square with the names of all these Traitors to the Minarian Protectorate on it, wanted dead or alive. A lot of them are on there from Sihma Harbor and Sihmad Shal. One name's on there three times. Can you imagine that? Busy fellow. He commanded that group, the Harbor Gnats you called 'em, and on top of that was a derna and an advisor to the king. Fancy that, will you?"

Nali stared at the shovel, running his fingers along the edge, reminded of Olna's prophecy about how rumors travel faster in a city than in the country, and in the same thought wondering who gave his name and for what price.

"Thought you might know some of them fellows since you're from back that way," Rathil added. "And a man might notice the farings of a fellow who happened to share his name."

Nali looked up at Rathil. "You suggesting we move on, Rath?"

"Never. Not unless I thought it was dangerous for you. It just might be something to think about. You know a man as busy as that other fellow might attract a lot of attention. You wouldn't be wantin' people makin' connections to a person who just happened to show up from back east with a similar name. Most people probably won't notice, probably not read it."

Nali nodded slightly and stared into the grain of the shovel handle.

"The other news is Sefresal finally fell. I thought you might be interested. You've asked about it often enough."

Nali bit his lip and closed his eyes as he thought of Arshal. Had they made it? Did they still have any hope of regaining Shande? He thought of all the shattered dreams staring at him from the faces of refugees in Peshal's Tunnel, the children and elders.

"Do you remember any other names on that list, Rath? There probably are folk I know – lived in the Harbor all my life," Nali said after a long silence when Rathil appeared about to leave.

Rathils's head bobbed. "Well, I guess there's a couple dozen under the heading of Gnats, can't remember all their names. And let me see – it was a long list – well, a lot of the royal family folks was on it. Kind of odd. What do you think of that?"

"Oh, I'd say maybe they knew they'd be killed on sight if caught and figured it would go easier on the defenders if they weren't around when the city fell," Nali said slowly, picking his words with care. "And maybe they figured if they survived, they might organize and fight back. I can tell you, we just weren't ready for what they threw at us. I think you said something was mentioned in the battle for Eilime about Minarians wanting to kill shawnsi and government folk. Knowing that, well, maybe it was just too much of a risk to have the entire government executed."

Rathil's gaze narrowed. He gave a slight nod to himself. "Well then, I guess they were pretty smart if that's what they did. Seeing how these people are, I guess it would go harder on a man if he wasn't just defending his home, but defending the enemy's arch-rival. Yep, I can see that. And I see where a covert resistance might use the time more wise. Well, I think I feel a bit easier about some things." Rathil smiled at him. "I knew there was more to you, son, than meets the eye. See how well you thought that piece out? I'd have never come up with an idea like that if it hadn't been throught of by someone else first." Rathil studied Nali for a long moment. "I bet there's a lot of things we could learn from a man like you, given time, and you having seen battle an all, a world of experience. All that's stored up inside of that head of yours, I bet we haven't seen the best yet.

With that, Rathil lay a hand on Nali's shoulder, gave it a squeeze and left, leaving Nali feeling naked, terrified, and yet somehow comforted and less alone.

43: Reunion

The figure stood before him, erect and patient. Arshal trudged ahead and grasped his cousin's arms in mittened hands.

"I thought we'd never meet again, Eithur," Arshal said, his voice hoarse. Several days had passed since his father fell, days his exiles had gone hungry.

The duke peered into Arshal's face. "I see hardship behind you. We were delayed by a patrol several days ago. They will not trouble us again, for a time."

"Then you gained for me vengeance for the death of my father," Arshal said, admitting a new emotion, a feeling so alien he had difficulty recognizing it. Not quite hatred, or malice, he couldn't accept those things yet. It came close, a consuming anger that made his breath burn. It troubled him that he hadn't felt it at Esthen's death. Perhaps the difference lay in the circumstances: he felt responsible for the king's death.

"I thought I recognized him," Eithurdon said. "He looked so old and thin, and without ring or crown. We sent his body to the Val."

"It's been too much, Eithur. Too much to understand."

Eithurdon looked away. "We will see to your people. There is time later to plan what must be done."

Arshal noted a fair-haired young man with hard emerald eyes urging his mount to meet him, a man from a tribe unknown to Arshal. He caught the look Eithurdon gave the young man dressed in the colors of the Lharan Guard, with huntsman's attire peeking from beneath his cloak, a look deferential, yet more than that. What strange relationship did his cousin have with such a cold-eyed and intense young man? Even while deferent and indulgent, Eithurdon's expression felt proprietary.

"Your Grace," the young man said as he dismounted, a hint of steel in his tone. He presented the Dyndevas standard and seal. He waited for Arshal's stunned nod before he spoke a word to his horse, then presented the reins of his mount to the prince and swung up behind another Guardsman. "Here is Fidra. She will bear you home to the Val with dignity, not as a haggard exile."

Arshal sensed the horse yearning for her true master, like a blossom reaching for the sun.

With that, Eithurdon led the ragged pilgrims on the last march to the Val. The wind's mournful howl fit the mood as they entered the valley, crews of Guardsmen hurrying out to conceal the paths they had beaten in the snow.

This might be a world far from Sihmad Shal, a place alien, cold and harsh, but as Arshal dropped his sack and scabbard on a cot in the bare alcove readied for him, he felt as if he'd finally arrived home.

Though they at last had found shelter, recovery for the exiles would take longer. Despite his duties, Arshal mostly slept and ate through his first hours in the Val, until forced to deal with yet another tragedy for his family. They had carried her those last days, hoping that once they found shelter and food she would improve. He never imagined he might next bury his mother in a shallow grave overlooking the lake beside his father, felled, he felt certain, by grief, for King Ebon, for Esthen, for Shande.

Arshal noted Peshal's arm around Resala's bent shoulders as they stood beside the frozen lake. How many more sacrifices must his family make? Above, the peaks gilded with late sun glowed yellow against a brilliant blue sky – a scene Queen Sala would have stared upon in awe. The air felt so crisp and dry, unlike anything in the eastlands. Even the wind in the trees seemed to mourn the passing of the queen. The trees closest to the lake's open water shook leaves that hadn't fallen, like the rattles of a death march pacing the Sijway. Waterfowl quacked and hissed and honked softly as they perched on the edges of the ice waiting for scraps of moldy bread or sprouting seed, like the soft murmurs of mourners on the march. A greater gust of wind fell from the peaks to push aside pine branches higher on the slopes where caves opened up, sending a soft hushing sound as if to still Arshal's grief. She hadn't even lived to see him named king.

A buzz grew among those gathered, broadening into cries of relief, delight, turning Arshal's attention to the west, where he knew Minaria lay somewhere beyond. The calls brought others rushing from the caves to call and cry out as a swift rapping, like cracking stone, raced along the valley to their ears.

Cupping his hands around his eyes, Eithurdon squinted at distant specks against the snow, Arshal awaiting his verdict. What strangeness in a land where news traveled so quickly! The young Guard officer stepped out of the ranks of Guardsmen to grip the duke's arm.

"My fa," he said, his words only a breath of mist.

Eithurdon turned to stare at his Lieutenant. "You are still an officer in the Lharan Guard, Khoti. By the gods, act the part." Eithurdon removed his arm from Khoti's grasp then glanced at the prince. "There are other peoples who have suffered, Arshal," he said quietly. "Yonder is one whose hatred runs deep. We shall see if he stood equal to the task he set himself."

Arshal stared at his cousin. What greater suffering could there be than the king's family, giving up its children, its home, its kingdom and trekking to barren lands with nothing but what they carried?

Having ridden to meet the newcomers, the Taschian Arshal understood to be the acting leader of the mountain people in the community, Konner, whooped so loud his cry echoed up the valley.

Khoti smiled a tight-clenched grin of victory. "That's Konner's way of saying he's done it."

Eithurdon brightened as Konner led the travel weary, half-frozen band to them, the clatter of the mountain calling stones echoing into the mountain peaks.

"Pician and Halieri," Khoti said.

Eithurdon gave him a wary glance. "I am sorry –"

"Hali was the last Lhatan. The last of an entire tribe," Khoti said.

Arshal lost his breath to see the menace lurking behind the cat glint in the young man's eyes. Arshal couldn't even contemplate such a statement.

"They exterminated a whole people like they were no more than ants in the larder."

Khoti's words struck Arshal a blow so hard he opened his mouth, but no words came. Khoti looked at the prince and nodded. The Guardsman understood. No one could absorb such a realization. It couldn't be undone, not like rebuilding villages and cities or herds of livestock. An entire people!

Khoti's father and his ragged band, dressed in tattered gear that might have been Minarian, reined in before Arshal. The man they named Tsevon gazed at them in stony silence, his features weather worn. Dark smudges and deep lines clung about his eyes.

"There's a story to tell here," the Taschian stated when his gaze fell on Khoti. Arshal glanced at the younger copy of the newcomer, seeing only a few battle scars, the buff and pewter trappings and a Lharan sword at the warrior's side. The Taschian headman seemed saddened by the sight.

"It has been many months, Tsevon, since you left him near death," Eithurdon replied, moving forward so that he stood a little in front of Khoti. Arshal narrowed his gaze on his cousin, who appeared to be challenging the man's own father to claim him.

Tsevon turned to Arshal, as quickly seeming to dismiss Eithurdon as if he were some merchant whose wares didn't interest him.

"Let me express my sympathy for your grief, King," he said, dismounting and bowing his head. The action appeared to stun Khoti, the duke, and all the mountain people gathered. A muttering began somewhere in the crowd and competed with the wind for dominance.

Arshal cleared his throat. "I'm not yet king, sir," Arshal said. "And today, there's no land for a king. But I extend my sympathies to you for the loss of your comrades, and promise I'll have back this land for its peoples." Though quiet, Arshal's sincerity softened Tsevon's stance.

The Taschian tugged a grimy bag free of his saddle. "I've brought you a gift, though I don't advise you to unwrap it." Arshal felt Khoti cringing from Tsevon's pained expression. "It comes to you by way of my lifemate, Amhese. We return with Mol Azezial's head." Shocked silence grew into an exhalation of excitement.

Arshal wanted to be sick, to shove the man away for the vile thing he had, for the thought that Shandean natures could be corrupted to such an act, or that any of his subjects would undertake such a horror. Though he could tell, with only the briefest glance, that Peshal, at least, approved.

"No gift could be greater," Arshal said instead of what he felt. "The more I see, the more I learn, many have tales of valor. I'm not alone. It gives me hope for the work ahead." He forced a wry smile. "I don't need to see it to believe it." He motioned to the sack as Tsevon emitted a humorless chuckle. "Sadly, as great as the deed was, and as much as I know it hurt them, it's isn't enough."

"We know," Tsevon admitted. "But were Pician and Hali lost for nothin'? Was Lagdche destroyed for nothin'? Was Amhese's grisly task, a thing that still haunts her dreams, unneeded? The Pladde have risen, has it been for nothin'?"

Khoti turned away at the plaintive tone in Tsevon's plea, held only by Eithurdon's command.

"It was the last week of the ripenin' moon. Lagdche was destroyed, and Mol Azezial – Has there been no change?"

"Three months," Arshal said. "Occupying forces are perhaps just learning of it. They may still be shaking out the leadership in Lagdche. I trust something will come of it, perhaps delayed reinforcements." He looked at the stone-faced woman sitting so erect on her mount. "It matters. It brings hope. It proves we have a sting, that we can sneak into our enemy's camp and destroy him at will. And if the Pladde rebel, it might just frighten a few of them to look over their shoulders and to their security at home."

The woman dismounted and stood beside Tsevon, her chin tilted upward to hear Arshal's evaluation of her efforts, revealing a tattoo at the base of her neck. Her face appeared worn, but not broken. If anything, her spirit seemed stronger, as if it fed upon Tsevon's. It made her appear much younger than her lifemate, though in spots Arshal detected a touch of frost in her dark braids.

"I'm told you're now a warrior and a healer," Tsevon said, his words aimed at Khoti, ignoring the prince as completely as he'd fawned on him before. He gazed at the Guard Lieutenant as if his entire story would be revealed.

Khoti shrugged, reddening beneath his father's stare as if merely a boy, not a Guard officer. Eithurdon set a heavy hand on Khoti's shoulder.

"He is the best kind of warrior, Tsevon," Eithurdon stated. "My aide. Quick-thinking. Nearly drove off an army with his temper and as a scout unmatched. Your boy is gone. He is my Lieutenant now."

Eithurdon's hand gripped Khoti's shoulder so tightly it had to hurt and the young man remained as expressionless as his mother. What were these people? Arshal doubted he'd ever witnessed such a stirring meeting that could be so devoid of outward expression. Was their pride so deep?

"We'll see," Tsevon said, turning to Arshal to hold up the stained sack. "We've carried this trophy for a month of days, Lord. Is there hope we can lose it."

Arshal nodded, emphatic. Tsevon tossed it away so that it rolled and bounced down the slope, a cursed thing no one ran to tend. What must it take to fetch such a trophy? What dedication? What vows made in moments of grief or pain? He glanced again at Amhese, who was smiling at someone she knew in the crowd.

Tsevon put a rough arm around Khoti, pulling him from Eithurdon's grasp to propel him toward the caves. And what prize could it be that Eithurdon sought in another man's son?

44: Fugitive

The barn door flew open with such violence it pulled the wooden guiderail from the wall. Nali stared, squinting into the brightness of the snow-covered yard, his hand reaching for a sword he no longer wore. A cold moon wind swept up the slope from the Dodfrenyen Sea and snuffed the lantern, bringing Nali a shiver as he let an awl fall in his lap. Nali rubbed his eyes as the figure searched for him in the darkened barn. Commotion grew in the yard as hounds yapped and doors slammed.

"Nali?" Rathil asked of the dark.

"'Bout scared me to death, Rath," Nali said, picking up his awl.

"If that didn't, this will. Pack your gear. They nabbed Banen – hoarding – and to save his skin he reported you."

"Banen! The snake! After all I've given him, the work I did!" Nali sputtered.

"Time later for curses! We got to get you out of here. There's a shepherd's shack about an hour back east from here. Atnil's getting' your folk packed –"

"It's bitter cold!" Nali protested. "Nalel –"

"They'll take the babe if you leave him. And if you stay, you're all gone."

Nali threw the awl against the wall with a bang, grabbed his mittens and pulled up his hood as he ran from the barn to find his family already bundled against the wind.

"We'll leave tracks. Step in each other's footsteps," Nali said as he hoisted Rena to his back and trotted in the direction Rathil pointed.

It took several hours to wade through the snow, slowed by the children's shorter legs and the bundles they all carried. At last, they found the hovel, unprotected by trees and standing stark against the sky.

Cold, drafty, the shed served as a summer house for shepherds. Only hides shielded the windows – for protection from summer rains, not winter cold. A small hearth beckoned, but no wood stood by. After doing his best to tuck blankets around the infant to keep him warm, without suffocating him, Nali called for Bertal.

"We need a fire. It'll be a long hike finding wood in these parts."

Bertal nodded in silence. He knew long hikes. The last had taken more than a month.

They trudged into the blowing snow without looking back.

They had barely crested the hill, bent from the load of wood on their backs, when they heard a screech. Nali looked up then dropped in the snow, pulling Bertal down beside him. Only three or four hours had passed since they left, but already Banen stood twitching outside the shack as shrieks and the smash of wood carried to their ears.

Nali's entire body clenched, his fists knotting snow into wet balls in the palms of his mittens. He buried his face, only looking up when Bertal gasped.

Rena and Kia huddled outside the shack under guard. Olna clutched Nalel, begging soldiers to leave the infant alone. One Minarian held Olna around the waist while another, tugging at the bundle, finally wrenched the child free and tossed him aside like a sack of seed. Olna still struggled to reach the two-week-old boy that nearly killed her to carry so far west. Her fight ended when a fist smashed into the side of her head, felling her like a tree before the axe.

Nali stuffed a fist in his mouth, clinging to Bertal to stop himself from charging the dozen soldiers. He especially wanted to get his hands on Banen. How he'd tighten them on Banen's neck if he could. Like no emotion he'd ever imagined came his desire to fly into the dozen soldiers with nothing but his fists and the wood on his back with which to strike them. But he had a duty to Bertal. He could only watch as they dragged Olna away, Kia and Rena following behind, Kia's movements stiff as she carried Nalel as if afraid to touch him.

A long time passed before Nali forced himself to stand. He hugged Bertal to him then wiped the tears from the boy's face. He could only briefly wonder what damage the event wrought in the boy's mind. Nali felt numb. Neither spoke as they turned into the wind for the long walk back to Rathil's. They had no other place to turn.

Dusk closed in on them before they reached the Hostler farm nestled in its shallow valley. The house remained dark as night descended, though soft sounds came from behind the barn. Nali's feet crunched in the snow as he approached. Without his family he just didn't care. Only Bertal gave him a reason to move, and the niggling hope he could do something to rescue them. When an eerie silence fell around him, he stopped. Two darker shadows poised over the dung heap with stumpy bone shovels in hand. If the moon hadn't briefly slid from behind a cloud, the four of them might have stood there until morning, each afraid to move. Nali saw the puff of mist as a long breath released.

"Nali, lend a hand. We've got to be moving on. They want us for harborin' fugitives. Banen was thorough. I thought at least I'd dig up the weapons I –" He looked behind Nali and Bertal, peering into the darkness. "You two alone?" He waited for Nali's stiff nod. "Then hop to it. Get a shovel."

Nali obeyed, not speaking, his limbs moving without his direction. He barely found the energy to lift the shovel. Rathil looked from Nali's blank expression to the tears on Bertal's face as the boy attacked the manure with vengeance.

"What happened," Rathil breathed.

"Banen led them to – gone, taken away."

"Olna! The childen!" Atnil's voice trembled.

Nali couldn't tell them how Nalel had been tossed about, how Olna screamed and struggled, collapsed, how Kia and Rena clung together, their eyes wide and terrified. The image stood before his eyes clearer than the dung heap he dug in.

Atnil buried her face in her hands and turned away, a small whimper the only lament escaping. Frozen for a moment, staring at the ground, Rathil absorbed the news then dug furiously into the pile, finally striking metal. He handed Nali the rag-wrapped sword the derna had carried from Sihmad Shal. It fit easily at his side, a missed friend.

"We've got folk in Sefresal. I got fake papers assigning me there. I'll claim you're my son. Somehow, we'll hide the boy. Family's allowed, and I'm sure my son won't mind if I adopt another. Better leave the name behind," Rathil said as he dug up knives, needles, an axe, broadheads and his own sword from a long-past stint as a Lharan Guardsman. "We'll call you Jani, Jani Hostler. Close in sound and like your friend's."

Nali nodded as Rathil kept talking, wondering how many more new names might come his way. Patter from the old farmer distracted Nali, soothed him like the relaxing chuckle of a brook.

Still, Nali couldn't put aside the image –

"I can't just leave," Nali choked as Rathil reburied the odds and ends they didn't need.

Rathil peered at him. "Jani," he said. "Alive or no, there's nothin', not a thing, you can do. They got 'em. They're probably holding 'em in that new lockup they built in Eilime. By the time you find a way to reach 'em they'll have already been sent away to labor like the others."

"Or killed."

"I've never seen or heard of 'em killing the young'uns. They want 'em too bad for work. From what you've let on about why you're here, maybe there's a hope this occupation'll end and you'll find them all safe, just a little worse for the wear. We can try to learn what we can, but from somewhere safe."

Rathil sowed hope. Nali wanted to believe the old farmer, just as he'd wanted to believe Sihmad Shal could hold on as long as someone fought for it.

"And then," Rathil said, "Then there's things you and I can do in Sefresal, better than here. Some of that teachin' you've been givin' might be needed there. And I mentioned to you some about my friends. They'd have a need for a fellow with sharp eyes and a quick mind, like you."

Nali averted his gaze. "I can't risk Bertal, Rath. He's all I've got left. If I get involved in something where I'd get caught stealing or hoarding – Don't tell me anything more about what you're up to. I don't want to know more than I need to."

Rathil shrugged, giving Nali a glance that said he expected Nali would come around. And when he'd spent his initial grief, he'd be looking for ways to get even.

Shoved into the back of the wagon, Kia sat hard on the rough floor and pulled Rena into her lap. She stared out at the snowy yard of the lockup. There, her mam hung by the neck from an old weathered swamp oak, twisting slowly in the wind. The notice beneath her read 'treason.' They had discarded Nalel – somewhere. He hadn't made a sound since she'd carried him from the shack.

Rena pushed against her as if to hide when the teamster climbed up on the broad wagon seat. Kia moved to the back of the wagon, as far from the teamster as she could get. No other children would join them on the journey. Few remained in Eilime when the Minarians swept in.

Kia didn't bother looking east anymore. Her fa had yet to come and probably wouldn't, couldn't. Days passed with no friendly face. Those few folk she recognized when she peered out the barred windows or when towed through the streets, turned away, unwilling or unable to help her as her fa had helped them. She swallowed hard but had used up all her tears.

A guard hooked a metal cuff around her ankle and locked it into a ring in the floor of the wagon. They had no fear young Rena would run off. The teamster tossed Kia a blanket, a waterskin and a half loaf of bread, then turned to whip up the team.

As the wagon jolted away, southwest along the dike road to find the southern mountains, the only image filling Kia's eyes, long hours after they left Eilime, was of her man's body turning on the bare black branch of a twisted tree, a look of deep sorrow, not fear, engraved on her face.

45: Vows

When Tsevon, Amhese and Khoti at last gathered alone, an expectant silence reigned. All had changed, Tsevon could see that. He hated treading unknown ground. He hated that things had changed, that strangers and royals and easterners who found mountain air too thin now crowded the Val.

Tsevon noted scars on his son's body, wounds he hadn't healed. The hardness in Khoti's expression he knew. But now it came from confidence, not stubbornness. A rift yawned between them as deep as the Staph-el mine. He caught a glimpse of a mark on Khoti's neck, his mark, made by Konner's hand. His son had a voice, and Tsevon hadn't witnessed it for the first time, as he had when he cut the tattoo into Amhese's neck, into Von's. The insignia of a royal officer clasped his buff and pewter cloak.

"Khoti, from all I've heard – the entire tale I'll demand later – I should be proud of you. And I am," Tsevon said when the three sat at the alcove's small wooden table. Khoti glanced at his mother, then away. What did he think of Amhese's feat? "If I didn't appear that way, it's because I'm sick for what's gone: that part of your life where you grow from boy to man, when you needed your fa."

"It's just war, Fa. Other countries separate men from families and send them off to battle. Kefta thinks I've a wealth of fas. Konner took a part, Eithur –" Khoti faltered when Tsevon leaned back and looked down his nose at him.

"And what part did they take, that your own failed you in?"

"The parts that kept me from making a fool of myself, getting myself killed," Khoti said, his hands clenching on the table. He looked up with a little of the fire smoldering in him and opened his hands to reveal the palms of a healer. "I've your curse, Fa. I didn't know what to do with it. I thought I could cure the world."

Tsevon reached across the table to touch the mark on Khoti's forehead. "Konner's work." He could feel something when he touched that mark, strong, pure, burning. Konner had not told him all the he could of his son. Khoti merely inclined his head. "And the lessons you learned?"

For an instant, Khoti's features took on a brutal cast, one Konner claimed drove armies from the field. Amhese's fingers dug into Tsevon's arm.

"It's a matter of choices," Khoti replied without elaboration.

Their alcove curtain stirred. They turned to the doorway to find a dark-haired young woman, her deep brown eyes on his son. She tossed her head to one side, sending waves of hair bouncing over her shoulder and revealing the mark of a shawnsi at her temple. When she realized they'd seen her, she entered with hesitation, yet a certainty as if the alcove were her home and she found strangers had come to visit. Tsevon's gaze narrowed on her as Khoti's mask dissolved into a bashful smile.

"I am sorry," she said. "I did not mean to interrupt."

Khoti held his hand out to her. She stood behind him, as if Khoti shielded her from Tsevon's stern visage, and Amhese's bemused smile.

"Lady Asteria of Lharan, my parents," Khoti said. "The duke allows suit." He grinned as he said it as if the phrase sounded odd even to his lips. Tsevon and Amhese stared.

Asteria laid her hand on Khoti's shoulder with a familiarity that made Amhese beam and Tsevon bristle.

"I will come back another time. You have much to discuss," she said. With a shy smile, Asteria declined Amhese's stammered invitation to stay. Khoti grinned at his feet.

"Yes, there's much to talk about," Khoti said with a wry smile and the half snort of a nervous chuckle as the curtain fell into place.

Amhese jumped up to fetch cups of wine to celebrate their reunion. Khoti maintained his covert smile until he looked up at his mother as she bent over him to give him his wine. He touched the tattoo at her neck, his smile souring.

"I haven't long. Tomorrow I'm off again," Khoti stated, then downed the wine and slammed the empty cup on the table.

"Doing what?" Tsevon had found his voice. It came thick with authority.

"Fighting for Shande." Khoti gave his father a slashing grin more ominous than Konner's. "I'm Lieutenant of the Guard, what's left of us. As second to Kefta and aide to the duke, I have duties and provide counsel. Me, counseling. Ha, now there's a frightening thought! It's all part of the game. Tomorrow, I must find out what happened to Lord Steadon when Sefresal fell. He didn't make it up the pass. Our conquerors tend to kill shawnsi with pleasure, but there's been no word of Steadon's fate."

"I'd thought we'd become a family again. Regain a little what's been lost," Amhese said.

"Nothing'll ever be the same, Mam," Khoti said more gently than his expression. "You can't make warriors, then expect them to put that nature aside the moment there's a lull in the battle, or relive the time lost. Look at yourselves. You know nothing'll ever be the same. All that died with Von and Grandmam. Though not what we wanted, we have to make what we can of it. We may have been defeated in battle, but it's only making us stronger. I'll be fighting until there's none left."

A horn call echoed through the drafty caves, coiling into niche and alcove. A few clacks of calling stones barely carried over the echoing song.

"King's to be coronated," Khoti said as he rose from the table. "We're special guests. I threw my lot with the Duke of Lharan, and he's bound to the King of Shande, whatever's left of it. It's your choice. Konner marked me a Tawnkat," he touched the tattoo on his neck. "I'm also a Lharan officer. I'd be happier if there was a stronger bond between the two." Khoti stared at Tsevon a moment before slipping from the alcove.

If Tsevon attended, he'd be bound to the king, the shawnsi and tribes his people had long kept at a distance. If he refused, he remained his own man. Who would he lead? Would people have to choose? A new, young king wanted his birthright, carried a fine weapon at his side and appeared capable of wielding it. What role would Tsevon have? Was the alliance best for his people? Did he even have a people to lead? They had taken Konner and Khoti to their hearts and those two had joined with Eithurdon. Tsevon turned to Amhese.

"He said you have a choice," she said. "I'll attend. You're welcome to join me."

The curtain dropped behind Amhese. He stood alone for many minutes, arguing with his pride. At last, he let out a deep breath, blew out the candle, and wound his way along the drafty cavern to attend the coronation of the King in Exile.

"We stand here united, people of the mountains, people of the plains, people of Sihmad Shal, Shandeans all," Arshal said to the bright sky above the Val, his voice carrying over the twilit lake and falling on the cloud of breath rising to the peaks.

He had heard many stories since he arrived in the Val, showing him he could have followed worse paths. Latest he heard the account of a young Taschian, Teckhan, of the journey to Minaria. He couldn't help but wonder how many more tales he would hear of the devotion and determination of his people.

"We remain here yet undetected," he continued. "Much of Shande has no such luxury, this sense of purpose. We know they suffer. Yet we had to preserve ourselves for the fight ahead. We owe it to those we left behind to bring purpose to their sacrifice. We were foolishly unprepared. We will not make such a mistake again. It will take time, months, perhaps years, but Shande will again belong to Shandeans."

An eerie silence reigned when Arshal ended. Each person had an idea of personal mission, but all stood united under Arshal's banner. He had become their hope. The tales of his visions and the fog in Sihma Harbor, of Khoti's strange powers of healing unheard of in generations coupled with his odd battle prowess, the unmasking of Cree: these signs and omens said the gods stood with them.

Cree had opened Ebon's grave for the formality that should have taken place in the royal tombs. Eithurdon stooped to retrieve the signet ring and circlet crown from the grave, where they had been placed that morning. Only cracking stone and the crunch of snow under foot broke the silence as Eithurdon passed the artifacts to Peshal, who then carried them to Cree.

Arshal knelt in the snow, thinking of Nali as he relived yet another moment from his visions. When Cree set the ring upon Arshal's finger and the circlet upon the young king's head and intoned the marriage rites of ruler to rule, land and people, the Visionary's eyes misted with uncharacteristic emotion.

Arshal stood and Cree blessed his joining with the realm. He looked his pupil in the eye and smiled, suddenly appearing like a god of old.

"It is said that after the Visionaries saw the devastation of the old world, they would never again find joy," Cree said, his words for Arshal only. "In you, Arshal, I have. We are not forsaken. In you I have seen the workings of gods who still care, though often it seems they do not."

Stunned by Cree's confession, Arshal could only nod. He grasped Cree's sinewy arm. "Then I forgive you the trials you've set me. You renew my faith."

Resala bore a pewter goblet on a tray, feet crunching snow, her face red with the cold. Zopher smiled at her concentration as she bore the filled cup. He took the tray as the wine passed from Asteria to Eithurdon to Resala to Peshal, each taking a sip in memory of Ebon and Sala.

Cree took the cup from Peshal, held it up and asked the gods' wisdom to fill it. Arshal took it from him with both hands. "I will never forget your sacrifice, Father, Mother, Esthen," he whispered before taking the remaining contents in one drink.

"I will not stand by and have this marriage broken," he called for all to hear, his voice hardened and the anger emerging. "In accepting my vows, I take an oath to do all in my power to restore Shande. I may live in exile, but I will not die an exile." His words carried on the cold air and gave hope to the grieving Val.

He tossed a fistful of frozen dirt and snow upon Ebon's open grave. "I will bear your heart back to your halls, Father. I promise," he whispered as he let the last grains fall from trembling fingers.

EPILOGUE

Occupied

Jan froze when a light tap fell on the farmhouse door. He'd managed enough warning each time the Minarian patrols came by to slip out and hide in the hay mow. While he hadn't heard horse hooves in the lane or the gruff calls of soldiers filled with self-importance, other dangers existed besides Minarians. People hadn't forgotten Jan's role in the city's defense. Already some folk found it more convenient to spurn their friends and cooperate with the occupation. He could only bide his time for the call he hoped would come soon from Nali, or even Arshal.

Ducking into the shadow behind the door, he pressed against the coat hooks. Cookie opened the door a crack.

"Is he here?" a voice whispered.

Jan stepped into the light. "You took a risk," he said. Olna's cousin, Tel, nodded as he stepped inside. "Your boy, Jali, they got him."

Cookie let out a small cry, clasping her hands over her mouth. Jan sank onto a stool as Tel closed the door.

"They caught him stealin' chickens from the governor's favorite farmer –"

"Favorite traitor." Jan snapped.

Tel nodded. "I heard they sent him off for schoolin' –"

"Labor."

"He gave 'em some story about bein' an orphaned waif that's hid out since the occupation and gave a false name so Aron wouldn't be onto him. He sold 'em. No doubt Aron Keeper's pleased another joins his young'uns in the camps. How he can be so blind! Though it looks like the man is thinkin' of regrettin' his words –" Tel stopped at Jan's furious gaze. "Jali's alive, Jan, an older boy, strong. He's got some smarts to convince 'em with, played all meek and stupid. He may find a way to escape if they think he's half-a-loaf short."

"Escape where?" Jan said sharply. He immediately held his hands out. "I'm sorry, Tel. Thanks." As Tel ducked back out into the night, Jan turned to comfort Cookie. As he held her, he wondered, not for the first time, if only a fool pinned all his hopes on Arshal and Nali who had disappeared west into who knew what. Daily, friends came by to tell him of changes in the lists naming fugitives of Minarian justice and Arshal's and Nali's remained. But for how long? What if both perished on their journeys?

He finally released Cookie and turned to the hearth to stir a thin soup as she dried her eyes. He'd have to go on, keep his promises to Nali. He'd find a way of being ready for their return, as long as he wasn't betrayed. He was a Harbor Gnat. The giant had yet to feel their bite.

THE END BOOK I

Cast of Characters

In order of appearance

WEST: Tasch-el, Sefresal, the Val, Eilime

Khoti of Tasch-el – Younger son of Tsevon and Amhese; Tawnkat; Lharan Guardsman; healer; favorite mount: Fidra.
Von – Tsevon's eldest son. Brother of Khoti. Dies in raid on Tasch-el.
Tsevon of Tasch-el – Headman of Tasch-el and the Independent Lharan Tribes; Tawnkat leader; healer; father of Von and Khoti and lifemate of Amhese; favorite mount: Kivik.
Eithurdon – Shawnsi. Duke of Lharan; provincial leader of Kishma; brother of Steadon; father of Asteria; nephew of King Ebon.
Ozer – Minarian envoy and friend of Eithurdon.
Kefta Salman – Captain of the Lharan Guard.
Geleg – Lharan Guardsman; scout; friend of Khoti.
Ytri – Lharan Guardsman; scout leader; friend of Khoti.
Toban – Lharan Guardsman; scout; friend of Khoti.
Amhese – Staphian. Lifemate of Tsevon; mother of Von and Khoti.
Latra – Taschian. Kinswoman of Tsevon and Khoti; sister of Tegi; lifemate of Ahrwesz; child: Jiata.
Tegi – Taschian. Tsevon's Second and cousin; brother of Latra; dies in rescue of Taschians.
Segan – Taschian and Tawnkat.
Konner – Taschian Constable and Second to Tsevon; Tawnkat; healer.
Halieri – Last survivor of Lhata.
Aibak – Shiadin border guard.
Ahrwesz – Taschian. Lifemate of Latra; child: Jiata; Tawnkat; Cousin to Khoti.
Davin – Taschian. Tawnkat.
Teckhan – Taschian. Tawnkat.
Tre the Imager – Taschian. Attendant to Khoti in the Lharan Guard.

Steadon Dodfrenyen – Shawnsi. Younger brother of Eithurdon; nephew of King Ebon.
Gelter – Tawnkat.
Pician – Tawnkat.
Velder – Tawnkat.
Jeret – Pladde resistance leader.
Dagon – Tawnkat.
Mol Azezial – King in Minaria.
Teshet – Pladde servant. Niece of Jeret.
Asteria – Shawnsi. Daughter of Eithurdon.
Mitte Salman – Younger brother of Kefta. Lharan Guardsman and scout.
Chati the Cooper's son – Taschian. Konner's nephew. Attendant to Khoti in the Lharan Guard.
Rathil Hostler – Eilimean farmer; former Lharan Guardsman; lifemate Atnil.
Atnil – Lifemate of Rathil Hostler.
Nalel Nalisson – Son of Olna and Nali born in Eilime.

EAST: Sihma Harbor, Sihmad Shal

Prince Arshaldon Dyndevas – Shawnsi. Eldest son of King Ebon and Sala; favorite mount Booty.
Javan – Shikoran Ship's Captain and friend of Arshal's.
Jan the Innkeeper – Owner of Sihma Harbor's Old Scow Inn; lifemate Cookie; son Jali; Harbor Gnat leader.
Azuth – Minarian ship's captain and friend of Arshal's.
Pedr the Drayman – Reve (officer of the peace) of Sihma Harbor; Harbor Gnat leader.
Cree – Advisor to the king; Arshal's tutor; Visionary; also known as Idenai.
Nali Drulson – Sihma Harbor fisher; derna (scholar); Harbor Gnat commander; lifemate Olna; Children: Bertal, Kia, Rena, Nalel; uses aliases Nali Bertalson and Jani Hostler.
Olna Rebertal – Lifemate of Nali. Mother of Bertal, Kia, Rena. Pregnant with Nalel (born in Eilime).
King Ebon Dyndevas – Shawnsi. King of Shande; lifemate Sala; children: Arshaldon, Esthenshaldon, Peshaldon, Resala.
Princess Resala Dyndevas – Shawnsi. Daughter and youngest child of Ebon and Sala.
Zopher don Saron – Shawnsi. Son of Baron Sipheron don Saran. Suitor of Resala's and friend of Arshal. Apprenticed Lharan Guard.

Aron Keeper – Lighthouse keeper/harbor pilot of Sihma Harbor.
Prince Esthenshaldon Dyndevas – Shawnsi. Second son of Ebon and Sala. Becomes a commander of the defense of Sihmad Shal.
Prince Peshaldon Dyndevas – Shawnsi. Youngest son of Ebon and Sala.
Yechan – Emissary of King Keyen of Shiad.
Marol – Consul of Otayr.
Queen Sala – Shawnsi. Lifemate of Ebon. Mother of Arshal, Esthen, Peshal and Resala. Sister of Habdelion of Mershy.
Bertal Nalisson – Sihma Harbor. Son of Nali and Olna. Twin of Kia
Jali Janson – Son of Jan the Innkeeper and Cookie.
Griag – Harbor Gnat and neighbor of Nali.
Drul – Nali's father.
Rena Renali – Youngest daughter of Nali and Olna.
Kia Renali – Daughter of Nali and Olna. Twin of Bertal.
Loch Asmodiel – Governor of the Minarian Protectorate of Shande.
Adesia – Lifemate of Loch Asmodiel; "Matriarch" of Shande.
Laria Keeper – Eldest daughter of Aron Keeper.
Lorem – Shawnsi official.
"Cousin" Tel – Sihma Harbor farmer; Olna's cousin.
Cookie – Lifemate of Jan the Innkeeper and mother of Jali.

TERMS

Taschian/Staphian/Lhatan – Shal tribes of the northern Lharan Mountains.
Second – The second in command to a Lharan headman.
Shawnsi – descendants of unions between the gods and shals prior to the Great War. Shawnsi are largely identified by a small star-shaped birthmark on their temple.
Independent Lharan Tribes – Federation of northern Lharan shal tribes.
Reve – Royal appointee who serves as town leader and constable.
Hogde – Ruling/higher caste of Minaria.
Pladde – Labor/lower caste of Minaria.
Derna – Scholars qualified to serve as advisors and cast auguries; recipients of Certificates Dernailye after many years of study; singular or plural term.
Stellan – A silvery metal softer than adanan mined in the mountains; often edges weaponry or is used for decorative purposes.

Adanan – An extremely hard metal mined in the Lharans.
Visionary – Term said to be reserved for the gods who remained behind after One called them home, but also a name given to the highest ranking derna.
Star-crossed – Pejorative. To be born under Kedtair despite proscriptions.
Sage – Term applied to high-ranking derna.
Shal – The people of Ea who survived the Great War; creations of Terremar and his children.
Merien – Sea people destroyed by Fyraer.
Osfothye – A plant with multiple medicinal, food and ritual purposes.
Lierye – The official history/documentation of the land of Shande.
Dynfearn the Lost – Historic shawnsi leader of renown from the Great War.
Harbor Gnats – Nickname for Harbor militia.
Eidhalt – Elite warriors of Minaria.
Tawnkat – Lharan tribal resistance fighter under Tsevon.
Tachi – Shal tribe of Tormor Wood.

DEITIES

One – The ultimate energy and fate (intent) of all that exists.
Terremar – One of two "offspring" of One.
Fyraer – One of two "offspring" of One; banished.
Maura – Daughter of Terremar who rules the sea; creations include water and the Merien.
Aziaris – God who cared for One's gardens; said to have been Maura's lover.
Ghyldus – Lesser god who aids Minaria after the Great War; known for enchantments; source of Ghyldism.
Luna – Daughter of Terremar who guides the moon.
Kedtair – Son of Terremar whose star rises every ninth year to create chaos as a sign from the gods; can mark those who will be good or evil if born during the month it's overhead.
Idenai – A lesser god who remained behind to become the Visionary Cree.

About the Author

A former journalist, editor, and farmer, M. Turville Heitz's short fiction appeared in anthologies and magazines before she took a break to collect a PhD and teach science and technical communications to undergrads. Her novel Black River was published in 2024 under the Mystique Press imprint of Crossroad Press. She lives on a defunct farm near Madison, Wisconsin where she coddles chickens and is kept by cats. She can be found on social media at MegT.bsky.social.

https://Oaklandhillsfarm.com

Other Books by M Turville Heitz

Black River
Dread Warrior (Book II of The Enchanter's Web)
The Rising of Kedtair (Book III of The Enchanter's Web)

www.ingramcontent.com/pod-product-compliance
Lightning Source LLC
Chambersburg PA
CBHW020507020726
47493CB00001B/223